"For a lady, you sure have a hell of a lot of wildcat in you. How come you've never bedded a man?"

Summer tried kicking him in the shin, but failed to connect. "Obviously, at some time in your life you were a gentleman, so how did you become such an obnoxious man full of so many horrid questions?"

"Horrid? I don't think they're so horrid, but I guess it depends on a person's viewpoint. I intend to be the man who beds you, so we might as well get these questions out of the way so we can concentrate on better things."

FOOL FOR LOVE

DeLoras Scott

AVON BOOKS ◆ NEW YORK

FOOL FOR LOVE is an original publication of Avon Books. This work has never before appeared in book form. This work is a novel. Any similarity to actual persons or events is purely coincidental.

AVON BOOKS
A division of
The Hearst Corporation
105 Madison Avenue
New York, New York 10016

Copyright © 1991 by DeLoras Scott
Published by arrangement with the author
Library of Congress Catalog Card Number: 90-93605
ISBN: 0-380-76342-7

First Avon Books Printing: May 1991

AVON TRADEMARK REG. U.S. PAT. OFF. AND IN OTHER COUNTRIES, MARCA REGISTRADA, HECHO EN U.S.A.

Printed in the U.S.A.

RA 10 9 8 7 6 5 4 3 2 1

Chapter 1

Rocky Mountains, 1863

It took several trips for Buck Holester to unload
the wagon and put away the grain and other
supplies he'd purchased in Mountain City. As soon
as the task was completed, Buck followed the narrow, rocky path that led down the side of the
mountain to the thick beams framing the entrance
of the Whiskey Hole Mine. He lit one of the oil
lanterns sitting on the ground just inside the dark
cavern, then grabbed the buffalo coat resting on a
peg.

The old, familiar shiver of apprehension ran
through him as he took off down the tunnel. It had
been a hot day up top, so the mine seemed even
colder than usual. Never missing a step, he pulled
on the coat, breathing in the shaft's musty smell,
mixed with the faint odor of blasting powder.

The light from the lantern cast eerie configura-
tions on the chiseled walls, reminding Buck of the
four years of muscle and sweat he and his partners,
Charley McMillan and Angus Comstock, had put
into this venture. At first, it had been because of
their ability to trap and hunt that they had managed to survive. Then, a little over three years ago
they had uncovered a small vein of gold that con-

tinued to produce enough ore to pay for mining equipment, staples, and a few pleasures. Still, they were all convinced the mother lode had to be nearby—it was just a matter of locating it. That's why they'd hung on instead of selling out to the big Eastern mining firms that were taking over claims all over the territory.

Where the tunnel forked, Buck veered left. As he neared the new digging area, it suddenly occurred to him that there were no sounds of striking picks. The silence unnerved him and made him pick up his pace. Were Angus and Charley resting, he wondered? Or could something have happened?

Just then, he rounded the last curve and saw his partners sitting on the ground, staring at each other as if in a daze.

Buck came to a stop in front of them. "What's the matter with you two?" he asked.

When neither of them responded, Buck tried again. "I said what the hell's the matter with you? You given up minin'?"

Finally Charley raised his hand and pointed to the opposite wall.

Buck turned around slowly. At first all he could see was a pile of recently dislodged rock and rubble. Then he swung the lantern up higher, and gasped.

There, in the solid stone wall, ran a vein of ore bigger than any he had ever seen or imagined.

"Damn," he said in a voice hushed with amazement, "we're rich."

Later that night the three men sat in the cabin around a wobbly table, the "thinking jug" strategically placed in the center.

"You know," Angus ventured, while stroking

his curly red beard, "I been sittin' here for nearly three hours and still ain't figured out what I want to spend my money on. The only thing that keeps comin' to mind is a woman."

"One with long brown hair," Charley added wistfully, "soft brown eyes, and a good deal of meat on her. Be mighty nice to have someone like that around,'specially when I feel an itch."

Sitting across the table from them, Buck focused his sea-blue eyes on Angus, a great bear of a man with a ruddy complexion, and much less given to chat than his garrulous friend, Charley. Buck was younger and taller than his two partners, but he knew they were all equal in strength.

He took a long swig of whiskey and passed the jug. "Hell," he said, a bit breathless from swallowing the liquid fire, "you two got enough money to spend a lifetime at Maybelle's. In fact, you'd probably save money by buying the damn place."

"Nope, that ain't what I'm talkin' about," Angus persisted. "I want a decent woman, not a painted one."

Buck released a disgruntled laugh. "When women are around—doesn't matter if they're decent or painted—you got nothin' but trouble. Hell, they nag you to death."

"That Old Man Larken that lives on the other side of the mountain says if a woman gives you trouble, smack her." Charley laughed. He knew he could never lay a mean hand on a lady. Women were meant to be loved. Fighting was for men.

"Old Man Larken is in his seventies, Charley." Buck impatiently brushed away a contrary tuft of thick black hair that had fallen over his eye. "He could probably get away with it, but I think he's all talk. Besides, what would you and Angus do if your women didn't take to that kind of treatment and some night, when you're sound asleep, a gun's put to your head and the trigger's pulled?"

Charley's grin broadened. "That sure as hell ain't bein' friendly."

Buck pushed his chair back and swung his muscular legs out from under the table. "I'm going outside to take a piss."

No sooner had he staggered out the door than Charley let out a long howl.

Angus jumped. "What the hell was that for?" he demanded.

" 'Cause I felt like it. Angus, we is rich!"

"I still got a woman on my mind," Angus said speculatively as he tipped back in his chair and balanced it on its two rear legs. Then suddenly he let it down with a thud. "Charley, let's get married."

"You serious?"

"Course I'm serious."

"What are you serious about, Angus?" Buck asked as he came back in, stopping for a second in the doorway.

"Gettin' married. We got enough money now to get everything a woman could want. What ya say, Charley?"

"Angus, you and Charley are drunk. This ain't no time to be decidin' on something like that."

"We're not drunk," Charley declared, pounding his fist on the table. "We're still sittin', ain't we? I agree with Angus. Gettin' married is a mighty good notion. I've never tried it before and it's high time I did."

"You don't gotta be so against it, Buck. Just 'cause we wanta marry don't mean you got to. Ain't that right, Charley?" Angus turned to his other partner just in time to see Charley pass out cold and slide to the floor.

* * *

For the next three weeks the men worked almost nonstop, digging and hauling hard rock to the smelter in Blackhawk. To their delight, the vein held. All during this time, Angus and Charley talked continuously about what it was going to be like having women around. Buck soon tired of listening to them. They reminded him of elk in mating season.

However, it didn't take long for Angus and Charley to realize they had a problem. As they saw it there were only three types of women in the area: whores; those who already had menfolk; and women no one cared to share a bed with.

It was Angus who came up with the idea of approaching Geoffrey Thorpe, an Englishman who'd come to the mountains several months back to paint pictures of the mining country.

"What's he gonna tell you that you don't already know?" Buck asked as they loaded another wagon to go to the smelter.

"He rides all over drawing them pictures. Maybe he knows of some women we ain't heard about."

"I doubt that, Charley."

"Buck," Angus snapped, "don't it make sense that since he's come all the way from across the water, he's seen a lot more than we have? Who knows? He could be just the one to solve our problem, or at least tell us how to go about it."

Buck considered the visit a bit of tomfoolery, but finally agreed to go with them the next morning.

Thorpe's cabin sat on the other side of the ridge, and it took almost an hour's ride to reach it. Fortunately, when they got there, Geoffrey was home.

"Good morning, gentlemen," the Englishman said as his guests dismounted. "It's good to see your scrubby faces." He gave them a friendly smile. "I seldom have visitors."

Now that they were here, Angus and Charley suddenly realized that saying you're going to do something and doing it were two different puddles of mud. The two men looked at each other, each waiting for the other to speak.

Sensing his company had come for something more than small talk, Geoffrey went inside to fix a pot of coffee.

Buck found himself thinking how out of place the Englishman seemed. He was tall and as skinny as a rail post, possessing thinning blond hair and a dapper air that set him apart from the miners and mountain men of the territory. Rumor had it that he paid a woman from town to come out and clean his place. Buck wondered how the man even managed to do his own cooking.

"Well, Charley," Angus said sharply, "why didn't you say something?"

"Me? It was your idea. And what's the matter with you, Buck? You're the one who usually does the talking."

Buck shrugged. He didn't want any women in camp, and both men knew it. But in all fairness, who was he to say it wouldn't work? He looked out over the high mountain range. Winter wasn't long off; some of the peaks were already topped with snow.

When Geoffrey rejoined them, the conversation turned to safe subjects: mining and hunting. They were on their third cup of coffee when Buck finally got around to saying, "Geoffrey, the boys have come to get your advice on something."

"Oh? What advice could I possibly give?"

"Decent women," Charley jumped in. "We aim to get married."

Unable to hide his shock, Geoffrey could only sit and stare at Angus and Charley. Both men had massive forearms and burly chests, and could probably wrestle down a mountain lion with their bare hands. In fact, because of their shaggy hair and beards, they could almost be mistaken for animals. Their clothes had probably never been washed since they'd left the store and were now permanently the color of dirt. And they wanted to marry decent women? The idea was so preposterous that Geoffrey broke out laughing.

"Just what's so damn funny?" Angus demanded.

The words brought Geoffrey's laughter to an abrupt halt. "I'm sorry, my friends, but look at this honestly."

"What you talking about?" Angus asked, trying to keep his temper under control. "We're rich. What more could a woman want?"

"Your question leads me to believe you know nothing about women."

"That's a damn lie," Charley countered. "The three of us has slept with a good many women, even shared some."

"Look gentlemen, you asked for my advice, but I don't want to make you angry by what I say."

"Go ahead and spit out what's on your mind," Buck ordered.

"Very well. First, you may have slept with . . . women, but apparently you have no understanding of the fair sex. If you want to marry proper women, you have to consider what it takes to make them happy, besides money. To begin with, take a look at yourselves."

Buck, Charley, and Angus did just that. They didn't see anything wrong.

"You've lived in the mountains too long, gentlemen. Quite honestly, you're unkempt and rough-mannered, which is fine under your present circumstance," he quickly added, afraid he'd overstepped his bounds. "But you'd have to change your ways before a lady would even look at you, let alone consent to marriage. Now if you want just any woman, that's a different matter."

"We thank you for your words," Buck stated simply. "We'll go back and think on 'em."

They rode home in silence.

"You think what Geoffrey said is true?" Charley finally asked as they sat around the table. He was disgruntled and made no effort to hide it.

"It makes me damn mad to think a woman wouldn't consider me good enough for her," Buck muttered. "Like I've been sayin' all along, we're better off without them."

"Your problem is you've always had any woman you wanted, so you can't see no reason for gettin' married," Charley replied. "Course there was that time you took up with Elly, but then you got tired of her and shoved her out of your bed. Never could figure out why you got so all-fired pissed when she took off with that Easterner afterward."

"Bastard was a woman beater. I don't want to talk about it, Charley."

"You just didn't like another man steppin' in your boots so soon," Angus said.

Buck jumped up and sent a big fist flying toward Angus, who was sitting across from him. Expecting the reaction, Angus easily ducked the blow, and Buck stomped out of the hut.

"You oughtn't push him like that," Charley commented, as he had on many other occasions.

"Oh, he'll get over it. Wasn't as if he gave a damn about her."

"Angus, if Geoffrey's tellin' us like it is, what we gonna do?"

"We could pay him to teach us what we need to know." Angus settled back in his chair and began twisting the end of his red beard. "Maybe Thorpe's got a point. It's been quite a while since I spent time with the kind of woman I'm wantin'. We need to talk about this. Why don't you see if you can get Buck back in here?"

"I will if I can find him," his partner said, and then sauntered out the door.

Buck always did his thinking in the mine, which was why he was there now, squatting on his heels in the semi-darkness, reveling in the silence— something he had little of, with Angus and Charley always around. It had been decided last week that since they could now afford it, they would hire additional men to help work the mine and thereby double the production. But with all the worry over women, it hadn't been attended to.

He picked up a handful of soft dirt, then let it slowly drain through his fingers. He'd known a lot of miners who became entirely different once they had a little gold in their pockets. Now he, Charley, and Angus possessed more gold than they had ever dreamed of, and the changes had already begun. Angus and Charley wanted to get married. Were these the same men who had vowed to remain single and sample the charms of every willing female who came down the road?

On the other hand, maybe it was only natural for Angus and Charley to be changing. Most men did eventually settle down and let a woman civilize them. Maybe he was the one who was out of step.

But Buck was different from his partners. He'd already been civilized once, and it hadn't agreed with him. Ten years ago he'd been a different man altogether, with a different name—John Holester, the twenty-three-year-old son of a prominent St. Louis banker, educated, well brought up, and stuck behind a desk in a stiffly starched collar, adding up figures in a ledger at his father's firm. He'd hated it, and every day he'd felt that collar tightening around his neck. How he'd yearned to be free of his family's expectations, and of the society women who dogged his path, conniving to trap him into marriage. That was when he got the idea of heading West to make a new life for himself. But when he'd broached the subject, his father had scoffed at the idea.

"Go West, indeed!" the old man had said. "You wouldn't last a month in the wilds. It takes more than knowing how to ride a horse to survive."

Buck had tried to reason with him, saying that he just wasn't cut out for the bank, but Elmer Holester had put his foot down. "If you take off on this ridiculous venture you'll never be welcome in my house again. Understand, I'm doing this for your own good. Tomorrow I expect to see you at work as usual." With that, his father had stalked out of the room, leaving Buck all alone to make the most important decision of his life.

He'd never intended to hurt his family. In fact, he still often wondered how his mother and two sisters were. By now Jane and Betsy probably had a dozen kids between them, all of them hanging on their mothers' skirts. He missed them sometimes, but he never regretted what he'd done. He couldn't have stayed in St. Louis. He'd sooner have died than become a replica of the demanding, unhappy man who was his father. So he'd simply walked out the front door.

Hunkered down in the chilly mine shaft, Buck

chuckled, remembering how ill equipped that rebellious young city boy had been. To this day he still couldn't figure out how he'd made it through those first two years in the mountains. But he had, thanks to the help of a few good-hearted trappers who'd taught him the fur trade. They used to tease him about being a young buck and eventually the nickname stuck. He'd been only too glad to give up his city clothes and city ways, and didn't care if he ever laid eyes on a fancy city woman again. As he saw it, they somehow epitomized everything that was wrong with civilization.

Now there was nothing left of John Holester. Buck found himself wondering whether anyone who knew him now would ever believe he'd once been a young gentleman. He could probably still talk and act like one if he put his mind to it. But what was the point, he decided, shaking his head. He was a mountain man now, and damned glad to be one.

He heard footsteps approaching down the tunnel and turned his head briefly to see Charley encircled in lantern light.

The older man put his hand on Buck's shoulder, knowing that his friend was deep in thought and coiled tight as a rope. "We need you up top," he said softly.

"You know," Buck said, not bothering to look at his friend, "I've been thinking that this gold's already started creatin' more problems than we're ready to deal with. Hell, we were better off poor."

Charley shoved his hands into well-worn pockets. "I reckon your point's well taken, but did you ever stop to think that havin' a woman around could be a good thing? And ain't nobody sayin' *you* gotta marry, Buck. Angus thinks we oughta pay Geoffrey to teach us manners, but you don't gotta be a part of that."

Deep down, Buck knew he wasn't being exactly fair. If Angus and Charley wanted to get married, that was their decision. Still, he couldn't stomach the notion of having a passel of women at Whiskey Hole Mine. "It won't work," he finally said.

"How about you coming back up so we can talk and be done with it once and for all?"

Buck let Charley lead him down the passageway and out into the waning sunlight. "It won't work," he repeated when they were back in the cabin.

"Why not?" Angus asked.

His anger gone, Buck grinned. He'd basically made up his mind not to try and stop their foolish scheme. So now he decided to offer them a piece of advice. "How is a *man* going to teach you about women? Anyhow, I got a hunch Geoffrey Thorpe doesn't know half as much as he makes out."

"How about one of Maybelle's girls?" Charley said and then exploded in a snicker.

"Maybelle's girls sure can't teach you about respectable women. I got a better idea."

Charley and Angus leaned forward, anxiously awaiting Buck's next words. Of the three, Buck always came up with the best ideas.

"If you're so all-fired determined to do this, I say you draw straws, and whoever gets the short one goes to Denver and hires a proper woman to do the teaching."

The other two grinned.

"You aimin' to draw, too?" Charley smiled.

Buck hesitated before finally saying, "Why not? Hell, if I end up going, at least I'll know a respectable female when I see one."

"I'll go get the straws," Angus offered.

He was back before Buck had a chance to think twice. And for better or worse, when they did the drawing Buck chose the short straw.

Chapter 2

A week later, across the foothills in the raw young town of Denver, Summer Caldwell climbed down from a stagecoach, her buxom friend, Milly Stern, following close behind. Since leaving Philadelphia, Summer had looked forward to seeing the place she would call home. But as she glanced around at the few ramshackle wooden stores lining what would hardly be called a proper street, serious doubts were already forming in her mind. The town looked like one big, ugly construction site, with rubble everywhere, uneven boarded walks, and muddy potholes in the road. Denver wasn't at all what she'd expected.

"So, this is where you'll be living," Milly said excitedly.

"I don't know why you sound so happy." Summer released an exasperated sigh.

"Try to remember, you're the one who chose to make this trip. You're the one who thought it would be such an adventure. I know I've said this thousands of times since we left Philadelphia, but why are you even considering marriage to William? As beautiful as you are, you could have had any man you wanted."

Summer adjusted the small blue hat adorned with artificial tea roses sitting atop her bright au-

burn hair, then made an effort to brush off her
traveling suit. The wrinkled blue linen looked almost white from the dust of the road. "Well, I told
William I'd marry him, and that's that. But whatever could have possessed him to practice law in
a place like this? Denver isn't much better than any
of the other small, dusty towns we stopped at during the trip."

"It's not so bad, Summer. Besides, it's a new
place. You know, I think I was just as tired of
Philadelphia as you were. When Lester died, I realized what a rut I was in. There I was in the same
town with the same friends who talked about nothing but the war. I couldn't care less about some
silly war, other than it took away too many young
and interesting men." Her gaze stopped on a perfect example of manhood, a tall, dark-haired fellow
standing several paces down the boarded walk. For
a minute she studied his broad shoulders and the
way his breeches rode low on his hips. "I find this
far more agreeable."

Summer knew the part about the war was a lie.
Milly was a strong supporter of Mister Lincoln.
Summer glanced about to see if William was anywhere in sight. It aggravated her that he had not
been waiting when the stage arrived.

Milly smoothed back her blonde hair and stole
another look at the big man. Suddenly he looked
her way and gave her a wide, heart-fluttering
smile. She was sure there were no men the size of
this one in all of Pennsylvania. At least she had
never seen any, and she knew a lot of men.

Apparently encouraged by Milly's attention, he
stepped forward. "Ladies," he said, tipping his
hat. "Name's Buck Holester. May I assist you with
your trunks?"

"Thank you," Milly replied, grinning from ear

to ear. "I do believe we could use some help."

"That won't be necessary," Summer snapped at the stranger. "Begone! You'll not be making money from us!"

The man moved away, and Milly groaned. Summer was not only high-strung and more than a little bull-headed, she was also such a snob. If a man wasn't dressed like a gentleman, or didn't come from a well established family, she wanted nothing to do with him. Milly watched her handsome admirer retreat down the boarded walk, then turned to her companion. At times Milly felt so much older and wiser than Summer, even though she was only two years her elder.

"At last. Here comes William." Summer tapped her foot impatiently while waiting for the slender, well dressed man to join them.

"My dear, I see you made the trip without any mishap." He kissed Summer's check. "Milly, how nice to see you again. I was quite pleased when Summer wrote and said you'd be traveling with her."

"I would never have forgiven myself if I'd let her make this horrid trip alone. You're looking well, William. Living in the West must agree with you."

"Yes indeed. Summer, I must warn you, I'm going to do everything in my power to convince you to stay. I suppose you noticed some burned buildings as you came in. We had a terrible fire last April that about wiped out the entire town. Of course everything is being rebuilt, and this time with brick."

Milly paid scant attention to what else was said as she studied William Nielson. He wasn't a tall man, standing only an inch or two higher than Summer. His blond hair looked almost white, and his facial features were sharp. As far as Milly was concerned, the man didn't even have a personality. He'd proven that when he was courting Summer back in Philadelphia. God only knew why she'd given in, though Milly suspected she'd affianced herself to him out of sheer boredom.

"Come along, ladies, the men are ready with your trunks." William guided the women toward the Palmer House hotel. It was a stone building, obviously recently built, that back East would have gone unnoticed. Here in Denver though, it seemed a veritable palace. The lobby gleamed with polished brass and a plush red carpet covered the steps leading to the second floor.

When they reached their suite of rooms, William stood talking to the manager while the two women walked through the apartment to make sure everything was satisfactory. Summer ran a slender finger over the furniture, checking for dust.

After requesting a tub, hot water, and help with the unpacking, William dismissed the manager.

Milly was glad when William said, "I know you ladies are exhausted, so I'll let you settle in. I'm sure you both could use a nap. I'll be back this evening to take you to supper." He kissed Summer on the cheek again. "Until tonight, darling."

Thirty minutes later the maid still hadn't arrived, so Milly volunteered to go back down to the lobby to check on it. "Our things need to be aired and put away," she said. "The clothes have been packed so long they'll probably never look decent again. While I'm about it, I'll find out when we can expect the bath."

Summer nodded her agreement before returning to the bedroom. Though she welcomed the feel of a decent bed, she couldn't seem to relax. At least William had arranged acceptable accommodations, even if the service at the Palmer House wasn't exactly up to standard. It was just like Milly to go down and get their problem taken care of. Summer smiled. How she loved her short and petite friend! They'd known each other since they were girls, and Summer was one of the few people who realized that behind Milly's flirtatious manner lay a sharp, inquisitive mind.

Summer rose and went to the window. Looking down, she watched dust rise as buckboards, spring buggies, and covered wagons moved to and fro. She felt disgust rise in her throat at the sight of men wearing articles of Union or Confederate uniforms. Probably deserters, she thought.

In his letters William had said Denver was booming because of the gold strike, which meant little or nothing to her. William Nielson could be a successful lawyer wherever he chose to live, so why would he pick an ungodly place like this? But he obviously planned on staying because in his last letter he said he'd opened a bank.

Suddenly Summer was filled with doubt. He'd come West not long after the war had broken out. Could he have done so to escape joining up? William had been after her for years to marry him, and when he'd returned nine months ago on a visit, she'd finally decided to accept his offer. At twenty-two she'd given up ever finding love, so what other choice did she have? Remain an old maid? None of her other suitors appealed to her, and William had waited so long.

In retrospect though, that didn't seem a good enough reason to get engaged. But there had been others. William was a man of consequence. Marriage to him meant an assured future, wealth, position, and the chance to see the West. Her parents hadn't been opposed to the idea so she'd simply said yes. However, halfway through her travels she'd started questioning her decision. Was she really ready to settle down and be William's wife? Milly was a good example of marriage without love: She'd had to pinch herself to achieve tears at her husband's funeral.

And what good was marriage without love, Summer asked herself now. Maybe it would be better to wait until the right man came along. And if he never did, maybe spinsterhood wouldn't be so bad.

All the way to Denver she'd told herself that once she saw William again everything would be all right. She'd closed her ears to Milly's disparaging comments about him. After all, how could she change her mind when she'd traveled across the country to be with him? But now that she'd seen him again she only felt worse. The feel of his lips on her cheek had left her completely cold.

Summer pulled back the lacy curtain for a better view of the street. William was going to be furious, and justly so. But she couldn't do it. She couldn't marry him. Somehow she had to find the courage to tell him so. And then what would she and Milly do, stranded in this godforsaken town on the edge of the wilderness? So much for adventure, so much for love. Summer lowered her head into her hands and sobbed.

"They promised me our baths would arrive in no more than fifteen minutes," Milly said as she entered the bedroom. But when she saw Summer's face, she stopped in her tracks.

"My poor, dear Summer," she said at last. "I can see we need to have a talk."

After eating a large supper, Buck returned to his small rented room to catch some sleep. It was going to be a long two-day ride back to the cabin. Though he had acquaintances in town, he'd contacted none of them. All he wanted to do was find a woman and get the hell out of Denver.

He stretched out on the bed and linked his hands beneath his head. Now that he'd found someone to take back to Angus and Charley, he felt as though a ton of ore had been lifted from his shoulders. The little blonde who had arrived on the stage today appeared to be amiable, and was obviously a lady. She had certainly given him plenty of encouragement, but that was a lot different than agreeing to take off with a stranger. So, he'd decided to just steal her and explain later. She'd be angry at first, but when she realized he and the boys meant her no harm and found out how much money she'd make, she'd settle down and get used to the idea.

"I must be drunk to even consider doing this," he grumbled, "but it hasn't been the best week of my life."

He'd spent the last couple of days approaching women about going to the high country, and for good pay. But apparently he'd been in the mountains too long, because he seemed to have lost his ability to communicate with city folk. Oh, the women had been happy enough to get his attention, batting their eyelashes and giggling like lunatics. But when he'd finally gotten around to explaining what he wanted, he'd had his foot stomped on, a parasol brought down on the top of his head, his face slapped, and a purse slammed into his gut. Of course, there had been the women who'd just raised their noses in the air and walked off, but most of them had had a few words to say before doing so. And they hadn't been pretty. But the worst had been the woman who'd screamed for the marshal. Buck had gotten off with a warn-

ing, though he sure hadn't relished having half of
Denver hear the man tell him that if he tried mo-
lesting any other women, he'd be stuck in a cell
for the rest of his life. God, how he hated women!
You just couldn't reason with them. The sooner he
could get out of town with one across his saddle,
the happier he'd be. More than likely, he'd have
to gag her, though.

It was nearly one in the morning when Buck
quietly entered the lobby of the Palmer House.
He'd been in the vestibule earlier that afternoon
when the blonde and her bitchy redheaded friend
had come in, and had heard the manager tell them
their room number. So locating it didn't present a
problem. Nor did he have any difficulty forcing the
lock. He just had to be careful to get the nice one,
because he'd rather waltz with a bear than tangle
with the other woman.

Oddly, when the door sprang open, he was mo-
mentarily at a loss for what to do next. It hadn't
occurred to him that they would procure a suite.
As his eyes adjusted to the dark, shadowy room,
he could barely make out a couch, chair, and two
open doors leading to the sleeping chambers. He
headed for the first bedroom, his years of hunting
enabling him to move from room to room with the
silence of a cat. He couldn't tell who was on the
bed because the quilt was pulled over her face and
she had a nightcap on. He decided to try the other
room. As he entered, his hand brushed against
something on the chest of drawers, knocking it to
the floor. Fumbling around, he finally located it. It
was a small hat with something on top. Remembering that the coppery-haired one had worn such
a hat, he returned to the first bedroom. As he
reached out to grab the woman, his knee hit the
side of the bed.

The woman stirred.

Buck clamped his big hand over her mouth and swooped her and the quilt up in his arm. She kept mumbling and trying to fight, but he managed to wrap the quilt tighter around her.

He hurried down the stairs and out the back entrance where two saddled horses waited. The reins of the bald-face were tied to the saddle horn of his sorrel. Buck continued to hold his hand firmly over the lady's mouth as he shoved a foot in the stirrup and swung up on the horse's back. With his wiggling prize easily held in one arm, he rode off, hell for leather.

It didn't take long for Buck to reach the foothills near the town of Golden. At least his captive had stopped struggling, which prompted him to slow his horse and shift the weight of his surprisingly soft bundle from his arm to his chest. "I'm gonna take my hand away real slow, lady," he said in a low voice. "As long as you don't scream or make trouble, I'm agreeable to keeping it off. I'm not going to hurt you. Do you understand?"

Feeling her head nod, he removed his hand. The next instant all hell broke loose. She fought harder and screamed louder than a cornered cougar.

"Damn, woman!" Buck snapped. "You sure do know how to make it hard on a man."

Because she kept flailing, scratching, and biting, Buck was barely able to regain his hold. The hellcat continued to release one shriek after another. To make matters worse, she had wiggled around so much that she was slipping out of the quilt. This was a fairly well-traveled road, and Buck knew if the confounded woman attracted someone's attention, he'd be in for trouble. No one would believe he meant the lady no harm.

He finally managed to scoot his captive up and

get a hand back over her mouth, putting an end to her infernal noise. Assured he once again had everything under control, he nudged his horse into a full gallop, wanting to get away from the area in case someone had heard her yowling. Even though it would take a little longer, he elected to circle around Golden instead of riding through it. He didn't want people getting curious about his cargo.

After a couple of miles of hard riding which left Golden behind them, Buck slowed the horses to a walk. The animals were now working their way up the narrow mountain path. The girl lay quiet. Silently, Buck cursed the darkness that made it impossible to see if she'd passed out. There was only one way to find out if it was a trick or if he'd smothered her, which at the moment didn't seem like such a bad idea. Slowly he removed his hand. Nothing happened. Figuring she must have dozed off, he transferred his burden to the other arm and leaned her against his chest. She smelled like flowers. He waited a moment to be sure she hadn't been disturbed, then began shaking his free hand. Besides being cramped, it was sore from all the times she'd bitten him. As they continued up the trail, the rhythm of the horses' steps lulled him into a peaceful, half-asleep state.

A sudden movement instantly brought Buck back to his senses. The sky was now gray and suffused with dim light. What he saw glaring up at him from beneath the folds of the quilt came as a shock. There was less bosom, and finer features than he'd expected. Somewhere along the way the woman's nightcap had fallen off, leaving him looking at a mass of reddish curls. Her wide green eyes certainly didn't look accommodating, though he had to admit they were a handsome color. In fact, right now they were sparkling with rage. He cursed under his breath. Damn if he hadn't gotten the snobbish harridan instead of the nice blonde.

"Just where do you think you're taking me?" Summer demanded, pushing against Buck's broad chest. She assumed her captor was a man, though he looked as much like a beast. She was so furious she considered socking him in the jaw; however, as big as he was he probably wouldn't even feel it.

"I tried telling you last night that I ain't gonna harm you, so you got no reason to fight."

"No reason? You kidnap me and I'm not supposed to be upset? You had better take me right back, because you're going to be in a lot of trouble if my fiancé finds you first. Let me off this horse!" She squirmed so hard she nearly fell off.

Unexpectedly, he lowered her to the ground. The moment her feet touched solid earth, Summer lifted her skirt and took off running. She didn't go far though. Pebbles dotting the ground stabbed into the bare soles of her feet unmercifully. The morning air was frigid, and the trail back down the mountain divided, leaving her unsure of which way to go. Looking back, she was surprised to see the big man still sitting on his horse, watching her silently. At that instant she realized she had nothing on but her nightclothes. "What are you staring at?" she cried, crossing her arms over her breasts.

"I was just wondering where you thought you were going."

Summer made a slow circle on the trail. On the right, craggy rocks and fir trees blocked her escape; on the left, a wide, boulder-strewn creek bordered the path. Seeing the water tumbling down the mountainside made her mouth feel as if it had been stuffed with dry wool.

"My fiancé owns a bank and is a powerful lawyer in Denver." She looked her kidnapper straight in the eye. "He'll see that the authorities put you in jail. But if you take me back to the hotel, I swear I'll never mention this incident."

"Never did like bankers," Buck replied. "Besides, I don't believe you'd keep your mouth shut."

"Surely someone saw you take me from the hotel. You can't expect to get away with this."

But the big man said nothing.

She tried licking her dried lips, but even her tongue lacked moisture. "Do you plan on letting me die of thirst?" she snapped.

He pointed at the creek. "There's more water than you could drink in a lifetime."

Loath to move, Summer glanced at the rocks she would have to walk over. Still, even if her feet did get cut, she had to have a drink.

She gingerly started forward when the stranger said, "Wait, I'll carry you."

Summer wanted to refuse, but her mind told her to be sensible. She watched him loosen two canteens that were tied with rawhide to his saddle then sling them over his shoulder. The man dismounted with the ease of someone who had spent a great deal of time on a horse. It occurred to her that he was very agile for someone so large.

None too gently, he swung a big arm around her waist and headed for the creek. When he stood her on her feet by the water's edge, Summer immediately dropped to her knees. Hands cupped, she dipped them into the clean, cold water. The taste was almost sweet, and decidedly refreshing. Once she drank her fill, she sank to the ground, releasing a long, deep sigh. But in the next instant, she was picked back up and returned to the horses.

Snatching the quilt from the ground, she quickly wrapped it over her shoulders. "I don't believe you've told me your name."

"Buck."

"Well, Mister Buck," she said sarcastically, "I will say that other than abducting me from my hotel room, practically smothering me to death, and bringing me to the middle of nowhere, you've done me no physical harm. Perhaps you would like to explain why you've gone to all this trouble. Am I to be ransomed?"

"I'm taking you to my cabin in the mountains. My two partners and me need a woman. We'll pay well, and you'll be none the worse for the experience."

Summer sucked in her breath. She tried to tell herself this was just a nightmare, but knew differently. How in God's creation had this bushy-haired animal managed to walk into her life? One look at him told her it was no use trying to talk him out of this. He was probably too simpleminded to realize what he was asking of her.

It took a considerable amount of effort to appear calm while maintaining a look of superiority. When she was sure she could speak without a quiver in her voice, she said, "If that is all you want, there are certain kinds of women who are more adept at that sort of thing. I'm sure they would be quite willing to accompany you. If you take me back, I'll make a point of locating one, or even two or three."

"Mount up," he ordered.

Summer spun around and started running, heedless of everything. But before she even reached the fork in the trial, Buck had his arms around her waist. It was hard for Summer to believe the man could move so fast, and he wasn't even panting.

"Please, Mister Buck," Summer pleaded, "take me back to my hotel. I'll pay you."

"I can't do that. What's done is done. I have to

admit, though, I hadn't planned on gettin' you. But that's the way the rock fell. Here's your horse." He handed her the reins. "We need to be moving on. And I wouldn't suggest tryin' to escape. You'd only get lost and I'd find you anyway. Or, considering how disagreeable you've been, I guess I could just leave you to the wolves." He mounted and urged his horse forward.

Summer remained standing in the same spot, wondering if he was lying to her. Could she escape? Which was worse, being eaten alive by wolves or having her body used by three men? Suddenly a hideous-sounding scream echoed through the canyon. A shiver shot through her like a lightning bolt. "What was that?" she called, trying not to make too much noise.

"Mountain lion," he called back over his shoulder. "They like women. Especially fiery-haired ones."

"All right. Don't ride off and leave me!" He continued on. "Mister Buck? You'll have to help me. I've never been on a saddle like this before!"

Buck turned his horse around and sat for a moment staring at her. "First put your left foot in the stirrup and grab hold of the saddle horn, then pull yourself up."

"But I'm used to a sidesaddle, and I don't even have a riding habit. While I'm thinking about it, just what am I supposed to do about clothes?" For the first time, she saw the man grin—a dazzling smile, full of humor.

"Since I don't happen to see a sidesaddle sitting about, I reckon you got no choice but to use what's available. As for something to wear," he went on, "I admit, I failed to think about it." With that, he turned his horse back around and moved off up the trail.

Again Summer heard the cat's menacing scream, and it sounded much closer this time. She amazed herself at how quickly she managed to get up on the saddle. Without any encouragement, her nag took off after Buck's horse. She tugged, yanked, and did everything in her power to turn the beast in the opposite direction. The horse just shook his big head, and once it caught up with Buck, continued to plod behind the other animal no matter what she did.

Because Buck showed no inclination to force himself on her right away, Summer was eventually able to settle down. It only made sense that somewhere along the way they would encounter other travelers. When that happened, she'd be rescued. But the trail soon became overgrown and they saw no one. She thought about Milly and how frantic she must be, and wished she could at least get a message to her.

It wasn't until darkness began to cover the canyon that Buck finally stopped. After hours in the saddle, Summer could hardly dismount. Her legs ached as she stumbled off to the side. The air had become chilly, causing her to pull the quilt tightly around her body.

It hardly took any time for Buck to unload the horses and hobble them. Summer silently watched as he gathered wood and proceeded to build a campfire. Though she was loath to go anywhere near him, she couldn't resist the fire's warmth. Her skin felt like gooseflesh. She sat on the opposite side from him and watched disconsolately as Buck set about busily preparing their food.

Summer had no idea what she ate, nor was she about to ask. It had a good flavor, and she was hungry. Her appetite satisfied, she placed the sleeping mat and extra blanket Buck had given her near where she'd been sitting, but well away from him. It was wonderful to be able to lie down and stretch. Exhausted beyond words, she knew she would immediately fall asleep.

But sleep didn't come. Without benefit of four walls and a bed, she felt unprotected. Smothered by the total darkness and silence, she tossed the quilt over her head while envisioning huge creatures ready to pounce. It also served to ward off the bitter cold. Anticipating Buck's footsteps headed in her direction added to the terror. But praise the Lord, he kept his distance.

Summer still had her quilt wrapped about her when they continued the journey early next morning. Because of the way she had to straddle her nag, her nightdress was hiked up almost to her knees. She could only hope that no one would see her like this. The beast in front of her didn't count. Nothing fazed him.

They rode the whole day without encountering another traveler on the trail, and by late afternoon Summer's hope of rescue plummeted. Should she jump over one of the many drop-offs they were passing by? Wouldn't that be better than allowing herself to be used?

But she quickly dismissed the thought of killing herself. She didn't want to die. She was still too angry at what this man had done to give him the satisfaction. Besides, he'd probably ride back to Denver and capture Milly. Why couldn't Buck at least let her rest or stretch her legs occasionally? The only time they stopped was when she had a need. He'd pull his horse to a halt and wait until she returned from behind some bush and re-mounted, a procedure Summer found thoroughly humiliating.

Now she centered her thoughts on the hateful

man ahead. His blue shirt and brown corduroy pants were covered with trail dust. He was obviously a degenerate, albeit a silent degenerate. He'd barely said two words to her since their first stop yesterday morning. Even without conversation though, she'd changed her mind about him being simpleminded. His blue-gray eyes were anything but dull, and he moved with a grace that left no doubt that he knew exactly what he was doing.

Thinking about Buck didn't help, so Summer tried to concentrate on the scenery. That didn't help either. She finally came to the conclusion that the only thing that would set her mind at ease would be a long knife planted deep in the broad back of the man ahead of her.

It was nearing dusk when Summer spied a large log cabin in a clearing. As they rode toward it, excitement began to build within her. Maybe now she'd meet someone civilized and with enough sense to get her out of this mess.

Buck let out some kind of strange whistle, and within moments two burly men came out of the dwelling.

"Oh, Blessed Mary," Summer uttered. "There are two more barbarians just like this one."

She gave the reins a hard yank, but the horse paid no heed. As they neared the cabin she got a good look at the men. One was brown-haired, the other a redhead, both slightly older than Buck, with chests the size of barrels and mangy beards.

Angus and Charley were so happy to see what Buck had brought them that they let out a war whoop. Eager to help the lady down, they ended up running into each other. It was Buck who finally picked Summer off her horse and deposited her on the ground.

"Howdy, ma'am," Charley said after shooting a wad of tobacco juice onto the ground.

Summer backed away.

"What the hell's goin' on, Buck?" Angus asked. "She acts like she's scared of us."

Angus' booming voice made Summer cringe visibly.

"Just look at her. She's tremblin'," Charley added.

At that, Summer turned and ran, but Buck extended his arm and, with one sweep, lifted her off the ground, leaving her feet still moving in the air.

"We need to talk," Buck stated as he headed for the cabin, holding Summer firmly by his side.

Candles had already been lit in the cabin, so when Buck dropped Summer to her feet, she had a decent view of the room. Never in her entire life had she seen such a filthy shambles or smelled so rank an odor. The place was as bad as a pigsty.

"Pull up a chair," Buck ordered. "You been askin' questions and I don't want to have to repeat myself."

"I need my quilt," Summer whispered, desperate to hide from the ogling eyes of the other two men. The redheaded man left, then returned, quilt in hand.

Buck pointed to a chair. Seeing the scowl on his face, Summer quickly took a seat. She was careful not to touch anything else.

When the men were finally seated around the table, Charley picked up the jug and offered it to Summer. "Would you like the first swig of whiskey?" he asked, trying to be friendly.

Summer opened her mouth to refuse, but words failed her. She shook her head instead.

After the jug was passed around, Charley and Angus were ready to listen to Buck's story.

"You might as well know right off," Buck began, "this woman was brought her against her will."

Angus frowned and Charley glanced at Summer.

"I tried every way I could think of to get a decent woman to come with me, but they all refused. So the way I saw it, if we was to have someone here, I had to take her whether she liked it or not. This ain't the one I'd picked, but what's done is done. This one can do the job just as well."

The other two again looked at Summer, then nodded in agreement before turning their attention back to Buck.

Summer wished there were some way she could just shrink into oblivion. Maybe she should have jumped off a cliff after all.

"Didn't you feed her?" Charley asked. "She ain't hardly got no meat on her bones."

"I fed her, she just came that way."

"Got a pretty face though," Angus commented, "and real good bosoms."

Feeling like a mare being discussed for auction, she pulled the quilt tighter about her body.

"Now I also tried to explain to this woman . . ." Buck looked at his prisoner. "What's your name?"

"Summer."

"I tried to explain what we wanted her for, but at the time she was in no mood to listen. So I decided to wait. You see, she's got it in her head we mean to share her."

"You got nothin' to worry about, Miss," Angus tried assuring her.

"We got plenty of money," Charley added, "and we aim to pay you well." Seeing the shocked look on her face, he rushed on. "You'll be rich when we take you back to Denver."

Summer grabbed at this first ray of hope. "When do you plan on doing that?"

"Well . . ." Angus said, giving it thought.

"I reckon they ought to be able to learn by summer," Buck answered. "Don't you agree, fellers?"

Summer gasped. Learn what? It was barely the beginning of autumn. That would be practically a year away!

Misunderstanding the reaction, Charley quickly added, "He's right, we can learn by then."

"Hell, they might be a little rough," Buck said, "but they ain't stupid."

Try as she might, Summer couldn't seem to make her mind function. Nothing they said made any sense.

"Are you all right?" Charley asked, suddenly concerned. "You need something to eat?"

Summer glared at the three men, still having difficulty believing what she was seeing. Clearly, they didn't own a razor between them, and lice had to be growing in those filthy beards. She took a deep breath. "Just what is it you want to learn?"

They all looked at her as if she were daft. Finally Buck said, "Manners."

Summer glared at him. Manners indeed! Did he honestly expect her to believe that? She turned to Angus and Charley. She'd had no success with Buck, but maybe she could make the other two understand. She gave them a soulful look. "As I told your friend, if you'll take me back, I'll do everything in my power to locate the type of woman you want. Believe me, you'll be much happier."

Buck shook his head. " 'Fraid we can't do that."

"I wasn't talking to you!"

"You'll stay here till the winter snow melts and the trail's clear again. You have my word that when that time comes, you'll be taken back, none the worse than when you came—and a good deal richer. We'll take care of you, and you'll want for nothin'. We ain't askin' much in return."

Charley slammed his big fist on the table, causing Summer to almost jump off the chair. "Couldn't have said it better myself. Buck's always had the silver tongue of the bunch, ain't that right, Angus?"

Angus agreed.

Summer had to accept that these men had no intention of letting her go. To run away could be foolish and possibly deadly. She wouldn't even know what direction to go. What was more, she felt desperately tired after the long hard trip into the mountains. A quick scan of the one room told her all she wanted to know about where they slept. There were three beds with furs of every description scattered over them. Just thinking about how many bugs were in them made Summer want to scratch her arms.

While Summer was taking stock of her surroundings, Buck proceeded to tell his partners what had happened in Denver. By the time the big man finished, the jug was empty and another put in its place. Summer found the part about Milly showing interest in Buck quite enlightening.

Then the others told him what had happened while he'd been gone. Summer had no idea who the people were that they spoke of, but it took no effort to determine what Maybelle's was. Summer's ears burned when Angus and Charley spoke of their visits, and how the girls had inquired as to when Buck would be back.

The men continued to talk, drink, laugh, and use language that wasn't fit for a woman's ears. They acted as if she wasn't there, and she sat perfectly still so as not to draw attention to herself.

When she could no longer sit up, Summer rested her head on the table, ignoring the dirt. Maybe later tonight she could steal a horse. Blissfully the voices began to fade and her eyelids grew heavy.

Chapter 3

M illy Stern sat twisting her handkerchief in the windowseat at the Palmer House. "What did the marshal say?" she asked without even glancing toward William Nielson.

"He hasn't found out a thing. Drink this, it'll help calm your nerves." William handed her a glass of brandy.

"The only thing that is going to calm my nerves is to have Summer return!" She rested her head against the windowpane. She hadn't slept for two days, and was convinced there couldn't possibly be a tear left in her. "Willy, would you please sit down? I'm tired of watching you pace the floor. This room is too small."

He lowered himself onto the footstool. He hated it when she called him Willy, and Milly knew it, which is why she persisted.

"The marshal said he'd make inquiries."

"That's all? What does that mean? Why don't *you* do something? You have money—hire someone to look for her."

"Milly, do you realize the position this puts me in?" He rose to his feet, toying with his watch fob.

"What are you talking about?" Milly scowled at her visitor.

"Thus far, I have a flawless reputation in town.

I know this might sound callous, but it's likely Summer has been taken away by a man, and ... well, you know what has probably happened. To tell you the truth it does me no good at all to become connected with this business."

Milly was so furious she wanted to hit the pompous ass over the head with something. She was even tempted to tell William that just before she'd disappeared Summer had decided against marrying him. But neither would help an already bad situation, and William was the only person Milly knew who might be able locate Summer. She took several deep breaths and tried to calm herself.

"Before this happened, Summer would have been a wonderful asset to my future, but now—"

A cold chill ran through Milly's body. "What you're saying is you don't love her," she interrupted.

"Oh ... yes ... of course I do."

The devil you do, Milly thought.

"But after all that's happened," William continued, "what would my clients think about me marrying Summer? I mean ... everyone will eventually find out she's been kidnapped, and the longer she's gone the worse it will be. I'm sure a lady of your breeding can understand my position. John Evans can't remain Territorial Governor forever, and I plan on taking his place. So you see, I must be very careful."

"Willy, you owe Summer something, whether you marry her or not! This trip would never have been made if it weren't for you." She paused for a minute, trying her hardest to keep from screaming at the man. "I can assure you, when Summer is safe, I'll take her back to Philadelphia, so your precious reputation will remain intact. But for God's sake! This once, stop thinking about yourself and think about her. What if she's being tortured by Indians?'' She took a sip of the brandy to avoid more tears.

"Marshal Bailey did remember that there was a man in town a few days ago looking for women to take into the mountains with him. Said he was a big man with black hair and a bushy beard."

Milly's hand flew to her mouth. Could it possibly have been the man she'd flirted with at the stagecoach stop? She collapsed back into the window-seat, welcoming the support. A feeling of giddiness was threatening to overtake her. "Go on," she said carefully.

"Well, he figures the man is either a miner or a trapper. In either case, he'd be practically impossible to trace."

"And?"

William sighed. "You're right, of course. I'll hire a man to try and find her." William sat down beside her and took her hand. "Now Milly, I know it's hard to accept but you must prepare yourself for the possibility that Summer could be dead."

"Summer is not dead. Something inside me says she's not."

"Let's hope so." He moved closer to her and placed his arm around her small shoulders. "My dear, should you remain in the hotel unchaperoned?"

Milly's head snapped up and she glared at William.

"Trying to get rid of me, Willy? Well, I won't leave Denver. However, I don't want to tax your pocketbook by remaining here. Perhaps I should move in with you." William looked as if he'd been stung by a bee, which under any other circumstances would have made Milly laugh. Clearly, he had no idea that she had ulterior motives for wanting to move into his house. It was the best way she could think of to make sure he kept up the search for Summer. "And don't tell me it wouldn't be proper," she added. "I know your Aunt Ruby is living with you, and I suspect your house is large enough to house several families. Like it or not, I shall remain until Summer is found. I know she will be found, Willy. When she returns, she may very well need me."

Seeing the hard look Milly gave him, William was positive that if he didn't do as she said, the woman would cause a great deal of trouble. "What would be a convenient time for you to move in?"

Milly's smile resembled a smirk. "This afternoon. When you go downstairs, have a girl sent up to do my packing. I will also be bringing Summer's things."

"I'll arrange for my carriage to come for you." Then he spun on his heels and left.

Needing a bracer, Milly downed the rest of the brandy, then poured some more. The moment William mentioned a man with black hair, she knew exactly who the marshal was talking about. Milly had always prided herself on being a good judge of character, and she didn't think that man would be the type to physically harm Summer. Why should he? Women probably chased him. His blue eyes were warm and his smile broad and full of devilish humor—though of course, because of his rough appearance, he wasn't the sort Summer would have looked at twice. Milly knew her friend well. Summer liked men she could lead around by the ear.

The more Milly thought about it, the more it all made sense. The man had been there when they arrived on the stagecoach. Maybe he'd followed them to the hotel. It would have been a simple matter to find out which room they were in. For the first time in days, Milly's heart-shaped lips curved upward. "And I thought he was interested in me." She laughed.

She chastised herself for her lapse into light-heartedness. But somehow she knew Summer would be all right. The girl had resilience—even if she'd never had to put it to the test. So Milly decided then and there not to dwell on the dangers, but to pray for the best. And if someone had kidnapped her friend, she hoped it was the big, black-haired man, because Milly was sure he was exactly the type Summer needed. A man who knew how to take control. She only wished she could be there to watch.

Slowly coming out of a deep sleep, Summer felt warm and deliciously comfortable. She stretched lazily, then opened her eyes. It came as a shock to discover she was in the cabin, on a bed, covered with one of those hides. Lord of mercy! This wasn't where she'd gone to sleep. Gritting her teeth, she jumped to the floor. Finally rid of the offensive skin, she began checking herself for bugs. There were none to be seen. Not convinced, she leaned over and carefully ran a finger through the long hair of the hide. Still none. She sat on the edge of the rope bed and studied the rectangular room. Was this to be her prison?

The sun filtering through the windows allowed her to see what had been cloaked in shadows last night. The place was filthy and cluttered, but a good deal of the clutter consisted of dirty, rusty equipment. A cold, wide-mouthed fireplace stretched across the far end of the room and looked large enough to accommodate an entire tree. The hewn table, chairs, narrow beds, and rudimentary stools were the only pieces of furniture. As she continued to scan the room, it occurred to her there were no kitchen facilities, nor water to wash her face, let alone rinse off. Of course, she had no clothes to change into, no shoes, and no brush for her tangled hair, either! The men looked, acted, and lived like animals, but that they actually expected her to exist in such an environment was inconceivable. The more she thought about it, the angrier she became. How dare they do this to her!

Hearing someone whistling outside, she stood. That she had nothing on but her nightdress wasn't about to keep her from confronting whoever it was.

In the clearing out front, Charley was running out of things to do. He'd been puttering around camp all morning waiting for Summer to wake up. Buck had insisted that someone keep an eye on her at all times. If she escaped and told the wrong people what had happened, Sheriff Cozens would come looking for them. Of course, Summer had no idea that they were under five miles from Mountain City, but Buck hadn't been about to tell her.

Charley was glad to finally hear the cabin door squeak open. Turning, he saw Summer standing in the doorway. She was a mighty beautiful woman. Her long auburn hair was spread out in disarray, descending down her white, high-necked gown. She looked to him the very picture of an angel. He smiled shyly. "How about a cup of coffee?" he called. "And now that you're up, I'll fix flapjacks. You could sure use some meat on your bones."

"Take me back to where I came from!" Summer demanded as she marched toward him. A rock stabbed the bottom of her foot, causing her to wince. She made a mental note to follow the worn path from now on.

"Now I can't do that, ma'am. Buck said you're to stay here, and we agreed on it." Charley scratched the back of his head. "Besides, what you got against stayin'? All we're askin' is that you give us some teachin'."

Summer placed her hands on her hips, ready to do battle. "Let someone else do the teaching. I refuse to be any part of this."

"Maybe you'll feel better after you get something in your belly."

"In my . . . ? Oh! You mean my stomach."

"What?"

"If you must refer to that part of my . . . anatomy, then call it by its proper name. Stomach."

"Stomach," Charley repeated. He couldn't understand what she was making such a fuss about. "You know, there ain't no sense gettin' that pretty head of yours all worked up. Like Buck said, you won't be going down the mountain till the next thaw, and that's a mighty long time to stay angry."

Summer had to force back the tirade that was about to erupt from her mouth. She didn't want to push the barrel-chested man into doing something she might regret. She was already making plans to escape. What was it going to take? A gun? She'd never even held one. She glanced at the hatchet that was sunk into a nearby stump. Don't be stupid, she chastised herself. What could you do once you got your hands on it? Kill the man?

Standing her ground, she was a little relieved when Charley sauntered over to a pile of rocks. What with the fire in the center, she could only conclude it was used for cooking. Next to that appeared to be a baking chamber. She studied her foe. Like the others, Charley was a big man. He possessed thick, unruly brown hair and was the heaviest of the three, but he was by no means fat.

From their obviously filthy habits, she thought it contradictory that all three men had broad smiles and surprisingly white teeth. She'd noticed last night that this man appeared to have an easygoing disposition. Could she convince him to help her get away?

Watching Charley slap a slab of bacon down on a flat, dirty rock, then start cutting slices with an equally messy knife, was almost more than Summer could handle. She turned away. She had to eat, if just to keep her strength up, but that didn't mean she had to torture herself by watching the food being prepared. A moment later the bacon was sizzling in a pan, and the delicious odor permeated the air. Her stomach growled, reminding her how long it had been since her last meal.

Charley's back was turned to her, and for a moment she considered giving him a good pounding with her fists. Then again, he might be the type that would hit her back. Also, instinct told her this was the wrong time to plead for help. She began walking around the clearing making a quick check of her surroundings and storing the information in her mind. Buck had brought her up the front slope of the mountain, so she hadn't realized that there was an almost sheer drop on the other side. Looking around, she saw huge peaks with thick forests of green fir that stopped well below the summits. There were no visible roads, no houses to be seen, nor anything that would indicate a direction she could escape toward. She was stuck in the middle of nowhere. Even the hope of rescue dimmed. Buck had been right. No one would have a clue as to where she was or who had absconded with her.

"Food's ready," Charley called genially to her.

Summer considered remaining where she stood just out of stubbornness. But knowing it would accomplish nothing, she capitulated and followed Charley back into the log cabin. There had to be a way of convincing him to help her. It was the only chance she had. She was sure Buck wouldn't do it, and she didn't know enough about Angus to even try. Though she made every effort not to dwell on her fear, it was always there, barely hidden behind a mask of bravery. Admittedly, so far the men had treated her with relative decency. But what did they have planned for her? "Teaching" seemed a lame excuse for kidnapping her. But why had she been brought here, if not to satisfy their lust? That was the frightening part.

Once inside the cabin, she took a seat at the table. It was so dusty she would have written her name on it with no difficulty. She looked down at the tin plate Charley placed in front of her, astounded at the tall stack of flat, round cakes. "I can't possibly eat all this," she half muttered.

"I reckon I didn't think of that." He sat a sticky can of syrup on the table and laughed. "I ain't used to fixin' for someone so small. Don't worry about it, just eat what you can." He pulled a chair out and sat across from her.

After having watched him cook, Summer's first reaction was to shove the plate aside. But it had been a long time since food had passed her lips, and besides, she could ill afford to insult the one man who was at least showing her a little compassion. Taking a bite, she found the food to be surprisingly good. However, she couldn't bring herself to eat the bacon.

"How does it taste?" Charley asked anxiously.

"Delicious. You're a very accomplished cook. Isn't your name Charley and the man with red hair Angus?" she asked between bites.

"Yep. Reckon we didn't get around to introducing ourselves last night.

"No, you didn't. Thank you for preparing my breakfast, Charley." She gave him the best smile she could muster.

Charley grinned from ear to ear. Buck and Angus were used to his cooking and seldom offered compliments.

Having eaten her fill, Summer turned pleading eyes toward the man. "Please, Charley, don't keep me here. Help me get back to Denver. I'll pay you. Don't you know I'd kill myself before I'd let any of you use me?"

A knot formed in Charley's throat. At that moment, he would have accommodated her gladly. Instead, he looked away and the moment passed. He wouldn't go against his partners. As Buck had put it, what's done is done. "I can't do that, ma'am," he replied sadly.

Slowly Summer placed her fork on the table. It wasn't easy to force back the threatening tears. She now knew, and had probably known all along, not a one of the burly men would help her.

It suddenly occurred to Charley what Summer had said. *Use her?* He certainly wouldn't have put it that way. Seeing the tears forming in her lovely eyes, he silently cursed himself and the others for being so damn stupid. "I been sitting here thinkin' that me, Angus, or Buck never really got around to spelling out just why we brung you here." He heard her intake of breath and quickly continued. "We do a lot of talkin', but sometimes don't really say much. Guess we've lived together for so long we know what the other's thinkin'"

Summer wondered if Charley had been outside to keep an eye on her. *If I can stay out of their way, maybe they'll leave me alone,* she thought, and tonight I can steal a horse. Anything would be better than remaining here, and how long would it be before one of them forced her into his bed? She'd been a ninny not to try it last night instead of falling asleep. Afraid her face might alert Charley to her thoughts, she poured more syrup over her flapjacks and made herself take another bite.

Charley placed his elbows on the table and leaned forward. "Now you might laugh, but you see, we're real serious about wantin' to get married to decent women. At least Angus and me are. Buck thinks we're loco. An English feller said no woman would have us unless we learned some manners and how to treat a lady properly. All we want you for is to learn us these things. I swear, nothing else. We didn't expect this to turn out the way it did."

Summer's eyes widened. Was he telling the truth? Suddenly she remembered manners being mentioned last night, but at the time she had thought they were playing with her.

"We're willing to do whatever you say," he said earnestly.

Her fork stopped in mid-air. "Anything?"

"Yep. That is, if it's gonna help us get women—and short of takin' you back down the mountain."

"Charley, I have a very dear friend in Denver. Can I at least send her a note saying I'm all right?"

"Can't do that either."

Furious, she realized she was absolutely trapped. The men wouldn't take her back to Denver or even let her get word to Milly. She was about ready to reach over the table and strangle Charley when she noticed his expression. He looked almost sorry, and half pleading. Suddenly, it occurred to her that, weak though she was, she wasn't exactly powerless. Apparently, the men wanted something from her. Summer's mind started ticking like a well-oiled timepiece. Maybe these three animals weren't all that different from ordinary men. And Summer never had any trouble handling them.

"Aren't you going to have something to eat?" Summer asked in a much friendlier tone.

"Nope. Me and the boys ate early this morning. See, I do the cooking, Buck goes to town for supplies 'cause he's good at talkin' to people, and Angus directs the buildin'. It's what each of us does best."

"And who's the boss?"

"Nobody. We vote if it's something important."

"Then all three of you decided to bring me here?"

"Not exactly." Charley chuckled. "It was Buck who came up with the idea of goin' to Denver to fetch a woman. Course, we didn't have anyone particular in mind, and sure didn't expect a kidnappin'."

"And who carried me to bed?"

"Buck."

"And . . . and did he sleep in the same bed?"

"Damned if I know. See, me and Angus was passed out. Reckon you'll have to ask Buck."

Summer wasn't about to ask that man anything. And it had been Buck's idea to bring her here. Though she was by no means feeling amiable, she smiled. "Yesterday someone said I would be paid. How do you plan to do that?"

"Hell, we're so damn rich it's goin' to take a mighty long time 'fore we can spend it all. See, we got us a fine little mine."

Summer took particular note of that. "Where are the others?" she asked casually.

"Working in the mine."

"I want to be sure I understand you correctly. I was brought here for only one purpose, and that is to teach you to be gentlemen? Nothing more?"

"That's right."

For the first time since her ordeal began, Summer's lips curved in a genuine smile. She had half a mind to take them up on their ridiculous deal, if only to exact her revenge. Oh, she could lead them on a pretty dance if she wanted to. For a minute she let herself imagine ordering the three bull-like men around, making them jump through hoops, having them buy her any and everything she desired. Summer especially relished the idea of putting Mister Buck in his place. He was such an abominable man! Now that would be an adventure well worth the trouble, and it would certainly save her from having to deal with William. Milly would be so thrilled to hear the story that she'd forget how worried she'd been during Summer's absence.

She'd do it—at least until she thought of something else. Before she could stop herself, she'd opened her mouth to speak.

"Charley, I'd like to have a meeting, and this time I want to do the talking. If all of you agree to my terms, I'll teach you what you want to know, and I'll promise not to run away." After all, she told herself, where would I go?

"Goddamn, Summer, I believe we got us a deal. I'll tell the boys."

When the huge noon meal was finished, Charley cleared the table and placed the thinking jug in its accustomed spot. Once everyone reassembled, the men looked at the woman who sat quietly with her hands folded in her lap.

Summer herself felt like a sparrow surrounded by vultures. Never in her wildest flights of imagination would she have pictured such a scene, especially with her barefoot and in her once-white nightdress. Since breakfast she'd given a great deal of thought to this venture, but she hadn't changed her mind. Now, with chin held high and back straight, she studied the enemy. This meeting was a big gamble. If they agreed to her plan, she had to make them think she was superior, at least in matters of conduct. To be sure, there could be no trace of apprehension in her voice when she laid out her agenda. She gently cleared her throat. "Gentlemen," she began.

Charley snickered.

"After talking to Charley this morning, I have finally come to understand what it is you want of me. I would have preferred to make my decision without being forced. However, since you have offered me no other recourse, I will agree to teach you to be gentlemen. But you must be willing to abide by my rules. I will be the sole authority in all matters that I believe pertain to your training. That is the only way it will work. I assure you, it's not going to be easy for you, or me. You will probably balk on more than one occasion, and I can be a hard taskmaster. However, if you give me your word . . . I assume you'll stand by your word?" She paused until they nodded. "If you give me your word you will not force yourselves on me physically and you'll listen and do as I say, I in turn shall promise to remain here until the winter snow melts. That is all I have to say. I'll step outside and you can discuss this between you. Call me when you've made your decision."

As Summer rose from her chair and left, she could feel the blood pumping through her veins. Power did have a strange effect on her. At the moment she felt more alive than she had in years.

It was a beautiful Indian summer day. Taking a big breath of fresh air, Summer caught the sweet smell of pine. All around her the mountains reached majestically for the sky. The scenery was truly a delight, she realized—though perhaps not so delightful that she wanted to spend the winter in this camp. On the other hand, who was to say she wouldn't enjoy that? She moved to one of the white-trunked trees that encircled the clearing and ran her hand across the smooth bark.

Inside, the three men stared at each other.

"What's there to discuss?" Angus asked. "Our minds were already made up when we decided to bring her here. Don't the both of you agree?"

Buck stood and went to the doorway. He watched Summer stop and inspect an old trap. "This is between you two and the woman. I never said I'd have any part of it."

"Hell, Buck," Charley spoke up, "it can't do nothin' but good. We all need to learn how to be gentlefolk. Even if you don't feel that way now, someday you might want to marry and settle down."

Buck snorted and shook his head. It would be a cold day in hell when he got himself yoked to a woman. He liked being his own man and living as he damn well pleased. Besides, he didn't trust the woman. She was just like the other pampered females he'd known back in St. Louis. Self-centered and conniving. He had a strong hunch Miss Summer wouldn't even be much pleasure in bed. Maybe she was after their gold now that she knew they were rich. He slowly turned. "I got a gut feeling that if you agree to her terms, you may be biting off too big a wad to chew. Another thing. Don't either of you think it's kind of strange that she's suddenly become so willin'?"

"What difference does it make?" Angus asked. "We're getting what we want."

"Then I suggest that if you accept her terms, you make damn sure it applies only when you're in camp."

Charley and Angus waited for Buck to go on, but he remained silent. So Charley went to the door and called Summer back in.

"We agree to your terms," Angus said, "but only when we're in camp."

Summer looked at Buck. She didn't like the smirk on his face. "All three of you?" she asked, her eyes never leaving his.

"'We' means Angus and Charley." Buck's words were clipped. "I want no part of it."

Summer looked at the other two shifting uncomfortably in their chairs. She couldn't let Buck out of this. He was the one she especially wanted to see eat mud. At any point during the trip up here, he could have told her what was going on. But no. He let her think the very worst and probably enjoyed every moment of it. "Then the deal's off," she stated firmly.

"What difference does it make?" Charley asked.

"It makes a big difference. Buck would be a bad influence on you and I want to feel safe." She heard him chuckle. "Keep me here if you can, but I guarantee I'll take off at the first opportunity. You can't keep watch on me the whole time until I'm to return to Denver." Summer silently prayed she wasn't pushing her luck. "All three of you must agree to my terms or I'll consider the matter closed." She crossed her fingers beneath the table. Seeing the angry looks Angus and Charley gave their partner, she had to bite her lip to keep from smiling. She couldn't wait to get Mister Buck under her thumb.

"Look, Buck," Charley said, "this means a lot to

me an' Angus. What's it gonna hurt you to go along with the deal?''

Buck was partly amazed that his buddy would pressure him, partly guilty about messing up the works. Most of all, he was mad as blazes at the way little Miss Summer had angled to divide them on this. He glared at her, but she only returned him a sweet, hypocritical smile.

"Yeah, Buck," Angus chimed in. " 'Member the time I pulled you out of that rock slide? Well, I'm calling the debt in."

At last he looked at his partners. "I should just knock some sense into the two of you—but I won't. Just don't come cryin' to me when you can't take it any longer."

Summer couldn't help gloating. "Am I to understand that you've decided to capitulate?"

"Capitulate, my ass," he growled. "All I'm sayin' is I accept your blasted terms."

Summer watched Buck squirm in his chair. She could almost taste her victory. Wouldn't Milly have loved witnessing this! But she knew she had to keep her wits about her. She decided now was the time to find out how much authority they'd allow her. "We might as well begin at once, gentlemen," she said.

Before the men had a chance to guess what she was up to, Summer grabbed the jug and tossed it out the open door. Everyone heard it break.

"There will be no more drinking."

"Son of a bitch!" Buck jumped to his feet and in two long strides was towering over her. "What the hell did you do that for?" he demanded.

Summer placed her hands beneath the table so the men wouldn't see them shaking. "And from now on, there will be no cursing."

"I've already had enough of this!" Buck was

tempted to throw her over his knee and give her a good spanking on the butt. Who the hell did she think she was to come here and start taking away their pleasures? What did that have to do with learning manners?

"Hell, it's only natural for men to drink and cuss," Angus explained. "You can't expect no man to do those things!"

"Those things are never done in the presence of a lady. Or are you already trying to find excuses to go back on your word?" With her heart in her throat, she gave them her best menacing look.

Buck sat back down. "Since you're goin' to be our teacher, we might as well start our lessons now. Tell me, do ladies go to bed with men and share in mutual delights?"

His blue-gray eyes had turned the color of stone. Summer knew he was furious, but she wasn't about to let him intimidate her. She glared back at him. "Very well. Your first lesson is that you don't ask such questions of a lady."

Buck sneered. He'd seen her cheeks flush. The woman was uncomfortable with the subject, no matter how much she tried to hide it. He now knew exactly how to knock the prickly Miss Summer down a few pegs. Out of all the women in Denver, how in the hell did he manage to pick the one virgin in the lot? He should have made sure it was the blonde he'd captured.

"Now let me get this straight," he persisted, determined to pay her back for what she'd done to their jug. "You're going to teach us to be gentlemen and how to act around proper women. Am I correct?"

Summer nodded.

"Well, accordin' to this friend of ours, we also have to learn to understand women. What pleases or displeases. Now how we gonna learn that if we can't ask questions without you gettin' all red in the face? I'm not interested in marrying a so-called lady if, when I get an itch, I gotta satisfy it in a place like Maybelle's."

Summer leaned back in her chair, trying to look relaxed. He was baiting her. If he saw he was successful, he'd pressure her unmercifully. She wanted him under her thumb, not the other way around. "You have a valid point," she said casually. "In reply, I can only teach you what women find attractive in men. What happens after that is between you and your lady. I will say that a decent woman saves herself for the man she marries. The thing to learn from this is that men do not bring up such subjects in front of ladies. It shows bad manners and makes the woman most uncomfortable." She dismissed Buck by looking at the others. "As I started to say, gentlemen, unmarried ladies do not sleep in the same cabin with men. Therefore, you shall all move out. Since Buck is the one who goes for supplies, tomorrow he can make a trip to town and get me dresses and shoes. As soon as I have those I'll go with him on his next trip and pick out the other things I'll be needing."

"It's a hell of a long way, *lady*, and not something I do daily. Just make a list and I'll fetch what you want." He wasn't about to tell her it was only five miles. She'd probably take off at the first opportunity.

Summer looked him up and down, clearly showing her distaste. It was obvious that Buck didn't like her any more than she liked him. "Very well, but you'll probably end up making more trips than usual. I'm not sure I can think of everything on the spur of the moment. Now, as of today you will start learning how to live like gentlemen. From this moment on I'm to be addressed as Miss Caldwell because we do not know each other well enough to be on a first-name basis. This cabin will be scrubbed from top to bottom and all this rubble tossed out. I can assure you, no bride would live in such a filthy shambles. Shall we begin?"

For a moment, Summer thought they were ready to attack. But slowly, one by one, they stood, Buck being the last.

"What does drinking, cussing, or movin' out and cleanin' have to do with being taught gentlemanly ways?" Buck demanded.

"What, may I ask, is your last name, sir?"

"Holester."

"Well, Mister Holester, to become a gentleman you must first learn to live like one."

"Where should we start?" Charley grumbled.

"Take out everything on the floor, then remove your personal things. I'll give further instructions when that's completed."

"But them's good traps and mining equipment," Angus said.

"Then I suggest you build some sort of storage shelter to put them in. I am not only going to turn you into gentlemen, I am also going to make this a place where a woman would be proud to live. I guess you know that more cabins will have to be built. You and your wives certainly can't all live together."

"If you're plannin' on havin' us do all these gentlemanly things, when are we gonna have time to work the mine?" Angus asked with no little amount of hostility.

"That's a fair question." Summer gave him a tolerant smile. "To begin with, I suggest you hire men to help, especially since you're supposed to have so much money. Not until the cabin is in decent shape will I begin instructions." She raised a finger to her bottom lip. "I believe evenings would be the best time for lessons. I'll have to think on it, but I can assure you I'll take your work into consideration. We'll discuss it further when the other things are completed."

Faces cast in steel, the men began picking up equipment. Summer discovered there wasn't even a broom, soap, or rags for cleaning. She did find paper and pencil and started jotting down what she wanted from town.

It was after the men had taken out the fourth load that Summer heard Buck say, "This is all your fault, Angus. You and Charley got a cockeyed idea in your head about gettin' married and just look what's happened. She's making jackasses out of all three of us! Every miner in the country is gonna be laughin' if it's discovered what's goin' on here. I'm not intendin' to bow and scrape for no woman."

"Ain't my fault! You're the bastard that came back with the wrong woman. Plus kidnappin' her!"

Hearing a loud smack, Summer ran to the door. Buck and Angus were rolling on the ground, dealing each other crunching blows. Charley stood to the side saying, "Hell, there ain't no use scrappin'. We done made a promise."

Summer walked to Charley's cooking area and picked up a sturdy skillet. It only took a rap on each man's head to stop the fight. Both men looked at her as if she'd gone crazy.

Summer froze. Had she lost her mind? Any one of these men could end her life with one hand tied behind his back. She'd have to bluff. "Gentlemen don't brawl, either," she stated, shocked at how calm she sounded. "Now if you're finished, we have a lot of work to do." She turned to Charley.

"Would you be so kind as to make a straw broom?"

Stunned that someone so little would dare do such a thing and get away with it, all Charley could say was, "Yes, ma'am."

"Come along gentlemen," Summer called as she headed back to the cabin. "There's still a lot of work to be done, and I don't want any more trouble." It wasn't until she had put some distance between herself and the men that her breathing returned to normal.

Chapter 4

Thoroughly disgruntled, Buck took off for Mountain City the next morning. He didn't like having to give up his bed again and he especially didn't like helping Lady Summer clean *her* cabin. When he left camp, Angus was hauling out the last of the traps. God only knew what else she'd take it in her head to make him do.

Buck rubbed his sore jaw while thinking about Summer's promise not to run away. He'd deliberately brought her up the mountain the long way, so as to avoid the other mines thereabouts. And he'd made it sound as if town was a long way away. All in all, he'd done a fine job of making her think she couldn't escape. Now, however, he wished she'd just disappear into the woods. For about two seconds after he'd agreed to take part in the ridiculous mess, he'd thought he might have some fun with Miss Caldwell. Then she'd thrown out the jug, taken over like she owned the damn place, and had them chasing around like a bunch of children. The lady had her nose up so high in the air, it was likely to get stuck.

But he had to admit that she bluffed well. For a moment yesterday, he'd actually thought he'd been wrong about her embarrassment when discussing intimacies between a man and a woman.

He knew now he'd been right the first time. She wasn't the first woman he'd seen displaying her morality like a pet dog. It was ironic, though. Most of the proper women he'd known—and especially the virgins—preached one thing, but were curious as hell about what went on between two hot-blooded people between the sheets. Was Queen Summer like that? He laughed at the possibility. Maybe he couldn't touch her, but he sure could tempt her. Tired of thinking about her and the lame-brained rules she'd laid down, he decided to make a stop at Maybelle's on the way back. After all, he wasn't in camp.

As he drove the team down Main Street, Buck was reminded of how Mountain City had changed in the last few years. The town had grown so fast that Buck often wondered if it was doomed to become another St. Louis. He didn't like living around so many people. In fact, if it hadn't been for the mine, he would have left long ago. But he'd stayed and watched it all, first the ten thousand boomers who'd rushed to Gregory Gulch dreaming of gold, and then the thousands of them who'd left penniless, to return to the states and enlist in the war.

He headed toward the mercantile store, suddenly wondering what he was going to tell the young widow who ran it. Lorna Templeton wasn't accustomed to him picking up needles, thread, china, and silverware, not to mention the other, more personal, items on Summer's list. At least one good thing would get accomplished. Today he'd hire men to help work the mine and get Lady Summer set up.

Buck entered the well-equipped store, the wooden floor creaking beneath his heavy boots. "Mornin'," he said to the owner standing behind the counter. He noted that as always, Lorna's brown hair was perfectly groomed, her cheeks rosy, and her skin the color of cream. A lovely woman and a terrible gossip.

"Howdy, Buck." Lorna turned toward the only other customer. "Do you plan on buying something, or are you just going to look?" she asked the small Chinaman. Her chin was set and her arms folded over a full bosom.

With a quick bow, the man left.

"They're always looking, never buying. Where you been keeping yourself, Buck? I hear tell you boys hit pay dirt."

"Yep, it's lookin' real good." Buck stopped and fondled some cloth remnants displayed on the counter. He knew he might as well get the matter of Summer Caldwell over and done with. "Guess you also heard we got us a guest." Looking up, he saw a tiny, excited smile flit across the woman's full mouth. Her cheeks even brightened.

"No. Who?"

"Charley's cousin. Looks like she's planning on stayin' till late spring. So, now here I am havin' to buy a lot of stuff that I know nothin' about."

"Well, don't worry, I'll handle it. You came at a good time. The men got through with the pack mules, so I'm pretty well stocked. Them Arapahoe and Cheyenne have been playing hell with the supply trains. There's been talk of getting some volunteers together to go after them."

"You don't say." Buck handed over the list.

"Why didn't Charley's cousin come with you?" Lorna asked while studying the order.

"She's busy cleanin' the cabin. You know how women are, they come to a new place and immediately want to change everything."

"What's her name?"

"Summer Caldwell. While you're gatherin' up things, I'll head over to the feed store. Then I got business I need to take care of. Probably be back in a couple of hours."

"Wait a minute. What size is the woman?"

He pointed to his chest. "She comes to about here."

Lorna went over and pulled a ready-made dress from the rack. "Would this fit her?"

"Hell, no. Much too big around the middle. She's got a real little waist." He chuckled. "The rest of her is just fine, too."

"Oh? Perhaps you can find one that would fit better."

Buck sorted through the clothes. A couple of times he had Lorna hold a dress to her so he could get an idea about size. Finally he settled on one.

"I'll let you pick out a couple of dresses 'bout this big. And there's lines on the back of that list. That's the length and width of her foot for shoes."

He was again headed toward the door when he caught sight of something in one of the cases. Halting, he looked back at Lorna and said, "Let me see that."

"Oh . . . I don't think you want that."

"You're wrong."

"But it's night clothing."

He reached behind the glass case and removed the article. Holding it up, Buck smiled. "I'll take it." Then he tossed the light piece of clothing to Lorna and walked out.

An hour later, Buck had just finished loading feed onto the wagon and was about to climb up on the seat when he heard someone call his name. Glancing around, he saw a short, balding man headed down the boarded walk towards him. The stranger's tailored blue suit led Buck to guess that he was from the city.

"I assume I have the right man," the gentleman said when he stopped in front of Buck. "Name's Elliot Toddle. I represent Pierson Mining Investments."

"Never heard of them." Buck started to turn away.

"I'm not surprised," Toddle persisted. "It's an Eastern company. If you could spare a moment, I'd like to buy you a drink and discuss an offer my company wants to make for your mine."

"How did you know my name?"

"I was asking directions to the Whiskey Hole Mine at the mercantile store, and the woman said I would find you here."

Buck was well aware that Eastern concerns were not only buying up mines, but putting pressure on some of the owners. "My partners and I aren't interested in selling, Mister Toddle, so there's nothing to discuss."

"A lot of miners in the area are finding times hard because they haven't the money it takes to develop their claims properly." Mister Toddle shifted his weight. He would have preferred to sit down with this man, which would at least put them on an even level. It was a strain on him to keep having to look up. "My company pays good money. At least the miners end up with a substantial amount to show for their efforts. Now I know the Whiskey Hole is doing well, but what about in years to come? At least let me discuss it with your partners."

"We've already talked about it, and like I said, we're not interested."

"Well, keep me in mind if you ever change your mind."

Buck swung up to the seat. He flicked the reins over the team's shiny rumps, not bothering to give Toddle so much as a nod.

As it turned out, there were a lot of miners around town who had fallen onto hard times, so it didn't take Buck long to hire good men. Satisfied with how the day had gone, he headed back to the mercantile store.

Apparently, since he'd left her earlier, Lorna had had time to think, so she was loaded with questions: What did Charley's cousin look like, how old was she, and on and on. She especially wanted to know why the woman needed clothes. Of course she didn't tell Buck she'd chosen two of the ugliest dresses in the store as well as a gaudy pair of red slippers— all because of the revealing nightdress he'd selected. On more than one occasion Lorna had tried to get Buck to take her to a dance, but he always found some excuse. Now it almost sounded as if he'd taken a shine to Charley's cousin. He certainly admired her figure.

Buck had to think fast to explain Summer's need of clothes. He told Lorna that the stage Summer had been traveling on was held up, and she had lost everything.

On the way home, Buck reviewed his conversation and decided he'd handled the problem of Summer quite well. Maybe he hadn't stuck to the truth, but close enough. And there was another matter that tended to tickle his ribs. By going to town he'd escaped a lot of the work Summer was making the boys do.

Back at camp, Angus' thoughts were running along the same lines. Standing by a water bucket, he watched Charley toting equipment around the clearing. Buck was the lucky one. He'd been permitted to leave. Angus had to admit, this entire mess was beginning to aggravate him. How could wanting to get married to a nice woman have brought all this on? Of course, he wasn't about to tell Buck of his misgivings. Buck was the one who had opposed this whole thing.

At least there was one good note to go with all the sour ones. He and Charley had finished cleaning the lady's cabin, and two of the beds were now in the shaft house. It would be a simple matter to have a third one built by nightfall.

Angus scratched his bearded chin. He was in the mood for a drink and a good fight. But the thought of another skillet coming down on his head had no appeal. During the day he had managed to sneak a couple of quick swings of whiskey, but even that had come to a halt. They were already low before Summer had arrived, and due to make a run to Hickory Joe's still. Now it looked like that pleasure was doomed. He started to kick the pile of equipment but changed his mind. The way things were going, he'd probably end up breaking a toe.

He glanced toward the cabin, where billows of dust were being swept out the doorway. Then he saw Summer and had to grin. His red bandanna was still wrapped around her head, and her hair was a tangled mess. But he could see why Charley thought she looked like an angel, even though at the moment her face and nightdress were thoroughly smudged with dirt. Admiration swept over him. The little lady may not have done any carrying, but she didn't back away from work. Drawing a dipper of water, he headed in her direction.

"Here, Miss Caldwell," he said gently. "I think you could use a drink."

Summer accepted the offering. The cool water

was a blessing to her parched throat. "I suppose we'd better get back to work," she said halfheartedly.

"Tell you what. Why don't we take a rest?"

She started to protest, but stopped when he took her wrist.

"We'll get back to the work. It ain't somethin' that's gotta be done in a day. How would you like to take a look through the mine?"

Though she wanted to very much, Summer hesitated. Charley was considerate, and she felt safe with him. She knew nothing about Angus. Like the others, his unruly hair hung well past his shoulders and the red beard reached down to his chest. She had noticed that Angus' hazel eyes changed color with his moods. Right now they contained a definite spark of orneriness. "Where is Charley?" she asked suspiciously.

Angus broke out in a hearty laugh. "Don't tell me you're afraid? Darlin', I admit I like women and you're about the prettiest little angel I've had the pleasure of meeting. But I made a bargain, and I'll abide by it." He smoothed the sides of his beard. "Now should you ever want to make some changes to that agreement, just let me know."

Summer had to grin at his brazenness.

"To answer your question, Charley went to the smokehouse to fetch meat."

"I apologize for the hesitation, Mister Comstock. I'd very much like to see the mine."

Angus reached down and swung her up in his arms.

"What are you doing?" she cried.

"Miss Caldwell, there's a path leading down, but I don't reckon your feet could handle the rocks."

To Summer's amazement, Angus didn't smell half as rank as she'd expected him to. Now that she thought about it, neither had Buck when he'd carried her to the creek. They had more of an earthy smell about them, which actually wasn't unpleasant.

As he carried her down the slope, Summer squeezed her eyes shut, convinced that any moment they were both going to topple to the bottom. And it was a long way down.

"You can open your eyes now. We're only a short ways from the mine." Angus stood her back on her feet. "The ground's smooth from here on."

Summer released a sigh of relief. Though she knew the trip had only taken minutes, to her it had seemed like an eternity. Even standing on the wide path, she refused to look out over the edge where the trail gave way to a cliff. Her eyes straight ahead, she surveyed the structure at the head of the mine. "What's that?" she asked, pointing toward it. She needed a moment to regain her composure and stop acting like a frightened ninny.

"That's a holding bin for ore. Look on over and you'll see the shaft house we've started. We're gonna have to add on to it now that equipment has to be stored there."

Summer refused to let him make her feel guilty. "It looked to me like the equipment hasn't been used for some time, so why not get rid of it?" They had started forward, and Summer made sure she walked on the safe side of the path.

"Well, it's like this. One minute we was makin' do, and the next minute we had all that gold. Our eyes tell us one thing, but after working so long and comin' up with almost nothin', our insides ain't quite convinced it's not gonna disappear. When we get used to bein' rich, we'll probably do just as you say. Get rid of it."

Summer would never have thought any one of

the men capable of such sensible logic. Because they lived so uncouthly, she'd assumed they had the mentality of animals.

"Did you know the name of the mine is Whiskey Hole?" Angus asked.

"Why would you name it that?"

"When we dug the air shaft, Charley accidently dropped a full jug down it. We figured it was a christening and named it Whiskey Hole. You know, we never did find that jug."

Feeling a little more secure, Summer was able to laugh.

Summer was a little disappointed when she saw the entrance to the mine. It was nothing more than a big hole reinforced by timber. She'd expected something more grand. At least she had enough sense to keep her mouth shut.

The coat Angus gave her almost weighed Summer down, but she felt thankful for its warmth once they entered the mine.

As they moved into the bowel of the mountain, Summer found the path smooth. She became fascinated as Angus explained some of the various procedures of mining. Among other things, he showed her a double-handed drill and told her how dynamite was set for blasting. And when he led her to the gold ore vein, Summer held her breath. She'd never seen anything like it, and now believed that this unlikely threesome was truly rich.

Summer was in a pleasant frame of mind when they came out an hour later. Angus had been both informative and entertaining. But she welcomed the sunshine and fresh air. Unlike the men, she'd never be able to stay underground for long periods of time.

Angus started back up the path with Summer in

his arms. As soon as they reached the top, he let her down.

"Where you been?" Charley called from the stump he was perched on. "I looked all over and was startin' to get worried."

Summer smiled. "There was no need for that. Angus was kind enough to show me the mine."

Charley slowly rose to his feet. "Is she sayin' you took her inside, Angus?"

"Yes, he did." Seeing the anger on Charley's face, Summer's happy mood evaporated.

"You're a damn fool Angus Comstock! You aimin' to get us all killed?"

"You listen to too many tales," Angus lashed back.

"Gentlemen, what is this all about?" Summer interjected. "As you can see, Charley, I'm perfectly fine."

"It's bad luck to take a woman in a mine. Ain't no miner around that would do such a thing."

"He's just superstitious. Pay him no mind. We got a lot of work to do, Charley. You comin', or are you goin' to stand around bitchin' like some old woman?"

"I'm comin', but if anything happens in that mine, it's damn well going to be on your shoulders!"

Summer watched the men until they disappeared from view. Angry words drifted back, but they were muffled. Though she had never been of a superstitious nature, Charley's words bothered her. Angus should never have taken her to the mine if Charley felt so strongly about such things. And what would Buck say when he found out? She shrugged. There was nothing she could do about it now.

The cabin was spotless when Summer heard

Buck return. At last she'd have decent clothes to wear. She started to leave the cabin when it occurred to her that in a few short days, she'd lost all sense of decorum. Before she'd come here, she would never have allowed a man to see her in nightclothes, even though the heavy material covered her completely. Yet without shame she'd boldly paraded in front of three burly beasts. She'd even allowed one of them to carry her to a tunnel. Well, that sort of behavior would have to stop. She wouldn't step foot outside again until properly dressed. After all, she was supposed to be the model, proper lady.

But all thoughts of propriety vanished as Summer watched Buck bring in the last of his purchases. Feeling like a child about to open Christmas presents, she waited for him to leave.

"The stove will have to wait," he said. "I need someone to help carry it."

Buck was about to walk out the door when the offensive smell of liquor reached Summer's nostrils.

"Just one moment!"

He stopped.

"I thought we made an agreement, Mister Holester."

Buck slowly turned. The prickly miss was a comical sight standing barefoot and ramrod straight in the middle of the room. He would have bet a good size poke that she'd never been so dirty in her entire life. "What is your complaint this time, teacher?" he asked. "I brung your things."

Besides everything else, the man's English is horrendous, Summer thought. "You have imbibed spirits and you needn't deny it!"

"Am I supposed to report all my activities to

you?'' He smiled. "If so, maybe you'd like to know what else I did at Maybelle's.''

Summer felt blood rush to her face. "That won't be necessary! You and your partners agreed to stand by your word, and now you've already broken that promise."

"Just how do you figure that?" His smile disappeared.

"We agreed that I am to have complete say about anything pertaining to gentlemanly conduct, and I said there would be no more drinking."

"That was only in camp. And besides, are you gonna stand there and tell me gentlemen don't drink?"

"Well . . . no. Just not around ladies."

Buck rubbed the back of his neck. "Then how can you rightly accuse me of breaking my word? Believe me, Miss Caldwell, there weren't no *ladies* around, if you get my meanin'."

"Oh, I get your meaning, Mister Holester. However, the next time you go to town I intend to accompany you. Like it or not, this won't happen again."

"And will you be aimin' to go along to Maybelle's?"

"I certainly will not!"

Buck was laughing as he went outside.

"Oh! Blast the man!"

Refusing to let him upset her any further, Summer turned and studied the copper bathing tub. Getting it had really been a last minute thought. She began checking the other things. Heavens! It looked like so much.

She found several bolts of material, and was already envisioning additional dresses. There was even chintz to make curtains. She never thought the day would come when she'd actually be grate-

ful for the stitchery instructions her mother had
insisted on over the years.

The clothes were at the bottom of the pile. Finally
she held up a cotton dress and was reminded of
something the servants in Philadelphia would wear
during their free time. The style was at least ten
years old. There was another dress just like the
first. But no matter what they looked like, they
were better than what she'd been running around
in. The shoes were another matter: bright red, soft-
soled slippers that clashed terribly with the frocks.
She just knew Buck had chosen them to spite her.

The pantalettes, chemise, and underskirts she
found next were plain and by no means of the
softest cotton she'd ever felt. And the corset was
little more than a waist cinch. Going through these
personal items, she was reminded of the embarrassment she'd felt when writing the list. But Buck
seemed to think nothing of it. How many other
women had he bought clothing for? Stop it! Summer chastised herself. Be happy you finally have
something to wear.

Summer was quite taken back when she discovered the nightdress. The pale cream silk had wide,
delicate alençon lace down the front and around
the long sleeves. She couldn't help but notice the
drastic difference between this piece and the other
articles of clothing. It was really quite lovely. But
it wasn't something a lady could ever accept from
a man. She should throw it in his face. Still . . .
maybe she'd keep it. She just wouldn't mention it
to anyone, especially Buck.

Needing privacy, Summer closed the door, then
shoved the wooden bar through the iron slot. It
took a little work to cover the two windows. When
she was convinced there would be no intrusions,
she slipped out of her clothes and poured the

bucket of water Charley had brought in earlier into the tub. The bath felt heavenly, and afterward, as she dressed, Summer was astounded at how well everything fit. All that was needed were a few tucks here and there. Of course the fit had to be coincidental. Buck couldn't possibly have guessed her correct size.

Combing out her tangled hair brought tears to her eyes. Finally she was able to weave the thick mass into a neat braid. She used a strip of material to tie the end. Looking proper for the first time since her arrival, Summer Caldwell was ready to face the world. But when she stepped outside there was no one around to appreciate her. The sound of hammering told her the men were at work. Disappointed, she went back in the cabin ready to place the china on the shelves Angus had put up.

When Charley returned to start supper, Summer was ready. The table had been properly set, including napkins, and tonight the instructions would begin. She had also worked out the schedule for lessons on deportment and proper grammar.

"Well, I'll be damn . . . dang," Charley said when he saw Summer headed his way. "You gotta be prettier than anything the Lord's still keepin' upstairs!"

"Thank you, Charley. I hope you're not still angry about my going into the mine." Seeing the sides of his mouth twitch, she knew he was.

"Ain't no cause for you to worry, Miss Caldwell. Weren't your fault." He proceeded to start a fire for cooking.

Summer knew better than to pursue the matter. Maybe while learning to be a gentleman he'd forget about the incident. "I have bowls to put the food in when it's ready, and a platter for the meat," she said.

"Yes, ma'am."

With nothing to do but wait, Summer took a stroll. Spying an outcrop, she walked to the end. It took a moment for her to get up enough courage to look over the edge. First she saw a road, and not that far down. Her eyes traveled up the far side. That was when she spied swatches of yellowish dirt splattered across the mountainside. A hard knot of suspicion began to form in her throat. She headed back to Charley.

"Shall I bring the platter?" she asked upon seeing steaks being cooked.

"Food ain't gonna be ready for another fifteen minutes or so."

"Tell me, Charley. What is that colored dirt spilling over the side of the mountain?"

"I reckon you're talking about tailings. It's what's thrown away after the ore's been washed out."

"Are you telling me there are mines across the way?"

"Yep. There's mines covering the land for miles around." He dipped a big spoon into a pan of water containing dried apples. "A lot of 'em have been abandoned, but others are still being worked."

Suddenly Summer realized she'd been tricked into staying, and knew exactly whose shoulders to put the blame on. Buck Holester. Furious, she went back to the cabin for the necessary dishes. Before too long, maybe she could talk one of the men into taking her to town. Then they wouldn't be able to hold her captive, and she would be free at last. On the other hand, maybe she would settle for making Charley, Angus, and especially Buck, miserable. She already had a good idea how it could be done. Come to think of it, she couldn't think of a better way to spend the winter.

When supper was ready, Summer watched the

men sit down at the table and start stabbing at the steaks Charley had put on a platter. "Stop it this very minute!" They were so busy talking to each other she had to yell to get their attention.

Forks and knives came to a halt in midair.

"As I said, gentlemen, the training begins tonight. Put the meat back on the platter."

Reluctantly, they returned the meat.

"If you will notice, I have yet to sit down. So, we'll start over. Gentlemen always stand until a lady is seated."

Buck scowled. "Damn it, we're hungry. We've put in a full day's work."

"So have I, Mister Holester. And please remember to watch your language. The sooner you follow my instructions, the sooner you'll eat. I thought that was why you brought me here and went to so much trouble to make sure I stayed."

Buck didn't miss the sarcasm in her voice. He smiled. He'd wondered how long it would take for her to find out there were other people in the area.

"Well? Are you going to get up?" she asked.

They rose as one.

"That's better. Now, push the chairs back in and stand behind them." Satisfied, Summer continued. "At each meal, a different man will seat me. Charley, we'll start with you tonight. Come here."

He ambled over.

Summer gave instructions on how to pull the chair out. Once seated, she permitted the men to return to their places.

Summer took a purposeful look at each of her subjects. "There will be no smacking of lips, the napkins are to be unfolded and placed in your laps, and your left hand should remain in your lap when you're not using it to cut your meat. Light conversation is permitted, but the lady at the table should be included. We do not start eating until everyone is ready. Angus, you may begin passing the food around."

It was a slow meal because Summer was constantly making comments about the men's behavior, especially Buck's. She was beginning to suspect he had to be related to a pig.

Meanwhile, Buck was quite enjoying himself. He rather liked frustrating the Queen Virgin. He noticed Charley and Angus looking at him questioningly, but they said nothing. The lady was a beauty and looked particularly handsome with her new dress and combed hair. But he rather preferred the way she had looked in her nightdress.

Though Summer maintained a calm demeanor, she was surprised to see how well the men were taking her nagging. In fact, off and on they even had the gall to tease her about it.

When the meal was completed and the men had placed their napkins on the table as instructed, she decided it was time to drop her cannonball. She cleared her throat, successfully drawing their attention. "Tomorrow night, gentlemen, I expect you to arrive with your hair properly cut and combed, and clean shaven. A trim mustache will be acceptable." Their silence pleased her. She'd finally gotten to them.

Suddenly Angus broke out laughing. "Look at it this way, boys. If we're gonna be rich, we might as well do it in style."

"I . . . I have the new shears Buck bought if you need them," Summer stuttered. This wasn't the reaction she'd expected. "Furthermore, you will be clean. That includes your clothes."

Buck combed his fingers through his black hair. "Guess after we get the new men started in the morning we'll just have to make a trip to town, boys. Ain't the gals at Maybelle's gonna be surprised to see us all prettied up?"

Summer winced. "So. You decided to take my advice about hiring extra help." She felt quite smug about it.

"Sorry, Miss Caldwell. We decided that before you came."

"I see. Well thank you, Mister Holester, for pointing that out to me."

"You had the right idea though, Miss Caldwell," Charley said, trying to make her feel good.

"I have decided that each of you should spend no less than five hours a week learning decorum and grammar. Let's hope that will be enough. If not, we'll have to take more time. Is that agreeable?"

They nodded.

"Then, gentlemen, you may stand. Mr. McMillan, you will pull my chair out."

Charley jumped eagerly to his feet. He grabbed the back of her chair and gave a hard tug. Summer fell forward, her face landing in the uneaten apples still on her plate.

"Are you okay?" Charley's brown eyes widened. "I didn't break anything, did I?" He practically whispered the words.

With as much dignity as possible, Summer straightened up. "Nothing is broken." She picked up her napkin and slowly wiped off the mess.

Seeing she was all right, the men almost doubled over laughing.

"Hell, Charley," Buck finally managed to say, "she's just a little thing. You gotta learn to be more careful."

"Good night, gentlemen," Summer stated flatly, dismissing them.

Lying on her bed that night, Summer thought

about what she must have looked like with stewed apples on her face. She couldn't help but smile. Had the shoe been on the other foot, she probably would have laughed also. How long had it been since she'd had a good laugh? Angus, Charley, and Buck seemed to find all kinds of things to laugh at and fight over. They shared a joy for living as well as a close bond.

For a minute Summer thought about what her life had been like before coming here. She'd been desperately bored and restless—not to mention undecided about William. The first genuine anger she'd experienced in years had come when Buck swept her away from the hotel.

In all honesty, it was hard to remain angry with Angus and Charley. Charley treated her like some one special, and Angus was a charmer, in a silent sort of way. When he took her in the mine, she had been shocked at how heavy a pick was. No wonder their arms were so big. Even after being told they usually put in ten to twelve hours a day, seven days a week, it was hard for her to picture how three men had doggedly carved so many long tunnels and shafts. Listening to Angus and seeing what they had accomplished had actually made her respect them.

She jerked up into a sitting position. "This won't do, Summer Caldwell. You've known these men a short time and you're already letting your guard down. Beware, girl! They've mistreated you, and you'd do well not to forget it."

As Summer fluffed the pillow, she made up her mind to insist on going into town tomorrow with the boys. She was in need of a warm coat and a decent pair of shoes. And it would be fun to make them worry that she might run away. She wasn't planning on it, though. She had a score to settle—

at least with Buck. Suddenly she remembered the way he'd sat at the table, trying to be delicate about cutting his meat. He'd never make a gentleman, but that didn't mean she wouldn't take great pleasure in trying to whip him into shape.

Chapter 5

The next morning, not long after sunup, Summer woke with a start, jumped out of bed, and ran to the window, convinced that all hell was breaking loose. She yanked back the makeshift curtain and looked out. Strangers were moving about, hammering and sawing, and in the distance she could hear trees being cut down. She knew they had to be the hired men, but weren't they supposed to be working down in the mine, she wondered. And why hadn't someone bothered to inform her that they would be arriving in the wee hours of the morning?

By the time Summer had dressed and stepped outside, wagons were arriving with equipment and lumber. Headed towards Charley's stove, she turned several circles in an effort to see everything that was going on. Bless you Charley, she thought when she saw the pot of hot coffee sitting in readiness. She was about to pour a cup of the steaming brew when the noisy sounds slowly ceased. Looking around, she saw the men staring at her.

"What the hell you doing?" Summer heard Angus yell to the workers. "Ain't you never seen a woman before?"

"Not like this one," a man hollered back.

Others agreed and some cheered.

79

Angus laughed. "I got no argument about that, but if you plan on bein' paid, you'd better get to work. I can always replace you."

Summer was taken aback until she suddenly realized she was being paid the biggest compliment of her life. Smiling, she curtsied. After whoops and laughter, the workers returned to their duties. To Summer's delight, a man began singing a lively song and others soon joined in. She poured her coffee.

"You've made the men happy. By tomorrow you'll be the talk of the territory."

Summer almost spilled her drink. Like a sneak thief, Buck had approached her from the back. "Mister Holester. You startled me. Shouldn't you be working?"

"That's why we hired help."

The big man was standing too close. Summer tried to step away, but the rock stove impeded her retreat.

"I noticed you were tapping your toe to the men's song. Do you like to dance?"

"Yes. Very much."

"Since we're on the path to becoming gentlemen, perhaps dancin' lessons could be included."

The right side of his mouth curled in a lopsided smile, giving Summer the distinct feeling he was teasing her. "I suppose so. I thought you hired the men to work the mine."

"I did, and I've already got them started."

"Then what are these workers doing?" she asked with a wave of her hand.

Buck chuckled. "Some are unloading track, cars, and switches, which Charley is seeing to, others are completing the shaft house, and some are building you a house, including a cellar and kitchen." He watched her green eyes light up with interest.

"A house?"

"Yep. Isn't that what you said we should do? When it's finished we'll move you in and take back the cabin. There's also going to be a barn with stalls for horses."

"A house," she said in awe.

Buck reached past her for a metal cup. Pinned against the stove, Summer had to suck in her breath to keep his arm from brushing against her. To her relief, he moved away and dipped the cup into the water barrel.

Summer decided now was a good time to inform him of last night's decision. "I'm going to town with you today to purchase some more things I need. While I'm there, maybe I can begin furnishing my new house." After being raised in a twenty-one room Philadelphia mansion it struck her as odd that a little wooden house would make her so excited. But for some reason it did. "There will be a dining room, won't there?"

"You'll have to take that up with Angus," he said, watching her speculatively. "So, you're going to town with us. Does that mean you'll also be going to Maybelle's?"

Summer choked on her coffee.

"There is a matter that I don't think you've given much consideration to, Miss Caldwell," he went on.

She wiped her mouth with the tips of her fingers. "And just what is that, Mister Holester?"

"We agreed to abide by your rules *in camp*. But we're healthy men, and we have certain needs."

Summer turned away.

"Now if you're plannin' to also take care of that—"

She swung back around. "How dare you speak that way to me! I'm not one of your ... women, Mister Holester! I'll ask you to keep a civil tongue!"

"I did. I could have been a lot more blunt. But now that we have an understanding, you're perfectly welcome to come along. A word of advice, though. There are some things we do you have no business interfering in—unless that is, you plan to join right along." He smiled. "And if that day ever comes, I'll be first in line."

Summer clenched her fists to keep from reaching out and slapping the man. "I'll be ready when it's time to go," she said, then headed back to the cabin.

Summer's hand clutched the edge of the wooden seat as the buckboard bounced over another rock. She was convinced that any moment she would be thrown off the side. "Isn't there another route we can take?" she asked Charley.

"It'll smooth out on up, but I'll try to drive more careful. The problem is you're too stiff. Turn loose and think of it as riding a horse. They call this 'Old Hell Road'."

"I can certainly understand why." Summer forced herself to relax and look around. The road down the mountain switched back and forth countless times and was bordered by thick stands of pine. As she watched the passing scenery, she realized Charley was right. Giving with the sway of the wagon made the trip much easier. Nevertheless, her hand remained curled around the edge of the seat.

To Summer's relief the road did eventually get a little better. Feeling considerably safer, she glanced ahead at the two men on horseback. Buck was talking and Angus laughing, making her wonder if Buck as relating their conversation from early this morning. She'd decided the man was deliberately trying to make her feel on edge, probably because he was angry that she had come along. With a lady in their company they wouldn't be able to stop at that . . . place of ill repute. She settled back, enjoying the crisp mountain air and sunshine.

"There she be," Charley said as he brought the team to a halt.

Sitting atop a hill, Summer looked down and had her first glimpse of town. It was much larger than she expected, with at least a thousand log cabins scattered across the valley.

"It's kind of hard to tell where it begins and where it stops. They sort of run together." Charley pointed to the right. "That east part is Blackhawk, the west Central City, and Mountain City is sort of in the center."

From Summer's vantage point, it looked like one big sprawl.

"All right, get on there," Charley called to the horses.

Summer gripped the seat as the buckboard jerked forward and descended the last long hill.

When they entered town, Summer grew excited. They passed hotels, shops, and she even saw a log theater. There were men everywhere, but few women. She noted that her presence seemed to be creating quite a stir.

Buck turned in the saddle just as the look of anticipation spread across Summer's face. How did they know she'd keep her word and not skedaddle, he asked himself. On the other hand, maybe it would be a good idea to let her go, considering how bleak their future looked.

As they continued down Main Street, Buck

pulled his horse in close to Angus. "Think we need to keep an eye on the lady?" he asked.

"I been wondering the same thing." Angus said in a low tone of voice. "Maybe we shouldn't leave her alone."

Buck slipped off his hat and mopped his brow with his sleeve. "As warm as it's been, I got a feeling we're in for a mean winter. Hell, Angus. What are we talkin' about, anyway? If the woman ain't gonna stick around, there's nothing we can do about it short of tying her up in the cabin. And even that probably wouldn't work after today. The new men will be asking about her. And if she's gonna run, we'd best find out now instead of later."

"I reckon you're right, but if she hightails it, I'm gonna be damn mad. I might even go lookin' for her! Buck, if we're takin' her to Lorna's don't you think she should know she's Charley's cousin?"

"Yep." Buck slowed his horse and waited for the buckboard to catch up. He pulled alongside Summer. "Thought you should know, Miss Caldwell, you're supposed to be Charley's cousin."

"I'll not lie, Mister Holester." She refused to even look at him.

"Don't matter to me. It's your reputation." With that, he spurred his horse and took off at a gallop.

"Just what was he suggesting, Charley?"

"Well you see, Lorna Templeton, who owns the general store, is quite a gossip. As Buck put it to us, tellin' Lorna you and me is related might prevent you from havin' a red face."

"Oh." Summer could kick herself. Was it because she'd been out of touch with civilization that she hadn't even stopped to consider what people would think of her situation? All her life she'd been taught to be careful of her reputation. Though she

hated to admit it, Buck's forethought had certainly
been better than hers. She turned to the man seated
next to her and smiled. "I would be proud to be
your cousin, Charley."

When Summer entered the mercantile store, the
men surrounded her, like Roman guard around
their emperor. Each knew this was the test. Would
Summer hold up her end of the bargain?

"Howdy, Buck," Lorna greeted him with a smile
that was too obviously coquettish. "You back so
soon? And Angus and Charley even came with
you!" Her grin broadened. "I haven't seen you
boys in a month of Sundays."

The men parted and Lorna saw Summer. Lorna
had to admit the woman was a real beauty. Even
the ready-made dress she'd sent back looked good
on the lady. Lorna could almost taste her own jealousy.

Normally Buck would have found the situation
amusing, but at the moment his attention was focused on Summer. Would she pull the curtain on
them?

Seeing Lorna's smile weaken, Charley stepped
forward. "Lorna, I'd like you to meet Summer
Caldwell. Whatever she charges on our account is
just fine."

Summer was surprised at how young Lorna
Templeton was. She couldn't be a day over thirty.
Rich brown hair surrounded a pretty face, and she
was quite tall. Summer would never have suspected the woman was a gossip. "Hello," Summer
said cheerfully. "Cousin Charley said you have the
largest and best mercantile store around."

The men looked at each other with relief. Summer wasn't going to cry for help.

"You have so many nice things," Summer commented as she browsed about the store. "What I'm

looking for, Lorna, is a good pair of shoes. Buck brought back these horrible red slippers I'm wearing, and the soles are too soft for the rocks." She stopped, looked at the owner, and smiled. "I just know you can show me the type of shoe I'll need."

Lorna had to admit, Summer was of a friendly disposition, and intelligent enough to ask for help. Of course the compliment about her store was duly appreciated, though Summer didn't need to know the truth about the shoes. "I sure do. You come over here and have a seat. I got some women's boots that will be just right for you."

"If you have things to do," Summer said to the men, "don't let me delay you."

"You gonna be all right?" Charley asked.

"Yes. I'm sure Lorna can help me with everything I need or direct me as to where I should go. Where shall I meet you, Charley? Here or someplace else?"

"Here will be fine. We won't be long."

"Good. There are quite a few things I want to order for the new house."

The men hesitated a moment, not sure if they should leave Summer and Lorna alone, but finally turned as one and walked out.

"According to Buck, you were on a stage that got held up, and you lost all your clothes," Lorna said when she returned with the boots. "Talked to Billy Updyke, and he said Buck had to be foolin' me. According to Billy, his stage has never been held up."

Summer sat on the chair to remove her bright red slippers. Obviously Lorna was fishing for information or trying to catch Buck in a lie. Summer was glad she'd been forewarned about the fact that she was to pose as Charley's cousin, but Buck could have at least informed her about what else he'd said. She took a deep breath. If she had to lie, she might as well make it convincing. "It happened on the way from Philadelphia," she began. "The bandits were absolutely horrible looking men, and I was scared half out of my mind!"

"I can sure understand that. It must have been a terrible experience."

"And so frightening. Believe me, traveling the rest of the distance in one dress wasn't easy. I threw it away when Charley had Buck purchase the other clothes." She gave Lorna a look of total innocence.

"Why would you want to leave Philadelphia to come here?"

"My parents died, and not having any other relatives . . ."

"That'll be a seventy-five cents for the haircuts and shave, and fifty cents for the bath, gentlemen. Except for you, Mr. Comstock. The Bingham Goose Grease I used on your mustache is five cents extra." The barber removed the white towel draped around Angus's neck and stood back.

"I don't know about the two of you," Angus said, rubbing his chin, "but I feel naked."

Behind him, Charley caught sight of himself in the mirror on the opposite wall. He straightened his stance and smiled at the fine-looking fellow staring back at him.

"Damn," Buck exclaimed as he paid his money. "I didn't realize just how good lookin' you boys were gonna be with new clothes and shaves. It's gonna be hell trying to keep all the gals at Maybelle's away from you."

Not wanting Charley and Angus to notice how skittish he was feeling, Buck went outside to await the others. Though he'd trimmed his hair and beard on occasion, this was the first time in six years that he'd been to a barber. Seeing himself in the mirror was like stepping back in time and looking at John Holester. Sure, he was older, but it was the same face.

He wondered whether, now that he looked more like his old self, he'd begin acting like it, too. He'd have to watch out for that. He sure didn't want Miss Fancy Pants Summer to start asking questions about his past.

"Well, Buck, you ready to head for Maybelle's?" Angus asked as he came out of the barber shop.

Buck laughed. "You're damn right."

A short time later, Charley entered the mercantile store to get Summer. He smiled when he realized no one recognized him. Then he saw Lorna give him the eye.

"Excuse me, Summer," Lorna said. "I have another customer." She hurried towards the handsome stranger. "May I help you, sir?"

Lorna reminded Charley of a bear with honey dripping from its mouth. "I came to fetch Summer."

"Charley?" Summer called from the counter. She started forward.

"Yep. You ready to go?"

Lorna was speechless.

"Oh, Cousin Charley, you look absolutely wonderful!" Summer said, her face mirroring her delight.

Charley walked tall as he proceeded to collect the angel's purchases.

She placed her hand in the crook of his arm, and they left the store. Still astounded at Charley's transformation, she was now looking forward to seeing his two partners.

Summer glanced around, but Angus and Buck were nowhere in sight. "Where are the others?" she asked while Charley stowed her things in the back of the buckboard.

"They went to Maybelle's." He circled around and helped her up.

Summer's happy mood quickly faded. So they had unloaded her on Charley. Of all the nerve! Of course Buck had claimed men had special needs. He referred to it as an itch. As Charley would say, hogwash. If a woman had . . . an itch, did she run into town to satisfy it?

"I'm sorry you didn't get to go with the others, Charley," Summer said as they were heading out of town.

"That's okay. It wouldn't be right to leave you at Lorna's. That woman can sure get under a body's hide."

But Summer could tell by the look on Charley's face that he was disappointed. At least he'd been considerate of her, which was more than she could say for Angus and Buck. "Charley, I want you to head for Maybelle's."

Charley was thunderstruck. "I can't do that! I can always come back later if I want. 'Sides, Miss Caldwell, you said it weren't decent for a man and a lady to be discussin' such places."

"I also said gentlemen do not argue with a lady."

He looked at her out of the corners of his eyes, wondering what kind of trouble was brewing in that pretty head now.

"Very well, then let me put it differently. If you don't head this buckboard towards Maybelle's, I'll start screaming. Surely there's a sheriff around here."

Charley didn't know what to do. He knew he shouldn't take her to Maybelle's, but he sure as hell didn't want the law breathing down his neck.

"It will be all right." Summer softened her voice. "I can wait outside. I'll be just fine." Then she put her hand on his forearm and lowered her thick lashes over her brilliant green eyes. "You have all been so nice to me, and I would feel guilty if I deprived you of at least a drink."

When she raised her head she was gratified to see that Charley was staring at her like a sick puppy. The lowered lashes almost always did the trick.

They were on the outskirts of town when Charley brought the buckboard to a halt. He'd stopped in front of a dilapidated house. Summer recognized Angus and Buck's mounts tied to the hitching rail across the street.

"I sure wish you'd reconsider," Charley pleaded as he set the brake.

"Nonsense." Summer adjusted the wide-brimmed straw hat she'd purchased from Lorna. "Charley, I owe you an apology. I really wouldn't have created a scene, but it made me angry to know Buck and Angus thought only of themselves. They had no right to saddle you with me. We all arrived together and should return together. Now I want you to have drink, then tell Angus and Buck we're ready to go. You may also remind them that gentlemen do not frequent such places."

Charley looked at her as if she'd lost her mind. "You ain't serious?"

"I certainly am!"

"I can tell you right now, this ain't gonna work."

She watched Charley jump down and hurry toward the narrow, two-story building. The big sign over the door declared it to be Maybelle's. Besides the two belonging to Buck and Angus, there were only a few horses standing in front of the place, and Summer knew there couldn't be many customers—probably because it was only two in the afternoon. Still, she could hear laughter coming from an open window.

As it turned out it was Buck. "She told you to do what?" he roared, slapping his hand on the bar. "Maybelle?" he called to the hard-looking brunette. "Bring a bottle and two glasses. You might as well join me, Charley."

"But what about Angel? It ain't right to leave her sittin' out there."

"Angel, hell. Let her sit for awhile and maybe she'll learn that teaching us to be gentlemen and running our lives are two different things. She's got to be the most bossy, self-righteous woman I've ever had the misfortune to meet."

"You ought not say those things about her, Buck." Charley countered. "It weren't her fault you brought her to the high country. She's tried to make the best of it. You just ain't givin' her a chance." He picked up the bottle and took a long drink.

"Think what you like. We've done nothing but kowtow to that woman since she arrived, and I damn well don't like it. But don't worry, Charley. We'll let her stew for a bit, then I'll take the confounded woman back to camp."

Just for the hell of it, Buck left Charley at the bar and strolled to the door to see what Summer was doing. He still didn't trust her, even though she'd gone along with their story about her being Charley's cousin. On the other hand, she was a slippery character. It might have been a means to throw them off guard.

Summer was gazing at the team of horses, wondering whether she could handle them. She glanced toward the bordello to make sure the men weren't coming out, then slid over to the driver's seat. Her hand curled around the brake and with considerable effort, she managed to release it. It isn't as if I have to keep my promise, she told herself. After all, I was tricked into it by three worthless men. I'm no longer stranded in the middle of nowhere and there are all sorts of people around who would probably be willing to help me return to Denver.

So what am I waiting for, she wondered. Suddenly she reset the brake. It was as if she'd known the answer to that question all along, but just hadn't been able to face it. She didn't want to return to Denver or see William ever again. Now that she was giving it proper thought, she didn't want to go back to Philadelphia either. The only thing that worried her was her parents and Milly, but she knew she could count on her friend to handle the situation reasonably. It occurred to her that maybe she should insist on contacting Milly now, but if she did that William would probably send out the cavalry to rescue her—when, frankly, she didn't want to be rescued.

Just thinking about how absurd her position was made her smile. Actually, she'd grown to like Charley and Angus, though she couldn't say the same for Buck. The two men had been good to her. She'd have her own house and spend the winter in a place she was beginning to enjoy. What was more, the challenge of transforming the scalawags was starting to appeal to her. She'd turn them into gentlemen, no matter what it took!

Buck had been ready to run out and jump on his horse the minute Summer inched the team forward, not just because he knew she wouldn't be able to handle the horses, but because it made him furious that she was devious enough to try to trick them. But when he saw her retie the reins and set the brake, he knew she wasn't going anywhere. He smiled. The lady might just work out after all. He returned to the bar.

Twenty minutes dragged by, and with each of them, Summer became angrier. She tapped her foot impatiently. How long did one drink take? Now that her mind was made up to truly take on the task of changing these men, she resented even more their staying in such a place. Gentlemen did not leave ladies sitting in the sun on a buckboard while they visited a bordello.

What would they think if she went in after them, she wondered all of a sudden. Charley, Angus, and Buck would probably hustle her out so fast she wouldn't even have time to sit. She glanced across the street at the open door. Maybe that was the answer. If they wouldn't come to her, she'd go to them.

Summer climbed down and quickly brushed the dust off her calico dress. No woman of proper breeding would ever consider entering such a place, but she was determined to teach the men a lesson. Head held high, she took a deep breath and she marched forward.

No one noticed she had stepped inside the doorway, which allowed Summer time to gaze around the room. It was nothing like she'd expected. Milly said she'd heard bordellos were very plush. But this place had a musty door, and though it was dimly lit, she could still see the badly scarred tables and chairs standing on the dirty wooden floor. Toward the back were narrow stairs leading to the second floor. As she'd suspected, there were few customers, which should have made her feel better, but didn't. She swallowed hard when she caught sight of several women with painted faces and bright-colored clothes that left little to the imagination. And good Lord! Some were actually smoking cigars!

Because of his red hair, Summer recognized Angus first. He was sitting at a table with a harlot on his lap. Then she noticed Charley standing at the long bar, talking to a man with black hair. The man's back was turned to her, but she felt sure it was Buck. Three ladies of ill repute surrounded them.

Summer was having second thoughts about being there when she noticed that two women sitting at a table nearby were blatantly looking her over from head to toe. Refusing to be intimidated, she headed straight for the table. "Hello," she said before pulling out a chair. Not sure what she should do, she said the first thing that came into her head. "My name's Summer. What's yours?"

"What the hell do you want, church lady?" the brassy blonde asked. "Don't you know you're not supposed to have anything to do with the likes of us?"

The other one giggled.

Summer felt her temper rise, but she was not going to let these women scare her away. "I would rather have your company than wait outside," she said politely as she sat down.

The women shifted nervously.

"Oh shit!" Charley blurted out.

About the same time, Angus also spotted Summer. He stood up so fast the woman on his lap fell to the floor.

Buck turned to see what everyone was staring at, and upon seeing their righteous teacher sitting with the whores, he broke out laughing. Never had he seen a more ridiculous sight.

"Do any of you know her?" Maybelle demanded. "If so, get her out of here."

Buck waved Angus back and placed a detaining hand on Charley's arm as the man started to move forward. Still laughing, Buck walked toward the table, a bottle of whiskey and two glasses in hand.

"When I asked if you were aimin' to go with us to Maybelle's, I didn't know how close I was to the truth."

Summer recognized the baritone voice of the man standing behind her. She didn't bother to turn. "I was thirsty, Mister Holester. Since you came here to enjoy yourself, I thought I might as well, too."

"Well, if that's how you feel, do you want to go upstairs?"

Summer's back stiffened.

"Would you mind moving to another table, ladies? Miss Caldwell and I want to have a private talk." The two prostitutes shoved their chairs back and left in a huff.

Buck moved around, and with a nonchalant grace swung a leg over the seat of the chair. He banged two glasses down, then proceeded to fill them. "You said you wanted a drink, so here you are." He shoved one in front of her.

Summer's middle twisted into a knot as she gaped at the devastatingly handsome man sitting across from her. His black hair was thick, his face perfectly sculptured, his lips full and sensual. Somehow, with his overgrowth gone, he looked taller, broader of shoulder, and intimidating in an indefinable way.

Buck had seen the look of admiration and curiosity on too many women's faces not to recognize it on Summer's. "Drink up. Isn't that what you came for, teacher?"

His mocking smile snapped Summer back to reality. She suddenly realized her fingers were toying with the glass. What had gotten into her? Had she so quickly forgotten that this was the same awful man who had kidnapped and misled her? Seeing movement out of the corner of her eye, she turned and watched a woman with bright red hair sally up to the table. Summer was appalled at the way the woman swung her hips from side to side.

"Sweetheart," the woman purred as she leaned down and placed her arms around Buck's neck, her full breasts pressed against his head, "I'd be more than happy to have a drink with you. Forget about her. I can make you happy."

Buck cocked a dark eyebrow at Summer.

Determined she wasn't going to back down, Summer picked up the glass and downed the contents. Her throat turned to fire, tears filled her eyes, and for a moment she had trouble getting air into her lungs. If this was how whisky tasted, why in the world did men drink it? "Well," she said brazenly, "that wasn't so bad. How about another?"

Smiling, Buck poured more. He watched her down that, her green eyes growing wider with each passing moment.

"You gonna come upstairs with me, Buck?" the redhead persisted.

"Go away, Jenny, I'm busy."

"With her?" Jenny demanded. She straightened up and glared at Summer. "You got no right to come in here and steal customers. Go find your own men."

"I'm not leaving unless the boys go with me." A hiccup escaped Summer's lips.

"You think you're gonna take them all?" the redhead screeched, closing in on Summer. "Why you . . ."

Buck caught the prostitute's hand just before it reached Summer's hair. Suddenly the room exploded with curses as the other girls headed for the table.

"Angus! Charley!" Buck hollered. "Take care of them while I get Teacher out of here!"

As Charley wrapped an arm around Jenny's waist, Buck picked Summer up and rushed out.

"Let me down!" Summer demanded as she pounded his hard chest. "I'm not leaving without Charley and Angus!"

"Oh yes you are." Buck plopped her on the seat of the buckboard and jumped up beside her.

Before Summer had a chance to scramble off the other side, Buck had released the brake and slapped the reins across the team's rumps. The ensuing jerk forward slammed Summer against the back of the seat.

"You don't have to drive so fast. At the rate you're going, I won't have a behind." Summer suddenly broke out laughing.

Buck glanced at her and shook his head in wonder. "Well I'll be damned. Summer Caldwell, you're drunk."

"Can't be. Proper women don't get drunk. And please do not curse." She started laughing again.

Summer was feeling less woozy and more humiliated as they neared camp. How could she ever have entered such a demoralizing place? Maybe at the time she thought her purpose was justified, but now she looked on it as pure stupidity. She'd done it to get even with them, but she had a strong feeling the tide was just about to turn. She didn't even want to consider what they would think after seeing her in a bordello.

As soon as Buck stopped the horses, Summer was ready to jump down.

"Just a minute, Miss Caldwell."

Summer hesitated.

"I thought you were supposed to be teaching us to be gentlemen."

"That's right, but you certainly do not make the task easy." Here it comes, Summer thought. He's going to make some snide comment about this afternoon.

"I admit I don't know much about such things, but ain't a gentleman supposed to help a lady down?"

"Well . . . yes," she mumbled, feeling discombobulated.

"Then just a minute and I'll do that very thing."

Summer steeled herself against his touch. All she wanted was to be alone.

Buck lifted her off the seat and slowly slid her body down his. He stopped before her feet touched the ground, his face even with hers.

"What are you doing?" Her words were jerky.

"You know," he said in silken tones, "you are one beautiful woman. I especially like your green eyes."

"Let me down," Summer whispered.

"I wish you had gone upstairs with me at Maybelle's. I could have shown you delights you've never dreamed of."

"Mister Holester," she gasped, "this conversation is uncalled for. Just because I went into that place doesn't mean—"

He moved his face closer to hers, their lips only inches apart. "I warned you that if you interfered with a man's needs, you should be prepared for the consequences. I really should teach *you* a lesson, Miss Caldwell."

Summer sucked in her breath.

"Damn if I'm not tempted to carry you straight into the cabin."

Summer didn't dare move even though her ribs hurt where he was holding her.

"I'll let you get by with a warning this time. But it seems that I should at least get a kiss." He started laughing, then dropped her to her feet. "Don't look so frightened. You might have enjoyed it. However, that wasn't part of our agreement, was it? Hope you enjoy the rest of your day, Miss Caldwell." Then he doffed his hat and walked off.

Summer felt totally humiliated. The conceit of the man! How dare he assume she would want to have anything to do with him, let alone enjoy it! Well, she couldn't think about that now. Her head was pounding unmercifully.

Thirty minutes later Angus and Charley rode into camp. The prostitutes had been mad as hell at Summer for invading their territory, and they weren't too pleased with Angus and Charley for keeping them from tearing her apart. Even if the woman hadn't been angry, neither man could have gone upstairs. After seeing Summer at Maybelle's, they'd lost their itch.

Angus and Charley found Buck down at the holding bin supervising a wagon being loaded. The three of them had a big laugh when Buck told them about Summer getting drunk.

At supper that night, Summer ate little, drank a great deal of water, and only spoke when there was a gross infraction of etiquette. She was waiting to give the no-account men a piece of her mind the moment they made some underhanded comment about this afternoon, but the incident was never mentioned.

Chapter 6

"William," Milly said after the waitress had cleared away her plate and left, "what has that man you hired been doing? He must have heard something by now. It's been two weeks since Summer's disappearance."

William cringed. He hated discussing the subject. "He's had nothing to report. I told you locating her wasn't going to be easy."

Noting his frown, Milly decided to change the subject. She'd learned that continual nagging made William tighter lipped. "Your Aunt Ruby says you didn't pay her your usual visit today. She so looks forward to seeing you. It must be terrible being old and bedridden."

"I'll go up when we return home," he replied. "By the way, you look very lovely tonight, my dear. Lavender is most becoming on you. I should take you out more often." His gaze dropped to Milly's voluptuous breasts swelling above her low-cut gown. Glancing back up, he saw her brown eyes studying him. He transferred his attention to the last bite of venison on his plate.

Milly dabbed her lips, then placed the napkin on the table. "Tell me, isn't your mistress satisfying your needs?"

"I . . . I don't know what you're talking about. I have no mistress."

"Nonsense. I saw you shopping with her yesterday when I came downtown. You were on Lawrence Street, if I remember correctly."

William cleared his throat. "Please keep your voice down. Someone might hear you."

"Exactly my point. From now on, keep your eyes to yourself."

"If we're speaking truths, Miss Stern, I may as well tell you that I heard a few interesting stories about you when I was visiting Philadelphia. It's my understanding you are of a very warm nature."

"If you're trying to embarrass me, Willy, it won't work. And if you're even thinking of suggesting I share your bed, the answer is no."

"Why should I be any different from other men?"

"Because I don't like you. I've never made a secret of it. You know I even tried to talk Summer out of marrying you."

His chest swelled with indignation. He couldn't believe she wasn't attracted to him. "A lot of women think differently about me. I can be most generous."

Milly laughed. "Willy," she said, stressing the pet name he so loathed, "money is the least of my worries. My late husband left me enough to live comfortably for the rest of my life. If I wanted baubles, I'd simply buy them. Now wipe that hungry look off your face. I'm ready to leave, and you must visit your aunt before she goes to sleep."

"I'm sure you'll change your mind about me."

"Don't count on it."

When they reached the door, a man who had just entered took her cloak from her arm. "Permit me," he said and started to place it on her shoulders.

William grabbed it back. "I'm perfectly capable of taking care of the lady's wrap." He performed the honor.

When they were in the carriage, Milly broached the subject of Summer again. "This man you hired to find Summer. If he's doing what you're paying him for, when will he report his findings?"

"Let me handle this. You know nothing about such things. I assure you he's doing everything he can. But if it will make you feel better, he's coming to the house tomorrow. I'll tell you if he's found out anything."

Milly retired to her room as soon as William went to visit his aunt. She didn't immediately pull the cord for the maid. She wanted time to think. She tossed her cloak on the bed and began removing the pins from her hair. It amazed her that William thought himself so irresistible, and that he'd begun to pursue her without so much as a twinge of conscience about Summer. She knew she'd have no trouble keeping him in check, but it infuriated her that he showed so little interest in locating Summer. One man indeed! He should have an army out searching for her. Well, if his man didn't produce some information tomorrow, she'd take matters into her own hands. Surely Marshal Bailey would be able to help her.

The next afternoon, Milly had just entered the parlor when the man William had hired arrived. "Well, I found her," she heard the man say.

"Let's talk about it in the study," William replied.

Milly hid behind an open door so William wouldn't see her.

"She's fine, and livin' with three miners just outside of Mountain City," the man went on. "They ain't holdin' her against her will and—"

"I said to wait until we're in the study!" William lashed out.

Relief flooded over Milly like a cool spring shower. Just as she'd suspected, Summer was all right. She'd even chosen to remain where she was! Milly could barely contain the bubble of laughter that threatened to burst from her throat. She knew in her bones that Summer was with the black-haired man. How she wished she knew his name and what he'd done to convince Summer to stay— although she could imagine his methods. As far as she was concerned, this was just the sort of experience her friend needed. What a waste it would have been if Summer had stayed in Philadelphia; she'd have withered away from boredom. And worse still if she'd gone ahead and married William Nielson!

She waited until she heard the door to William's study close before she ventured out of her hiding place and went to her room. Her steps were appreciably lighter than they'd been before. She didn't exactly relish staying on in Denver with William. But nothing would budge her from here now. She'd wait however long it took for Summer to return. She wanted to hear the story of her adventures from her own lips.

"Now, Mr. Click, tell me everything you found out," William said as he moved behind his desk and sat down. But as the man proceeded, William grew more and more appalled. Click had actually seen Summer in Mountain City in the company of three miners. The man even reported a story that had been circulating around town about her visit to a bordello called Maybelle's. Given Summer's upbringing, it amazed William that she could have sunk so low.

But what concerned William most was that his associates in Denver knew about his engagement. He'd bragged extravagantly about his beautiful fiancée from a wealthy, well-established Philadelphia family. If they found out about her escapades now, his reputation would suffer. In fact, he could probably say good-bye to his political aspirations. What right did Summer have to do this to him? He couldn't possibly let it become known that his fiancée had run off with a miner and was living with him in a cabin in the mountains. It was all too unseemly.

By the time Mr. Click had finished his report, William was seeing red. He stared up at the ceiling for a long moment before finally speaking. "Is there someone up there who might like to make a little money?" he asked Click.

"Depends on what you want."

"What I want is to have the lady and her three friends out of the Colorado Territory!" He brought his fist down hard on the desk.

"Well, there's a man by the name of Toddle," Click began. "He's wantin' to buy that mine real bad. I'd be willin' to bet he'd be more than happy to solve your problem."

William paused. He'd been involved in slightly shady dealings once or twice before, but paying someone to get rid of Summer Caldwell was different. Suddenly he felt consumed with guilt. But what else could he do? No matter which way he turned, all he saw was trouble. He cursed Summer silently, then opened a drawer and pulled out some money.

"Here's your pay, and extra to get word to Toddle that I want to see him."

Click nodded, pocketed the money, and left.

When the door closed behind him, William rose and began pacing the floor. What was he going to tell Milly? The woman never let a day go by without bringing up her friend's plight. For the moment, he'd keep the truth from her. Then, when Summer was taken care of, he'd make up some lie. She'd be shocked, but that would give him the opportunity to console her. He closed his eyes for a moment and imagined her deep, inviting decolletage, then recalled the fact that she'd told him she had a sizable income. How convenient that she was living under his very roof. Once Summer was out of the way, he felt sure he'd have no trouble convincing her to stay and become his wife.

Lorna put out the new sadirons, butter churns, axes, and other items that had arrived yesterday. Also in the shipment was the order Summer had placed over a month ago. It seemed to Lorna that during that time, Summer's name had been on absolutely everyone's lips. Lorna wished the woman would fall down a mine shaft. Nonetheless, at last week's women's social, she'd swallowed her jealousy and told the ladies how sweet and innocent Summer Caldwell was, and that she was Charley McMillan's cousin.

The very next day, stories of a different nature drifted in. A man claimed that a woman fitting Summer's description had been in Maybelle's trying to steal customers. It had to be Summer because the man talked about the fight that almost took place and Buck having to carry her out. Then men who worked at the mine began talking about how beautiful Summer was, which made their wives start complaining about her flaunting herself in front of their husbands.

The women of the social were appalled. Lorna was mortified when they accused her of lying about Summer and said she was a fool if she believed Summer was decent. After all, the woman was living alone with three handsome, single men. Ever since then it seemed to Lorna that the ladies had looked down on her—and all because Summer had put on an act that she'd been dumb enough to believe. Lorna couldn't wait for the hussy to pick up her order. She had every intention of telling Miss Caldwell that from now on, she could take her business elsewhere.

The bell over the door jingled, drawing Lorna's attention.

"Mornin'."

Lorna recognized that timbre of voice first, and Buck Holester second. She was flabbergasted. He looked taller and so handsome her heart began to palpitate. First Charley, now Buck. Had Angus also changed? In the two years she'd been in Mountain City, Lorna had never seen the men cleaned up.

"I thought while I was in town I'd drop by and see if Summer's order had arrived."

Hearing Buck speak Summer's name made Lorna nauseous. He was too good for the likes of that woman! "It's here. You'll have to come get the rug. Can't carry it myself. Summer said you was building her a house. Is that right?"

"Yep. It's finished." Buck followed her to the back.

"She also ordered crystal glasses. She's gettin' pretty fancy, don't you think?"

"Summer's folks had money. Reckon she's just used to those kind of things."

"Just a darn minute!"

Lorna turned so fast Buck almost ran into her.

"We've known each other two years, Buck, and

though you and the boys have been paying customers, I hate to see you spend your money like this."

"What are you getting at?" he asked warily.

"Summer's not what you think she is. She may have told you she was from a wealthy family, but I don't believe it because ladies don't behave the way she does. More than likely she also lied about her clothes being stolen. The dress she arrived in was probably the only one to her name. You and your partners are too good to be used like this."

"Now just how did you come to that conclusion?"

Lorna didn't like the way his eyes had turned steel gray. She lowered her head. "There's been talk."

"You, of all people, should know not to believe rumors."

Her head jerked up, causing strands of brown hair to fall from the bun atop her head. She impatiently shoved them behind her ears. "Summer was seen in Maybelle's by more than one person, and it's my understanding you had to drag her out. We already have enough of her kind around. Now you, Angus, and Charley are welcome in my store, but if that woman sets foot in here, I'll throw her out!"

"Is that the rug she ordered?" Buck asked, pointing to the bundle on the floor.

"That's it."

He swung it over his shoulder.

"Buck, you know I took a liking to you the first time we met. I just hate to see you wastin' your time on the likes of her."

"I'll be back for the glasses."

When Buck returned, he grabbed Lorna's arm and roughly escorted her to the side of the store so the other customers couldn't overhear their conversation. "Since you say you're concerned about me," he said, coming to an abrupt halt, "and since you've always been fond of gossip, I'm going to tell you a couple of things. I suggest you remember them. The only reason Summer went to Maybelle's was to get Charley, Angus, and me out. No other reason. As for her being *that type of woman*, you couldn't be more wrong. She's colder than a judge's gavel. And if you can't be hospitable to her, then I reckon the boys and me'll take our business elsewhere. Sean MacIvere just opened a mercantile store in Central City, and I'm sure he'd be more than happy to welcome our account."

"Well, I didn't mean—"

A bitter smile creased Buck's lips. "You probably think you know me, Lorna, but you don't. There's very little I haven't done over the last ten years, and believe me I can be a mean bastard when I'm crossed. On the other hand, I do have a healthy appetite for women. If Summer were passing around favors, I'd be more than ready to wait in line." He slowly ran a finger along her jaw, and his voice softened. "So you have a liking for me? Tell me, Lorna, since you're a widow, do you ever feel a need to have a man share your bed?" Seeing the pleased look on her round face, he added, "Before you answer that you'd better think real hard about what you'd be getting into."

Lorna opened her mouth to say yes, but nothing came out. There was something dangerous about Buck, a side she'd never seen before, and it frightened her.

"Wise decision." Buck tipped his hat and walked away.

*   *   *

Buck was near camp by the time his anger subsided. Though reluctant to accept it, he had to admit things were changing in the Mountain City area. Just a few weeks ago he'd seen Reverend Mr. Porter trying to collect money to build an Episcopalian church. His congregation included a small group of self-righteous, churchgoing women who were determined to run the town and the people in it. Apparently, Lorna wanted to be a part of that group and used gossip as a wedge in. There was nothing so surprising about that. So if he understood all this, why had he become so damn angry? Certainly not because of what Lorna said about Summer. If the circumstances were different, Summer would probably be the leader of the biddies' social group.

Coming to a small glade, Buck drew the horses to a halt, and shoved his hat back. He could feel the definite nip in the air that presaged snow. Relaxed, he listened to the rustle of pine trees as a breeze kicked up, then died. He reflected on how Summer had reverted to her old self after her visit to Maybelle's. For the last month she'd been more high-handed and bossy than ever. From the first moment he'd seen her standing barefoot in the trail, defying him and the world, he'd had an overpowering desire to put the plucky woman in her place. He smiled. She had been avoiding being alone with him, which told Buck that his occasional amorous advances were having an effect on her. Did the woman have needs that she was afraid to acknowledge? Possibly. So he'd just keep on riling her, if only to see what it took to make her react like a woman instead of a haughty, rich bitch. He chuckled, suddenly remembering how she'd looked sitting at that table in Maybelle's. Too bad *that* Summer hadn't stuck around a little longer.

What the hell, he thought as he picked up the reins, it was fun giving her a hard time and watching the blush spread across that beautiful face.

Summer wrung her hands as she continued to pace. Buck was late for his lesson. Had he stopped at Maybelle's? Not that she cared. She just didn't like having to wait until he decided to make an appearance. She crossed over to the small mirror on the bureau, but before looking at her image, she turned and walked away. What difference did it make how she looked? She began pacing again. And furthermore, the new dress she had on had nothing to do with the devilish brute.

She had to admit Buck radiated masculinity, and it frightened her. Ever since he'd said those terrible things when she had been a bit intoxicated, she'd made sure they were never alone together. But hadn't she felt a tingle in her stomach? Absolutely not! It was the whiskey. Buck had been absolutely too bold, yet she couldn't honestly accuse him of doing a thing. No touching, no kissing, nothing. He'd remained true to their agreement.

She went to the stove and poured a cup of tea. After several slow sips, the fresh brew helped settle her nerves somewhat. The stove was such a pleasure, especially after Charley had taught her how to build a fire. Maybe she should get him to teach her how to cook.

Cup in hand, Summer strolled into the parlor that contained six chairs, only two of which were fairly comfortable and had arms and high backs. A low table sat in the center of the room. Though her new house was small compared to the mansion in Philadelphia, she liked it much better. It had a warmth to it. There was a dining room, kitchen, parlor, and three bedrooms upstairs. She'd been told that the gingerbread trimming was similar to a house in Blackhawk. Now all the place needed was more furniture.

Hearing a noise outside, she gazed at the door, waiting. But no one knocked. Why was she so fidgety? Knowing she couldn't avoid Buck forever, she'd arranged this private lesson because he needed help with his grammar. Of course, her real purpose was to show him she was in complete control of the situation.

When the knock finally came, it made her jump. Setting her cup down, she went over and opened the door.

"Mister Holester," she said to the man filling the doorway. "You're twenty minutes late. I'll overlook it this time, but please make sure it doesn't happen again. Do come in."

Buck was tempted to remove his knife from his boot and cut the woman's tongue out. "You know I had to go to town."

"Did you make a stop at Maybelle's? Is that why you're late?"

"I thought about it."

"Are you coming in or not?"

Buck took notice of her new green dress that matched the color of her eyes, and her crisp white pinafore. All very proper. The only skin showing was her face and hands. Her shiny hair was twisted into a figure eight at the base of her head, but short strands had escaped and hung in curls around her face, softening it—something he felt sure she had not intended. No matter how severe she tried to look, Summer Caldwell was still a very beautiful woman. "Would you rather I bring in your rug first?"

"You have it?" she asked excitedly. Catching herself, she made her face look stern again. "Yes.

Bring it in. Then we can proceed with your lesson."

When the rug was in place and chairs positioned atop it, Summer was delighted. "Doesn't that look better?" she asked Buck.

"I reckon."

"What a gracious reply," she said sarcastically. "And how many times do I have to tell you that *reckon* is an improper word? *I agree* or even *I disagree* would be better." She released a heavy sigh. "And why haven't you removed your hat?"

Buck slid his hat off and placed it on the peg by the door. "We alone?"

"Charley and Angus will join us shortly. When they arrive, we'll have instructions on having tea. Please be seated, Mister Holester." Once he was settled on the clair, she circled behind him. "Sit straight!" she ordered as she poked a stiff finger between his shoulder blades.

It took every bit of willpower Buck could muster to keep from jumping up and twisting the woman's finger off.

Summer sat across from him, back ramrod straight and hands properly folded in her lap. She was quite pleased with herself for taking control of the situation right away and had every intention of keeping it. "The reason I'm taking extra time with you, Mister Holester, is because you don't seem to grasp things as quickly as your partners." He was glaring at her now, but she enjoyed his anger. This time the shoe was on the other foot. "I realize it isn't something you can help, so we'll take it a little at a time. I'm particularly referring to your speech."

He started to smile, then forced his lips back down and slowly shook his head. "I just can't seem to figure out what I do wrong."

"Can you read?"

"Somewhat. I'm real good at figures." His gaze slowly traveled from her eyes to her shoulders to her breasts.

Summer ignored the innuendo. "I have made a list I want you to study."

"You know, you sure have pretty green eyes."

"You're not here to flatter me, Mister Holester. Now, if we may proceed? Perhaps it would be to your advantage to work with Angus or Charley, whose speech has improved considerably."

"Is there a particular way gentlemen kiss ladies?" he said, leaning toward her in his seat.

Summer held her knees together hard and clenched her teeth. "If it's not too much to ask, could we stay on the subject of grammar?"

"I'll study the list, and you might just be surprised how quick I can learn things if I set my mind to it."

"Good."

Buck stretched out his legs and Summer noticed how the material of his pants clung to his muscular thighs.

"But so far, all you been teachin' us is how to eat and talk. When do we get to the part about what goes on between a man and a woman?"

"Is that all you can think of?" Summer asked in disgust.

"Pretty much."

"I think you should leave." Summer jumped up. "It is obvious we're accomplishing nothing, and I have no desire to sit here and listen to your bestial thoughts." She walked to the door, but before she could open it, he was in front of her, much too close.

"You see, I ain't had no woman for goin' on a month, and believe me, that's a long time. So naturally I'm anxious to learn the other stuff so I can get me a wife and not have to worry when I get an itch.''

Summer was horrified. ''You can't be serious!''

''Why not?'' He let his breath ruffle the wisps of copper hair beside her ear.

''Gentlemen don't get married just to satisfy animal lust, Mister Holester,'' she said, desperately trying to control the tremor in her voice.

''Then why marry?''

''For love,'' she said honestly. ''You wait until you find the woman you want to spend the rest of your life with. Someone you want by your side, to take care of, make happy, protect, and tell your deepest thoughts.''

''Do you really believe people fall in love?'' he asked quietly.

''Of course I do.''

''Have you ever been in love?''

''I don't find that question pertinent.'' She shifted uneasily.

He put his hands against the door on either side of her. ''Afraid to answer the question?''

''No, I have never been in love.'' She whispered. ''Are you satisfied?''

''Then what you just explained about marriage don't apply to you?''

''What are you talking about?'' She tried to avoid his probing eyes by looking to her side, but all she could see was his muscled arm.

''If I remember correctly, when I brought you here you said you were betrothed to a banker. If you've never experienced love, how do you explain why you was gonna get married?''

''There were extenuating circumstances,'' she said, trying to barge past him. But he caught her by the waist and held her fast.

''Like what?'' His lips were close to her forehead,

his voice as soft as silk. She fell a vague stirring in her breast.

"I want you to leave. We've gotten completely off the subject of—"

"Not really. How you supposed to teach us about love when you haven't even experienced it yourself?"

She could feel his hand creeping up her spine, coming to rest at the sensitive nape of her neck. It took all she was made of not to succumb to the dreamy smooth circles his thumb was making there. "Love's not something you learn," she said angrily. "It comes naturally. I'm not here to be interrogated, Mister Holester. Let me remind you that I was brought here against my will because *you* were the one who wanted me to play teacher! Since I foolishly agreed, I'm holding up my end of the bargain, like it or not!"

He smiled. "I reckon you got a point. Now back to the original question. Is there a particular way gentlemen kiss ladies?" He moved so close that his chest was almost touching her bodice. "For instance, do they ask permission, or is this something else you've never experienced?"

"I've had enough of this!" She tried to break away, but he blocked her escape. "Obviously I made a mistake by thinking we could—"

"Well? Have you ever been kissed?"

"Yes. On quite a few occasions. I'm not entirely innocent, Mister Holester."

Buck doubted that. "Do gentlemen take the woman's hand first?" He took her hand in his. She snatched it away. "What words do they use? Please, Miss Caldwell, may I have the pleasure of a kiss?"

She laughed nervously. He sounded so sincere.

Was he actually asking? "It just depends on the gentleman," she said breathily.

"Or do they just catch you in an off moment and take what they want?"

For no explainable reason, Summer suddenly couldn't take her eyes off of his full lips. There was no smile now. She made the mistake of looking up. His blue-gray eyes held hers, and her senses began to reel,

Slowly he leaned down, his hands playing at her waist. "Show me how they do it, Summer," he murmured.

Summer raised her hand to her face, and he gently moved it away. "Surely one kiss wouldn't be wrong—in the interests of education."

Mesmerized, she started to lean toward his lips when a knock on the door snapped her back to reality.

Buck straightened and gently moved her away from the door. He grabbed the knob, then turned. "Like it or not, Miss Caldwell, you were sorely tempted. Beware. Next time you might not be so lucky."

Summer started to make a tart remark, but his smile stopped her. Her eyes became hard emeralds. "It's difficult to believe a shave and haircut can change a man so drastically."

"I'm the same. You're just getting to know the real me."

Another loud knock sounded. Buck opened the door, and with a wave of his hand, bid Charley and Angus enter.

Get a hold of yourself, Summer thought as she stumbled toward the kitchen to fix tea. Since when did you let a handsome face throw you off balance?

The men sat on their usual chairs, making sure their posture was correct. Buck didn't have the heart to tell Angus and Charley that a lot of the things they were learning didn't amount to a hill of beans. Was she fixing to teach them how to pour tea? Maybe their next lesson would be a class on how to sew. He wasn't in the mood for this. He decided to change the agenda. "In two weeks there's gonna be a hell of a shindig—"

"Please, Mister Holester, watch your cursing." Summer said as she brought in the tea tray.

"I ain't meanin'—"

"Hell, Buck," Angus blurted out, "how many times has Miss Caldwell gotta tell you not to use the word *ain't*?"

Summer groaned.

Looking properly reprimanded, Buck continued. "I was tryin' to say there's gonna be a dance in a couple of weeks. I was thinkin' Miss Caldwell might like to go. I know I would." He watched Summer's face light up with interest. "So, I was also thinking maybe we should start dancin' lessons. You know, like real gentlemen do."

Angus and Charley began jabbering at the same time.

"Just a minute, gentlemen," Summer interrupted. "We have no music."

"Charley, where's your harmonica?" Buck asked.

"In the shaft house. I'll go get it."

Summer didn't argue. She could also use a change of pace. She did, however, hope that the men knew something about dancing or her toes would surely suffer.

Angus was the first to pair off with Summer, and to her delight, he handled the waltz quite well and had no trouble with some new steps she showed him. When Charley moved forward, Angus sang a lively song while Buck clapped his hands. Charley also proved to be light on his feet. Then came Buck's turn. Watching the big man move toward her, Summer wanted to refuse, but couldn't think of a plausible excuse. To her shock, Buck reached out and crushed her to him. He was holding her so tight, she could hardly breathe. He started moving to the music, and Summer was positive the man had ten feet, all in the wrong place. In desperation, Summer shoved him away.

"Men do not hold their partners so close, Mister Holester! Nor do they step on a lady's toes. Weren't you watching Angus and Charley? Let's try again."

Charley and Angus broke out laughing.

"Come on, Buck," Angus finally said, "the lady isn't going to have any feet left after you're through with her. You might fool her, but you're not fooling us." He started laughing again.

It took a moment before Summer realized what Angus was saying. Her eyes became bits of stone as she glared at Buck. "You know how to dance and you've put me through all this torture?" She raised a foot and brought her heel down hard on top of his boot. "How do you like having your toes stomped on, Mister Holester?"

Seeing Buck jumping around holding his foot, Charley and Angus laughed all the harder.

"Now," Summer said, "shall we try again, or can you stand?"

Buck placed his foot on the floor. Deciding nothing was broken, he again pulled Summer roughly to him, but not as close this time. His eyes never left hers. "Let's have a hoedown, Charley, and make it fast."

All of a sudden Buck was expertly moving Summer around the room. His feet moved faster than hers and they had to stop several times and start again. Charley continued playing, Angus clapped his hands, and Buck kept dancing until Summer could no longer catch her breath. Suddenly Buck stopped, stepped back, and with a slight bow said, "Gentlemen, I think Miss Caldwell could use a drink of water."

Summer collapsed onto the nearest chair, then gladly accepted the water Angus delivered. When her breathing returned to normal and she'd had a moment to think, she started laughing. Seeing the puzzled looks on the men's faces, she laughed even harder, causing tears to run down her cheeks. When she finally managed to get control of herself, she said, "Gentlemen, I owe you an apology. I think you should be teaching me to dance. You know steps I've never seen before. It's been a long time since I've had so much fun. Shall we try again?"

They danced and laughed well into the night. When the men left to go to their cabin, a light snow was falling.

Chapter 7

The next morning, after cleaning house, Summer decided a walk would be invigorating. Even though the weather had turned cold, the sky was blue and clear. Looking forward to stretching her legs, she quickly tied a scarf around her head, then slipped on her heavy coat.

The ground crackled beneath Summer's feet as she stepped outside. It was still morning and the bright sun hadn't yet melted the thin crust of ice covering the clearing. A heavy silence seemed to loom over the area now that the buildings were completed and the workers had left. She buried her hands in her pockets and took off at a brisk pace.

The beauty of the scenery made Summer quickly lose track of time. The aspen leaves had turned color. Thickly interspersed with pine, the surrounding forests had become beautifully splashed with brilliant gold. The ground was still covered with thick grass, except for the rocky areas. Summer was glad when the sun finally melted the ice and she didn't have to walk so carefully.

She had stopped to rest when a movement ahead caught her attention. Not more than twenty yards away a bald eagle stood on the ground over its kill. A group of magpies were attacking, trying to get the prize for themselves. They kept coming at the eagle from all directions until the big bird had enough and flew away. Summer wanted to rush forward and scatter the black and white birds, but didn't. It wasn't fair. The eagle should have had the kill.

"That just proves the mighty aren't always the ones to reap the reward."

Summer groaned, aggravated at having her solitude invaded. She turned to look at the tall, handsome man wearing a heavy coat and carrying a rifle. "Were you following me, Mister Holester?"

"Not exactly. When I discovered you weren't in the house I had to track you down. I didn't want you dropping into some abandoned mine shaft. We'd never know what happened to you. There are shafts all over this area. It's especially dangerous during winter 'cause the snow hides the holes."

"You're just saying that to scare me."

He stuck a foot on a fallen tree and pointed straight ahead. "Go about ten steps that way, then look to your left."

Just to prove he was lying, Summer did exactly that. When she turned and saw the gaping hole, she immediately stepped away. "It's really there!"

Buck joined her. "This is mighty pretty country, but you gotta respect it. Shafts aren't the only things you should be worrying about. You'd do good to remember that mountain lion screaming when I brought you up here, and bears don't take kindly to someone getting in their way."

"I . . . I didn't stop to think."

"Just make sure the next time you decide to take a walk, someone else goes along."

For once, Buck wasn't being flippant and Summer could actually hear concern in his voice. He was right of course, she shouldn't have left alone.

"Tell you what. I saw some elk the other day. Why don't we see if we can find some more? They're starting to head down with winter comin'."

Summer followed alongside and Buck showed her animals she would have missed had he not been there to point them out: a marten with a beautiful bushy tail, whistle pigs that kept gibbering at them, and even a fox that darted between the trees. But when Buck put his arm out to stop her, then pointed ahead, Summer was speechless. They were standing at the edge of a small, grassy meadow, and on the far side was a magnificent stag scratching a tree with his gigantic antlers. The tree was sturdy, but still shook. Nearby the females had their heads down clipping grass as they slowly moved about.

Summer was able to watch the stag join his herd before Buck motioned to leave. She hesitated, wanting to remember every detail. What a truly marvelous morning this has been, she thought. I'm falling in love with this vast, untamed land.

They weren't even halfway back to camp when Summer had to stop and rest on a stump. She hadn't realized they had gone downhill to get to the meadow, but she certainly noticed they were climbing now. It was even difficult to breathe. Didn't Buck ever tire, she wondered as she removed her scarf and opened her coat.

When her breathing returned to normal, Summer studied the man sitting nearby on the ground, knees bent, with the rifle laying by his side. He was looking off into the distance, his mind appearing to be elsewhere. As had Angus and Charley, he'd remained clean shaven and was keeping his hair well trimmed. She took in the broad shoulders, the chest hairs peeking out the open collar of his blue shirt, his strong body narrowing down to slim hips. . . .

Suddenly she realized that his blue-gray eyes were focused on her. Embarrassed at being caught staring, she said, "I take it those were elk we saw?"

"Yep."

"I never had any idea they were so large. Even the females."

Buck grinned. "The males are called bulls, and the females are cows."

"Oh. You seem to know so much about such things. What did you do before taking up mining, Mister Holester?"

Buck's grin broadened. "Well, *Miss Caldwell*, I guess you would have called me a mountain man. What did you do before going to Denver?"

"I lived in Philadelphia with my parents."

"It's hard to believe that a beautiful woman who has spent her life under the protection of a family would come all the way out West just to marry." He straightened out his long legs. "And from what I saw of your fiancé, the trip was a waste. Surely there're better men than that back East—or are you running away from something?"

Summer thought about that for a moment. "I guess you could say I ran away, but not for any reasons you might suspect."

Buck smirked. "So your folks didn't want you marrying that banker. Can't say as I blame them."

Summer wondered how the man could be so astute. "He's not a banker, Mister Holester, he's a lawyer who owns a bank. What do you have against banks? You've made more than one derogatory comment about them. Did you used to be a bank robber or something?"

"You don't know how close to the truth you are.

Let's just say I've done business with them."

Summer noted that faraway look in his eyes again. She was about to suggest they return to camp when a sudden realization hit her with the power of a heavy rock. She glared at him, wondering where in heaven's name she had been all this time. *Mister Holester*'s words were devoid of any mountain slang! She tried thinking back on other conversations. Yes. There had always been a vaguely cultured undertone to his voice, albeit off and on. She even knew why she hadn't picked up on it sooner. Any time the man was around he managed to keep her in a turmoil. He never asked the meaning of words like Charley and Angus did, or questioned etiquette procedures, other than to harass her. She also remembered yesterday when he said, *You'd be surprised how fast I can learn if I put my mind to it.*

The nerve of him saying he just couldn't figure out what he was doing wrong! Even Angus and Charley had become aggravated at him for being so slow. Since he obviously knows English, does that mean he's familiar with gentlemanly ways, Summer wondered now. The liar! He'd made a fool of her, and she was absolutely furious.

Rising, she walked over and cuffed him hard across the head. "You bastard!" she accused. "All this time you've deliberately—"

Buck looked up just in time to dodge another blow. "Damn it, woman, what the hell's wrong with you?"

Summer started to swing her hand again, but before she could connect or even finish giving him a piece of her mind, he grabbed her legs and her knees buckled. The next thing she knew she was on the ground with him sitting on top of her. "Let me up!" she demanded. She struggled, but it was no use. He was far too strong. "You swore not to do me any physical harm," she quickly reminded him.

"In camp, Angel. Only in camp."

Frantic, she began pounding on his chest, but he easily grabbed her arms and pinned them beneath his knees. Knowing she was about to be kissed, Summer squeezed her eyes shut while flinging her head back and forth. When nothing happened, she stopped and slowly opened her eyes. He was just sitting there, watching.

"Are you through?" he asked calmly.

Summer tried biting his leg, but she couldn't quite reach.

"You know, Miss Caldwell, I ain't—"

"Save your slang. I know you can speak English as well as I can."

He noted the beads of perspiration above her brow, her auburn mane spread out on the ground, flashing green eyes, rosy cheeks, and especially her heaving breasts. A most tempting situation. There was no question that he wanted her, but not like this. He had it in mind to make her come to him with no reservations, and that took time. "Very well, then let's stop the pretending. When you were waiting in front of Maybelle's, why didn't you take off like you started to?"

She gaped at him. "You saw?"

"That's not answering the question."

"Let me up and I'll tell you."

"Oh, no."

"It's none of your business!"

"Don't go getting haughty with me, Angel. You're hardly in the right position."

"At least let go of my arms. You're hurting me."

The moment he raised his knees, Summer twisted. Because he was off balance, a good shove knocked him to the ground. Immediately Summer grabbed for the rifle. Her hand curled over the barrel, but before she could yank it to her, a boot clamped the weapon to the ground. With lightning speed, Buck had managed to get to his feet and was now standing over her. Summer yanked herself up into a sitting position and scooted backward. Her coat impeded her progress, and he reached down and picked up the rifle.

"All right! I felt that remaining here was better than returning to Denver."

"You don't want to marry the banker. Is that it?"

"I wanted time to think about it. Can I get up now?"

"For a lady, you sure have a hell of a lot of wildcat in you. How come you've never bedded a man?"

Summer gasped. "That isn't any of your business!"

"Never found the right man, huh? Haven't you been tempted or at least curious? How old are you?"

"Twenty-two." She managed to scoot back a little farther. He stepped forward.

"Are you planning on dying a virgin, or was the banker your last hope?"

Summer tried kicking him in the shin, but failed to connect. "Obviously, at some time in your life you were a gentleman, so how did you become such an obnoxious man full of so many horrid questions?"

"Horrid? I don't think they're horrid, but I guess it depends on a person's viewpoint. I intend to be the man who beds you, so we might as well get these questions out of the way so we can concentrate on better things."

He leaned the end of the rifle on the ground, still standing over her, providing Summer with a heart-stopping view of his sinewy thighs. "As for being a gentleman, that was a long time ago," he went on. "Believe me, I have no qualms about taking what I want or asking whatever questions I want answered."

"I want to go back to camp," she demanded.

"What you really want is to run back to safety because you're afraid to face being a woman. You're afraid to let your body dictate to you. But I know, as sure as I'm standing here, you're curious. And it's that curiosity that's going to be your undoing, teacher." He rubbed the back of his neck. "I'll let you up, on one condition."

Summer's back met a tree.

"I get that kiss you were trying to avoid a minute ago, and I don't mean a peck on the cheek."

"I won't do it! I'm not about to so much as touch you!"

"That's fine with me. I'm in no hurry. Of course when it gets dark I might set my sights on something even better. It's up to you."

Summer didn't like the way he was looking her up and down. "If I do this repulsive thing, will you let me return to the mine?"

"If you make it real good, Angel. If not, we may never make it back." Seeing her horrified expression, it was all he could do to keep from bursting out laughing. She was acting as though she'd just been asked to forfeit her life. He stepped back, giving her room to rise.

Summer slowly stood, not sure she could do what he was demanding. Forcing, was a better word. She brushed the pine needles from her coat, stalling for time. She had no idea how far from camp they were, but what difference did it make? There was no escape. He continued to stand there, one hand on his hip, waiting. Summer moved for-

ward until she stood directly in front of him. Closing her eyes, she raised up on her toes, ready to
perform the hateful task.

"Stop right there," Buck said. "I like my woman's arms here." He placed them around his neck.
"And keep your eyes open. I wouldn't want you
to miss my lips. We'd just have to do it over again."

Summer yanked her arms back and gnawed on
her inner cheek. Her hands tightened into fists,
ready to strike.

"Don't do it, Miss Caldwell," Buck warned.

With the realization that she might as well get
this over with, Summer again stood on her tiptoes
and placed her arms around his neck. Because he
was so tall, her body pressed against his and she
could feel the hard muscles beneath his shirt. "If
I must do this, at least bend down!"

He obliged her, but to Summer's disappointment, he still didn't initiate the kiss. She placed
her lips on his, expecting him to wrap his arms
around her, but he didn't. As she started to pull
away, he said, "Is that really the best you can do?
Maybe I just found out why you haven't married."

Her pride smarting, Summer again placed her
lips on his, suddenly wanting to prove she was
every bit a woman. His mouth was soft, yielding,
then he was nibbling on her bottom lip. It caused
a wave of sensation she'd never experienced before. His arms curved around her, drawing her
harder against him as he returned her kiss. A delicious feeling coiled deep down inside her. Her
mouth opened slightly, allowing his tongue to caress the soft inner surfaces of her lips. She didn't
want him to stop. His kiss became more demanding, and she was lost in the pleasure of it.

All too soon she felt him lower her arms to her
sides and gently push her away. She was disap-

pointed. But when she opened her eyes, the first thing she saw was that devilish grin of his. She wanted to slap his smug face. Instead she also grinned, trying to act as though the kiss was of no consequence. "I hope that will do?" she said in an offhanded manner.

"It won't work, Angel. You liked that as much as I did. Besides, you broke the rules, you closed your eyes."

"That's not so."

"Maybe you'll learn a couple of things from this. A man likes to have the woman come to him, and secondly, it's always better when both parties share in the pleasure."

"If you're through with your lecture, I'm ready to go."

Buck broke out laughing. "You are such a hypocrite."

Summer tried not to think as they headed for the mine, but more than once she caught herself wanting to touch her lips. Though she'd never say so to Buck, it had been a glorious kiss, far better than those she'd gotten from her Philadelphia beaux. Were her lips swollen? Had Milly told the truth when she said having a man make love to you was a delightful pastime? Suddenly Summer felt shocked at the direction her thoughts were taking. Like it or not, she'd just have to stay in camp so as to prevent this from happening again. Buck was dangerous. He'd said that he intended to bed her, a warning she would be wise to heed. Of course, he'd also accused her of not being a woman, but hadn't he just contradicted that? If he didn't think of her in those terms, why would he have kissed her like that? Not for the first time she wished Milly were there so they could talk.

When Summer and Buck arrived back at camp,

Charley and Angus were conversing with a gentle-man Summer had never seen before. Glancing at the two armed men on horses directly behind him, a shiver ran through her body. They were gaping at her boldly. One had beady eyes and an ugly scar that went from the top of his head to his jaw. The other one had rotted, black teeth.

"We have a visitor," Angus called when he saw Buck and Summer walking up.

Buck headed toward the group as Summer took off for her house.

"Hello, Mister Holester," Elliot Toddle said in a friendly manner. "I figured your partners had a right to speak for themselves."

"Very well. Go ahead. Tell them what you told me."

Toddle adjusted his glasses. "The company I represent, gentlemen, is willing to pay a handsome sum for your claim. Think of it. Never again will you have to work underground. You'll have enough money to live like kings."

"We can do that anyway," Charley said. "We ain't . . . we're not interested."

Angus nodded his agreement.

"But, gentlemen, I haven't named the amount we're willing to pay."

Angus stepped forward. "Get back on your horse, Toddle. Buck told you, now we've told you. We're not interested. We don't want to see your face near this mine again. If we do, we won't take kindly to it."

Toddle smirked, then mounted. "You're going to be sorry you didn't take my offer." His words were laced with anger.

"Is that a threat?" Buck asked.

"Would I be that foolish? Let's just say you should give it further thought." He jerked his horse around and rode off, his two henchmen following.

"What do you think?" Buck asked as the cloud of dust caused by the departing horses settled. "Should we post guards?"

"Don't think we have any choice," Charley answered. "What about you, Angus?"

"Didn't trust the man the minute I saw those strange glasses he wears." Angus snorted. "Whoever heard of glasses being square? I agree about posting guards. I didn't like the looks of those riders Toddle had with him."

"It might be a good idea to put a few rifles and shotguns in Summer's cellar. That way they'll be close by if anything should happen."

Summer wasn't at all pleased when Buck began bringing weapons into her house. But when he explained the reason for it, she simmered down.

"I want you to come to the cellar with me," Buck said when he had finished.

"Why?"

He laughed. "You sure are one suspicious lady."

"I've learned to be with you around."

"I need to explain what to do if there is trouble," he said, taking her by the elbow.

"Is it necessary? I don't like being around weapons, and surely we're not going to be attacked."

"I don't trust Toddle, so yes, it's necessary."

The trapdoor in the hall was still open, and Buck led the way down the wooden steps. There was a candle already lit, so it was easy for Summer to follow. The small room had a musty smell due to the earth walls.

"Now sit on that last step and listen carefully to what I'm going to tell you," Buck instructed.

But Summer had trouble paying attention as Buck proceeded to explain the difference between a rifle and a shotgun. She was more interested in the way his broad shoulders tapered down to his narrow hips. How could it have taken so long for her to realize how handsome he was? Of course, looks aside he was the devil incarnate.

"Are you listening to me?" he asked sharply.

"Yes."

"I'm leaving a shotgun by the stairs." He hoisted one up. "It's loaded, so be careful. If you have to, just carry it to the front door and pull the trigger." He held the butt against his shoulder. "Hold it like this, because if you don't, it's going to kick the hell out of you. Why don't you come over here and try it?"

"That really won't be necessary. If I do need it, I'm sure I'll be quite capable of handling the situation." Summer stood. "Is that all?"

Buck was tempted to have her hold the shotgun anyway, but ended up standing it up where she'd have easy access. "That's all," he finally said.

Summer went back upstairs, convinced this whole thing about guns was ridiculous. Besides, she needed to get away from Buck. Though she'd wanted to deny it, Buck had an irresistible attraction. And he knew it. How she could so dislike the man and yet be drawn to him physically, she'd never understand. It was as if she were spellbound. Aggravated at herself, she chose to concentrate on the shirts she was making the men for Christmas.

Toddle and his men rode into Central City, stopping at a small office with "Pierson Mining Investments" painted on the front window.

"What we gonna do now, boss?" Tucker asked when they were inside.

Toddle ran a hand over his bald head. He hadn't been at all pleased to see the Whiskey Hole Mine in full production, and having to deal with three men instead of one made him more edgy still. He removed a handkerchief from his pocket and began cleaning his glasses. "Well, we can either get rid of them or shut down production." He placed the glasses back on his nose, hooking the wire ends over his ears. "We don't want to do anything that might make us look suspicious."

He hadn't told either man about his meeting with William Nielson. Some things were left better unsaid. Nor did Tucker and Victor know that Pierson Mining Investments was his, and not an Eastern concern. It kept the two men from getting greedy.

"We should shoot them and toss 'em down one of the old shafts," Tucker said.

"I think a little accident in the mine might just start things rolling in our direction." Toddle took a seat behind his small desk.

"When we gonna do it?" Victor asked.

"I'm not sure. In the meantime, I want the two of you to camp on the other side of the ravine so you can keep an eye on the mine. If you see anything interesting, let me know."

"When this job's done, do we get the woman?" Victor drawled.

Toddle glanced at the man who was by far the meanest of the two. Considering William Nielson's desire to get rid of the woman, Toddle could see no reason not to let them have her. "Why not? Now get going. One of you report back so I'll know where I can find you."

It was nearing midnight when Buck entered the dark cabin. Charley was snoring, and Angus was still out making sure the guards stayed alert. Buck stripped and climbed into bed. Pulling the blanket over him, he was reminded of Summer. The blankets had been her idea. *Gentlemen don't sleep under hides,* she'd said. Buck had to admit it was a hell of a lot more comfortable, but the hides were warmer.

There'd been so many changes around the place in such a short time. Their encampment now included a house, barn, and a shaft house, all completed. Ten men were working twelve-hour shifts and the motherlode kept producing. By any standards, he, Charley, and Angus were rich. Charley and Angus were starting to buy *city clothes* and even talking about going to Denver where they'd have more of a selection. Even the cabin had remained clean.

At the hub of it all was one small female with a big cat's temper. From the beginning she'd represented everything he'd rejected all those years ago. Even though he had brought her here, he'd resented her intrusion and especially her uppity ways. He'd wanted to pay her back by getting her in his bed and hearing her beg him to make love to her. But somewhere along the way, the coin had turned. He was finding it more and more difficult to keep his hands off her. He could still picture her on the ground beneath him this morning. There was no doubt in his mind that he could eventually have her, but then what? She'd start hanging around all the time, wanting to know when they'd marry. Like so many other women, she wouldn't be content with just a romp; she'd want to own him. Then he'd have a hell of a mess on his hands. Angus and Charley would be on his back saying he should do right by her.

He decided the time had come to back off. Besides, she'd remember what he'd said this morning and start running scared. He chuckled softly.

Teacher, he thought, you have no idea how close you came to losing your maidenhood. Don't go tempting me, because I won't back off the second time. Just stay out of my way.

Chapter 8

Milly tried to concentrate on her cross-stitch as William bragged about his lunch with Territorial Governor John Evans.

"We dined at Peoples on Blake Street. Excellent food. I must take you there soon. But back to what I was saying. John is quite sure..."

Milly paid scant attention. She found his political aspirations unimpressive, considering that back east she had dined with senators and even President Lincoln.

"William," she interrupted, "would you place another log on the fire? It's getting chilly. I'm already learning to dislike the winters here."

Instead of performing the task himself, William pulled the service cord. When the butler entered, William ordered him to do it.

"You still haven't heard anything about Summer from that man you hired?"

"Thank you, Henry." William waited until the butler had left before saying, "I wish you would refrain from mentioning such matters when the servants are about, my dear. You know how they carry tales. To answer your question, I have heard nothing." He managed a grieved look. "I know this is going to upset you, but I've released the man I employed. Surely you can understand that

136

it makes no sense to spend good money on such a hopeless endeavor."

"I see."

"What? No argument?"

"Would it do any good?"

William crossed over and dropped to one knee. "Dearest Milly, I hate to see you suffering, but I'm doing what I think best."

What Milly wanted to know was why he continued to hide the fact that Summer had been found. "Of course you're suffering as well, Willy," she returned sarcastically.

He reached over and placed her hand in his. "Yes, my dear. I'm saddened at what has happened to Summer, but because of you I've come to realize I never loved her."

"Oh?"

"Milly, it's you I love, and you I want to marry." He put his hand to her lips before she could interrupt. "Please, don't say anything until I've finished. I know I'm speaking out of turn, what with the matter of Summer remaining unsettled. But at least, while you're recovering from the loss, you'll have time to consider my proposal. I'm a very good catch, you know, and have a strong chance to become the next territorial governor. Surely being a governor's wife must have considerable appeal."

It took every ounce of willpower Milly possessed to keep her anger from boiling over. After several deep breaths, she managed to produce the serious look he expected. "Yes, I'll consider your proposal, though it's still too soon for me to make any decisions. Now, what were you saying about Governor Evans?"

William rose to his feet, quite pleased at how well he'd handled everything. Though Milly had been previously married, she'd still make a fine wife. "Well," he said, returning to the fireplace, "John was saying . . ."

Milly shut her ears. William was such a fool! How could he think she'd ever seriously consider marrying him? It was the most ludicrous notion in the world. And she'd tell him so once Summer returned. But until then she was determined to keep him dangling. She definitely didn't like the fact that he was keeping what he knew about Summer a secret. She didn't trust William and wanted to be around to see just what the sneak might do. And Summer would come back eventually, she was positive of it—though with winter approaching, it looked like it was going to be a while before Summer could come down from her mountain. Milly groaned at the thought of having to remain under William's roof that long.

"Did you say something?" William asked.

"No, just clearing my throat. Please go on." She smiled at William, her thoughts quickly turning to Gus Slaterly, the man she'd hired to go to the mining camp and locate Summer. She'd done so on the advice of Marshal Bailey, and of course without William's knowledge. Milly had every intention of finding out if Summer was really staying up in the mountains by choice.

Summer was upset at the way Buck had been acting of late, and couldn't concentrate on her work. She set her needle and thread aside, then carefully placed the dress she was sewing across the back of the bedroom chair. Thinking a cup of tea might settle her thoughts, she went downstairs.

After stoking the fire in the stove, Summer added more wood before putting the kettle on top. She sat at the table to wait for it to boil. It was a wonderful stove, and with Charley's tutoring she

was becoming quite a fine chef. Though Charley
cooked most of the meals, she now helped. He still
preferred his old outdoor stove, but at least now
he made sure the cooking area and utensils were
kept clean. Placing her elbows on the table, Summer rested her chin on her hands and contemplated the strange things that had been happening
over the past few days.

The day after Buck had *forced* her to kiss him,
she'd decided to make a new dress for the dance.
Oddly enough, it was Charley who had driven her
to town, not Buck. Then, instead of going to Lorna's, he'd taken her to a store in Central City, in-
sisting it had a better selection of material. Now
how could Charley have known that?

What more, Buck hadn't shown up for dinner
that night, nor the two following—leading her to
suspect he was avoiding her. Angus and Charley
excused Buck's absence by saying there was trouble
in the mine. A likely excuse. Nothing had ever kept
Buck away before. At first she'd wondered if he
were angry, but quickly dismissed the idea. If anyone had a reason to be angry, it was her.

Hearing the water boiling, she returned to the
stove and placed the tea leaves in the teapot. Covering them with hot water, she set the teapot aside
to let the tea brew. So why is Buck staying away,
she wondered as she returned to the table. She
could remember their kiss as if it happened yesterday. It probably meant nothing to him, though.
Just another means of giving *teacher* a lesson. What
else could she expect from a man of his sort? Or
was her kiss so inexpert that he'd lost interest?

Summer rose again, aggravated at herself for
wasting her time thinking about such a worthless
man. She poured a cup of tea, then strolled to the
parlor window. It was a dreary day. Dark, clouds

hovered above. Last night Charley had said they were going to get more snow. A thin layer already covered the land.

Summer leaned her cheek against the cool pane of glass and let her thoughts fly. Suddenly she wondered why the men had never married and what their pasts were like. Several weeks ago Charley had said he and Angus were around thirty-seven and that Buck was thirty-three. Buck was an educated man, so why had he come West? To make his fortune? He would have been twenty-nine at the time he arrived. Where did he come from? Summer sipped her tea and grinned. He certainly wasn't a banker, because he didn't seem to like financial institutions. She remembered asking him if he'd been a bank robber and he'd said, *You don't know how close to the truth you are*. Summer's mouth dropped open. Could he really be a robber who'd come to the mountains to escape the law? She turned so fast her tea sloshed, spilling onto the wooden floor. She hurried to the kitchen to get a cloth to wipe it up, her mind racing with possibilities. Had Buck ever been in jail? Of course, it was all pure speculation. Maybe Charley could provide more information.

Since she had to fetch a bucket of water, Summer chose to do it before Charley arrived for the private lesson he'd requested.

As Summer headed toward the wooden pipe that brought water down from above Blackhawk, she was surprised to see the devil himself casually leaning against Charley's stove, holding a cup of coffee. Summer avoided looking at him and continued on her way. When she returned, he was still there.

"Morning, Miss Caldwell."

Though he didn't move a muscle, his smile spoke volumes. Summer just knew it was his way of reminding her of his warning. Well, if he still felt her curiosity would be her undoing, he was in for a big surprise. She stopped and looked him in the eye. "Good morning, Mister Holester. Have you lost weight? Perhaps you should try coming to supper some night, not that we've missed you. Oh, and since I haven't talked to you in some time, I want to express my thanks."

"For what?"

"For letting Charley take me to town the other day. I do so enjoy his company, and he's becoming quite a gentleman. At least with him or Angus around I don't have to put up with your tiresome efforts to prove you're a man. Good day, Mister Holester."

Buck gripped the mug so hard his knuckles turned white. His gaze remained fixed on the woman's back until she disappeared into the house. I should have taken her when we were in the woods and been done with it, he thought angrily. Tiresome efforts to prove I'm a man? That certainly wasn't what their kiss had been about. The lady possessed the tongue of an asp.

He tossed out the remaining coffee, slammed the metal cup down on the stove, and headed for the shaft house. He'd made a big mistake saying he'd take her back to Denver after the snow melted instead of before it fell.

Summer smiled at Charley, who had spent all of the last hour practicing talking to a lady. More than anyone, he was determined to be the finest gentleman in the Colorado Territory. "See, Charley," Summer said, "you'll do just fine."

"Talking to you is different."

"Not really." She leaned forward and patted his

hand. "Call me Summer, Charley. Good friends call each other by their first names."

Charley was so pleased he started to howl, but restrained himself just in time.

Summer continued stitching the dress laying across her lap. "I'm curious, Charley. How did you, Angus, and Buck become partners? You're so different from each other."

Charley relaxed, but made sure he was still sitting properly. "It was back in '59. We'd all tried our hand at placer mining and had nothing to show for it. We didn't know each other then. Well, one night we was—"

"We were."

"One night we were standing beside each other at the bar in the old Bishop Saloon, and we got to talking about our bad luck. It was Angus who come up with—"

"Came, or suggested."

"Angus suggested we work together and try shaft mining. So, that's what we did."

"But surely you haven't spent your life searching for gold? Where did you come from?"

"Texas."

"What did you do in Texas?"

"There ain't much to tell."

Seeing he was embarrassed, Summer didn't correct his grammar. It wasn't easy for someone to change speech habits after thirty-seven years. "Please tell me about it."

"Well, my pappy was a cowhand and we moved around a lot from one ranch to another. Ma died givin' birth to the last of five children, and Pappy made a living the best he knew how. Because I was the oldest, it fell on my shoulders to take care of the others. Not that I minded; they were good kids. I did all the cooking and such, and they helped.

When they'd all left to find work of their own, I took to cow punchin'." He rubbed the side of his chin. "I was working for the Bar L when the chuck wagon boss got stabbed by a bull, and old Shorty up and died. Since I'd been cooking for my family for years, I took over Shorty's job and worked steady from then on. Eventually Old Man Wheeler passed away and some big Eastern concern took over his ranch. They brought in their own hands, so I headed for the gold fields."

If anyone deserved the comfort of a good wife, it was Charley. And he wouldn't have any problem finding the right woman if Summer had anything to say in the matter. He wasn't bad looking, with thick brown hair, warm brown eyes, white teeth and a ready smile. In Philadelphia, the women would have flocked to him, and she could see no reason why the same wouldn't happen in Denver. "Were you ever married?"

"No, never had anything to offer a woman."

"Except your wonderful self. Have Angus or Buck ever been married?"

"Not that I know of. Men around here don't talk much about their past, and I don't ask. It's private."

"I agree, and I had no right to pry."

Tired of sitting in the uncomfortable chair, Charley stood. "That's a mighty pretty dress. You making it for the dance?"

Summer smiled. "If I can just get it done in time." She looked out the window at the heavy snowflakes starting to fall.

At supper that night, Angus didn't take kindly to Charley and Summer calling each other by their first names. Summer still called Angus, "Mister Comstock." He tried calling her Summer once; however, the hard look he received put an end to that.

* * *

As the days passed, Summer began to get used to Buck's surly disposition. She eventually found out he'd been complaining about Angus and Charley spending too much time with teacher and not enough in the mine. When Summer heard that, she started seeing red. How dare Buck say such things? Angus and Charley weren't neglecting their work and Buck was well aware of why she'd been brought here!

The following week became a nightmare for Summer. Angus and Charley were miffed at Buck for not attending any of the classes or supper. According to the two men, Buck was now demanding production be stepped up. Angus was even threatening to land a fist in Buck's face, while Charley wanted to tie Buck up and let him simmer. And not once during that period of time did Summer see or talk to the insufferable man himself. In fact, now that she saw the problems Buck was creating for his partners, Summer felt sorry she'd insisted he be included in the lessons in the first place. He was nothing more than a bull-headed egotist! How could she possibly have been attracted to him?

But one good thing did come out of all this; Summer was growing much closer to Angus and Charley. She now let Angus call her by her first name, too, and because they sopped up every bit of information she could give, they were progressing by leaps and bounds. Both men proved to have good minds and quick senses of humor. She enjoyed their company immensely.

Summer felt privileged when Angus spoke freely of his past one night.

"My grandparents came from the old country and ended up as Ohio farmers. My pa, their only son, was dedicated to the land. For years I worked alongside him and my two brothers. I managed to get a fifth grade education due to my ma's insistence, but once Pa found out I could read, write, and do numbers, he put his foot down and said I was needed on the farm. See, Pa never had an education so he could see no reason for it.

"One day, while I was in town getting supplies, the Indians came and killed the entire family. That was a rough time for me. I had to bury them.

"I was in my twenties then and had my fill of farming, so I sold the land and took off to become a gambling man. All things considered, once I learned the game I lived pretty well."

Summer found it interesting that neither man expressed any apparent sorrow for the past. They accepted their fate and lived one day at a time, deriving as much pleasure from life as they could. Like Charley, Angus was reasonably good-looking, in his own way. His red hair was curly and full, and his hazel eyes twinkled with mischief. He was a devilish tease. He'd have no trouble finding a woman either.

Charley and Summer laughed when Angus finished his story. "Things was going just fine until the sheriff caught me in bed with his wife," he concluded. "I had to hightail it out of town, leaving everything behind. That's when I decided to try my hand at mining."

It wasn't until the day before the dance that Summer happened to see Buck pass by her window. She threw on a warm shawl and rushed outside, the snow crunching beneath her feet. She followed him into the barn.

"Mister Holester!" She watched him turn and wait for her to catch up with him. His nose and high cheekbones were red from being out in the cold, his sculptured lips set. She could tell he wasn't at all pleased to see her.

"Yes, Miss Caldwell, what can I do for you?"

Summer ignored his frosty reply. "I want to know what is going on."

"What do you mean?" he said shortly.

"You can be quite dense when it's convenient. Why have you been riding Angus and Charley about spending too much time on lessons and not enough time attending to business? I can accept that you consider me an intruder in your little world. But be so kind as to remember I didn't exactly volunteer to come here. And Charley and Angus have been your partners for four years! How can you treat them like this?"

"It's not the first time we've had differences, Miss Caldwell, and most likely it won't be the last. Angus and Charley know that."

"Is it because of me?"

"I reckon that's between the three of us."

"So it *is* me. I thought you were a bigger man than that, Mister Holester, though of course you've proven me wrong on more than one occasion. Well, you'd better start adjusting because like it or not, I'm going to be here for awhile. I owe it to Angus and Charley."

"What the hell does that mean?"

"If you don't want to explain your unforgivable attitude, I do not feel obliged to explain my honorable one."

As she turned to leave, he grabbed her arm and spun her back around. "Just a damn minute. Let's get something straight. What goes on between me and my partners is none of your business. You were brought here to teach. Nothing more, and that includes meddling."

Summer yanked her arm free. Even though the

color of his eyes had turned steel gray, she wasn't
about to let him intimidate her. "It is my business
because I care about those men and I don't like
seeing you upset them."

"Who the hell do you think you are to dictate
how I'm supposed to act? From the time you came
here you've placed yourself so high in the clouds
the devil couldn't reach you with a pitchfork. Don't
preach to me. What you need is a man to teach
you once and for all what being a woman is all
about, and right now, lady, I'm sorely tempted to
take on the task."

Summer hit him across the face with every ounce
of strength she possessed. The sound of the slap
resounded throughout the barn. "You've needed
that for a long time, Mister Holester. Too bad I'm
not a man because instead of a palm it would have
been a fist."

She again turned and marched away, and Buck
didn't stop her. Instead he said, "I warned you
once, teacher, then backed away. You're not going
to be so lucky the next time."

Summer spent the next day keeping busy with
washing and cooking. She was still furious with
Buck, but at the same time eagerly anticipating the
pleasure of going to a dance. As soon as the sun
slipped behind the mountains, she decided it was
time to get ready. She wasn't going to let Buck's
attitude deprive her of having fun. She was about
to go upstairs when someone knocked on her door.

"Where's your bathing tub?" Angus asked when
Summer let him in.

"It's upstairs in the front bedroom. Why? Do you
want to use it?"

Angus didn't reply. Instead, he headed up the
stairs two at a time. A few minutes later he returned

with the copper tub and placed it in the middle of the parlor. Going to the fireplace, he added more logs until the fire crackled and flames shot up the chimney. Summer watched, not daring to believe what she hoped was about to happen.

Satisfied, Angus headed back to the door. He swung it open and called, "You ready, Charley?"

Then Charley entered, carrying two large pails of steaming water, and Angus left and returned shortly with two more. They continued doing this until the tub was full. Summer laughed and clapped her hands. She was actually going to have a bath!

Standing outside about ten paces from the open door, Buck had no trouble watching the scene. Summer's delight made him grin, despite himself. He walked away.

"Now don't stay in there all night," Angus warned, "or we'll be late for the dance."

"Thank you, Angus, Charley, for this wonderful surprise."

"Though we'd like to take the credit," Charley said, "it was Buck's idea."

Summer was immediately suspicious. Why would Buck do something nice for her? "Is he going to the dance?" she asked.

"Not that we know of," Angus replied.

"Good. We'll have more fun without him."

As soon as the door closed behind the men, Summer pulled the heavy drapes. She ran upstairs to fetch what she'd need, then back down to stoke the fire in the kitchen stove. Quickly placing the curling iron on top, she rushed back to the parlor, afraid the water might cool. Feeling terribly wicked, she removed the pins from her hair and let them fall to the floor, then stripped in the middle of the room. The water was still hot enough to sting and it took a few minutes before she could climb in. Knees bent, she submerged her body, delighting in something she'd taken for granted most of her life—a hot bath. It was heaven.

An hour later, Summer stood in front of the mirror. She was more than a little proud of the dress she'd made. It fit perfectly, and the green and silver vertical stripes made her narrow waist look even smaller. It was very proper, with a high neck, long sleeves puffed at the shoulders, and the front of the waist forming a V. Yards of material had gone into the skirt, which draped in folds to the floor, her wired petticoats giving it fullness. Originally she'd thought to make something daring and fashionable, but decided that would be frowned upon by the mountain women. She'd pulled her hair high on her head, then twisted it around several times and let the tight curls cascade down. One last touch of rouge and lip coloring and she'd be ready.

Turning away, Summer lifted her new cloak from the bed. It was much heavier than the one she usually wore and had a hood, which she'd need for the cold night.

When the men were ready, they knocked on her door. Summer opened it. She couldn't believe what she saw standing in front of the house. A sleigh, with bells and all! Even a driver. She looked questioningly at Angus and Charley. "Did Buck think of this also?"

"No, I did," Angus answered, beaming all over. "I rented it from the livery stable. A buckboard just isn't good enough for a woman dressed so lovely."

Summer leaned over and kissed his cheek. "Thank you, Angus. and thank both of you for my bath."

Charley pulled a small bouquet of flowers from

behind his back and handed them to Summer. "For you," he said simply.

Tears filled Summer's eyes. "Where did you ever find flowers this time of the year?" She kissed his cheek also. "You're both too good to me."

"Well, what are we waiting for?" Charley opened the door. "Are we just going to stand out here all night?"

They all laughed, and Angus helped Summer inside and made sure she was well covered with the rugs. As the driver moved the horse forward, Summer listened to the bells jingling and knew that this had to be the best night she'd ever known.

The dance had just started when the threesome arrived. It was being held in the fire house, and the fire wagons had been moved outside. The good-sized room was crowded around the edges, the center being used for dancing. Summer noticed the long table against one wall, with cookies, cakes and various other delicacies. Several large punch bowls sat at the end with glasses nearby. What really surprised her was the liquor bottles lined up. Men stood about in groups talking while the women sat on chairs chatting with one another. In the center, sawdust had been sprinkled on the floor and couples were already dancing to the music supplied by five men. While Charley attended to Summer's cloak, Angus led her to the dance area.

A short time later Summer saw Lorna enter on the arm of the short, bald man that had tried to buy the Whiskey Hole Mine. They stopped, said something to each other; then he went back outside. Lorna had stopped to talk with an older woman as Summer headed toward her.

"Lorna!" Summer said excitedly when she

reached the woman's side. "It's so nice to see a friendly face."

"I didn't expect to see you here." Lorna would have dearly loved to have given Summer a piece of her mind; however she refrained from making a scene. Neither Buck nor the boys had been to her store in weeks, and she resented it mightily.

"Buck didn't mention the dance until two weeks ago." Summer smiled. "I wasn't sure I'd be able to finish my dress in time. That's a lovely gown you have on, Lorna. Blue is a most becoming color for you."

"Excuse me, I see some friends." Lorna brushed past Summer.

Summer could tell when she was getting the cold shoulder, and it upset and confused her. She'd tried so hard to get off on the right foot with Lorna Templeton. She glanced about to see where Angus and Charley were. Maybe they could explain why the woman had been so standoffish. Spying Angus, she was about to head in his direction when she heard a woman behind her say, "Isn't that the Caldwell woman who's living at the mine with three men?"

"It certainly is," another replied. "She has her nerve coming here among decent folks!"

Summer felt as if she'd just been stabbed with icicle. Her cheeks went pale and her palms deadly cold. Shoulders back, she turned and faced the two women, whose face were pinched in smug expressions. "Ladies," she began as calmly as she could, "it has been my experience that people who spread malicious gossip usually do so because their lives are boring."

The two women were too astonished to reply, so Summer moved away. But having said her piece hadn't helped to soothe her pain. In fact, she'd probably only incited them. She knew she couldn't tell Angus or Charley what had happened because it would only stir up more trouble. Besides, the two men were surrounded by women, quite the center of attention. It made her proud to see what she'd taught them actually being put to use. She had to smile at the ridiculous sight of Charley's little finger pointed straight out as he held a dainty cup of punch.

All of a sudden, though, her pleasure evaporated. Buck was standing by the door and Lorna was hurrying toward him. Summer was appalled at the unfamiliar pang of jealousy that shot through her when Buck gave Lorna an ingratiating smile.

Buck wasn't dressed any differently than the other men, except for the wide-brimmed hat he'd bought in town from a man named Stetson, and the fine-looking sheepskin coat she'd never seen him wear before. Still, there wasn't a woman in the room who didn't turn and look. Even Summer had to admit he was the handsomest man in the place. Not wanting Buck to see that she'd noticed him and irked at the way Lorna was flaunting herself, Summer gladly went out on the dance floor when an elderly gentleman asked.

Just as the small group of musicians began playing the Shoe & Shuffle, Buck cut in. The white-haired man who'd been partnering her was too polite to object. Even though it was a fast dance, Buck still pulled her into his arms as though she belonged there.

"Don't you think you're holding me a bit close, Mister Holester?" Summer tried pulling back, but his arm held her in place.

"No, Miss Caldwell, I don't."

"There's already too much talk going around about me."

"To hell with them. May I say you look especially beautiful tonight?"

"I thought you weren't coming to the dance."

"And miss holding you in my arms? Not likely. Did you enjoy your bath? It's too bad I couldn't have joined you."

Summer tried stepping on his toes, but missed. "Is that the only thing you ever think of?"

"Is what the only thing I think of? Taking a bath with you?" His eyes were sparkling with amusement.

"I refuse to let you bait me, Buck Holester." She tried to pull away, but he wouldn't let her. "Why not save your energy for dancing with Lorna," she said caustically.

"Do I detect jealousy?"

"Not over the likes of you."

He moved her around the floor, putting an end to any further conversation. He danced with ease and grace, and Summer had no trouble following him.

A tall, blond-headed man claimed the next dance and Summer was angry at herself for being disappointed that Buck readily stepped aside. She smiled at the stranger. Her insides were still quivering from the pleasure of Buck holding her so close. Why did the man continue to have such an effect on her?

The stranger wasn't as good a dancer as Buck. He moved her right arm up and down to the music, making Summer feel like a water pump.

"I have been given to understand your name is Summer Caldwell. Am I correct?"

"Yes." She waited for some sly remark to follow.

"Name's Gus Slaterly, ma'am. I was hired to seek you out by Milly Stern."

Summer tripped over his feet. "Milly? Is she—"

"Please keep dancing. I was told not to make anyone suspicious."

Summer tried looking off into space. "How did Milly know I was here?"

"I didn't ask, and she didn't say. I'm to tell you Miss Stern is still in Denver, staying at the house of a man named William Nielson. She will remain there till you come back. If you need help for any reason, you can contact her there. Also, I'm to ask if you want me to help you escape."

"Dear Milly," Summer whispered. "She always manages to help when I'm at my lowest ebb. No, Mister Slaterly, I'm not ready to leave. I would like you to take a message to Milly, though. Tell her that she would be envious of me. I'm actually teaching some wonderful miners to be gentlemen. I have agreed to stay until the snows melt. That's when I'll come to William's house. Ask her to please wait." Summer grinned mischievously. "You can also tell her that if she's trying to steal William, she's welcome to him."

"Is that all?"

"Yes, and thank you for delivering the message. You have no idea how much it means to me."

Gus guided her back to a chair, and a few minutes later she saw him go out the door.

After her talk to Gus Slaterly, Summer began enjoying herself, especially once she realized her partners paid little heed to the women's malicious gossiping. She even danced several more times with Buck who, wonder of wonders, acted the perfect gentleman and made no further objectionable comments.

It seemed as if every man in the place wanted to claim Summer for at least one dance. But after two of her partners made offensive remarks about her moving in with them, Summer refused to dance with anyone except Angus, Charley, or Buck. When she took time out to catch her breath, she could see the envy in other women's eyes. That was why they were being so rude to her, she decided. But for the moment, she was having too much fun to let it prey on her mind.

When the musicians took a break, Charley escorted Summer to the punch bowl. She was enjoying a piece of chocolate cake when a woman stepped forward. She looked to be in her twenties, with friendly blue eyes and a wide smile that brightened her face.

"Miss Caldwell, I've never had the opportunity to meet you before, but my husband works down in the Whiskey Hole. I had to thank you for the coffee you've had ready when the men come out of the mine. My Freddy said he'd already thanked you. I felt I should, too."

"How very nice of you, Mrs. . . ."

"Allen. Ina Allen."

"I'm surprised you were bold enough to speak to me after some of the whispering I've heard going around."

"I'd be mighty proud if you'd call me Ina. I've heard the talk. I don't pay any cotton to what them women say. Believe me, there's a lot of other women here tonight who don't think that way. You just watch, they'll be comin' around."

A short man joined them and placed his arm around Ina's shoulders. "Evening, Miss Caldwell, I hope you're enjoying the dance."

Summer recognized the man, but hadn't known his name. "Yes Mr. Allen, I am. It's nice to get away from the mine for awhile."

The Allens were in the process of introducing her to other couples when a loud smack was heard

by everyone. A man went sliding across the floor
on his back, out cold.

"Now," Angus announced, "if any more of you
bastards has something to say about Miss Caldwell,
just step right this way!"

In a flash, Charley, Angus, and Buck had surrounded Summer, waiting for the first man to step
forward. But it soon became clear that no one was
about to take on even one of them, let alone all
three.

"Please don't do—" But Summer didn't get to
finish before Charley pushed her behind them.

"I'm going to tell you once, and you'd damn well
better take notice," Angus continued. "If I or my
partners hear another slander against this lady, and
that includes you biddies," he said, looking toward
Lorna and her friends, "we'll either buy you out
of town or kick you out, and everyone here knows
we can do it. I've given fair warning." He took
Summer's arm. "We're getting the hell out of here.
There's a lot of people I don't care to be around."

As Charley and Angus escorted Summer outside, Buck passed by Lorna, stopped, then tipped
her chin up with his finger. "I warned you." He
cocked a meaningful eyebrow before walking
away.

Other than a brief apology from Angus and
Charley, the ride home was in silence. The three
passengers were lost in thought. The night was
bitterly cold, but the wool rugs kept them comfortable. Buck followed behind on his horse.

Toddle and his two henchmen slipped back out
of the mine. The guard had been asleep when they
passed him the first time, and still was when they
left. The three men walked for some distance before arriving where they'd tied their horses.

Toddle mounted. "All things considered, boys, I think we've done a good night's work." He moved his horse forward. "It just goes to prove what I've always said. You have to have patience.

"For instance," he continued when his companions had pulled alongside, "if I hadn't put you to watching the mine, we wouldn't have known about Holester's habit of going in the old entrance. And when I saw the three at the dance, I knew it was the right time to strike. Yes, patience. Weakening those support beams with that log barley holding them in place is the perfect way to rid ourselves of Buck Holester. Maybe one or even both of his partners will go in with him. Tell you what. Because you boys have done such a good job, I'll buy you a drink when we get back to town."

Buck stood beneath a leafless aspen and watched the light flicker out in Summer's bedroom. He could picture her in her nightgown, snuffing the candle out and climbing into bed. The more he thought about the bed, the stronger his need became. Just knowing there wasn't a damn thing he could do about it was enough to make him want to kick the blasted door down. The evening hadn't ended the way he'd planned. Summer most definitely was not lying naked beneath him. All night he'd watched her gracefully move around the dance floor in other men's arms, seen them ogle at her beauty and admire her dress that failed to hide a single curve from the waist up. She'd bestowed quite a few breathtaking smiles on strangers that night, but not a one on him.

In an effort to get his mind off the woman, Buck strolled aimlessly around the clearing. He didn't know what he wanted to do. He damn sure couldn't go to sleep. The thick snow reflected the moonlight, making the night almost seem like day. He watched a fox pop its head around the pile of firewood and scurry off, then he looked up at the sky, drawing pleasure from a sight that never ceased to amaze him. Being so high in the mountains, it felt like he was almost standing among billions of stars—especially on a clear night like this. But try as he might, nothing captured his interest.

He returned his gaze to the upstairs window and suddenly smiled. For a fleeting moment he'd seen Summer looking down at him. He hoped like hell her need was as strong as his and that she was just as uncomfortable. It was her damn fault. The woman was made of stone. Buck chuckled softly. However . . . that stone was slowly chipping away.

Since he couldn't sleep and it was too cold to keep standing outside, he decided to go down to the old part of the mine and try to figure out a way of bedding the elusive Miss Caldwell.

Standing back from the window so Buck wouldn't see her, Summer watched him head down the old mine path. A soft ache spread through her body as she studied the tall, powerfully built man. After the angry exchange of words at the beginning of the evening, she'd actually enjoyed dancing with him, being held in his arms, smelling the pleasant scent that belonged only to him. He'd made it quite clear he still wanted her. If she allowed him to have his way would she lose her self-respect? Would he think less of her? She brushed her bottom lip with her fingertips, remembering his kiss. Her hand slid down her neck and over her breasts, making them tingle. Hadn't she often wondered what it would be like having a man make love to her? Hadn't she been tempted at times by men back in Philadelphia? Still, she'd never

found it hard to keep them—and herself—in
check. So why in the world did she feel such desire
for someone who could be a bank robber? Because
he was handsome, willing, mocking, and dangerous—a combination that was hard to ignore. She
remembered his comment about them sharing a
bath and was instantly consumed by the wicked,
raw thrill of it. Her hand started to move down
further, but stopped. Buck was right. Curiosity
could very well be her undoing.

Chapter 9

As Buck ambled down the old passageway he felt nothing but disappointment. The old anticipation and excitement that used to come when he entered the mine were no longer there. That had changed like everything else. Now they owned a business. Nothing more. Oh, it was making him and his partners rich all right, and providing jobs for men who had been desperate for an income. But the miners had to be watched closely to keep them from stealing, and they'd had to hire additional guards because of Toddle's threats. It didn't make sense that the man had backed off so easily. Time would tell, he guessed.

A partially filled car sat on a track that was no longer in use, and Buck felt the urge to be just a miner again. He grabbed a discarded pick and started striking at the small vein glistening in the lantern light, knowing that it would probably only yield fool's gold. But after a while, the strain of his muscles and the sweat trickling down his body felt good. He worked steadily until the car was filled.

Setting the lantern atop the ore, he proceeded to push the car down the track. When the wheels struck something and ground to a halt, Buck cursed. Lifting the lantern, he saw a log blocking the track and was about to move forward to remove it when dirt and pebbles started raining down on him. Then he heard the beams creak and knew he was facing a cave-in. Seeing he couldn't make it by running forward, he turned and ran toward the back of the tunnel. A huge billow of dust engulfed him and behind him he could hear the crushing sound of boulders and the snapping of beams. Buck slammed against the back wall gasping for breath, when the deadly silence fell. He turned and faced the barricade of dirt and rock not ten feet away. He was trapped. He laughed aloud upon discovering he was still carrying the lantern, then cursed the devil upon seeing the flame flicker weakly.

When the men working the late shift in the other section of the mine heard the rumbling, they shuddered, knowing exactly what had happened. They lived day in and day out with the worry of a cave-in. It took every ounce of control to keep from panicking, and not until it was determined the collapse had occurred elsewhere did they settle down. After work resumed, Cinnamon Pete went up top to inform the owners what had happened.

The heavy pounding on the cabin door woke Charley and Angus. As soon as Cinnamon Pete had given his report and left, the two men quickly dressed. Even though the cave-in was apparently in the old section, they decided to check it out.

"Wonder where Buck is?" Charley asked Angus as they headed out the door.

"He's probably waiting for us below."

The minute the two men entered the mine, they could smell the loose dirt. Cautiously they moved forward. It didn't take long to discover where the cave-in had taken place.

"Damn it, Angus!" Charley whispered. "I

warned you something like this would happen when you brought Summer down here. We're just lucky no one got killed."

"That didn't have a damn thing to do with it." Angus held his lantern up, taking a closer look. "I can't figure out how this happened, Charley. You know as well as I do, this tunnel was strongly reinforced. Look here at this beam. Sturdy as hell."

"I'm telling you, you put a curse on it."

"Jesus! Can't you think of anything else?" Angus turned and looked at his partner. "What's wrong with you? You've turned white as a ghost."

"Angus, something just occurred to me. Wasn't there a lantern missing? And how come Buck ain't down here yet?"

"God almighty! You don't . . . you find out if he's in the other section, and I'll check around up top. I'll meet you in front of the cabin."

Summer tossed on her robe and hurried downstairs. Who would possibly be pounding on her door at this time of night? Opening it, she was surprised to see Angus and Charley standing there.

"Summer," Charley said, "I hate to ask, but it's the only thing left we could think of. Is Buck here?"

"Of course not. Why would you even imagine such a thing?"

Charley spun around and swung a big fist at Angus, catching him squarely on the jaw. Angus flew backward and hit the ground with a thud. "Damn it, Angus, I warned you this would happen, but you wouldn't listen."

Summer's hand went to her mouth.

Charley reached down and grabbed Angus by the front of his shirt then jerked him back on his feet. "Before you go nursing that jaw, I suggest you jump on a horse and get help. I'll set the men in the mine to diggin'."

Angus hurried off, cursing a blue streak.

"Charley, what's going on?" Summer demanded.

"There's been a cave-in in the old section of the mine, Summer, and we think Buck's in there."

"Oh, no. Please God, no."

Charley pulled her shaking body into his arms. "Maybe we're wrong," he said gently.

Summer pulled away, tears already streaking her face. "Charley, the last time I saw Buck he was headed down the path toward the old mine."

Charley nodded, accepting what now seemed a certainty. "We'll get him out, Summer, don't worry. I have to go." His voice was husky with emotion.

Summer ran back into the house to get dressed. "Please, God," she begged, "don't let anything happen to Buck."

A half an hour later, men began to pour into the area to help, others to watch. Behind them Summer saw the women, including Lorna.

"Summer," Lorna said when she caught up with her serving coffee to the cold men, "I want to apologize for the way I acted at the dance."

"I'm busy, Lorna."

"I want to help. Please, let me do this. I have to keep busy or I'll go crazy with worry."

Summer could see the dark circles under the woman's eyes. It was obvious she'd been crying. Why had it never occurred to her that Lorna was in love with Buck? "Some of the women are in my kitchen cooking. I'm sure they'd welcome the help."

"Thank you."

Like Lorna, Summer also needed to keep busy

as the long night dragged on. She tried not to think about Buck being buried beneath tons of earth. It was an impossible effort. She wanted to scream at the men to work harder and faster, but didn't. They were doing the best they could. She saw men sweating while ice was hanging from their beards and mustaches. She doctored cut hands, and still they continued to dig. Charley and Angus worked side by side, refusing to rest.

It was dawn when Summer staggered to Charley's stone stove. Though she was bone tired, she refused to lie down. Any time now they could be bringing Buck to the top. He can't be dead, she tried to assure herself. The only man I've ever loved can't . . . no. She straightened up and made more coffee. Her exhaustion was making her delirious. In love with that contrary scoundrel? That was the most preposterous thing she'd ever heard of. Naturally she'd feel bad if something happened to him but that was a lot different than being in love. Besides, he was going to be fine.

Summer was still standing at the stove when two men arrived to fill their cups. Their clothing was filthy, their faces red and chapped from the cold.

"Angus and Charley been working all night. I don't know how they can still be standing," one of them said.

"They ain't gonna quit till they reach Buck. I'd feel the same if I was in their shoes."

"Think Buck's gonna make it?" the first one asked.

The gray-headed man slowly shook his head. "I don't see how it could be possible," he said sadly. "There ain't enough air down there to stay alive this long."

Summer fainted.

* * *

When she came to, she was lying on her bed and Lorna was patting her face with a damp cloth. Summer tried to rise, only to have Lorna gently push her back.

"I can't stay here," Summer insisted angrily. "They might reach Buck any time, and I have to be there."

"They've already reached him, Summer. Buck is alive."

"Alive?" Summer couldn't stop the flood of tears. A sudden thought occurred to her. "You're not just saying that to keep me here?"

"No, I wouldn't be so cruel. Apparently the large rocks fell in such a way that it allowed just enough air in to keep Buck from suffocating. He was unconscious, but Doc Willaby feels sure he's going to be all right."

"Thank God," Summer whispered. She accepted the handkerchief Lorna gave her and blew her nose. "Can I see him?"

"No, he's in the cabin resting, and the doctor, Angus, and Charley are with him. What you need to do is rest so they won't have to be worrying about you as well."

"How long have I been here?"

"About thirty minutes. They were bringing him up when you passed out."

Nothing had ever given Summer as much relief as hearing that Buck was going to be all right. Her tears were tears of joy.

Lorna dropped the cloth in the bowl of water. "I suggest you take a nap. I've brought up a bucket of warm water in case you want to clean up first, and there's some broth beside your bed. I'll be downstairs if you need anything else."

"Why are you doing this, Lorna? At the dance I thought you wanted nothing to do with me."

Weary herself, Lorna sat on the chair by the bed, a frown creasing her brow. "I guess to make amends."

"I don't understand."

"I've done a lot of thinking since last night. When you told Esther and Estelle Chambers off for the comments they made, I admired your courage. You stood up to them, something I've never had the nerve to do. Then when I arrived last night, saw your concern, and watched you work tirelessly, I knew you had more quality in your little finger than all those biddies in the social group put together."

Summer was embarrassed at receiving such high praise.

"I just hope from here on out we can be friends. There is, however, one question I've been dying to ask."

"What?"

"What really happened at Maybelle's?"

"I made a fool of myself." Summer smiled and propped herself up with pillows.

By the time she'd finished the story, both women were doubled up with laughter.

The weeks passed and Summer was overjoyed to see Buck back on his feet, apparently none the worse for his experience. However, it bothered her that the partners were no longer speaking to one another. Suppers were eaten in silence. Charley still blamed Angus for the cave-in, Angus felt he was being unjustly accused, and they both snapped at Buck, who was leaving them alone so they could settle the matter by themselves. She tried talking to Angus and Charley individually. It didn't do any good. As a last resort, she decided to approach Buck.

All morning, Summer kept glancing out the window in hopes of catching sight of him. She derived some pleasure from watching the icicles hanging from the roof glisten in the cold sunlight. She was about to give up hope of seeing Buck when he appeared from between the trees and headed for Charley's stove. He put something that looked like a large bird on top of it, leaned his rifle against the rocks, then continued on toward her house. Summer rushed to the door and opened it so he wouldn't have to wait outside in the cold. "Hurry," she called, "before the room gets cold."

As soon as he'd brushed his coat off and kicked loose the snow packed on the bottom of his boots, Buck entered the house.

"What did you leave out there?" Summer asked, shutting the door behind him.

"A turkey." He smiled as he pulled his gloves off and stuffed them into the pocket of his coat. "Isn't that what people eat at Christmas?"

"Oh Buck, how wonderful!" she cried. "Are we going to have a real turkey?"

"I'd hate to think I'd shot something else. How did you know I was coming?"

"I've been watching for you."

Buck cocked a dark eyebrow.

"Not for any reasons you might come up with."

She watched him hang his coat on the peg by the door, then move to the fireplace to warm his hands. It was good to see him looking strong and healthy. His presence filled the room. "I have coffee. Would you care for some?"

He nodded. "Maybe it'll warm my insides."

Summer returned shortly and handed him a cup of the steaming brew.

"You know," he said as she sat down, "you could warm me up if you were of a mind to."

Summer didn't miss the familiar twinkle in his eyes. Yes, Buck was definitely his old self. "I want to talk to you about something serious."

"If you think I'm not serious, you're dead wrong. I'd like nothing more than to carry you up those stairs. That bed Angus made is big enough to hold the two of us."

"I want to talk about Angus and Charley," she protested.

"Summer, you've a coward." He laughed at the cold stare she gave him. "All right. What about Angus and Charley?"

"It hurts me to see them feuding. I've had no success talking to them about it. I thought you might."

"Perhaps you haven't approached it in the right manner." He sat his cup on the narrow mantel and turned toward her. "Why don't you slap them the way you did me? That should get their attention."

"That's not fair, Buck Holester. I slapped you because of the way you were treating me. You had it coming."

"Maybe so." He stared into the fire. "Now, as far as Angus and Charley, they both have a valid point."

"How can you stand there and say that?"

"Even though Angus doesn't believe in superstitions, he had no business taking you inside the mine, especially when he knew how superstitious miners are. Believe me, if the men we hired knew what he'd done they wouldn't be working for us, no matter how much they need the money."

Summer's mouth dropped open. "You can't be serious."

"I'm serious."

"Surely you don't give credence to that foolishness?"

"I'm not sure what I believe right now, but that's not the point. Charley believes that's what almost cost me my life. Neither of us is going to change his mind with talk." Seeing her shoulders slump, Buck was tempted to gather her in his arms. He had his own suspicions as to what caused the cave-in, but he wasn't about to tell Summer.

"I didn't realize the ramifications," she said. "I just love those two men, and hate to see them at odds with each other."

Buck's back stiffened. "Don't you think love is a pretty strong word to use?"

Summer sank back in the big chair. "I don't think so," she said softly. "They're wonderful and caring."

Buck's eyes narrowed as he surveyed Summer. It didn't make much sense to him that she was this wrought up about his partners. Suddenly he remembered Lorna saying something about Summer being after their money. She'd claimed to be from a wealthy family, but how did he know that was true? He took a drink of coffee. What it all boiled down to was that he didn't know a damn thing about this woman. He'd just assumed. A bad error on his part. The whole thing could be an act, including the engagement to the lawyer as well as her embarrassment over the subject of bedding. Was she out to snag Angus or Charley for money? That would explain why she hadn't taken off when she had the opportunity.

"Since tomorrow is Christmas," Summer said, "maybe they'll put aside their differences." She looked up at Buck. "We'll have a big dinner and I'll collect pine branches and make wreaths. I can use turkey feathers and pine cones for a table decoration."

Seeing the way her eyes sparkled with childlike

glee, it tore at him to suspect her. But he couldn't help it at the moment. Well, there was one way to tell for sure if she was what she seemed—and it was something he'd been wanting to do for a long time.

"Sounds like a good idea. Tell you what. I happen to know where there are a bunch of pine cones on the ground, so why don't you bundle up and I'll take you there."

It wasn't until they'd left camp that Summer began to have reservations about taking off with Buck. Her concern about Angus and Charley had made her let her guard down. Why, just a minute ago he'd been talking about carrying her upstairs!

The more they walked, the more leery Summer became. They'd left camp behind, so he was no longer constrained by their agreement. Would he take advantage of that fact, as he'd threatened to do? A part of her was excited at the possibility, but another part was suffering from stark fear. "How much longer?" she asked nervously.

"Down the next hill and we're there."

Summer could see the thick forest of fir and pine ahead.

Buck led her into the tree where the snow was sparse and she could see the pine cones lying about. She knelt down and started picking some up.

"You know, Summer, I'm considered handsome. I'm certainly wealthy and I can be most considerate under the right circumstances."

"What are you bragging about?" Pricking her finger on one of the cones, she gently sucked the wound.

"If you want a man, why didn't you choose me instead of setting your sights on Angus or Charley?

Or do you think you're more apt to get one of them to the altar?"

She had just reached down to pick up another cone when her hand stopped. "Just what do you mean by that?"

"I thought I made myself quite clear."

Holding the cones in her arms, Summer stood. She felt a small degree of safety at seeing Buck standing a good five feet away. "I'll ignore your insinuations this time. Just don't make them again."

"It's me you want in your bed, Angel, so why do you continue to fight it? You know I'm more than agreeable. As for the money, Angus, Charley, and I have already agreed on the amount we're going to pay you. You'll be able to live comfortably the rest of your life. Or maybe you're greedy and that's not good enough."

"I should have known there was a reason why you agreed to bring me here." She practically spit the words out. Instead of trying to run away, she stood her ground and glared at him. "I've never met a more despicable man than you! What have I ever done to make you dislike me? Nothing. You're right about one thing, though. I did have visions of you making love to me, but not any more. You make me sick. What's made you hate women so? Your mother? Or maybe some woman from your past?"

Buck flinched. "I don't hate women."

"So it's just me you dislike. Then why do you keep trying to take me to your bed? To humiliate me? Fine! Go ahead and have your way with me if you're that kind of an animal. I'm certainly not strong enough to prevent it."

He watched the fire dance in her bewitching eyes, and contemplated the way her small chin jutted out in defiance. She was angry as hell. But the corners of her mouth twitched ever so slightly which told him that she was also afraid. Yet she continued to stand there, holding those damn pine cones. Buck realized he'd misjudged the lady. She wasn't acting. Goddamn if she didn't have more courage than he'd ever seen in a woman. The entire situation was so ridiculous he broke out laughing.

Summer was at a complete loss. Had the man become addle-headed? Maybe the cave-in had damaged him after all.

Still smiling, Buck stepped forward, expecting her to turn and run. Seeing the fear jump into her eyes, he stopped and expelled a heavy sigh. "All right," he said soberly, "I owe you an apology. I shouldn't have made those remarks. As for the part about wanting you, I won't apologize for that. You're a beautiful woman, Summer Caldwell, and I wouldn't be a man if I didn't desire you. At least you were finally able to admit you have similar feelings, even if it was in a fit of anger. Come here and let me hold you. I promise not to do anything else if that's what you want. Or are you more worried about yourself?"

Not sure what she should do, Summer said, "I want to go back."

"Go ahead. I'm not stopping you. But just holding you isn't going to take away your maidenhood." He extended his arms toward her.

Summer almost swooned. His voice was deep and his words were like being caressed with velvet. His blue-gray eyes held her green ones as she slowly lowered her arms. She wasn't even aware of the pine cones falling to the ground. Without willing it to, one of her feet moved forward. He reached out and drew her to him, then she was enveloped in his arms. It felt so right. Her head rested against his powerful chest and he moved his hand gently up and down her back. Wonderful sensations were beginning to take hold when her eyes snapped open. "No," she whispered, more to herself than to him.

Buck's need was strong and he wasn't about to back off this time. If he had his way, Summer was about to become a real woman. "For once in your life, let your desire take over. Don't you know how badly I want you? Look at me, Summer."

She shook her head.

"Look at me," he said softly.

No longer in control of herself, Summer slowly looked up. His lips were parted . . . waiting . . . wanting. When they gently touched hers and withdrew, she lifted onto her toes, needing more. She heard him groan softly as his tongue traced her mouth and he sucked on her bottom lip. He kissed her again, but this time it was more demanding. She was engulfed in flames when his hand cupped her buttocks and he pulled her hard against him, leaving no doubt as to what he wanted. She tried telling herself to put a stop to this, but his hand had reached into her cloak and was now cupping her breast and his fingers manipulating the sensitive nipple. Her entire body became weak. With reckless abandon, she returned his kiss, calling upon every feminine instinct she possessed as her hand covered his, not wanting him to stop. His tongue trailed down to her neck as unbuttoned the front of her dress. She became entrapped in total bliss as her swollen breasts were freed from their confinement and his mouth closed over her pulsating flesh.

Hearing her moans of pleasure, Buck lifted her skirt. Expertly he untied the strings holding her petticoats and let them fall. The pantalettes followed. He removed her cloak, dress and chemise, then gently laid her on a bed of soft pine needles. "God, you're beautiful," he murmured, then covered her so she wouldn't be chilled.

To his surprise, she boldly watched him undress, then held the cloak up for him to climb under.

He lay down beside her and placed his arm under her head. His hand roamed over her perfect breasts, then traveled down her flat stomach and on to the moist area between her legs. When his finger found the small button of pleasure, her body twisted and her hips lifted in encouragement. It was like stoking a fire. Underneath her proper, virgin-like behavior, she blazed.

"Summer," he whispered huskily in her ear, "I don't want you to say I took you against your will." He continued to manipulate the silky folds of her skin, knowing she couldn't refuse him.

"Don't stop," she groaned, her breathing coming in gasps.

Removing her hand from his chest, Buck placed it on his rigid manhood. "See," he uttered, "my need is every bit as strong as yours. I've never wanted any woman the way I've wanted you."

His words released what few inhibitions Summer still felt. So this was how it was between a man and a woman. She loved touching him, even though she could barely concentrate on anything beside the way he was making her body feel. The relentless throbbing in her stomach and between her legs was driving her mad. When he mounted her she was ready, only vaguely recalling the sharp pain Milly had said she would feel.

Buck entered her and felt her stiffen, but she didn't cry out. It was all he could do to keep from releasing his own satisfaction. Beads of perspiration covered her upper lip and her hair was spread out on the ground like a halo. He leaned down and kissed her lips as he moved in and out, drawing almost unbearable pleasure with each thrust. Her hips moved beneath him, and he smiled at how naturally her responses came. She was consumed with raw need. She was his. He moved faster and she met every thrust.

Summer suddenly stilled, afraid to move or breathe. Then every imaginable color exploded in her head as Buck took her to the height of fulfillment. Afterwards she felt his warm body relax on top of her and she dozed.

Summer awoke with her face buried in Buck's chest. Though his mat of chest hair tickled her nose, she remained perfectly still. A rush of emotion swept over her when she realized where she was, and what she'd just done. With each passing moment, images collided in her brain—of herself lying naked on the pine needles, thrashing, begging Buck to go on. How had she gotten here? Had she willed this to happen? Was she no different than the whores at Maybelle's? At least they did it in a bed instead of rutting on the ground! Tears stung her eyes and she turned her face away from him.

"So you're awake," Buck said kindly. He leaned over to kiss the top of her head and felt her body stiffen.

"Can we go back now?"

It angered Buck to hear bitterness in her voice. It had been wonderful experience for both of them, so what was she angry about? Next she'd be accusing him of taking advantage of her against her will. He loosened his arm to give her more room, but not enough to let her up. "You may be having second thoughts, lady, but if you'll remember, I gave you every opportunity to stop."

"I have no argument with that. I take full responsibility. If you don't mind, I'd like to get dressed and I'd prefer you didn't watch." She struggled to get free, but he continued to hold her down.

"At this point, there's very little I don't know about your body, so why the sudden need for privacy?"

"You think because you mounted me I no longer have the right to privacy? Very well, if that's what it takes I'll dress in front of you, only let me up!"

"First I want to know what's going on in your head, lady."

"That's my concern, not yours."

"You may be right, but if we have to stay here . . ." He caught her wrist before she struck him with a pine cone, then rolled back on top of her. "As I was saying, if we have to stay here a week making love, I intend to find out what's wrong."

Summer gasped. "You wouldn't!"

Still angry because she couldn't even accept the pleasure they'd shared, he said, "I've already proven I keep my word."

Summer's fury knew no bounds. She leaned forward and sunk her teeth in his shoulder while striking him with her free hand.

"Son of a bitch!" Buck yelled. He could feel blood drip from where she'd bit him. It didn't take long to get her flailing body back under control.

"You . . . bastard . . ." Summer accused between labored breaths. "I know what I've become, but you don't have to remind me!"

"What have you become, Summer?"

"A trollop!" Tears streamed down her cheeks.

"Why? Because you enjoyed this?"

"If you must know, my . . . actions were unforgivable. Now, will you please let me go?"

"So that's it." Buck's gut told him to let her go and be done with it, but for some ungodly reason, he couldn't. Maybe because he owed it to her or the man she'd marry someday. "Summer, listen to me. You did nothing to be ashamed of. Actually you should be proud."

"Leave it to a man to say something like that."

"Would you have derived as much pleasure if I'd lain here like a dead fish?"

"What kind of a question is that?"

"Just answer it honestly."

"Well . . . no."

"It's the same for a man. The more a women reacts to his lovemaking, the more pleasure he gets. There's no need for you to feel embarrassed, Angel." He rolled off of her. "If you don't take what pleasure life has to offer, it makes for a damn sad existence. Now let's get dressed. I'll turn my back."

Summer knew she should do the same, but for a brief moment she allowed herself the pleasure of seeing his muscled body and lithe movements. She felt considerably better after what he'd said. Maybe she was being too hard on herself.

"If you don't stop watching me," Buck said over his shoulder, "I'm going to be very tempted to rejoin you, and I won't take no for an answer this time. You know, the second time is even better than the first."

"Really?" Summer even surprised herself when she didn't move. Buck's words had made sense. Why should she feel guilty? Milly didn't. She watched him slowly turn and face her. All he had on was a heavy flannel shirt, still open in the front. He wasn't the least ashamed of his nakedness.

"I'm not going to get caught up in your guilt, Summer. If you want me, you'll have to ask."

Summer swallowed hard. She'd expected him to come straight to her. "That's not what you said a minute ago," she said, trying to make a joke of it.

"A few minutes ago I was teasing. I'm not teasing now. When you're ready to shed your guilt and admit your needs are as strong as mine, you know where to find me. Now get dressed." This time he didn't turn his back. He watched her put every stitch of clothing on.

"Are you still sorry?" Buck asked as she finished dressing.

"No," she answered honestly.

"At least that's a start."

Summer knew now that even if she could, she wouldn't have changed what had happened. Such rapture was too exquisite. Even the thought of how she'd saved her precious virginity seemed to have little merit at the moment. But she couldn't tell him that now, just as she couldn't ask him to make love to her again. At least not yet.

Chapter 10

William blanched when he heard what his visitor said, then rushed to the library door and opened it to be sure no one was eavesdropping. Satisfied, he closed it again, moved back into the room, and looked down on the small man seated comfortably on the large leather chair. "You tried to kill them?" His eyes were as round as cannonballs. "I said nothing about killing anyone! How could you have even considered such a thing?"

Toddle removed his glasses and calmly began cleaning them. "And just how do you propose to make them leave the area, Mr. Nielson?"

"Buy them out!"

"They won't sell," Toddle said flatly.

"Then scare them."

Toddle's grin was malicious. "Obviously you don't know the men you're dealing with. I wouldn't be the least surprised if they had all escaped from prison. They're hard, and they don't scare. I feel sorry for the woman because I'm sure they've put her through every sort of hell. No man will ever want her." Seeing Nielson wince, Elliot Toddle began to understand what this was all about. A prominent man like Nielson could ill afford being connected to such a woman.

"Then kidnap her and get her on a stagecoach out of here," William persisted.

"She's been kept in a cabin with three men who seem to enjoy their pleasure with—"

"I don't need details."

"To do what you say, I would have to get past the men and their guards, which isn't possible. And don't forget, it is her decision to remain there."

William began to pace. "I'm sorry I got involved in this mess. But one thing is certain, I will not be a party to murder. So stop everything, and I'll just wait and see what happens." With that he collapsed onto a chair.

"Mr. Nielson, why don't you look at this honestly?" Toddle replaced his glasses. "You've worked hard to get to where you are. Surely you're not going to let these men and a worthless woman ruin everything. Why, I've even heard rumors that you'll be the next territorial governor."

"You're right. What do you suggest I do, Mr. Toddle?"

"Please call me Elliot." Toddle noticed the man didn't return the offer. "I suggest you let me handle matters in my own way. I'll make sure everything is taken care of. In return, when I get control of the mine you can pull strings and make sure it's legally put in my name. Of course, with you holding five percent of the shares, you'll benefit by it." Naturally, Toddle would make sure Williams never knew the true value of the mine.

"And perhaps in the future you'll have other jobs you'll want me to take care of, and I will have other mines. I'm sure we can create a most profitable and equitable arrangement. We never get anywhere if we don't take what we want. Don't you agree, *Governor*?"

Hearing the man address him as Governor was all William needed to make up his mind. Toddle was right. You had to take what you wanted. As for Summer and the men, as long as he didn't have to know what happened, his conscience wouldn't bother him. Even if he did know, it only made sense to remove scum from the earth. "We have a deal, Elliot." He rose from the chair and the two men shook hands.

While they were clustered in the library, Milly was talking to the cook about what to serve for supper. She suddenly began laughing, and the cook looked at her strangely.

"Pay me no mind, Margaret," Milly said. "If you have any further questions, I'll be in my room. I have several letters I need to write."

In her room, Milly went directly to the small desk and pulled out paper, fountain pen and ink. She'd waited entirely too long to write to Summer's parents. At least now she'd have good news for them, though she wouldn't tell them exactly what was going on—perhaps just that Summer was spending the winter in the mountains. She laughed, again thinking about Slaterly's report. So Summer said she was welcome to take William. Apparently Summer was now well aware of William's faults, or had her eye on one of the miners.

Milly sat down, feeling quite pleased at how thorough Slaterly had been. The money she'd paid him was well spent. He'd found out about the Whiskey Hole Mine, and even provided a detailed description of the handsome and wealthy miners. Milly was itching with envy. How she would love to be in Summer's shoes instead of stuck here with the insufferable William. She still wondered if there was any way she could get up to see Summer even though Slaterly had informed her it was a hard ride. She never had cared much for horses. She sighed. Why butt her head against the wall? She'd just have to wait until Summer came to her.

Christmas wasn't the happy affair Summer had hoped for. However, everyone at least acted civil. What with Angus and Charley refusing to talk to each other, she became the center of attention. The hardest part of the day was trying to act normal around Buck. His handsome face, knowing eyes, and quick smile made her body ache with desire. On more than one occasion she'd actually pictured him with his clothes off.

Summer presented each of the men with a flannel shirt she'd made, and broke out laughing when they tried them on. All the shirts were too small. They tried to assure her the fit was perfect, then also laughed at the absurdity of it. Charley gave her a new kettle for cooking, and Angus presented her with a lovely shawl. Buck's gift was a beautiful bedspread, and she didn't fail to recognize the innuendo.

Two days later a blizzard hit. Summer kept looking out her window, wondering when it would stop. But the wind kept howling and the snow continued to fall. Even the mine had been shut down. Angus or Charley came by occasionally to be sure she was all right, but Buck never made an appearance.

Try as she might to prevent it, Summer's need for Buck grew with each passing day. She could even understand why the men referred to it as an itch. The nights were the worst. In her mind she couldn't stop picturing everything that had happened on that fateful day, and her hands would roam her body just from the remembering. It only served to increase her need for the physical release Buck alone could give.

Buck sat at the table sharpening his long knife on a whetstone, trying to ignore Angus and Charley's constant arguing. Being confined in the small cabin with the two of them was getting on all their nerves. The men did agree on one thing. They had never seen a storm to equal this one.

"You should be thanking the good Lord that Buck is alive!" Charley barked at Angus.

"I've had enough of your goddamn caterwauling, Charley. You know I would never wish Buck any harm, and I still haven't forgotten that fist you landed on my jaw. If it's a fight you want, then just step forward 'cause I'd be more than happy to oblige you. If not, shut your damn mouth!"

Charley, who had been sitting on one of the beds, jumped to his feet. Fists raised, the two men started circling each other.

Buck jammed the knife back into the scabbard and looked at his partners. "Listen to me! I haven't said anything before because I have no proof. But I'm tired of listening to the two of you. As you know, I've had a lot of sleepless nights since that cave-in. But by having to relive it, I also started paying attention to some things." Seeing the two men had lowered their fists, he continued. "When I was pushing the load of ore down the track toward the old bin, the car struck a log. I guess I wasn't paying attention when I entered the mine and I had to have been walking on the wrong side, because I didn't see it. Well, I finally asked myself what the damn thing was even doing there. It wasn't the type we'd use for supports or anything else I can think of. I now believe it was used as a brace."

"Are you saying what I think you're saying?"
Angus asked.

"Remembering back, after the first support beam
fell, the others cracked."

"You're thinking someone did some tamper-
ing." Charley looked at Angus, then back at Buck.
"Toddle?"

"That's my guess." Buck pushed the whetstone
aside. "It would make sense, especially after he
made that threat. I don't think he would say something like that and then back off."

Angus and Charley pulled out chairs and joined
him at the table.

"You sure about the log?" Charley asked.

"Yep."

Charley tugged at his earlobe while giving
thought to the matter. "Looks like I owe you an
apology, Angus, even though I still think taking
Summer in the mine was wrong."

"You're right. I shouldn't have done it, even
though I consider that whole mess about women
in mines to be hogwash. Nevertheless, it won't
happen again."

Charley was satisfied.

"If it was Toddle," Angus said, "he'll be trying
again. We're going to have to be more careful.
Wonder how he got past the guards?"

"Considering when it happened," Buck added,
"I'd say it was done while we were at the dance."

Charley leaned forward. "You know, I saw him
at the dance, and now that I think about it, I didn't
see him later."

"Well," Angus said as he stood, "we have no
choice but to wait and see what his next move will
be." He started to walk away, then stopped.
"Guess this is as good a time as any to tell you
boys I've decided on a wife."

Charley laughed. "You don't say. So have I. I plan on asking Summer as soon as this storm blows over. Who did you choose?"

Angus gave him a fierce look. "Summer? Son of a bitch, Charley, I had the idea first."

"The hell you did!" Charley shoved his chair back. "I've had it on my mind for a long time."

To Buck's horror, he suddenly realized he didn't want either man to have her. Damn it, he'd already staked his claim. But marriage? He paid scant attention to the two arguing again. His thoughts were on the emerald-eyed beauty across the clearing. Over the last few days he'd given a lot of consideration to her different reactions during and after they'd made love. She hadn't even pursued him the way he'd expected. "I also intend to marry the woman." The words slipped out before he realized what he was saying.

Charley and Angus stared at him in total disbelief.

Buck grinned nervously. "Well, I guess it was bound to happen some day."

"But why Summer?" Charley asked. "I want to marry her because I love her."

"Me, too," Angus chimed in.

They waited for Buck's answer.

"Who's to say she'll have any of us?" Buck asked, avoiding the question.

Angus' hazel eyes turned hard. "All right, then it's every man for himself. But I think there is something else we need to take into consideration. We've been partners and friends a long time, and even though we've had our differences, we've always ironed them out. Some have taken longer than others." He glanced at Charley. "I wouldn't like losing that friendship because Summer chose me."

"He's got a point." Charley sat back down, a woebegone look spreading across his face. "But if Summer were to choose me, I wouldn't let our friendship stop me from marrying her."

"*If* she picks one of us," Buck said, "the other two have to be willing to back off with no hard feelings or cracking of skulls."

"I'm agreeable," Angus said begrudgingly. "But she's not to know about our agreement."

"All right," Charley said. "But there has to be one more provision. No one forces Summer to do anything against her will. Angus . . . Buck?"

They were all in agreement.

The next morning, upon seeing the bright blue sky, Summer leaped off the bed and looked out the window. Never had she seen anything quite so beautiful. It was a white fairyland. The snow reached almost to the roof of the cabin, making her wonder how the men were going to get out.

After dressing, Summer hurried downstairs, eager to go outside and make a snowman. But when she swung the door open she was facing a white wall. She stuck her finger in it, then watched her entire hand disappear. She'd expected the snow to be hard, not soft. Closing the door, she checked all the windows downstairs and found them also covered with snow, except for a couple, where she could see a little light at the very top. She went back upstairs and looked down at the cabin again. This time she saw three men on snowshoes, pick and shovels in hand. She waved, but they weren't looking up. At least there was no longer any question of Buck, Angus, and Charley being able to get out of their cabin.

By the time the men had tunneled to her door, Summer had hot coffee and a waffle about ready to take out of the cast-iron waffle maker. She told them to sit at the table but they wouldn't hear of it. Instead they made sure she was properly seated. Charley removed the waffle and put it on a plate before pouring batter for the next one. Angus grabbed the plate and some silver and brought it to her. Buck delivered the maple syrup with a spoon already in it. Then all three stood watching her eat. Though Summer rather enjoyed the attention, she couldn't figure out why they were acting so strangely.

Charley went to the stove and flipped the waffle iron over. "There'll be another one ready in just a minute," he said, returning to the table.

"Thank you, Charley, but this is all I can eat. Why haven't any of you drunk the coffee I fixed? I made it for you."

Charley and Angus rushed to the stove and poured a cup.

"Charley, I've finished my breakfast. Now I insist you, Angus, and Buck sit down and let me make the waffles."

The men took their places at the table.

Later, when everything had been washed and put away, Summer asked, "Would it be possible for me to go outside?"

"I don't know why not," Buck replied. "It's not really that cold. There are snowshoes in the shaft house. I'll go fetch a pair. Besides, I need to check and see if everything is all right."

Angus stood. "I'll go with you."

"Then let's go."

"I would have thought you'd want to stay there," Buck commented when they were outside.

"I could say the same thing to you."

"We're not going to get anywhere if we keep butting heads."

"I suppose you're right." Angus smiled at his partner. "How come you wanted to be a part of this, Buck? Never thought I'd hear you express a desire to marry."

Buck laughed. "To tell you the truth, Angus, I've been asking myself the same thing." He inhaled deeply, enjoying the fresh, crisp air. "I like the life I live, and I'm not anxious to change it. Marriage scares the hell out of me. I never saw any happiness in my mother and father's marriage. And I've known too many married women who like to warm themselves in other men's beds. Of course, married men aren't much better."

Angus was quite taken by Buck's words. In the four years he'd known Buck, there had never been mention of anything about his past other than telling stories about when he was a trapper—some too grisly for remembering. Angus also knew Buck had killed, albeit in self-defense. But so had he. "Not that I want to encourage you into courting, but do you really think Summer's that kind of woman?"

"Maybe not. I have to admit the thought of her marrying you or Charley doesn't sit well with me."

Angus grabbed Buck's arm and stopped him. "Shit, Buck, I think you're in love with her, too, but don't recognize the symptoms."

The two men stood staring at each other, their breath looking like puffs of smoke.

"That's the problem, Angus. Maybe my pride's just wounded because she hasn't latched on to me the way other women do."

"You ever been in love before, Buck?"

"No, can't say as I have. How about you?"

"More times than I care to admit. I think I've loved every woman I've ever known, and that even includes some of the whores."

"What if Summer's not a virgin, Angus?"

Angus looked at Buck with a keen eye. "You trying to tell me something?"

"Nope. Just asking a question."

Angus broke out laughing. "I'm sure as hell not one either."

They continued on to the shaft house. Climbing the stairs proved a bit difficult, but the house sat high enough that it didn't take much effort to open the door.

When they returned, they discovered Charley had already managed to get Summer out of the house. The two men laughed uproariously upon seeing Summer and Charley lying on their backs. Charley was showing her how to make angel wings in the snow.

They all pitched in and made a huge snowman, then flat boards were brought out that allowed them to slide down the gentle slopes away from the cliff's edge. They even threw snowballs. At one time Summer stepped off into a drift and Angus and Buck each grabbed a wrist and pulled her out. Summer would never have believed three huge, grown men could have so much fun. Even Buck was relaxed and gladly joined in the activities.

For Summer, the day passed too quickly. It wasn't until she returned to her warm house that she felt cold and worn out. She put more logs in the fireplace before going upstairs. After removing her damp, flannel dress, she laid on the bed and pulled a quilt over her to keep warm. It was wonderful, seeing Charley and Angus finally at peace with one another, though she had no idea what had brought it about. Spending this special day with them had meant a great deal to her.

She had no problem bringing Buck to mind, remembering his laughter and friendly teasing. Even though at one time she'd accused him of not caring about his partners, she knew that wasn't true. He cared a great deal. Why else would he have gone along with Angus and Charley's desire to learn manners, or suggest they get a teacher? He also loved the land. She had seen it in his eyes many times when he would look out over the mountains. Buck possessed many good qualities. Unfortunately, trusting women wasn't one of them. Her eyelids grew heavy and she permitted herself to take a short nap. The short nap lasted until dawn the next day.

Summer was sad when everything returned to normal. The partners spent a good deal of time in the shaft house or underground, and Buck made no effort to rekindle their lovemaking. But they really hadn't made love. Lust was a much better word for it.

But Summer soon learned that contrary to what she thought, things really weren't the same. It all started when Charley presented her with a gift. Summer opened the small box and discovered a beautiful gold locket and chain nestled inside.

"How thoughtful of you, Charley," she said as she lifted the beautiful locket into the air for closer examination. "Where did you get it?"

"At a jeweler's in Central City. Went there yesterday."

"It's so lovely, but you really shouldn't be giving me a gift."

"I want you to keep it." Charley dropped to his knee so fast, he knocked the chair over. He stood and put it upright. This wasn't the way he'd practiced asking Summer for her hand.

Summer sat staring, trying to figure out just what he was doing.

Again Charley fell to his knee in front of her, and placed his hands over his heart. He tried to ignore the slight rip he heard. He was wearing his best outfit and his pants were quite tight.

"Summer . . . dear Summer," he stammered, "I'd like you to be my wife." The words were blurted out, and Charley silently cursed himself.

Summer couldn't have been more surprised. "I'm sure you don't mean that."

"Yes, I do. I love you. I've been thinking about it for some time. I don't expect you to give me an answer right now, but I'd be pleased if you'd at least agree to think on it."

"But. . . ."

"Wait until it's time for you to go back down the mountain. I'd make you a good husband, Summer, and although I know you're not interested just in money, I'd have us a grand home built in Denver where we could raise children properly. Would you please think about it?"

Summer's heart went out to him. He looked so adorable in his black frock-coat and checked trousers. Even his shirt was well starched and the slender tie matched to perfection. She knew she could never marry him, but she couldn't bear to hurt his feelings by turning him down cold, so she said, "Charley, I'll give it proper consideration, but I can promise nothing."

"That's all I ask." He rose carefully so his pants wouldn't tear any more. A big smile stretched from ear to ear. "May I place the locket around your neck?"

Summer nodded, knowing it would seem childish to refuse.

As soon as he'd fastened the clasp, Charley leaned down and kissed her on the cheek. He grinned. "Now don't get mad at me, I just couldn't resist."

Not knowing what to say, she changed the subject. "Have another cake. I admit they're a bit flat, but they are tasty. Perhaps my next effort will prove more successful."

"I think they're perfect." He took another of the small cakes before returning to his chair.

"Come, come, Charley, you may be courting me, but we are friends as well. You don't need to lie."

"But I'm not lying. I do enjoy the cakes."

Summer studied his warm brown eyes. "I think I taught you too well, but we'll leave it at that. Did last week's snow damage anything at the shaft house?"

"No, everything is fine." He took a sip of his tea. "I do believe Angus and Buck took your suggestion about letting others do the work."

"Oh?" She'd suggested earlier that the partners just oversee the digging, since they were now such rich men. But she hadn't thought they'd paid any attention to her.

"They took off and said they'd be back when we see them."

Summer's first thought was Maybelle's. "Did they go together?"

"I don't believe so. I have a hunch Buck is headed for Denver."

"With all this snow on the ground? He'll never make it!"

"He'll make it, and when he returns he'll look none the worse for wear. I don't know much about Buck, but I do know he was a trapper for a good many years. He knows these mountains like the back of his hand. I've seen him go out hunting on days that Angus and I had trouble just making it from the cabin to the mine. He'll be just fine."

Summer wanted to get off the subject of Buck. She'd already spent too much time thinking about him, and it only made her miserable. "And where do you suppose Angus went?"

"My guess is he's taken off for Central City or Mountain City, because he took the buckboard. The only reason I said Buck could be headed for Denver was because of the gear he took, and a packhorse."

"How strange."

"Not really. Buck's always been prone to wanting to get off by himself and think."

When Charley left, against her better impulses, Summer found herself giving serious thought to his proposal. He was a good man, probably better than any she knew. She would very much like to have children someday, and she'd fallen in love with Colorado. She had no desire to return to Philadelphia unless it was to visit her parents, and she certainly didn't want to marry William. Charley was a hundred times better than William. But what about Buck?

She was terrified of the effect he had on her. What if his comment about discovering how much she wanted him when it was too late were to come true? Every time he was near she became weak, and the hardest part was knowing all she had to do was ask. The offer was always there, in his smile, the way he looked at her, even though he never made mention of it. Would it be fair to marry Charley knowing she felt that way about Buck.

It occurred to her now that she didn't know the first thing about love, even though she'd gotten engaged to William and was actually considering marriage to Charley. But everytime she thought about love, it was Buck who sprang to her mind. Was what she felt for him love? Then why was she so afraid? Because it hurt her to think that he only wanted her for the pleasure she gave him? He certainly didn't love her, and she could never be happy hanging on to him, afraid he would leave. That was her biggest fear about letting him possess her body again. He had said the second time was even better. If that was so, would she have the strength to leave him, or would she become his slave?

"Is there anything else I can do for you, Mister Comstock?" the clerk said.

Angus thought a moment. "No, I believe this will do for now."

"Everything is loaded in your buckboard, sir, and ready to go."

After lighting his Cuban cigar, Angus left the store feeling quite pleased with himself. He stood on the boarded walk and enjoyed his smoke while watching the wagons and men on horses going up and down the muddy street. Some tipped their hats in acknowledgement as they passed, and several smiled sheepishly. Angus narrowed his eyes, recognizing them from the dance, the night he'd become so angry. Things had changed a lot since then. Even Charley and Buck had commented on the respect everyone now showed them, and on more than one occasion people had inquired as to Summer's well being.

Cigar clenched in his teeth, he took off down the boarded walk towards the bathhouse. He wanted to look his best when he proposed to Summer.

Chapter 11

Summer stood staring at the cherrywood secretary and delicate brocade chair sitting in the back of the buckboard. They were lovely and normally she would have been thrilled to receive such expensive additions to her rather barren house. But coming so soon after Charley's gift this morning, and seeing Angus dressed in city clothes with his red hair and mustache trimmed to perfection gave her cause for thought. She saw his expression turn from excitement to disappointment and felt guilty.

"Don't you like them?"

"Oh, yes. They're beautiful. Whoever lives in this house will certainly appreciate such fine furniture."

"Good. I'll have Charley help me put them inside shortly. In the meantime, I thought we might go for a walk. I imagine you get pretty tired staying in the house most of the time."

The old sparkle was back in his eyes, and Summer had to smile. "You're not planning to take me to the mine again, are you?"

Angus laughed. "Not in a thousand years. I still don't believe in that hogwash, but I'm not about to get Charley on my back again. I thought we could follow the meadow. The snow isn't as deep since the melt, and it's a nice afternoon."

"I'd like that."

"Wait here while I get my rifle."

They strolled for some time in comfortable silence.

"Buck said you have a man waiting for you," Angus said after they'd stopped to watch a hawk circling overhead. "Are you looking forward to returning to Denver?"

"I don't know, Angus. I have mixed feelings. I've really come to love the high country. It's so beautiful, though I'm not too sure about the winters."

"What about the man?"

"When I go back down, naturally I'll have a talk with him."

They started walking again.

"Do you still plan on marrying him?"

"I'd made up my mind not to marry him before Buck took off with me. I have to admit that part of that decision was based on the fact that Denver seemed like such a scrubby town compared to Philadelphia."

"Do you still feel that way?"

"No." She laughed softly. "My values have changed considerably since I've been here. You, Buck, and Charley have actually taught me more than I've taught you. I'm ashamed to say that before coming here I wouldn't have given any of you a second glance. You see, proper dress, social etiquette, and family status were all I cared about. I guess that was pretty obvious. As for William— that's the man's name, William Nielson—I wouldn't even consider marriage to him now. He's a pompous bore."

"Would you consider marriage to me?"

Summer lowered her head for a moment, but

kept on walking. "Is that why you bought the secretary and chair?"

"Probably. I once heard a man proposing marriage should come bearing gifts."

Summer had always considered Angus' straightforwardness one of his most attractive attributes. "Charley proposed to me this morning." She waited for a reply, but none was forthcoming. "I take it you're not surprised."

"No. I expected it."

"And you're still asking?"

"We're grown men, Summer, not young pups. We're well aware of the gambles in life. None of us have ever let another man stand in our way when we wanted something. If I had asked first, I can assure you that wouldn't have stopped Charley. I'm in love with you, Summer, and if there is a chance you could find it in your heart to return that love, I'll continue asking until I get an answer."

"I can't say I'm not flattered. You know I love all three of you, but that's different than being in love. Any woman, unless she was addle-brained, would be proud to be your wife. You're handsome and personable. I just never thought about either of you asking for my hand. Now that you've asked, I find myself already worrying about hard feelings developing between the two of you again. I was sick with worry when you and Charley were arguing about the cave-in and just knew you'd never settle your differences. I don't want to be the one who ends that friendship, Angus."

"What did you say to Charley when he proposed?"

"I said I would give it serious consideration and he'd have my answer by the time I'm to return to Denver. I had no idea you'd be asking, too."

"Can't you give me the same consideration?"

Summer stopped and looked at him. "I won't marry anyone unless I know I can return that man's love. It wouldn't be fair to either of us."

"I wouldn't have it any other way."

"Then I'll consider your proposal." After all, what else could she do? She felt she had to treat the two of them the same way.

"You know I'm going to do everything in my power to win you over."

Summer smiled. "Yes, and I have a strong feeling Charley is going to do the same."

For a minute it looked to Summer as if he were going to ask her for a kiss. But he didn't. She guessed he was too shy. But as they walked back, Angus took her hand and she let it remain there, hoping above all that the two of them weren't comparing notes.

Charley wasn't too happy about having to help Angus carry the secretary into the house, and even less happy when he found out Summer was also considering Angus' proposal. But he managed to keep his tongue in check.

The lovely secretary and chair looked out of place in the otherwise sparsely furnished room, but Summer cherished them, just as she cherished Charley's locket. They'd been offered with so much love.

However, two days later, when a Queen Anne sofa and chair were delivered as a gift from Charley, followed by a large cherrywood four-poster and matching chifforobe from Angus, Summer knew she had a problem.

The next night Charley, Angus, and Summer sat on the chairs around her new dining table—Charley's gift. She didn't wear the diamond earrings Angus had given her.

"Gentlemen," she began when supper was over, "I must refuse any further gifts. It's not that I don't appreciate them, because I do. However, plying me with gifts isn't going to help me make my mind up." She gave each man a hard look to get her point across.

"But I enjoy buying you things," Charley said, a hurt expression on his face.

Angus laughed. "You know, Charley, maybe we should build a shed outside Summer's door. We'll just put her gifts in there, and if she needs anything she can go get it."

Summer gasped. "You wouldn't!"

"Or maybe we should just buy her a store." Charley grinned. "I always wanted to buy a store."

"Stop it! Stop it right now!" Summer demanded.

"The only thing wrong with that, Charley, is she'd always be taking off to town. Then how would we court her?" Angus took another sip of the brandy Summer now allowed them after supper, then stared at the crystal snifter. "Can't say that I really care for this. I still prefer a good drink of whiskey."

"Guess your idea about something to put our gifts in is a better idea. What size do you think we should make it?"

"I don't know. What all are you planning to buy?"

Summer fidgeted in her chair. "You . . . you can't do that."

"Why?" Angus asked.

"What if I decide not to marry either of you? What would you do with everything?"

The two men thought about that.

"As I see it," Charley said, "we have several

choices, the first one being that you take it all with you. The second would be that we could just leave it sitting there, and if any of us decided to marry, that woman could have it."

"Or . . . we could just set the place on fire and watch it burn," Angus added.

Summer smiled. "You're both playing with me. You wouldn't burn it."

"No?" Angus crossed his legs, looking the perfect dandy. "When a man's in love, he's not accountable for what he does. Don't you agree, Charley?"

"Absolutely. I might just be in the mood for a good fire. By the way, Angus, I rather like the brandy."

Summer kept looking from one to the other, not knowing what to think. They seemed serious, and it would be just like them to set everything on fire. What had happened to the backwoodsmen she'd met when she'd come here? The two of them had worked hard to become gentlemen, especially Charley. But this was ridiculous. Now she was facing a pair of very polished men who had no intention of letting her dictate the rules of courtship to them. Her eyes narrowed. "I will not let you blackmail me, gentlemen. Either the gifts stop, or I'll leave." She saw panic leap into Charley's brown eyes, but Angus just sat there studying his glass.

"It's too late for that, darlin'," Angus finally said. "Now. Do we build the shelter, or—"

The knock on the door startled all of them. Charley went to answer it.

When Buck walked in, Summer was sure her entire body had turned to jam. A heavy, lined coat covered his buckskin clothing. Beneath his hat was a bandanna wrapped around his head to keep his ears warm. A thick stubble of whiskers lined his strong jaw, and even looking like that, he had to be the most handsome man she'd ever seen.

While Summer looked at Buck, Angus looked at her. He watched her eyes light up with interest and wondered if Summer had already made her choice or if there was still a chance to win her love.

"You look like you've been riding hard," Charley commented.

Buck glanced around at the new furniture and the way Angus and Charley were dressed. The corners of his lips slowly curved upward. "And it looks to me like you boys have been busy while I was gone."

"And just where did you go?" Summer asked. Though he wasn't obligated to explain his whereabouts, it still galled her that he hadn't at least had the decency to say he was leaving.

"I took a little trip to see a friend of mine in Denver. I know I'm too late for supper, but is there anything left over? I swear I could eat a bear."

"I'll fix something." Summer rose and headed for the kitchen. As she warmed Buck's food, she could hear the men talking but couldn't make out what they were saying. Occasionally they'd laugh and Summer felt left out. Had Buck's friend been a woman? Had he even thought about her while he was gone? He certainly didn't look overjoyed to see her. He seemed more interested in Charley and Angus. She slammed a plate down so hard it broke. Apparently the men didn't hear it because no one came to help pick up the pieces scattered on the counter and floor. Even that made her angry.

The men sat around the table talking about some type of new equipment Buck had seen in Denver. It galled Summer even more that Buck didn't so much as say thank you or even give her a glance when she put the food in front of him. Of all the ungiving men in this world, Summer thought, how could I ever have made the mistake of thinking I loved this one? Angus and Charley are far more caring and considerate. At least they had the courtesy to say hello when they entered her house!

Finally Charley got up to help her in the kitchen. "There's a piece of china on the floor," he said, reaching down to pick it up. "You must have broken something."

"Nothing of importance," she snapped at him. Seeing Buck was finished, she went over and snatched up his plate. "Why don't you men continue this conversation in your cabin? I have a headache."

"Before you go to bed, I brought something back from Denver that I thought you might like to see. If you have a headache, I guess it can wait until morning."

"Why would I want to see anything you brought back?"

"Because it's for you."

Summer could have bitten her tongue off for saying she had a headache. Buck had actually thought about her while he was gone! "What did you bring?" She tried to appear nonchalant, but her curiosity was killing her.

"You'd have to see it."

He gave her a smile that would normally melt ice, but Summer was still put out with him. "Very well, but can't you bring it inside? It's cold out."

"Let's just forget about it. Tomorrow will do. This is a nice table and chairs. Did Angus or Charley give them to you?"

"I did," Charley said proudly. "The gift you brought Summer, do you need help carrying it in?" He was also curious.

Buck chuckled. "No, it'll be just fine where it is."

Summer was tempted to break another plate, this time over Buck's head. How could he say he'd brought her something and then turn right around and dismiss it as something of little importance? He'd never given her anything before. At the same time she didn't want him to think she was excited. What could it possibly be that didn't need to be bought in?

"Well, let's all go out and take a look," Angus suggested. "I'm curious now myself."

"No, I think Summer should see it first. Like I said, it can wait until morning."

Summer couldn't stand it a moment longer. "Very well. Let me put my coat on and we can get this over with."

"If you're going to be so damn secretive, I'm heading for the cabin." Charley wasn't the least bit happy with this situation. He didn't want Angus or Buck giving his Summer gifts. Unfortunately, there wasn't a damn thing he could do about it.

"I'll join you," Angus said.

When Summer stepped outside with Buck and glanced about, she saw nothing unusual. She suddenly wondered if this was just a ploy to get her alone. She was about to tell him she was going back inside when he took off walking toward the barn. At first she was hesitant, but then she followed. What with the full moon and the snow on the ground, it wasn't hard to see where she was going.

When they entered the dark barn, Summer inhaled deeply. She always enjoyed the earthy smell of hay. Suddenly she was pulled into Buck's arms and he was kissing her. She tried fighting him, knowing it wasn't right, especially now that she had agreed to consider Angus and Charley's proposals. Buck's hand covered her breast and raw passion shot through her like a bullet. I can't let this happen, she kept telling herself. Out of desperation, she bit his lip. He didn't pull away. She could taste blood, but his kiss became even more demanding. On the verge of losing control, she shoved him with all her might. He wasn't expecting it, so she managed to get free from his arms. "Stop it!" she demanded. "I don't want your kisses or your hands on me."

"What's wrong, Angel? Running scared again? Or are you back to thinking that acting like a real woman is wrong?"

Though she couldn't see him, his voice sounded like a caress and she detected a hint of humor. He was so sure of himself that what she had said and done hadn't had the least effect on him. "It has nothing to do with any of that. I never want what happened to us to be repeated again. Charley and Angus have—"

"Before you continue, let me show you what I brought back from Denver. Wait here while I light the lanterns."

By the time Buck had four lanterns going, the barn looked as if it were ablaze. Again Summer glanced about and saw nothing unusual.

"Follow me."

He headed toward the back, holding one of the lanterns high. Summer had to hurry and had just about caught up with him when he stopped and hung the lantern on a nail.

"Come here," he said.

Not daring to trust him, Summer moved forward cautiously. He was standing in front of a stall, and when she looked inside she stopped breathing. Standing inside was the most beautiful, unusual mare she'd ever seen. The glossy coat was solid

black, and her mane and tail cream-colored. The
deep chest and long legs told Summer the mare
was fast. "Where did you ever find her?" she asked
in awe.

"Believe me, it took some looking. A friend of
mine in Denver finally told me about her."

"What's her name?"

"Wind."

"I like that. It seems to fit."

"She's yours," Buck said, "and the foal she's
carrying. I figure the little one will arrive about
spring."

"Mine?" Summer was so taken with the gift, her
word came out as a whisper.

"All yours. I remembered when I brought you
here, you said you didn't have riding clothes or a
sidesaddle. The saddle is on the rail over there,
and the clothes are in the bundle on the ground.
The outfit is green to match your eyes."

Summer couldn't remember ever receiving a gift
that meant more to her. That he had remembered
what she'd said on the trip up was enough to bring
tears to her eyes. The mare moved forward and
Summer gently stroked the soft, velvety nose.
"She's so beautiful." Summer had to fight back the
tears. When Angus and Charley had brought her
their gifts, they'd proposed. Was it possible Buck
was about to do the same? She waited, but the
words didn't come.

"You do know how to ride, don't you?"

"Yes." It wasn't easy to hide the emotion she
was feeling.

"Good. Then we can start taking rides together.
You may be tempted, but don't go out alone, Summer. It isn't safe."

"I won't. Buck, there's something I have to tell
you." She couldn't even force herself to look at

him. "Angus and Charley have asked me to marry them, and I said I'd think about their proposals." Again she waited for him to make the offer, but again she was disappointed. "Because of that, I couldn't possibly let you make love to me again. I can't tell you how much your gifts mean to me, but if you want to keep them for yourself, I'll understand."

"Don't you think I'd look rather silly in a woman's riding habit, clinging to a sidesaddle?"

Summer had to smile. "Yes, I suppose you would." She gave the mare another pat and turned. Seeing the big grin on Buck's face, she laughed. "Buck Holester, you are impossible."

"You don't laugh enough, Angel. It lights up your entire face. However, I bought the mare for you. Now why would I want her back? I've missed you, Summer."

She tried not to let his words affect her, but they tempted her like rich icing on a cake. "Why did you buy me the gift?"

He took the lantern off the nail and they started walking back to the front of the barn. "While I was gone I gave a lot of thought to us."

Summer held her breath.

"We have a strong attraction for each other. It may just be physical, but there's nothing wrong with that. Summer," he stopped and turned to face her, "I'd like you to tell Angus and Charley you won't marry them. I'm asking if you'll let me move in with you. We could just see what happens from there."

Summer was shocked, then furious. "That is the most immoral thing any man has ever said to me. Well, you can just rot in hell. If I decide not to marry Angus or Charley, it'll be my decision and it most certainly won't be because I'm going to keep your bed warm." She marched away.

"Wait just a damn minute, lady!" It took only a couple of long strides for him to stop her. "What's the difference between that and getting married?"

"Something you seem to know nothing about. It's called commitment."

"Contrary to what you seem to think, I consider living with a woman a commitment."

"How absolutely wonderful!" Realizing she was starting to yell, Summer lowered her voice. "Make someone else the offer, *Mister Holester*. Not only am I not interested, I find the idea repugnant. Furthermore, I don't know how you could have the gall to make such a suggestion."

"It's very simple. I want you in my bed, not another man's."

"You told me the next time we made love, I'd have to ask. I haven't asked, have I?" She watched the muscles in his jaw flex.

"As sure as I'm standing here, you will, lady. Maybe not tomorrow or even a month from now, but you will. Every time a man kisses you, you're going to compare it to my kisses. And if you marry, you're going to compare his loving to mine. I put my mark on you, Angel, and you'll be a long time forgetting it. Don't try telling me that at night you don't relive the ecstasy we had. Call it desire, need, love, or whatever you like. And if you're married when you come to realize you want to share my bed, the guilt will be on your shoulders, not mine. If you don't marry, you'll be long gone, and it'll be too late for us."

"I call it lust!" Summer said as Buck left the barn, but she doubted he heard her. "I won't let you do this to me," she muttered. She slapped her hand against her thigh. "I won't." The mare neighed and the other horses snorted as she grabbed her package and turned out the lanterns.

When Buck climbed in bed, he thought Angus and Charley were asleep until he heard Charley quietly ask, "Well, what did you get her?"

"A mare," Buck growled.

Charley snickered. "From the way you're acting, she must not have been too impressed."

Buck had half a notion to drag Charley out and knock the hell out of him. Instead Buck rolled over on his side and forced himself to think about the investments he'd made in Denver. He'd stayed with Howard Jackson and his wife Molly. Howard used to be a trapper, but once he saw Molly, his trapping days were over. They'd moved to Denver, and Howard had done quite well there in real estate.

By the time Buck left his friends, he was the owner of a great deal of land on the outskirts of Denver, as well as downtown. He particularly liked the five hundred acres he'd purchased that covered a small portion of the foothills. There was a sturdy house that needed only a few repairs. Tomorrow he'd tell Charley and Angus about Jackson in case they might also be interested in getting land.

Buck tossed in his bed. Why couldn't he get the woman out of his mind? It seemed like everywhere he turned he saw those stormy green eyes and smelled her flowery scent. God, if only he had her here now. . . .

She was weakening him, no doubt about it. Only once before had he lived with a woman, and when that hadn't worked out he'd sworn never to do it again. Summer didn't realize how he'd had to compromise his principles to suggest even that. No,

Miss Summer wanted something more. She wanted to get hitched.

He punched his pillow and listened to his partners snore.

Chapter 12

Hearing several sharp, loud whistles, Summer slid her window up and looked out. Below, Buck sat atop his horse holding the reins of her saddled mare.

"Wind needs to be exercised," Buck called. "Dress warm."

"I wouldn't go anywhere with you."

"You want this mare or not? Because if you do, you've got to take care of her." He adjusted his Stetson.

Summer closed her window, still undecided about going riding with Buck—especially after their argument in the barn over a week ago. Because of his insulting proposition, it had taken that long for her anger to settle down to a simmer. Nevertheless, a brisk ride appealed to her, and Wind did need exercise. What with the chilling cold and deep snow, they couldn't possibly ride for very long.

Convinced Buck would make no advances as long as she remained atop Wind, Summer pulled out the heavy velvet riding suit he had given her and quickly changed clothes. Actually, she'd been looking forward to taking the mare out, but hadn't thought it possible because of the snow. Apparently Buck didn't consider that a problem.

Summer had come to realize that though the mountain weather had a harsh bite to it, the sky was usually clear and bright blue. Today was no exception. When she came out, Buck gave her a hand up, and without exchanging any words at all, they rode off.

Though Wind was frisky after her long rest, Summer was pleased to discover the mare reined easily. She had to keep her in tight control in order to guide her safely through the snow. In some places the depth was considerable, and the animal had to lunge in and out. More than once Summer thought she would fall off, but because of her years of riding, she managed to keep her seat. Due to the strenuous workout, she soon felt perspiration beneath her heavy clothing.

Buck continued to lead and occasionally Summer saw him turn back to make sure she was still following. She had no idea where they were, and though more than once she was tempted to turn back, she knew she'd never find her way on her own.

To Summer's relief, Buck topped a hill and finally stopped. She pulled up alongside, grateful for the moment's rest. Leaning forward, she stroked Wind's damp, powerful neck while uttering soft words of praise.

"I give you credit, Summer. When you said you could ride, you were dead serious."

"Did I have to go through all this to prove it?" she snapped.

Buck laughed. "When I saw how well you were doing, I decided to take a shortcut to town."

Summer looked ahead, and sure enough Central City was only a short distance below. "How did we get here so fast?"

"It's a lot shorter if you don't take a buckboard

down Old Hell Road. How does a good bowl of soup and a cup of strong coffee sound?"

"Absolutely wonderful."

Riding through town, Summer felt like a queen as people stopped and stared at her beautiful mare. Boys started running along the boarded walk, following them as they made their way down the street. When they stopped in front of the restaurant, the boys watched excitedly.

"Can I tie the reins to the hitching post?" a freckle–faced one asked.

"Where did you ever find a mare that looks like that?" another inquired.

"Skedaddle," Buck said in a joking manner. "We've come here for a meal." Seeing their disappointed faces, he added, "However, if you boys want to keep an eye on the horses for us, I'd be willing to pay a nickel."

"We'd be right proud to do it, Mister."

Maggie's Kitchen was crowded when Buck and Summer entered, but they managed to find seats at one of the long tables. Everyone seemed to know Buck and either waved or said hello while tipping their hats at Summer.

Summer liked the friendly atmosphere, warm room, and the pleasing aroma of food—especially the soup that was placed before her. Large chunks of meat and a variety of vegetables swam in a hearty broth. Thick slices of bread for dunking accompanied the meal.

"That was wonderful," Summer said, pushing her empty bowl aside. She couldn't quite figure out why Buck was being so amenable, but she decided to take advantage of it while the mood lasted. "Buck, if you're not in a hurry, I'd like to see Lorna."

Buck raised an eyebrow. Only when they had

made love had she called him by his first name. "After the way she's treated you?"

"We settled all of that when you were in the cave-in. I now think of her as a good friend. Are you aware she is in love with you?"

"She *thinks* she's in love with me. There's a big difference between that and the real thing."

Summer couldn't help but wonder if she also just thought she was in love. She glanced at Buck, who was talking to a man who had stopped at the table. What woman wouldn't? He was devastatingly masculine.

"If you want to go there that's fine with me," Buck said when the man had left. "While you visit, I'll take care of some business."

After paying the boys their nickel, Buck took Summer to Lorna's mercantile store. Promising to be back within an hour, he rode off.

Lorna was overjoyed at seeing Summer, but quite taken aback when she saw the mare. "She's so beautiful," she said. "I've never seen such unusual coloring. Where did Buck ever find her?"

"I don't know. To be honest, I never thought to ask. It must have been in Denver."

They went to the back of the store. Once seated and drinking coffee, Lorna filled Summer in on what was happening around town. Summer in turn told her friend of the proposals, and how Charley and Angus had been plying her with gifts.

"When Buck gave you his presents, did he propose, too?"

"Buck?" Summer said lightly. "I can't picture Buck asking anyone to marry him. Can you?"

"Probably not, but if he did, it would be you."

"Why do you say something like that?"

"I guess it's the way I saw him looking at you at the dance." Seeing a frown on Summer's lovely face, she quickly added, "Don't worry, Summer. I'll never catch Buck."

Summer toyed with her cup. "You could be wrong."

"No. I know it and so do you. Accepting the truth has helped. I've actually started looking at other men. Elliot Toddle has been most attentive and—"

"Oh, Lorna. You shouldn't have anything to do with that man."

"Why? He's very much a gentleman. I know he's quite a bit older than I am, but maybe that's what I need. My husband was fifteen years my senior and we got along fine."

"He wants the Whiskey Hole, Lorna. He even made threats, and the two men he has working for him look dangerous. You shouldn't be seeing him. Ask Buck, he'll tell you."

Lorna grinned. "I'm sure Elliot didn't mean it the way they took it, and after all, you know those boys are always ready for a fight. Elliot's just not that type of man, Summer. If you knew him you'd see what I mean. He works for an Eastern company, so naturally he's trying to purchase all the mines he can get. That's what he was hired to do. As for the men who ride with him, you can't judge them by their appearance. Elliot would never have anything to do with shifty types."

"Surely there are other men around who have piqued your interest?" Summer said, holding her cup out while Lorna poured.

"None as sweet as Elliot."

On the way back to Whiskey Hole, Summer didn't get a chance to tell Buck of her talk with Lorna. And by the time they arrived, the entire conversation had slipped her mind because her attention was trained on the shiny black buggy sitting at the side of her house. There were even men building a structure to house it.

"Looks like the boys have been busy again," Buck said slowly. He dismounted, then helped Summer down. "I'll take the mare to the barn and give her some oats. See you later, teacher."

Summer didn't miss the sarcasm in his last words. As Buck led the mounts away, Summer marched over to the men's cabin and pounded on the door. Purchasing a buggy was going entirely too far! How was she even supposed to use it in a place like this? When no one answered, she searched the area around the clearing, but Angus and Charley were nowhere to be found. Seeing the buggy again, she couldn't help but wonder where they were finding all these things. Having no other recourse, she returned to the house to change and wait for one of them to show up.

Not until she came back downstairs and entered the parlor did Summer see the blue wool cape lying across the arm of the Queen Anne sofa. When she picked it up she discovered it was lined with mink. Something had to be done to put a stop to this, but she didn't know what.

Half an hour later, Angus and Charley arrived with broad smiles.

"How can you refuse our gifts when you accepted Buck's?" Charley asked when Summer had managed to get them seated in the parlor.

"I also accepted gifts from the two of you, on the condition that I would consider your proposals." Summer was so frustrated she was having a hard time controlling her temper.

"Has Buck proposed?" Angus asked.

"No, and you're skirting the issue. "I—"

"If he didn't propose," Charley butted in, obviously perturbed, "then why did you take his gifts?"

Summer's head was swimming. She took two deep breaths and tried again. "Let's look at this from a different angle. Where is all this leading to? I'm going to need a mansion to hold everything."

Seeing Charley's eyes light up, she sucked in her breath. Oh, please, Lord, she thought silently, don't let him get any ideas. She tried again. "What I'm trying to say is that instead of allowing me to make my decision, you're forcing me to turn away. I don't want to be married to any man who thinks the only way he can win my love is with gifts."

At that moment Buck strolled into the parlor. "Thought I might as well join this little group," he said casually.

Everyone just sat staring at him.

He walked over and placed a narrow box on Summer's lap, then moved to the fireplace to warm his backside. Seeing that Summer hadn't even picked it up, he asked, "Aren't you curious?"

With considerable reservation, Summer opened the box. Her eyes grew huge upon seeing the beautiful diamond necklace inside. "I can't accept this," she managed to choke out.

"Oh, yes you can. When you started thinking about getting betrothed to Angus and Charley, you accepted theirs. Since I'm throwing my hat in the ring as well, it's only fitting."

Never had Summer been at such a loss for words. Her heart leaped with joy until she saw Angus and Charley's grim faces. Charley rose from his seat and left without a word.

"I take it you're asking the lady to marry you?" Angus asked smoothly.

"That's right."

Summer gasped.

"I have to admit, my friend, that if I were a woman and I received a proposal like that, I'd give you a flat no."

"Get the hell out of here, and I might just do it properly," Buck countered.

"You've got all the charm of a rattlesnake. This lady deserves better," Angus said, getting to his feet.

Before Summer knew precisely what was happening, Buck swung at him and the two men were rolling on the floor, cursing and grunting. All she could think to do was scream, which succeeded in bringing the battle to a standstill.

"Get up, both of you," she commanded, her hands trembling.

They did, looking rumpled and sheepish.

"I'd like you both to leave," she said quietly.

"But I thought—"

"No, Buck. I want to be alone." Summer watched the muscles in his jaw flex. Finally he dropped his eyes from her and left, with Angus following.

Summer remained in her chair, temples throbbing. She slowly picked up the beautiful necklace and clutched it to her heart as tears trickled down her cheeks. How many nights had she dreamed of Buck asking for her hand? And he didn't even have the decency to get her alone. Certainly, there'd been no words of love. If she'd let him stay, she felt sure he'd have come up with some lie about loving her, if only to keep her out of his partners' beds, and get her in his own. If she wouldn't live with him, he'd marry her. None of it had anything to do with love.

And what she'd feared most was happening at last. She'd already heard little tiffs erupt between Charley and Angus, and now that Buck had proposed they were at war again. She groaned inwardly. The one thing she could never do was make enemies of the three men she'd come to care for so much.

Summer wiped the tears away. Unless things changed, she wouldn't be marrying any of them. She should never have decided to remain here in the first place.

Buck found Charley standing by the edge of the cliff facing the whitened mountain range. Buck stood beside him, respecting his need for silence.

"Why did you do it?" Charley finally asked.

"It wasn't as if I didn't tell you I might."

"You know, there's not much that means more to me than Summer. You could have shown her more respect in the asking."

"Asking didn't come easy."

"So you think I should be understanding? She's a lady, Buck, and she has every right to expect us to treat her like one."

"I have no quarrel with you, but we made an agreement. If you think I'm going to back off because your britches are crusty over the way I asked for her hand, you'd better think again. Damn it, Charley, in your head you've made her into some creature to be worshiped. She's a woman, nothing more. Apparently you haven't had to deal with that temper of hers. I've been slapped, cuffed over the head, and even spit at."

Charley turned toward Buck, his face red with anger. "What the hell did you do to make her so damn mad? You talk about agreements; we also agreed no one would force her."

"Shit! There's no sense in trying to talk to you. You're so damn in love you can't see past your nose."

Charley raised a big fist and took a swing, but Buck ducked.

"Don't do that again, Charley," Buck warned, "or you're going to end up getting the hell beat out of you. Now let's just leave it at that."

Charley took another swing. Again Buck ducked but this time his fist moved forward, landing hard on Charley's chin. The blow sent Charley staggering backward toward the edge of the cliff, but in the next moment he charged. Head down, he hit Buck in the stomach, his momentum landing them both in a snowdrift.

"Damn it, Charley," Buck said, trying to catch his breath, "don't do this."

Charley was too enraged to listen. Again he raised his fist, but this time Buck lifted a foot and kicked him square in the chest. Charley's bull tactics were no match for Buck's agility and accurate fists. The fight was soon over, and Charley lay on the ground with Buck standing over him.

"Now, are you going to listen to me?"

Charley looked up, blood trickling from his nose and mouth, and suddenly smiled. "Don't reckon I got a choice. Hell, Buck, in all the time I've known you, I've never really fought with you. Why didn't you tell me you were so good?"

Buck laughed and reached down to help Charley up. He realized his mistake too late. Charley's fist landed on his jaw hard.

"Hell," Charley muttered seeing Buck passed out, "I thought you were too smart to fall for that." He laughed as he rubbed snow on Buck's swollen face. The minute Buck came to, he was ready to tear Charley apart.

"Hold on," Charley said.

Buck's fist was raised, but he held it in check. "You going to tell me you've had enough again?

It might have worked once, but it won't work again."

"I admit you're better than I am, but it was worth two loads of gold to get that punch in. Yeah, I've had enough. I don't want my face so ugly Summer won't want to look at me."

Buck broke out laughing as he sat up, but he still kept an eye on Charley sitting beside him. They were both covered with snow from head to toe.

"Charley, you already look like hell," Buck said.

"Then I guess Angus has an advantage, because you don't look so fine yourself." Charley chuckled. "Did she really slap you and do those other things you said?"

"She sure did."

"Wish I'd been there to see it. She must have really got under your skin, because I don't know another living soul who could do that and get away with it. It wasn't you declaring yourself that made me mad, Buck. Angus I could accept, because I know he loves Summer. But I figure you're doing it just to satisfy an itch. I know how you have a way with the women, and I didn't want Summer to fall into your trap." Charley stood and put his hand down to help Buck up. Charley didn't even see the fist coming at him.

"Now we're even," Buck said to his unconscious friend.

Summer was appalled when she saw Buck and Charley that night, with their bruised faces and black eyes. Nonetheless, as usual, the men were most attentive, even Buck—but she couldn't allow herself to show favoritism.

Summer's nights were becoming a living hell. Sleep was impossible. Never had she wanted Buck as badly as she did now. He had lit a flame in her that she couldn't extinguish. She wanted him to take her in his arms, reassure her that everything would be all right, tell her how much he loved her—because she knew now without a doubt that it was love she felt for him. But that wouldn't happen. She couldn't let it happen, because if she did, they'd all end up hurt, and Angus, Charley, and Buck would never be friends again.

Over the following weeks, the men continued to give Summer gifts, the strangest being a cow by the name of Lady Bug from Charley and chickens from Buck. Because cows and chickens were a rarity in the mountains, Summer asked where they had found them, and as usual, both refused to say a thing. At least she now had the pleasure of milk and eggs. Learning to milk that cow presented Summer with more than a few problems. The cow's tail kept slapping her in the face, and eking milk from the udder seemed an impossible task. When she finally managed a small portion, the cow knocked the bucket over. With Charley's help, however, she finally mastered the task.

Summer grew quite fond of her animals, but even so, she became withdrawn. She knew she was going to have to face the inevitable. Marriage to any one of the men was impossible. When the snow melted, she'd simply have to go.

Thinking her mood stemmed from the gifts she had said she didn't want, the men agreed among themselves to stop giving them. But Buck couldn't really believe the presents would make Summer so withdrawn, though he had no idea what was going on in the woman's head. He intended to find out. However, one way or another, she managed to keep him at a distance. She never allowed him to be alone with her and only went riding with Angus or Charley. If she kept this up, how was he going to find out why she was acting so strangely?

Buck gave a lot of consideration to what Charley and Angus had said about loving Summer. Maybe he was in love and just too stubborn or scared to see it. One thing was sure, though: He didn't want Charley or Angus to have her. Not just Charley or Angus—any man.

As the days passed, Buck watched Summer change from a happy woman full of fire to a lady who forced smiles and did a poor job of acting cheerful. Both Charley and Angus approached him and asked if he knew what was bothering her, and he had to tell them no. But the truth was dawning on Buck. As sure as the sun rose, Summer was running scared. Could he be the reason? If so, why? Hadn't he committed himself properly?

As Buck guided his horse toward Templeton Mercantile Store, he recognized Toddle's horse tied up in front and recalled that Summer had mentioned Lorna was seeing the man. For a moment Buck considered riding on and coming back later, but he wasn't in the best mood and decided it was as good a time as any to have it out with the crooked snake.

When Buck walked in the store, he saw Toddle leaning over the counter talking to Lorna. Lorna smiled, and Elliot Toddle turned to see whom she was smiling at. Anger flashed across his smooth face for a brief moment, but his recovery was quick.

"Hello, Mister Holester," Toddle said amiably. "It's been awhile since we saw each other. I heard about that nasty cave-in. Glad to see you came out of it all right."

Buck's anger grew with each step he took. This was the son of a bitch that had put him through hell. He walked straight up to Toddle, grabbed him

by the front of his coat, and lifted him off the
ground.

"Buck!" Lorna yelled.

"Someone should have beat the shit out of you
a long time ago."

"No!" Lorna hollered. "You'll hurt him!"

It was too late. Buck threw the man on the other
side of the counter, then went around the corner
after him.

Lorna moved between them. "You'll have to go
through me to get to him," she said bravely.

Buck picked her up and sat her on the counter,
then reached down and snatched the quivering
man to his feet. Toddle's glasses fell to the floor.
"Take a good look at him, Lorna," Buck growled.
"The perfect weasel."

"Buck, you don't know what you're talking
about." Lorna tugged on his shirt.

"I know exactly what I'm talking about. You're
the one he's been leading down the primrose path.
Has he proposed yet? If not, I guarantee he will.
Having control of your store would be just the
thing to make him happy." Buck let loose with a
list.

Lorna jumped down and knelt beside Toddle.
"You've knocked him out," she cried, "and I think
you've broken his jaw."

"If that's all I've done, he should consider himself lucky." Seeing the tears in Lorna's eyes, Buck
pulled her into his arms and stroked her hair. "Listen to me, Lorna," he said gently. "Even though
we've had our differences, I would like nothing
more than to see you married, but to a man who
can make you happy. I heard about how you
worked all night at the cave-in and how you looked
after Summer. You have a lot of heart, lady, so
don't let someone like Toddle steal it."

"But you don't know him, Buck. He's a good man."

"He's a sneaky bastard. He threatened us at the mine, and three men didn't *mis*understand him. After that, the cave-in happened. He may talk a good line, but behind all that is a ruthless man." He let her go and went back over to Toddle. "Now I'm taking him out of here." Buck went on. "If you decide to continue seeing him, that's your choice."

Buck picked Toddle up and slung him over his shoulder. Outside he placed the man face down across his saddle then mounted his own stallion and grabbed the reins of Toddle's horse. By the time he reached the Pierson Mining office, Toddle was moaning. Buck released the reins and moved his horse around until he was beside Toddle's head. "I know you can hear me, so you'd better listen real good. You tried to kill me, and you're damn lucky I didn't return the favor. But if you ever try anything like that again against me or my friends, you're a dead man." With that, Buck kicked his horse into a gallop and rode out of town.

"Gentlemen," Summer said after supper, "there is something I have to say. I have been honored to have had three wonderful men ask for my hand." She looked at each of them. "However, I have decided that marriage is out of the question."

Angus leaned forward. "Are we permitted to ask why?"

"Yes, you may." Summer continued to sit ramrod straight, not allowing any emotion to show on her face. "After much thought, I have come to realize that I cherish each of you, but as brothers. That's not what I should be feeling going into marriage. You see, I know now I'm in love with another man."

"I'll castrate the son of . . ." Charley cleared his throat.

"You'll do no such a thing." Summer hated seeing the hurt look on his face, but she had to do what was best for all of them. "His name is William Nielson," she lied.

"But you told me—"

"I know what I told you, Angus, but I was angry with him. I've come to realize that I can't let a little fight destroy my happiness. And, yes, he is occasionally pompous, but he's going to be the next territorial governor." She made it sound as if she found that exciting.

"And being a governor's wife means so much to you," Buck said sarcastically.

"Of course. It's what any woman of breeding would want."

"I had honestly begun to think you weren't like the other women of your so-called class." Buck's words were scathing. "I should have known better. Now if you'll excuse me, madam, I have work that needs to be done. But before I go, remember what I said would happen when you married. There are some things you can't deny."

When Buck left, Summer refused to let Charley and Angus see how heartbroken she was. Buck's words had cut to the bone.

"Well," Charley smiled, "if marrying that man is what you really want, then I for one wish you the best. I can't say it doesn't hurt, but I'd rather see you happy."

"You'll find the right woman, Charley. I'm sorry it wasn't me. We can still be friends, can't we? You can always come to Denver and visit."

"Oh, I don't plan on losing touch. Will we be going for a ride in the morning?"

"Absolutely."

After Charley left, Summer looked at Angus, who was still staring at her. "Do you have anything you want to add?" she asked. The evening was starting to take its toll.

"You're lying," he said simply.

"I . . . I don't know what you're talking about."

"You know exactly what I'm talking about. If it's because of the gifts . . ."

Summer lowered her head. "No, this has nothing to do with that." She raised her head and straightened her spine.

"Well, if you change your mind and want to talk about it, darlin', I have a pretty big shoulder." He stood. "There's something else I don't think you've given much consideration to."

"What's that?"

"You've still got awhile before you leave. Sometimes it's surprising how things can change over time. Maybe for the best, maybe for the worst." He walked over, leaned down, and kissed her on the forehead. "Good night, Angel."

Summer cried the entire night. How could she possibly hold out until the snow melted?

Chapter 13

"**W**illiam, I am tired of you constantly trying to put your hands on me. Either this stops, or I will move back to a hotel!" Milly slid to the far side of the carriage and adjusted her bodice. Not for the first time did she wish she'd told Summer she'd wait at the hotel. At least spring was near, so hopefully it wouldn't be too much longer before Summer returned.

"Fine," William pouted. "Go right ahead. I'm equally tired of you leading me along."

"What are you talking about? I've done nothing to lead you on."

"And just what would you call it? You haven't returned to Philadelphia, so naturally I'm left to assume it's because you find me and my offer of marriage attractive."

"That's an awfully big assumption. You know I have remained only because of Summer."

"I also know Summer is a closed subject and it's time you accepted that." He reached for her again. Milly tried to shove him away, but he persisted.

"I could introduce you to pleasures you've never dreamed of. Your body was made for a man to enjoy."

"That's enough!" Milly could hear his heavy breathing, and for the first time she felt a tinge of

227

fear, even though she knew William was an absolute coward. The time had come for her to put him in his place, once and for all. "I think you had too much to drink before we left."

"It's because you are driving me to desperation!"

"I wonder if the governor would understand that."

"What are you talking about?"

"The governor, Willy. Remember how you commented on the attention he paid to me at his last supper party? Now what do you suppose he would think if I told him about Summer?"

"You wouldn't do that!"

"Oh, I would indeed. He might find it as curious as I do that you have continued to hide the fact that she is alive and well."

"I don't know what you're talking about."

"There's no use lying."

He shifted about and the side of his mouth began to twitch.

"I overheard that man you hired say she was at the mining camp, and that she had no desire to return. To satisfy myself, I also hired someone. I finally received word from Summer. Why were you so cruel not to tell me she was alive?"

"Do you realize the embarrassment it would cause me if she were to return and my political colleagues discovered my fiancée had spent the winter with three men? I'd be ruined! I want her out of Colorado." William suddenly realized that in his anger, he had said more than he meant to. "If you knew she was alive, why have you remained?"

"Because I promised I'd wait for her. And she will return, Willy, like it or not. I believe you owe me an explanation. What did you mean about wanting Summer out of the territory?"

The carriage came to a stop. "We have to go in," William said, eager to end the conversation. He needed time to think.

"One last thing," Milly persisted. "From here on out, you'd better be a good boy, or I will personally see that your political career comes to an end."

The driver opened the door and helped Milly out.

Summer went about the house humming as she attended to her daily chores. Now that she'd come to accept her fate, she was beginning to relax. With each passing day, there was less strain when she was around the men. However, she knew she still wasn't strong enough to risk being alone with Buck. That was going to take time. She couldn't fool him as easily; he was too perceptive. So was Angus, but at least he'd said nothing more. When Charley didn't know she was looking, she saw sadness in his eyes, but hopefully this would change when he started associating with the women in Denver. At least, as a whole, Charley and Angus were back to being good friends, and they laughed and teased her again.

Her work completed, Summer set off for the barn to give Wind some sugar. As she crossed the clearing she could smell spring in the air. The mare's head was sticking out of the stall, and she nickered in recognition as Summer headed toward her.

"Hello, my lovely," Summer greeted her. "Look what I've brought you." She held out her hand and let the mare feast. "I wish I had an apple or a carrot to give you, but I'm afraid that's something you're going to have to wait for. How would you like to go exercise in the corral?"

"And what would you like to give me, my lovely?"

Summer's spine became rigid. "I didn't see you when I came in, Mister Holester."

"Mister Holester? Not Buck? You didn't see me because you didn't look. And had you seen me, I'm quite sure Wind wouldn't have received that tidbit."

Summer started to leave, but Buck stepped in front of her, effectively blocking her path.

"You know, Angel," he said smoothly, "I've been asking myself a lot of questions. For instance, why don't you look me in the eye anymore? Why do you avoid being alone with me? And most importantly, why didn't you tell Angus, Charley, and me individually about your decision not to marry any of us?"

"It was easier that way."

"I don't think so. Summer, look at me." She continued to keep her eyes averted. "Very well, then I'll tell you what conclusions I've reached. To begin with, you had no problems until I asked you to marry me."

"I don't seem to recall you asking. You stated it." She tried to retreat, but her back met the stall. Buck placed a hand on either side of her. She could feel the warmth from his body. He was too close.

"You once thought I didn't know the meaning of commitment. When I proved you wrong, you ran scared."

"That's not true."

"It's true. I'm your problem, and you're afraid to admit it."

Summer tried ducking under his arm, but he grabbed her around the waist, pressing her body to his. "Let me go! I told you I love another."

"I don't believe that either. I am of the opinion you love me, and that's what scares you."

"Then you're living in a fool's paradise."

"Prove it."

"I don't have to prove it."

"Oh yes you do, lady. Kiss me, then look me straight in the eye and say you love your banker."

Summer tried pushing him away, but he grabbed her wrists and pulled them behind her back. Her breasts were pressed against his strong chest, and she could feel her nipples harden.

"You can't do it, can you?"

Angry at her weakness and at him for putting her in this position, she steeled herself and looked up into his blue-gray eyes. Suddenly she wanted nothing more than to run her fingers through his thick black hair and feel his hands on her body. "I love another," she whispered weakly.

"You got it backward. First the kiss." His voice was deep and husky.

"Please, Buck, don't."

"The kiss."

"Angus and Charley—"

"This is between us, not them." He released her wrists and slowly lowered his head.

When Summer's lips met his, she felt a searing desire in every fiber of her being. Her arms curled around his neck. It had been so long.

His lips possessed her, proving once and for all, she was his.

"Ask me," he murmured.

Summer moved her head to allow Buck access to her neck. She was no longer capable of fighting him, no longer able to think about endangering his friendship with Angus and Charley. Nothing was as important as being with the man she loved. "Please, Buck, make love to me." Raising her head to capture his lips again, she saw Charley standing not more than twenty feet away. Before she could say anything, he turned and left the barn. "Buck! Stop!"

"Stop? After you just asked me to make love to you?"

"Charley. He was right there. He saw us!"

"Forget about him." His hand cupped her swollen breast.

"I can't. I could see his pain." Her breathing was already shallow.

"He was bound to find out eventually."

His kisses were compelling, coaxing, and Summer was having difficulty thinking. She knew she should go after Charley and explain, but Buck's hands and mouth had already set her on fire. "Don't make me do this," she whispered, wanting him to stop, yet afraid he would.

"I want to run my tongue across your body. I want to feel you throb with desire as I enter you and watch you lose control until nothing matters but your need for me." He pulled her dress open, freeing one of her breasts so he could tug on it with his moist lips.

Summer arched her back, unable to deny the pleasure. His mouth returned to hers as he continued to fondle her. She was convinced he was driving her mad. "Buck," she moaned, "I need you."

He picked her up and carried her to the back of the barn.

Slowly, and with great deliberation, he took off her clothes. But even after she lay naked he still continued to tease and coax until she was begging him to possess her.

"You're so beautiful," he said, his eyes devouring her. He stripped, then joined her in the sweet hay, rolling over on his back, taking her with him. "I couldn't stop if I wanted to, my love." He smiled warmly. "Have we an agreement? Will you be my wife?"

At this moment, Summer would have said yes to anything he asked. She nodded, still engulfed in desire, but she hadn't missed him calling her his love.

He entered her, then told her to raise herself up and straddle him. Summer hesitated, unsure of herself. Slowly she moved to a sitting position. The penetration was deep, causing her to gasp with pleasure. She moved her body, discovering that each new motion seemed to take her to the edge of a cliff. Then the glorious spiraling colors burst forth, and she collapsed on top of him.

Summer spent the rest of the day in a delirious haze; waiting for Buck to get through in the mine. It wasn't until suppertime that she thought of Charley again. She wanted to look for him and explain how much she loved Buck, but suddenly found herself embarrassed. If Charley had waited outside the barn, he'd have guessed what had happened. She couldn't stand the thought of him thinking she was free with her favors, especially knowing how he'd put her on a pedestal. There was also Angus. Could she make both men see how much this meant to her, and thereby avoid any more fighting?

When Charley arrived to help prepare supper, Summer screwed up her courage. "Charley," she began. "we need to have a talk."

"I don't know that there's anything to talk about." He put fat in the hot skillet, then moved it around to grease the bottom.

"Please, let me explain."

"Are you going to marry him?"

"That's part of what I want to talk to you about.

Why don't we sit at the table and . . . ?"

Charley slapped the meat in the cast-iron pan. "Thought you said you were in love with that man in Denver? Were you lying?"

Since Charley obviously wasn't going to join her, let alone look at her, Summer pulled out a chair and sat down. "I guess you could say that, but I had a good reason. You see—"

"Anyone home?" Angus called.

When Angus entered the kitchen, Summer could tell from his happy expression that Charley had said nothing to him.

"Is that pies I see?" Angus went over and smelled. "Apple?"

Summer glanced at Charley's back, not sure if this was a good time to approach the subject of her relationship with Buck. But since they were both here . . . "Ah . . . yes. I baked them this afternoon. Angus, there's something I'd like to—"

Charley turned and forced a laugh. "Don't believe a thing she's fixing to say, Angus. Maybe I showed her how to make a pie, but now she makes better ones than I ever did."

Seeing the hard look Charley gave her, Summer knew he was telling her to keep quiet.

"When you came in, Summer and I were wondering why Buck had asked her to marry him. We all know he's not the sort to get tied down to any woman, let alone be faithful to her."

Angus twisted the end of his mustache in thought. "Why even wonder about it since Summer turned us all down?"

Charley shrugged. "Just curious."

"As I see it, that's Buck's business."

"I suppose you're right." Charley returned to his cooking. "Summer, did you hear that one of the cars ran over Freddy Allen's foot?"

"Is he all right? How did it happen?" Charley's manner made her edgy, but she kept playing along with him.

"Crushed a couple of toes, but other than that, he'll be all right. I sent money home with him so that sweet wife of his won't have to worry about food until he can work again. As I heard it, he stepped into the path of the car when it was already moving down the track. I have no idea why."

"How terrible. Poor Ina. That was awfully nice what you did, Charley."

Summer found supper stressful. Fortunately, Buck and Angus seemed not to notice that Charley was out of sorts. She avoided looking at Buck for fear her eyes would mirror her feelings for all to see. It hurt deeply to know Charley was judging her. She made a vow that even though he had avoided talking with her in the kitchen, she would corner him alone soon.

After the men had left, Summer sat in the parlor and tried to work on her embroidered tablecloth. To her aggravation, her mind kept jumping from one problem to another. She'd hoped Buck would come back and they could spend most of the night together. Her body became warm just thinking about their lovemaking earlier. Buck had been right. The second time was even better than the first, which she would have thought impossible. She smiled, wondering what it would be like to awaken in the morning with him lying beside her. "So many things to think about. Why can't life be more simple?" She set her work aside, then rose from her chair—Charley's gift.

By the time Summer climbed into her big bed, she was exhausted from so much thinking. She closed her eyes, but it took awhile before she drifted into a fretful sleep. When she awoke a third time, she climbed out of bed. Maybe a warm glass of milk will help, she thought.

The floor was cold beneath her feet. She quickly slipped on her red slippers, then threw on the heavy robe that had been hanging on one of the bedposts. She headed for the kitchen, not bothering to light a candle.

As Summer descended the last step, she saw a strange glow in the parlor. She hurried to the window and, to her horror, saw riders silently approaching the cabin, torches in hand. She ran to the door, flung it open, and tried to scream, but no sound came forth. Buck, Angus, and Charley were going to be killed! Just as she started to run out the door, she remembered Buck telling her that if anything happened, she should use the loaded shotgun in the cellar.

Tripping over her feet, Summer managed to make it back to the hall. She yanked the trapdoor open and started to go down, only to discover she couldn't see in the pitch black. It seemed to take forever to get a candle lit. Protecting the flame with a cupped hand, she returned to the basement stairs. Halfway down, the toe of her slippers got caught in the hem of the robe, but by some miracle she managed to catch herself.

"Oh, God, oh, God!" she moaned upon seeing the firearms piled on one side of the small room. She didn't know a shotgun from a rifle. Why hadn't she paid attention when Buck had explained the different weapons to her? Turning, she finally spotted one by the stairs. She grabbed it and ran back up praying she had the right weapon.

Returning to the front door, Summer saw men tossing the torches to the roof and the base of the cabin. She lifted the long, heavy gun, pointed it in the direction of the cabin, and pulled the trigger.

The butt hit her so hard it knocked her to the floor, and her ears rang from the blast. The night riders started yelling, but she paid no attention to what they were saying. Her eyes were focused on the cabin door. She hurried to her feet, her heart pounding, what she saw next made her catch her breath. The cabin door slowly opened and she could see the barrel of a revolver appear through the crack.

At that moment, all hell broke loose. Everyone fired their revolvers, and Summer saw men fall from their mounts. At least Buck, Angus, and Charley have good aim, she thought anxiously. Summer kept glancing from the riders to the flames that were now creeping across the roof. Charley was the first to run from the cabin toward the house, with Buck and Angus covering his back. Then the other two made a run for it. On his way, Angus slipped in the snow. She held her breath until he jumped back to his feet. Summer stepped out of the doorway just in time for Charley to rush past her. Buck and Angus followed.

As Charley slammed the door shut and shoved the bolt, Buck grabbed Summer's candle and he and Angus headed for the cellar.

Bullets shattered Summer's windows, one hitting the chair beside her.

"Get down!" Charley hollered. Seeing her wide eyes, he knew she was frozen to the spot. He made a flying leap, knocking them both to the ground, then quickly covered her body with his.

"Get the torches," someone yelled from outside.

The words terrified Summer. She started shaking so badly Charlie couldn't hold her still. Shots were ricocheting off the walls around them.

"Easy, Angel," Charley soothed, patting her hair. "It'll be over soon."

Summer heard his comforting words and clung to him, her fingers digging into his shoulder. Then she felt Charley's body stiffen. "Charley, are you all right?"

"I'm fine, darlin'." He kept his voice calm, trying to keep Summer from becoming more frightened than she already was. "Now listen carefully." He eased his body off hers. "I want you to get to the hall where the shots can't reach you. All right?"

"They're going to burn us alive!"

"Everything will be just fine. Go now. As fast as you can."

She nodded.

"Good girl."

Summer got to her hands and knees and frantically tried to crawl, but her gown tripped her. Suddenly someone grabbed her wrist and dragged her into the hall. Scrambling to a sitting position, she saw Buck hurrying away to hand Charley a couple of rifles before positioning himself at the kitchen window. Charley braced himself at one of the parlor windows. Both men had revolvers in hand, and rifles standing beside them.

Summer circled her arms around her knees, trying to get control of herself. She was still shaking, but unable to turn away as the men fired back at the invaders. She heard shots from upstairs and realized Angus had made his way up there. The room was alight from the burning inferno of the cabin, and she could smell the smoke. She waited for her house to catch fire, too, and tears of fear streamed down her cheeks.

During a moment's lull, Summer heard the horses screaming, and Lady Bug bawled. Summer clenched her fists. The riders had set the barn on fire! The horror of Wind and the other animals being burned alive spurred her into action.

It wasn't difficult to sneak to the back door, as the men were too busy to keep an eye on her. A rifle stood nearby, and she picked it up before peeking outside. Seeing no one, she took off running.

"Nooo!" Summer screamed when she saw the big barn engulfed in yellow and orange flames. The fire was already shooting up into the black of night. She tried to rush in, but each time the heat and smoke forced her back. There were no longer any sounds coming from within.

Summer collapsed to the ground, pounding her fists on the blackened snow. "Damn them! Damn them all!"

Somewhere in the back of her mind, she heard the pounding hoofs of an approaching horse. As she watched a rider heading toward her, she was consumed with fury, the likes of which she had never felt before. Not knowing if the rifle was loaded, she grabbed hold of the barrel. Suddenly calm, and with cold-blooded determination, she stood and waited.

His horse in a full gallop, the man leaned down and extended his arm, ready to swoop her up. When he was almost upon her, Summer swung the weapon with every ounce of strength she possessed. The heavy stock hit his skull with a sickening thud, and the rider toppled to the ground. Other riders raced by, but left her alone. Silence descended, and Summer heard nothing except the crackle of the fire eating wood. Then the barn collapsed, sending sparks in all directions.

Summer turned and headed for the house. It wasn't until she neared the door that she looked up and saw Buck standing there, rifle in hand, watching her. She had no idea how long he'd been

240 DeLoras Scott

there, nor did she care. He moved aside, and she
went in.

"Is she all right?" Angus hollered as he started
down the stairs.

"I think so," Buck called back, "Summer," he
said softly, "the fighting is over. Sit at the table
and let me look at you." The soot covering her
clothes and dark blotches of reddened skin on her
arms told him that she'd tried to save the animals.
"Charley has grease that works on burns." Buck
suddenly remembered there was nothing left in the
cabin. "Charley!" he hollered. "Go to your stove
and fetch some of that stuff you use for burns.
Summer is going to need it."

"Damn it to hell!" Angus said when he entered
the kitchen and saw Summer.

"She'll be all right, but she needs these burns
taken care of."

"I didn't hear Charley leave, so I'll go see what's
keeping him. Don't worry, Angel," Angus assured
her, "we'll have you taken care of right away." He
ran out of the kitchen.

"I killed a man," Summer whispered.

"It couldn't be helped, darling," Buck crooned.
"It was either you or him." He dampened a cloth,
then gently began cleaning her face.

"Why would they set fire to the barn, Buck? The
animals couldn't do them any harm."

"Buck!" Angus called. "You'd better come
here."

Summer knocked Buck's hand away. There was
not a single doubt in her mind that something had
happened to Charley. She was out of her chair and
headed for the parlor before Buck had a chance to
stop her.

The moment she entered the room, Summer saw
Charley lying face down on the floor, the back of

his white shirt soaked with blood. She knelt beside him. "You're going to be just fine, Charley dearest. I won't let anything happen to you." He didn't open his eyes. She looked to Buck. "Is he . . . is he alive?"

"For now," he said gruffly.

"Carry him to my bed," she whispered, "then one of you will have to walk to the doctor's. The horses are all dead."

"How the hell did he get shot in the back?" Buck asked Angus as they carefully maneuvered Charley's unconscious body up the steps.

Summer answered, "I think it happened when he was protecting me from the bullets."

Buck insisted Charley be taken to one of the spare chambers. He knew that if Charley died in Summer's bed, she would never be able to return to her room.

By the time Angus had left to get the doctor, the miners were coming up from the hole to see what had happened. It was up to Buck to explain, and after assuring them there was nothing they could do, he sent them all home. For the second time in four years, the mine was completely shut down.

Buck returned to the house and helped Summer strip Charley's clothes off. He tried to get her to let him do it alone, but she was like a woman possessed, paying no heed to her burns or anything he said.

Buck left the room to fetch a bucket of water. When he returned, Summer shoved him aside, then snatched up a washcloth and began cleaning Charley's back. Even though he couldn't hear her, she kept talking to him. "You can't die, Charley. You have to keep fighting. . . . You're a big man and nothing can keep you down. . . ." She saw the hideous opening in his back. "Charley, I've come to realize it's you I love. . . ."

Buck blanched, but he knew exactly what she was doing. Charley's wound was near his heart. He hurried downstairs to replace the bloodied water. When he reached the kitchen, he opened the back door and vomited. Finally the retching stopped, but his chest was still tight with pain. He'd seen wounds like Charley's before, and knew it was fatal. He'd also watched men die over the years, but none had been as close to him as his good-hearted partner, and it hurt like hell!

He tossed the dirty water out and headed for Charley's stove. Not even thinking about what he was doing, he soon had a fire going. After piling the bucket full with snow, he set it over the flames to melt. He'd never known such deep misery.

It seemed ironic, considering just tonight he'd come to realize how much he loved Summer. It had happened when he'd discovered she was missing from the house. When he'd seen the man riding toward her, his heart had stopped beating. The man had leaned over, too low for him to get off a shot. He had thought he was going to lose her, and at that moment he wanted to die. But Summer had shown more courage than he had thought possible. As she walked toward the house, he'd wanted to take her in his arms, tell her of his love, and vow he would keep her safe for the rest of her life.

Chapter 14

Although Charley's life was hanging by a thread, Summer was convinced that if she could keep him alive until the doctor arrived, he'd live. She talked continuously while taking care of him. Buck had located the salve for her burns, but she'd refused to let him apply it. Her wounds were nothing compared to what Charley was going through.

Buck tried relieving her, and Summer knew he was angry for not letting him help. She didn't care. *It was because of her that Charley had been shot!*

"Just think how beautiful our children are going to be," Summer said as she removed a damp compress from Charley's forehead and replaced it with another. She watched Buck leave the room before resuming her seat and placing Charley's hand in hers. "And I want a big wedding, Charley McMillan, with lots of flowers and . . ." She thought she felt Charley squeeze her hand, but thinking she was hallucinating, she continued. "I think . . ." Again she felt the squeeze and her gaze darted to Charley's face. His eyes were open, and joy filled her bosom. He was going to live! She took a quick glance around the room to tell Buck, but found he wasn't there.

"Charley dearest," she said softly.

His lips moved, but she couldn't hear what he was saying.

"Try not to talk, you need to save your strength."

Again his lips moved.

"Are you trying to tell me something?"

He nodded.

Summer stood and leaned over so she could hear better.

"I love you," he whispered, "but I know I ain't the man you'll marry."

"Nonsense. You haven't been listening to me."

"Shh. I don't know if I'll be able to say this again, so please listen." He coughed, and his face twisted in agony.

"You have to be quiet."

"I knew I wasn't gonna win your love, but I didn't want to admit it to myself."

Summer waited for him to continue, but when he said nothing more, she straightened up. His eyes were closed and his breathing labored. "Have faith, Charley, we'll marry." She started to sit back down, but he suddenly reached out and grabbed her arm.

"Summer, it's Buck you should marry. Funny, I can see it so clearly now."

His voice was stronger and his soft brown eyes were clear. Her hope for his recovery soared.

"But promise you won't marry him until he says he loves you." He gave a hoarse chuckle. "That's gonna be hard as hell for him."

"We'll see, Charley. Now I want you to rest."

"Promise me."

"I promise."

There was a smile on his lips as he drifted back into unconsciousness.

When Summer realized that at some time Buck had reentered the room, she smiled. "Charley was conscious," she said proudly. "He's going to be all right."

Buck was not only surprised that Charley had regained conscious, he was also surprised his friend was still alive. Even he was starting to feel a slight ray of hope. "Did he say anything?" he asked.

"He said he loved me."

Buck watched her attention quickly leave him and return to his partner. He'd had a lot of time to think. He'd even prayed, something he hadn't done since he was a boy. He felt so damn helpless. Summer continued talking on and on, her voice cracking. She looked worse than Charley. Not once since discovering Charley had been shot, had she shed a tear. He knew that it was because of all that had happened over the last few hours. Her hurt was too deep. He studied the dark circles under her eyes and her pale face whose beauty even burns and smudges couldn't hide. He wanted to hold her. Instead he went downstairs to pour her sa bowl of the meaty broth he'd made. He shrugged. Maybe not as good as Charley's, but palatable.

When Buck tried to hand the bowl to Summer, she refused. He'd had all he was going to take. Charley's condition was bad enough, but having to put up with Summer as well was suddenly more than he cared to handle. He placed the bowl on a small table beside her.

"Either you eat this broth," he said in a hushed but firm voice, "or I'll carry you to the kitchen and force it down you!"

"Carry me? How can you be so thoughtless? I have to stay with Charley."

"Then eat, because I don't want to have to take care of you, too."

"You don't care about Charley," she accused. "If you did you wouldn't be thinking about food and you wouldn't leave his bedside!"

Buck grabbed her by the arm, jerked her out of the chair, and forced her into the hall. Closing the door in case Charley might hear, he spun her around so she was facing him. "What in the hell makes you think you're the only one hurting? I've known Charley a lot longer than you have, lady, and my suffering is every bit as deep as yours. But there is a difference. Yours is mixed with guilt. You now feel you should have accepted Charley's marriage proposal and made him happy. But what if he hadn't been shot?"

"You don't know what you're talking about," Summer snapped at him.

"You think not? For three hours I listened to you plan everything, from getting married, to building a house in Denver, and even the children you would have! How am I supposed to feel about that?"

"I don't care how you feel about it! Don't you understand? Charley wouldn't be close to death if it hadn't been for me. I owe him my life."

"What are you talking about?"

"He protected me with his body. If he hadn't, I would be the one on that bed."

Buck raked his fingers through his hair. "When we first came into the house?"

"Yes. He had just rolled off of me when I was trying to make it to the hall."

"If you knew he was shot, why didn't you say something instead of letting him stand by the window shooting back at those damn raiders?"

"I didn't know he was shot."

"You aren't making a damn bit of sense, but I'm

not going to stand here and argue the point. You are going to eat."

As angry as Summer was, she knew that if she said no, Buck would take her away from Charley. She'd already been gone too long. "Yes. I'll eat!"

"Fine. And after that you will let me finish cleaning you up and taking care of those burns. I warn you, Summer, don't say no to me again because I'm in no mood for it." He moved away and allowed her to go back in the room.

Summer didn't even taste the food she was putting into her mouth. Her gaze followed Buck as he tenderly removed the bloody pàd made from ripped sheets atop Charley's wound and replaced it with a clean one. He fluffed a pillow for Charley's head. Suddenly Charlie's hand jerked up and caught Buck's wrist in a death grip, but Buck didn't flinch. He stood there until Charley let loose. Summer could see the red welt around his wrist.

It was almost noon when Angus returned with Doctor Willaby. "Are we too late?" Angus asked Buck as they entered the bedroom.

"No, he's still alive. How, I don't know."

Oscar Willaby went straight to the bed. "I want everyone to leave the room," he ordered. "And make some strong coffee. I've been up all night."

Summer tried to stay with the doctor, but Buck quickly put her efforts to a halt.

"What took so long?" Buck asked as he, Angus, and Summer headed down the stairs.

"The Doc was off attending to a dying man who had been found by the road, shot. I've got a strong hunch that bullet came from one of our guns. As luck would have it, the man died. He could have told us who was behind all this. While I waited, I picked us up a buckboard, some feed, and horses.

I'll put them in the old shed. At least that didn't
get burned."

As Summer turned to go into the kitchen, Angus
motioned Buck into the parlor.

"How bad is it, Buck?"

"I wouldn't have believed he'd last this long."

Angus collapsed in a chair.

"All I can say, Angus, is the longer he continues
to fight, the better his chances are."

"And Summer?"

"She's like the walking dead. I did get her to eat,
but I had to threaten her to get her to do it. She
thinks this is all her fault."

"You have any idea who the bastards were that
did this?"

"Only a hunch. I'm sure it's the same with you."
Buck looked at Angus' haggard face and stubble
and knew he probably looked just as bad. "I'll tell
you one thing, if I get the least inkling of proof,
I'm going after them, and they won't live to see
another day."

"And I'll be by your side. When Charley gets
better, we'll get to the bottom of this."

While the doctor attended to Charley, Angus and
Buck loaded the six dead riders onto the buckboard. There hadn't been a recent heavy snow, so
Buck had no trouble driving them to Blackhawk.
He and Angus had discussed the need for guards
again, so Buck also attended to that. They were to
start work that night.

When Buck returned home, he found Angus and
Doctor Willaby sitting at the kitchen table. Angus
informed him that Summer was back up with Charley.

"Oscar was just fixing to tell me about Charley,"
Angus said, motioning Buck to take a seat.

"I've removed the bullet," the doctor said as he

started on his third pot of coffee, "and patched him up. But I'm sorry to say that without a miracle, Charley isn't going to make it, boys. I told Miss Caldwell the same, but she accused me of lying. I did finally manage to get her to let me look at those burns. The ones on her hands are the worst, but I don't believe there will be any scars. She's ready to collapse, gentlemen." He reached down and pulled a vial from his black bag. "I'm going back up to check on Charley now, and I'm sending Miss Caldwell back down. Would one of you get me an empty cup?"

Buck handed him one from the hutch.

"She has to get some rest. I'm putting laudanum in this cup. I suggest one of you lace it with coffee and get her to drink it, then you may have to carry her to bed. If there is another bed in the house, I'd also like to get some sleep."

"There are three bedrooms, Oscar, and you're welcome to stay," Buck said. "Follow me. Angus or I will remain with Charley, and if there are any changes, we'll wake you."

"It wouldn't hurt either of you to get some sleep, too."

"I don't want any coffee," Summer insisted as she joined Angus at the table. "I've already drunk five gallons of it."

"Buck said Charley was conscious."

Summer smiled weakly. "He's going to live, Angus."

"I hope you're right, Angel. You know, you're looking awfully tired."

"Don't you start on me. I'm not going to bed."

"I wasn't going to suggest it. I was simply going to point out that if you want to remain awake and not fall flat on your face, you'd better drink another cup of coffee."

"Oh, very well. If it will make you happy. Honestly, you're as bad as Buck. I tell you I'm fine, but neither of you will listen to me."

Angus went to the stove, poured the coffee into the cup with laudanum, and set it in front of her. He watched her hands shaking as she raised it to her lips. It didn't take long for the drug to take effect.

"Angus," Summer said, resting her elbows on the table, "I can't seem to keep my eyes open." She rubbed them in an effort to dispel the drowsiness.

"That's because you've been up too long, darling. I'll carry you to bed so you can get some sleep."

"No. I need to stay with Charley."

He pushed her empty cup aside. "Then why don't you lay your head on the table and take a quick nap. If Charley's condition changes, Buck or I will wake you."

"Well . . . maybe for just a minute." Her speech was slurred.

In no time, Angus could hear her even breathing. He released a tired sigh. The little one was hurting as bad as the rest of them. She'd been so protected that what she'd seen and been through over the last twenty-four hours were bound to take a heavy toll. He picked her up in his arms and carried her to the stairs, thinking how wrong they'd been to bring her here. If they'd left her alone, she might never have had to experience the harsher side of life.

When Summer awoke, her head felt fuzzy. She had no idea how long she'd been asleep and couldn't seem to concentrate on anything. As she walked to the door her steps were unsteady, but she grew stronger as she entered the hallway. She quietly opened the door to Charley's room and peeked in. Buck sat slumped in the chair, his long legs stretched out in front of him. He turned his head to see who had come in, and for the first time Summer noticed how haggard he was, as well as the hard, dangerous look in his eyes. They softened a bit when he saw her.

"How is Charley doing?" she asked quietly when she reached the side of the bed.

"He regained consciousness once."

"Why didn't you wake me?"

"It was only for a few minutes and you wouldn't have had time to get here."

Pain ripped through her as she looked down at her gentle Charley. His face was drawn and had a strange pallor about it. He looked so much older. "Did he say anything?"

"He said if you didn't marry, you were to have his share of the mine."

"I couldn't do that!"

"It's his wish, and that's the way it will be."

"Go get some rest, Buck. I'll stay with Charley."

He nodded and stood, though he knew sleep was impossible. He had decided that he was going to kill every man who had anything to do with the raid. It might take time, but eventually he'd find out exactly who they were. "By the way, Lorna's downstairs," he said before leaving. "She arrived shortly after you fell asleep. I'll have her bring you up some food."

Charley died in the wee hours of the morning, his hands slipping from Summer's grasp.

Reverend Porter conducted the service the next

day, and men and women from all around stood
on the hill to say their final good-byes. It was the
same hill the three partners and Summer had all
slid down the day after the blizzard—which now
seemed like ages ago to Summer. She paid scant
attention to the people or what the minister was
saying. She was remembering how Charley had
been the first one to show her any kindness when
she arrived, the big stack of flapjacks he'd made,
his determination to be a gentleman, his patience
in teaching her how to cook, him lying on top of
the snow showing her how to make angel wings.
. . . And as a final gesture, he'd left her his share
of the mine, so that if Buck didn't declare his love,
she'd be secure for the rest of her life.

Hatred for this place welled deep within her. She
wanted out of Colorado, never to return again. She
needed to go home to Philadelphia and get away
from the senseless killing of men and animals.

Buck and Angus stood on either side of Summer.
She knew they were trying to give her support,
but she still felt cold and alone. A hard knot formed
in her throat as the coffin was lowered into the
deep pit. Earlier, Angus had told her he and Buck
had ordered a tombstone. The inscription was simple.

CHARLEY McMILLAN
1827–1864
A GOOD FRIEND AND PARTNER

As men began shoveling dirt over the coffin,
Buck and Angus escorted Summer back to the
house. Seeing the devastated camp only served to
strengthen her determination to leave. Even part
of the shaft house and some surrounding trees had
been consumed by the fire. Her house looked

strange standing amid the rubble and ashes.

The dining table was covered with food, brought by the mourners. There were slugs embedded in a lot of the pieces of furniture, but no one commented on it. Lorna sat Summer in the most comfortable chair, not knowing it was a gift from Charley, and someone brought her a plate of food. Very little reached her mouth. Nothing seemed real to her. People were introduced to her, but she didn't bother trying to remember names. There wasn't any need. She'd be leaving soon, no matter what the roads were like.

The only person who did briefly attract Summer's attention was a tall, slender Englishman by the name of Geoffrey Thorpe. Summer enjoyed listening to him speak. He was obviously a well-educated man, and she couldn't help wondering what he was doing in the Mountain City area. Naturally, she didn't ask, but he supplied the answer when he told her he was an artist and had come West because the doctors in England had told him he had tuberculosis. And yes, he did feel much better. He very much wanted to paint Summer's portrait, but she declined.

While everyone ate and visited, Buck stepped outside. At least for a few minutes, he needed to get away from the sea of smiling, sympathetic faces. It seemed everyone had some memory of the things he, Angus, and Charley had done. A wry smile crossed his full lips. The three of us made damn good hell-raisers, he thought. He couldn't remember the number of saloons they'd torn apart simply because they were in the mood for a good fight.

Buck's anger over Charley's death festered. He knew it was the same with Angus, and he kept asking himself if Elliot Toddle had been the culprit behind it. He wanted revenge, and had half a notion to ride into town and kill the son of a bitch and be done with it once and for all. Frustration eating away at him, he strolled over to the pile of ashes and wood that used to be their cabin and kicked around pieces of burnt logs to see if anything was left to save. As he turned away, the sun hit a square piece of glass, causing it to sparkle. Even before he leaned to examine the cracked lens, he was bent on murder.

It was night by the time everyone had left and Summer went to her room. There was nothing there to remind her of Charley, but in her mind she could still see him. She could still hear the bullets and the screaming of Wind. She even thought about the sweet foal her mare never had.

Hearing Summer close her door upstairs, Buck turned to Angus, who was in deep thought while smoking one of his cigars.

"I'm heading out in the morning to kill Elliot Toddle and his two cohorts," Buck stated simply.

Angus' eyes were squinted as his glaze landed on Buck. "You know something I don't?"

"I found his glasses a short distance from the cabin this afternoon. The wire frame is all bent out of shape, but it was recognizable."

"What time do we leave?"

"In the morning, after I've told Summer."

"Maybe we should leave her a note."

Buck grunted. "It would be the easiest way for us, but we both know we couldn't leave without an explanation."

"It's times like this that I would prefer being a coward, but you're right. She's not going to take this well."

"Nope."

"You think she'll be all right while we're gone?
It could be a long trip if Toddle's gone into hiding.
He's got to be considering the possibility that we
found his glasses, and knows damn well that if we
did, we'll go looking for him."

"She'll be all right. The guards are good men,
and they're not about to let anyone slip past them,
especially after what happened. And Summer
needs time to herself to work the devils out of her
head. After all she's been through, we could lose
her, Angus."

"I know."

Though Summer's bedroom door was closed,
both men heard her sobbing when they went upstairs. It was good to know she was finally letting
her grief spill forth.

Summer was still asleep when Buck entered her
room at dawn the next morning. He stood by the
bed gazing down. With all his soul, he wanted to
join her, feel her body against his, and say to hell
with everything—but that couldn't be. Nor could
he tell her of his love, because he might not return.
He studied her beautiful face, still a bit swollen
from crying most of the night, then reached out to
stroke her hair. Instead his hand dropped to her
shoulder. He gently shook her.

Summer was in such a deep sleep, it took a moment to realize where she was. "Buck?" She sat
up and rubbed her eyes. Looking at him again, she
noted the Stetson, brown shirt, leather vest and
pants. A gun belt was strapped around his slim
hips with a revolver nestled in the holster. Saddlebags were slung over one of his shoulders. But
what frightened her the most was the cold look in
his eyes. "Are you going somewhere?" she asked,
knowing it was a ridiculous question.

"Angus and I are going after Toddle and his partners."

"Why?"

"I found out he was behind the raid. None of us will have any peace until he's dead."

Summer flung the covers off. "You can't do that. You'll both be hung for murder! Listen to me, Buck. We can leave. We can get married. Let the sheriff handle this."

The muscles in Buck's jaw flexed as he worked to control himself. "I owe it to Charley."

"But—"

"What about Angus? You going to marry him, too? If our lives are in danger, you'll marry us all? Is that it?"

"I didn't mean it that way." She struck her fist on the bed. "Why do we spend most of our time arguing? Go ahead. Get your head blown off. I don't care!"

Buck spun around and left.

Summer remained on the bed feeling sorry for herself and wondering why Buck had to be so stubborn. Didn't he realize what he would be putting her through? Suddenly she thought about what she had said to him. Frantic, she leaped off the bed. Before they left, she had to tell Buck she didn't mean it. When she ran out the front door, the two men were already riding away.

"Wait," she hollered, but they didn't hear her. "I didn't mean it, Buck," she whispered.

Angus and Buck headed straight for town. After stopping at a lawyer's office to have papers drawn up that made Summer sole owner of the mine should they both die, they set out toward the Pierson Mining Investments office.

Later that morning, they found out Pierson Mining Investments was no longer in business. The rest of the day was spent trying to find where Toddle was staying. That also drew a dead end. He had moved out. Convinced Toddle had gone into hiding, the partners knew they had their work cut out for them. They could only hope he hadn't headed back East.

Summer had to keep busy because she felt so lonesome with Buck and Angus gone. She came to the conclusion that there wouldn't be a better time to do the spring cleaning. The house was filthy after all that had happened. The smoke alone had covered everything with a black grime. She would make sure the next woman who moved in couldn't accuse her of being a bad housekeeper. She stripped all the beds, washed, starched, and ironed the sheets and pillowcases. The windows came next, then the furniture received a good beeswaxing. She scrubbed the floors thoroughly, and took the rug and feather mattresses outside to give them a good beating. The guards waved and occasionally came by to share a cup of coffee, but it wasn't the same as before. She dreaded the nights because there were always the nightmares that awoke her, usually in a cold sweat. On top of all that, there was the constant worry that Buck and Angus might not return. However, it did give her a slight lift to see the chickens come home, one by one.

The one thing Summer couldn't do was visit Charley's grave. She didn't want to relive the funeral and picture him being lowered into the ground.

Summer hardly left her house. The land that she'd thought so beautiful now seemed cruel and harsh. She wanted desperately to ride to Central City and catch the stage to Golden, then on to

Denver. But she couldn't until she knew Buck and Angus were all right. She even made up her mind that if Buck still wanted to marry her, he'd have to move to Philadelphia. She could no longer consider this her home.

By the seventh day, Summer was a nervous wreck. The men should have been back by now. She tried not to dwell on them being hurt or lying dead somewhere. At the same time she hated them for leaving and putting her through more misery. As a matter of fact, there was little she didn't hate.

As one day followed another and spring stole over the mountain, Summer began to face the likelihood that Buck and Angus were dead. With little else to do now that everything was spotless, Summer began taking an honest look at herself. Since Charley's death, she'd thought of no one but herself. Never once had she taken into consideration what Buck and Angus were going through, nor had she offered them a single word of sympathy. Each, in his own way, had always been there when she needed him. Though she'd found out from the doctor about the laudanum Angus had tricked her into taking, it had been for her own good. And what about Buck? He'd let her have her way until he knew she had to eat and her burns had to be nursed. He'd been so gentle, even though she'd hated him for interrupting her vigil over Charley. Each thing she thought of led to something else, and by the time she had taken everything into consideration, she didn't much like herself. She also came to another, very important conclusion. Even after all that had happened, she still had not accepted the fact that Charley was dead.

Late one afternoon, she walked to his grave. She was surprised to see a beautiful smattering of wildflowers on the hill. Spring had arrived early, and was already in full bloom. She picked a few of the blossoms and knelt, placing them on Charley's grave. "Oh Charley, how you would have set the women's hearts aflutter. Rest in peace, my dear friend. You will always be in my heart. If I could ask a favor, I'd ask you to look after Buck and Angus and bring them back safely to me. You were right, I'll never love anyone the way I love Buck, but I will keep my promise. I'll not agree to anything unless he says he loves me."

Then Summer stood and took a fresh look at the lovely glade below, the tall pine trees, the majestic peaks in the distance still covered with snow, and the brilliant blue sky. How could she have ever thought she wanted to return to Philadelphia? She hadn't even begun to live until Buck had kidnapped her.

Weary, angry, and bitter, Buck and Angus knew they had no recourse but to give up the search for Toddle. For two weeks they'd combed every gully, mountain, and ravine, but the man continued to elude them. They knew that as of three days ago, Toddle and his men were still in the area because a few miners had seen them. The two partners decided they would have to draw Toddle to them.

It was midmorning, and Angus and Buck were following the deer path up the side of a mountain, single file. They were headed for home. Buck, who was leading, suddenly jerked his mount to a halt. Angus glanced ahead to see why he'd stopped. Not fifty feet up the trail were the three men they'd been searching for, but someone had gotten to them first. Their wrists and ankles had been tied, and the ropes around their necks squeaked as the strong breeze coming from the canyon caused the bodies to slowly swing back and forth. They were hanging from a large beam of an old mine shack.

Flies were buzzing around everywhere, and the bodies had already started to smell. It was obvious the hanging had taken place sometime early this morning because of the color of their faces, and because, as yet, the wild animals hadn't gotten to them.

Their hate spewing forth, and feeling they had been cheated of their just revenge, Angus and Buck drew their revolvers and unloaded them into the dead bodies.

When the two men rode into camp the next day, they were dog tired. Last night they'd gotten the first decent sleep they'd had in a long time. They both knew that as of tomorrow, there'd be a lot of work to do.

"I sure hope Summer has something to eat," Angus said as they stripped the gear and saddles from the horses and led them into the old shed. "Of course I don't know why she would after we've been gone for so long."

Buck laughed. "Last time I talked to her she said she didn't want to see my face again."

"Good. Maybe she'll be happy to see mine."

After rubbing the horses down and giving them grain and hay, the men headed for the house.

Angus and Buck were surprised that no one was home, but gave it no more thought as they went to the kitchen for grub. They quickly devoured half the cake Summer had left on the counter while they waited for their meat to cook.

When forty-five minutes had passed and Summer still hadn't made an appearance, they began to worry. They were even more concerned after checking with the guards and finding out they'd seen her leave camp alone—though they assured

Buck and Angus she'd been doing a lot of walking of late.

"Maybe she's gone to Charley's grave," Buck said. "You go looking in that direction, and I'll take off the other way."

After grabbing a couple of rifles, the men split up.

It wasn't long before Buck spotted Summer's footprint in a small patch of snow. He started moving faster. She was moving directly toward a nest of old shafts. He was both angry and desperate as he ran to catch up with her. Damn it, Buck thought. Why didn't she ever listen?

Meanwhile Summer continued to stroll along, occasionally leaning down to examine a wildflower. She was very careful where she walked. She hadn't forgotten Buck's warning about the shafts, but this was the warmest day they'd had in months, and she needed to get away from the house or she would go crazy. She was sick with worry that she'd never see Buck or Angus again.

Having been gone longer than she'd planned, Summer knew it was time to go back. What if Buck and Angus had returned? But how many times had she thought the same thing, only to have that day pass uneventfully? Spying a different kind of flower near the forest line, she took off in that direction to have a look. From a distance it reminded her of a cattail, except it was orange. She had almost reached it when she heard the loud cracking of a limb. To her horror, a bear came waddling out of the forest. At the same time she saw it, the bear saw her. The big beast growled and reared up on its hind legs, its paw looming larger than her entire head. But Summer's gaze was now fastened on its teeth. It growled again, swinging one of its huge paws in the air. Summer wanted to turn and run, but her feet seemed nailed to the ground.

A shot rang out. It hit the bear in the chest, but only seemed to make the creature twice as angry. Another shot was fired just as it came down on all fours. The bear's roar echoed through the woods. Then it started running toward whoever had fired the shots.

Summer turned and saw Buck take the barrel of the rifle in his hand, waiting for the bear to attack. She threw her hands to her mouth to keep from screaming, instinctively knowing that it could do more damage than good. Buck was going to hit the bear just as she had struck the rider who had attacked her. All she could do was stand and watch.

Buck waited, but before the bear reached him, the animal reared again. Buck cursed himself for not having brought more ammunition. He took several swings at the big animal, connecting effectively. He knew he had hit the bear in the chest with the first bullet and could see blood matting the thick fur. His second shot had taken out an eye, so the bear wasn't as accurate when it swung its paw. If Buck could hold out long enough, the huge beast would eventually drop. The question was, how long would it take?

Summer held her breath when the bear managed to knock the rifle from Buck's hands. She started yelling, trying to draw the beast's attention. She'd rather die than see the man she loved killed. But it didn't work. The bear wanted Buck. Almost quicker than her eyes could see, Buck pulled a long knife from the scabbard attached to his belt. He circled the shaggy animal, and each time the bear reached out, Buck slashed with his knife, careful not to lose his only weapon. When one thrust caught the beast's haunch, it staggered and came down on all fours. For a minute it looked like the bear was going to retreat, but it quickly swerved and ran for Buck. Again it stumbled. Then it reared, and Buck lunged forward, sinking the knife deep in its massive chest. Buck didn't jump back in time to keep from being hit and knocked to the ground. The bear collapsed on top of him.

"Buck?" Summer whispered. "Buck?" she screamed as she ran forward.

"I'm all right," he said when she reached him, "but you're going to have to help me get out from under this goddamn thing!"

Summer started laughing from sheer relief. "What's wrong, Mister Holester? I thought you were the big mountain man who could handle anything?"

"Damn it, Summer, this isn't funny. He's heavy as hell. You're going to have to roll him over before I can get free."

Suddenly she became serious. "Oh, darling, what should I do?"

"Grab his paw and pull. I'll push."

Summer stared at the big paw and long nails. Tentatively, she reached out. The paw suddenly jerked, and she screamed. "He's still alive!"

"No, it's just a reflex," Buck assured her.

Steeling herself, Summer again reached forth. Satisfied Buck was right, she grabbed hold and pulled. With Buck's help, the beast was moved enough for Buck to crawl out. Pain shot through Summer when she caught sight of the blood on his clothes. "You're hurt!" She dropped to the ground by his side, both of them gasping for breath. "Lie still. Oh my darling, where did he hit you?" she asked, gently unbuttoning his shirt. "What should I do?"

"Make love to me."

"What? You must be out of your head! You're—"

"Fine."

"But the blood—"

Laughing, he pulled her to him. "Is from the bear."

"Of all the . . ." She couldn't finish because his lips were on hers.

Buck led Summer to a small stream then, and once he washed off, they made love with wild abandon. They couldn't get enough of each other. After her need had been satisfied, Summer was surprised when Buck showed her he could still be aroused.

"You're not serious," she said in awe.

"I'm quite serious." He smiled. "I am a man of strong appetites. I just haven't had the opportunity to show you before."

Summer had never known a woman could reach so many heights of pleasure, all in one afternoon.

"Angel," Buck said as they lay satiated in each other's arms, "as much as I'd like us to get married right away, I'm afraid it's going to have to wait a week or so." He felt her body stiffen. "It's only because there are so many things that have to be taken care of at the mine."

She pulled away and began dressing. "I can't marry you, Buck."

"Are you saying you don't love me?"

"I've never said I love you."

"I see." He began putting on his clothes. "You've enjoyed the frolic, but don't want the muzzle. Or is it because if that happened you'd lose Charley's share of the mine?"

Summer turned on him with the fury of a wildcat. "As I recall, you were the one who didn't want to be tied down. Then, out of the clear blue, you toss your hat into the ring just because you didn't want Charley or Angus to have me. Isn't that what you said?"

"Yes, but it's different now."

Summer glared at the handsome man standing in front of her. "Because we've made love? I also remember you telling me all about a man's needs. Give me one good reason why we should get married!"

He smiled. "Because I love you."

Summer's anger floated away like a drop of water in a river. "Why didn't you tell me that before?"

"I don't exactly remember having the opportunity."

Summer laughed. "No, I don't suppose you did. I've dreamed of you saying you love me, because I've been in love with you for an awfully long time."

He grabbed her in his arms and started swinging her in circles as they both laughed.

Because they were so carried away with discovering their love for each other, it wasn't until they were close to camp that Buck again suggested they marry within a week.

"Darling," Summer said, "please don't be angry, but I want to have our wedding in Denver. There are a few things I need to clear up before I would feel right about our getting married."

"Like what?"

"I owe it to William to explain what has happened and why I can't marry him."

"You don't owe him a damn thing."

"Try to understand. I want our marriage to start off right, and this is something I feel I must do. Also, I'd like Milly to be at our wedding."

Buck had deep reservations, but finally agreed

to what she asked. He had fallen in love with the woman she'd become in the mountains. He was more than a little worried that she would revert to her old self once she returned to civilization.

Chapter 15

As Summer made biscuits so they would be ready when the men awoke, her mind was on her beloved Buck. After they had returned to camp yesterday, Buck had taken Angus aside and told him of their forthcoming wedding. She had been surprised at how well Angus took the news. The fight she'd anticipated never took place. It was as if Angus already knew. After an early supper last night, the men had gone to bed. Buck had wanted to sleep with her, but she sadly refused. With Angus still living in the house, it didn't seem proper. Fortunately, Buck was too tired to press the point, but tonight might be a different matter.

She had slept very little. All she could think of was Buck saying he loved her, and that soon they would be spending their lives together as man and wife. But in the middle of her rapture, she started looking at some simple truths. She and Buck needed to take the remainder of her time in the mountains to get acquainted. She still knew nothing about his past or what his thoughts were about their future.

The men finally came down and Summer felt like a giddy girl when Buck pulled her to him and kissed her thoroughly.

"Good morning, lovely lady." He gave her a wicked smile.

"Good morning. And good morning to you, Angus," she said over Buck's shoulder.

"Did you miss me last night?" Buck asked as he and Angus took their places at the table.

Summer turned red with embarrassment and wouldn't look at Angus. "I'll have your breakfast ready shortly."

After a good night's rest, Angus was also in a fair mood. It hurt like hell knowing he had lost Summer, but he'd been around too long not to know he'd eventually get over it and find a wife. However, he was in no hurry now. "I have to say, Buck, I was more than a little surprised to see you in your own bed. I thought you would move right into Summer's."

Summer dropped a pan.

"She wouldn't have me. Said she didn't feel right with you still living in the house. Tonight, though, I plan on changing her mind."

Summer swung around, threatening them both with the pan. "How can you sit there and talk about me like that? I'm not some..."

"No one said you were, darlin'," Angus said, "but when a man claims a woman in these parts, he beds her. The winters can be pretty hard, and it might be awhile before they make it to the preacher."

"That's heathen!"

Their laughter was infectious and Summer couldn't help but smile. In the time she'd known them, neither man could be accused of not speaking his mind.

Summer soon placed the platters on the table and joined them for breakfast. She'd long since become accustomed to the volume of food they ate.

"Where did you find the eggs?" Buck asked as he slid four of them onto his plate.

Summer grinned. "The chickens came home."

After breakfast, the men went out to hitch up the buckboard while Summer washed the dishes.

"Have you and Summer decided where you're going to live?" Angus asked as they were leading the horses to the buckboard.

"No."

Angus was well aware of Buck's dislike for towns. "What if Summer wants to live in Denver or with her family?"

Buck hooked the rigging on and turned to his partner. "Why are you asking, Angus?"

"Because if you're not going to live here, there isn't much sense in building the place back up."

Buck's gaze fell on the mountain peaks he loved so much. "We'll let you know."

"You know, Buck," Angus went on, "I've been doing a lot of thinking since Charley's death, and I've come to the conclusion that it's time for a change."

"What are you talking about? Are you planning on leaving?"

Angus pulled a cigar from his shirt pocket and lit it. "I'm not sure." He took a long draw and slowly let the smoke trail from his lips. "The war can't last much longer, and when it's over, there are going to be a lot of people heading west. Denver is going to grow, Buck. I think I'd like to be a part of it. I have half a notion that you were thinking the same thing when you bought up that land."

"If you like, when we take Summer back down, I'll introduce you to Howard Jackson." Buck chuckled. "We could end up owning Denver."

"I didn't know Summer was going back."

"I thought she'd want to get married right away,

but she wants to have a talk with that Nielson fellow and have her lady friend attend the wedding."

Angus saw the concern on his friend's face. "Why should that bother you?"

"What if she changes her mind? She could very easily decide she's missed the life she knew before coming here."

"What difference does it make? Hell, you've got enough money already to give her everything she could possibly want."

"You know, it's strange. I don't think she has any idea just how wealthy I am. I haven't told her anything about what I've bought." He rested a hand on the horse's rump and looked at Angus. "There's one spread that has good grass for grazing cattle and a fine little house nestled in the foothills. Be a good place for raising children. I want it to be a surprise for Summer. Kind of a wedding present." He proceeded to hook up the rigging.

Angus moved to help him. "And you're going to spring it on her when you get there?"

"That's what I'm planning. We've had an easy winter. So unless a heavy storm comes along, I figure we can head back to Denver by the end of this month. The sooner I get Summer to a preacher, the better I'll feel."

"But what if she has it in her mind to return to Philadelphia?"

Buck didn't get a chance to answer. Wearing a bonnet, Summer walked out the door and headed toward them.

It was a beautiful spring day, and the three rode on the front seat together. They sang one song after another practically the entire distance to town, their loud voices scaring away the wildlife.

As usual, Angus and Buck dropped Summer off

at Lorna's while they left to tell the miners they were going to reopen the mine.

"Summer!" Lorna called excitedly from across the long room. She glanced back at the customer she was waiting on and said, "Gertrude, I'll send Margaret right over to help you."

As soon as she had one of the girls helping the customer, Lorna headed straight for Summer—the gold watch chain around her neck bouncing from side to side over her ample bosom. "It's so good to see you. How are you feeling?"

"Fine. Oh, Lorna, I have so much to tell you."

"And I have a lot to tell you. It's been so busy today, I was just thinking about getting away and going down the street for a cup of coffee." Her brown eyes grew large. "You do have time to go with me, don't you?"

Summer laughed. "Of course I do. You know Buck and Angus always have a hundred and one things to do."

"Let me tell the girls, and I'll be right back."

Lorna soon returned, her round face flushed from hurrying.

When they were seated at the restaurant with their coffee, Summer said, "Business must be good. I see you've hired two more women."

"Yes, it is—especially since I stopped gossiping with that little social group. Oh, Summer, I owe you so much."

"I don't know why. You've done far more for me than I've done for you. You took care of everything while Charley was dying, and helped after the funeral. Because you've been such a good friend to all of us, Buck, Angus, and I want you to accept a gift as a thank-you."

"I did it as a friend," Lorna said, trying to contain her excitement. "What is it?"

Summer laughed. "That new black buggy that Angus said you so admired. I guess having that carriage house built was a good idea after all. The buggy looks as new as the day it arrived."

"I can't take that. It was a gift to you."

"I'll never use it."

"Let me pay you for it."

"Absolutely not. Now, what was your news?"

Summer watched Lorna dab her rosebud lips and replace her napkin in her lap. She was beaming all over.

"I'm getting married, Summer."

"Oh, Lorna. I'm so pleased. Who's the lucky man?"

"Norman Picket. He's from New York and works for a large Eastern concern. He's here to buy mines."

Summer groaned. "Not again."

"No, it's true this time. I know several people that have sold to him, and they were quite pleased with the arrangement. We were coming to see you tomorrow because I wanted you, Buck, and Angus to meet him and attend the wedding."

"When do you plan on getting married?"

"A week from Sunday."

"So soon? Have you known him for long?"

"He came into my store the day after Buck lit into Elliot." Seeing Summer's puzzled expression, she asked, "Didn't you know Buck beat the tar out of him?"

"Buck didn't say anything about that." Summer took a drink of her coffee, feeling quite proud of her future husband.

"I have never heard Buck bad-mouth anyone, so when he was furious at Elliot, I knew he had to have a valid reason."

"Yes, he did. Lorna, are you sure you want to

marry this man when you've known him for such a short time? You're inclined to quickly attach yourself."

"This is different. I knew it the moment I laid eyes on him."

"You're still going to come to the house like you planned, aren't you? I'll fix a grand lunch."

"I wouldn't want to put you to a lot of trouble."

"Nonsense. I'd enjoy doing it and love the company."

"Then, yes. We'll be there about noon."

"And bring along an extra horse to pull your buggy."

Lorna laughed. "Won't I look grand driving it down Main Street?"

"Indeed you will."

"Now what was your news?"

In light of Lorna's happiness, Summer felt telling her about the engagement to Buck could wait one more day. "We'll talk about it tomorrow. How would you like to help me select a new dress for your wedding? Or do you have to get back to the shop?"

"Be serious—I own the store."

The two women left the restaurant.

On the way back to camp, Summer told Buck and Angus about the forthcoming wedding. They were both surprised. Though neither of the men had met Norman Picket, they had certainly heard of him when they were traveling the country in search of Toddle. They said he had a reputation for being a fair and honest man.

"Tell me," Angus said as Buck brought the team to a halt, "you two planning on staying in separate bedrooms until you get married?"

Summer's face turned scarlet and the men laughed.

"That's an issue I plan to discuss with my betrothed as soon as I can get rid of your ugly face,"
Buck replied.

That night Buck moved into Summer's bedroom.
She protested, but not hard enough to make him
change his mind.

It wasn't until almost dawn that Buck and Summer lay satiated in each other's arms. Summer was
positive there was nothing as wonderful as having
the man she loved remain in bed until morning.
Buck did indeed have a most healthy appetite, and
there would no longer be nights of wrestling with
unfulfilled desires.

"Do you still love me now that I'm a scarlet
woman?" Summer teased.

"Especially now that you're a scarlet woman. It
makes the loving so much easier." He hugged her
to him.

"Buck, since we're going to be married, don't
you think we should start out by not keeping secrets from each other."

He ran his hand up her bare thigh. "You have
such soft skin. I never tire of feeling it."

"Please, Buck, can't we talk?"

"Very well, if we must," he said jokingly. He
rolled over on his back. "Now, sweet love, what
terrible dark secrets have you been keeping from
me?"

"I wasn't referring to myself."

"Oh? Am I the one with the dark secrets? Pray
tell, where did you come up with that notion?"

"If you were a wanted man, you would trust me
enough to say so, wouldn't you?"

Buck was at a complete loss as to what she was
talking about. "What makes you think I might be
wanted?"

"You're avoiding my question."

"Answer mine, and I'll answer yours."

"Buck, please don't do this. If we can't share our feelings with each other, we'll never have a happy marriage. I couldn't stand it if I thought you would keep things from me. For some time now, I've considered the possibility that you may have been a robber—especially since it's obvious you despise banks." She propped herself up on her elbow and looked down at him. "You are an educated man, but you never discuss your past. Now, in case I've added two and two and come up with five, I want you to tell me why. If you are wanted, then naturally that would affect where we are going to live."

He laughed. "I'm not wanted, Summer, so you have nothing to worry about along those lines. I was born and raised in St. Louis and worked for a bank. From the time I left, I have never wanted to live in a city again."

"Oh." Summer shifted to a more comfortable position.

"What does that mean?"

"Nothing."

"I thought you were the one who just said we should discuss things."

"Well, I thought we might live in a town, or at least nearby."

Philadelphia immediately came to Buck's mind. "Maybe we could buy some land and build a house on it."

Buck knew that if she continued this line of thought, she was going to end up ruining his surprise. He leaned back on the pillow and let the little white lie slip like silk from a spool. "I thought we could just pack up and go into the mountains. We could build us a nice little cabin and there wouldn't be a soul to bother us."

"Away from civilization?"

"There will be nothing for you to worry about. We'll be just fine."

"How would I have children? You do want children, don't you?"

"Oh, I think about a dozen would be just right. Women have babies in the mountains all the time. The question is, do you love me enough to forego the luxuries you were raised with?"

"Do I love you enough? Oh, I love you enough to go anywhere you say, but I just can't understand why it's necessary. Why can't we live in Denver, or even here?"

"I would never be happy. But it's your choice. If you choose Denver, that's where we'll live."

Summer curled up against him. "I couldn't ask that of you if you feel so strongly about it. We'll live in your mountains." She yawned. "But maybe someday we can visit my family in Philadelphia."

"We'll see." Buck came close to telling her it was all poppycock, but didn't. He couldn't wait to see her face when he told her the truth. And if she got mad at him for leading her along, well, he'd know just how to smooth her feathers.

Summer was in a state of euphoria as she prepared for their guests. Sharing a life with Buck was the most beautiful thing she could possibly think of. Living in the mountains away from people didn't have much appeal, but they would be together. Besides, she'd felt the same way when he had brought her here, and she had come to love the mountains. If living away from everyone meant Buck would be happy, then that's what she wanted.

When their guests arrived, Summer was pleasantly surprised to see how young and nice-looking

Lorna's fiancè was. He had blond hair, sky-blue eyes, and a most ingratiating smile. While the men discussed mining, Lorna and Summer went out to see the buggy.

"It's so beautiful," Lorna said, as she ran her hand along the glossy black front. "Are you sure you want to give it to me?"

"More than ever now."

Lorna looked at her friend. "Now? What does that mean? Oh, Summer. Don't tell me you're going back home!"

"I didn't want to say anything yesterday, what with you telling me about your marriage plans. But I want you to know that Buck and I are also getting married."

"How wonderful!" Lorna practically screamed the words. "I knew it! I absolutely knew it. When?"

"I have some business to take care of in Denver, so we'll be married there."

"Oh, Summer, I'm so happy for you. Buck is such a wonderful man. I'm glad to hear you'll be living nearby."

"I'm not sure where we'll be living, but it won't be here. Buck wants to live in the mountains away from everyone."

"That's ridiculous. A woman like you can't be happy living in the wilds."

"What do you mean, 'a woman like me'? I've certainly managed to do fine here."

"Now, don't go getting your dander up. I simply meant that with Buck's money, I would think he would want to give you the conveniences you're used to."

Summer smiled. "Lorna, if Buck is happy, I'll be happy. You might be surprised at what I can adjust to."

"You're probably right," Lorna said, but she still

had strong reservations. Seeing Summer standing there dressed to perfection in her pink day dress, her thick auburn hair perfectly styled atop her head, it was very difficult for Lorna to visualize it.

Everyone came to the wedding, which was held in the firehouse. Lorna looked beautiful in her white wedding dress, and Norman was handsomely attired in a gray suit. Buck held Summer's hand while she cried, and there were still tears in her eyes as she wished the bride and groom happiness.

A party followed, with plenty of food and music. Summer danced with most of the men, and this time there were no snide remarks. These were people she'd come to know and like, and she knew she'd be sad to leave what she now considered her home.

Though it hadn't been so long ago that Summer couldn't wait to return to Denver, the days now passed too quickly. The two partners went back to spending most of their time in the mine, but Summer knew that, come nightfall, her beloved Buck would be by her side.

Lying in her arms, he had finally told her of his past. Summer felt his pain when he spoke of his family, and she came to understand why he thought of women as being shallow and materialistic.

Most of all she loved listening to his stories about when he was a trapper. She was amazed to find out he had actually made friends with a wolf pack.

Too soon, the day had come for them to head back to Denver. While Angus and Buck loaded the pack horses, Summer walked through her house.

There were so many memories. The furniture from Angus and Charley, the stove, the table where they'd all sat and enjoyed suppers, and even the bed on which she and Buck had shared so much bliss. She would never see them again, because Buck planned on going straight into the mountains when they left Denver.

"We're ready to go, Angel," Buck said softly.

Summer jumped. She hadn't heard him enter the bedroom. "I want to say good-bye to Charley, then I'll be ready. Is everything in order in the mine?"

"Yes. The men we left to run it are honest and will do a good job."

Even though she tried to sound cheerful, Buck could see the sorrow in her emerald-green eyes. Again he almost capitulated and told her about the spread near Denver. But he stopped himself just in time. Angus had given him all kinds of hell for what he was doing, but Buck remained steadfast.

"Good-bye, my sweet Charley," Summer said as she stood over the grave. "You'll always be in my heart." She turned and walked away.

Perched on a sidesaddle atop a horse much better than the nag she'd arrived on, Summer followed Buck and Angus out of camp.

It was a glorious morning, and she soon went to work trying to cheer herself up. After all, she told herself, I'm beginning a new life that will be full of adventure. She looked at the two broad backs ahead, and suddenly realized there was something she had failed to take into consideration: Angus.

Over the past weeks she'd thought of very little except the love she shared with Buck. She hadn't given any thought to Angus not being with them when they left Denver.

Whenever she had looked toward the future, it had always included the three of them together, or four if Angus took a wife. It didn't seem right that she and Buck should leave him. Saddened again, she tried concentrating on Milly and how good it would be to see her.

"I think you've carried this bit about returning to the mountains too damn far, Buck!"

"You've already told me, Angus." Buck turned in the saddle and glanced back at Summer. She did seem a little glum.

"Did you see the look on her face when we rode out of camp?" Angus continued. "Hell, she even said she'd go with you up into the mountains, though I haven't the faintest idea why. It must be because she loves you, you damn ass."

"All right," Buck finally said, hating to give up his surprise, but seeing his friend's point. "You're right, Angus. I'll tell her."

"When?"

"Tonight."

They made camp that night beside a swiftly flowing stream. "The water's much higher than when I came up last year," Summer said when Angus brought her water for cooking. She watched him place it on the hook rod above the campfire.

"They call it Clear Creek, and this is Clear Creek Canyon. The reason the water is so high is because of the melting snow. I always thought it was awfully pretty through here, with the rock towering up to the sky."

"I agree. What do you plan on doing after we leave, Angus? Will you stay at the mine?"

"I haven't decided. I do know I'm going to remain in Denver for awhile. It wouldn't be right if I didn't give the women a chance to chase me."

"I have no doubt that is exactly what will happen. I shall miss you."

Angus cursed silently. By all that was holy, if Buck didn't make things right tonight, he'd take care of it the first thing in the morning. "We should reach Denver around noon tomorrow. So before that happens, I want to say I'm sorry for all we put you through Summer. I wouldn't change it for a moment, though. You did more for us than we could've ever expected."

Summer reached over and took his hand. "I wouldn't change it either, Angus. And I should be the one thanking you. I'm sorry I couldn't have fallen in love with you or Charley, but you know I will always hold a place in my heart for you."

"I know. Where's Buck?"

"He went down to a place where he said he could bathe in the creek. How he can even stand putting that cold water on him is beyond me." She dropped the cooked meat she'd brought into the water. "Food's going to be sparse tonight." The statement was more to herself than to Angus. She sat on one of the bedrolls while the meat was heated. "Angus, is something wrong with Buck? I mean, is he upset about something?"

"He'll be fine when you take him to bed."

"You are terrible!"

Angus let out a robust laugh. "You wouldn't have teased me like that when you first came to the cabin."

Summer smiled. "Heavens, no. I didn't dare."

They all bedded down early that night. As always, Summer felt quite safe in Buck's arms. She hadn't realized how exhausted she was from the day's ride. "I'm going to miss Angus," she mumbled, her eyelids already heavy.

The night air was cold and she snuggled close to Buck, his body heat keeping her warm. Even the bright moonlight wasn't going to keep her awake.

"Honey, I know you're tired, but I have something important to tell you."

"Can't it wait until tomorrow?" she asked, already half asleep.

"No, you need to know this now."

"Very well, what is it you want to say?"

"We won't be moving to the mountains to live, Angel."

"All right."

"I know I was wrong to lead you along, but . . ."

"What do you mean by, 'leading me along'?" she asked drowsily.

Buck decided to spit it out and get it over with. "I never had any intention of us going to the mountains to live."

Summer was suddenly wide awake. "You mean you lied?"

"I guess you could say that. But there was a reason."

Summer jerked away and threw the covering off. "Reason or no reason . . ." She jumped to her feet. "Do you have any idea what I suffered just knowing I would never see my friends again, or Angus? Let alone trying to adjust to the fact of living in the wilds! How dare you do this to me!"

"If you'd just let me explain—"

"Of all the stupid, arrogant men I've ever known, I think you, Buck Holester, are the prize! Angus, move over. I'll be sleeping with you."

"But, darlin'—" Angus sputtered.

"Summer, you come right back here!"

"Don't order me around, Mister Holester. I'm not your wife yet. And at the moment, I'm not sure

I ever will be. Angus, are you going to let me share your bedding or not? It's not as if we are in our nightclothes!"

"You do have a point."

Buck stood, looking like an avenging angel. "You let her sleep with you and I'll beat the hell out of you."

Angus raised the cover for Summer to climb under.

"If you start a fight, Buck Holester, I promise I will never speak to you again."

Buck was so furious, he went to one of the horses, slipped the hobble, then looped a lead rope around the horse's neck.

"You can't just ride off!" Summer demanded.

Grabbing a handful of mane, he easily swung himself up. The horse leaped forward, then suddenly Buck neck-reined him around. Before Summer even had a chance to duck, Buck reached down and snatched her up. "Meet you down the trail," Buck hollered as he rode off.

Angus laughed. Now this is the Buck I know, he thought.

Summer felt like she was in a jar of pickles, being bounced up and down. Buck's arm was around her waist, the horse was in a full gallop, and she could actually see the ground flying beneath her. This was even worse than the first time he'd ridden off with her. She was scared half to death, and tried saying something, but couldn't. The air kept getting knocked out of her. Then, with seemingly no effort, Buck raised her up and sat her sideways in front of him. Summer became more terrified as she remembered that the rocky trail could be treacherous during the day, and this was night. "Buck," she pleaded, "the horse might stumble!" He began laughing, and Summer couldn't help but wonder if he had lost his mind.

"Tell me you love me, sweet Summer of mine, and I may just give it some consideration."

"Yes! I love you!"

"How much?"

She also started laughing when she realized he was playing with her. "Not enough to get killed for," she teased back.

Buck slowed the horse down. "Have you ever been made love to on a horse?"

"You know I haven't." The very thought of it made her body come alive.

"If you didn't have those heavy riding clothes on, I'd show you how it can be done." He brought the horse to a halt. "I'm more than a little tempted to just rip them off."

"It would be my pleasure to have you tear my clothes off, sir, but don't you think I'd look pretty ridiculous when we rode into town?" She curled her arms around his neck. "Oh, Buck, why didn't you tell me the truth?"

"I wanted to surprise you, honey." But he couldn't wait a moment longer to claim her lips. His tongue entered her mouth, and she moaned with pleasure as she rubbed her breasts against his chest. "Woman," he whispered as he pulled away, "do you have any idea what you do to me?"

"If it's anything compared to what you do to me, then it must be truly glorious. Buck, show me how it's done on a horse."

"I can see I've made you into a wanton woman. Unfortunately, it would be too dangerous here. But rest assured, my love, it will be something we'll share in the future." He started unbuttoning the front of her riding jacket, his loins already throbbing. She hadn't worn a corset because of the rigors of the ride, and her silk chemise was smooth beneath his hand. "God I love feeling your nipples. You have such beautiful breasts." He leaned over and suckled on the pointed tips, molding the silk to her like a second skin.

"Oh, Buck, I don't think I can wait for you to undress me."

He gently lowered her to the ground before sliding off the horse's back. As he secured the animal, Summer undid the buttons at the waist of her skirt and let the heavy material fall to the ground. She watched him remove his boots, then his pants as she untied her pantalettes.

Unexpectedly, he turned her around so her back was to him. "What are you doing? Please Buck, take me now," she pleaded, her voice husky, her desire demanding.

His arms circled her and with a swift jerk, the silk chemise tore and his hands were cupping her bare breasts. Summer shivered with delight. He leaned her over the boulder in front of her. It felt rough against her stomach, but she paid little heed when, to her surprise, Buck entered her from behind.

As one powerful thrust followed another, her head began spinning with unbelievable pleasure. "Yes," she encouraged, "oh God, yes." He was driving her mad each time he moved rapidly in and out. Then with a hard thrust, lifting her off her feet, he remained deep within her, and she screamed as one sensation after another exploded within her.

Buck could feel her throbbing inside. Never had she given herself to him so thoroughly, caring not a whit that she might be heard. Her scream caused him to grow hard again, and slowly he began moving in and out, still feeling her pulsing against his manhood. When he pushed deep within her and waited, he was delighted to feel her hips begin to rotate—she was using him to recapture the rapture she'd just experienced. Though the night was cold, he could feel the moisture trickling down between her breasts. He slid his hands down to her narrow waist and lifted her up and down. They were both gasping for breath as their desire reached wild, uninhibited proportions.

Unable to remain still another moment, he withdrew and turned her around so she was facing him. His urgent need became even stronger as he gazed at her damp body glistening in the moonlight. Her tongue circled her parted lips and she brazenly pushed her breasts forward.

Standing before him was more woman than he'd ever believed possible. The lioness was forever released from her cage. He pressed her against the rock and slid into her with a wildness that was matched by hers. She sucked on his neck and her fingernails dug into his back, then she stiffened and arched, her wide eyes staring into his. Buck grinned, and gave one last, hard thrust, his seed spilling inside her as wave after wave plunged over both of them.

Chapter 16

The next day, as the threesome and their pack horses neared Denver, nothing looked familiar to Summer. She couldn't recall having crossed the Platte River or the Larimer Street Bridge so many months back. But it had been dark and at the time she wasn't exactly paying attention to where Buck was taking her.

As they continued down Larimer Street, Summer thought Denver now looked like a utopia instead of the hole in the road she remembered. It was so big. Even the clothing the people wore seemed fashionable to her now. It was amazing how her viewpoint had changed since living in the mountains.

Summer swelled with pride as sophisticated-looking women offered friendly smiles to Buck and Angus as they rode by. However, when they acted the perfect gentlemen and nodded their acknowledgement, Summer felt a twinge of jealousy, particularly over Buck. But she certainly wasn't excluded from the attention. Gentlemen readily tipped their hats to her.

It wasn't until the small group dismounted in front of the Tremont House that Summer suddenly thought about their accommodations. "Darling," she said, taking Buck's arm, "don't be unhappy with me, but I really think I should have a private room."

Buck frowned. "Why?"

"I expect Milly or William to be visiting."

"I don't give a damn what they think."

"Please, Buck, try to understand. It's important to me."

"She has a point, partner," Angus chimed in. "Why start a lot of gossip?"

"Very well," Buck conceded. "Angus and I will room together."

"Sorry, but I'm getting my own room. I rather liked that attention we received when we came into town, and I don't want you around if a lady is gracious enough to share her favors. It's been a long dry spell."

As they entered the lobby, Summer noted the polished furniture and hardwood floors with expensive rugs scattered about. Well dressed men and women were coming and going, making Summer feel dowdy.

"You could have visited Maybelle's, Angus," Buck commented.

Angus laughed. "Not as long as I thought I had a chance with Summer. But since you snatched her from under my nose—"

"Both of you hush," Summer scolded. "Someone might hear."

After informing the smiling clerk that they wanted three rooms on the same floor, Buck, Angus, and Summer each signed the register.

"I'd like a bathing tub and water sent to my room immediately," Summer ordered the clerk. "Also, would you happen to know where the lawyer William Nielson lives?"

"No, but I can find out for you."

"Good. Send a boy up as soon as possible. I'll have a note I want delivered there."

"Make that two baths," Buck said.

"Three," Angus added.

"Buck," Summer said as they headed for their rooms, "I would very much like to go shopping. I want to be appropriately dressed when I call on William and Milly this afternoon."

His saddlebags slung over one shoulder, Buck stopped and looked down at Summer. Was he mistaken, or did Summer sound like her old haughty self? "What's wrong with the clothes you have?"

"It's only natural that I would want to look my best."

Buck tipped his hat back. "Do you feel a need to impress someone?"

Summer resented his innuendo. "Why are you being difficult about this? You can take it out of the money I'm supposed to be paid for my services, or even my share of the mine!"

Buck eyes turned metal gray. "Don't do this, Summer."

"What are you talking about?"

"I don't like it one damn bit when the woman I'm supposed to marry wants to look special for another man, and you become snippy about *your* money."

"It is my money!"

Buck flexed the muscles in his jaw. "I'll see to it that a buggy is at your disposal, as well as a line of credit."

"Thank you." Summer entered her room and slammed the door behind her.

"I'll be glad when you two get married," Angus said. "Maybe then you'll both settle down."

"If she keeps this up she may live in the mountains after all."

"You think Summer is getting decked out for William?"

"Sure seems like it."

Angus shifted his weight and stared at Summer's closed door. "We could always make sure he leaves town."

"Don't tempt me. While Summer's shopping, you want to pay Howard Jackson a visit and see about buying land?"

"As soon as I get this trail dust off."

The errand boy, copper tub, water, and Summer's satchels all arrived at the same time. She gave the note she'd already written to the errand boy, then proceeded to shoo everyone out. Still angry with Buck for the way he'd acted, Summer quickly undressed. The moment she sank into the hot foamy water, her body relaxed. Why was Buck acting this way? He'd known all along she planned on seeing William and Milly. She suddenly laughed. Buck was jealous!

William sat at the imposing desk in his office, his face red with anger after having read Summer's note saying she was at the Tremont House and would be paying a call to his residence at three this afternoon. Toddle was supposed to have taken care of that problem. But Toddle had failed him and had even threatened him with blackmail, which is why he'd been forced to have him taken care of. At least the two men William had working for him now seemed more adept.

William felt reasonably certain he had assuaged Milly by apologizing for the way he'd acted. He'd even managed to excuse himself by saying he'd acted out of his obsessive love for her. He'd been afraid she'd leave him once she found out Summer was safe. Milly still looked at him with a glint of suspicion, so from the time she'd threatened him, he'd made a point of conducting business at his law office in town.

He leaned forward and glanced again at the handwritten note still in his hand. Summer would have to be dealt with soon. There were people at the Tremont House who were aware they were acquainted, so at the moment, removing her didn't seem wise. On the other hand, he could always say she was seeking legal advice. Still, if Milly got the least inkling of something happening to Summer, he would be the first one she'd accuse. The one thing he didn't want was Summer staying in his home. If Milly was correct about Summer not wanting to marry him—and obviously Milly wasn't inclined in that direction either—hopefully they would leave on the next stage. If not, he would eventually have to make some sort of final arrangement for them.

He quickly scribbled two notes, one to be delivered to the O'Leary boardinghouse where his hired men were staying. The other one was for Summer, saying he'd send a carriage for her at three.

When Summer left her room, Buck was leaving his.

Summer smiled. "You know we're both acting silly. Buck, William means nothing to me."

"You'd damn well better be right, Angel." He pulled her to him and kissed her. "I've turned into a possessive man," he whispered in her ear.

"I love only you."

"I'll try to remember that." He kissed the tip of her nose, stepped back, and smiled. "Since you're off to purchase clothes, why not buy something special for when you and I go out tonight?"

"Maybe," she said mischievously.

Buck laughed aloud. "I'll be looking forward to it."

Summer couldn't believe her luck when she went into a shop and found exactly what she was looking for. The seamstress had just completed a town dress that she claimed was an exact copy of a gown by Charles Worth. She had made it to show to a wealthy customer, but since only a few tucks at the waist were needed, she gladly sold it to Summer at an outrageous price.

After the crinoline cage was placed over the lace-trimmed pantalettes, two petticoats followed. The third was white with several starched flounces. Then came the last underskirt of muslin. Over that went a white, beautifully embroidered tunic. The seamstress boasted that the bottom was four yards in circumference. The bodice, pale blue with a darker blue skirt, allowed the tunic to peep out at the bottom. The bolero jacket matched the skirt and was trimmed in an even darker blue. A sash of the same color circled her waist and tied in a large bow with long wide tails. Even after refusing to wear the horsehair underskirt, Summer felt weighed down. She certainly didn't remember everything being so heavy before. At least her corset was much lighter than the ones her mother used to wear. But all things considered, Summer left the small shop feeling elegant and self-assured. Unfortunately she was running short on time and wasn't able to purchase a dress for that evening.

Ernie walked straight into William's office and closed the door behind him so the clerk couldn't overhear their conversation.

"Well," William impatiently asked the dark-skinned man, "did you deliver my message to Miss Caldwell?"

"No. According to what you said in my note, Miss Caldwell was alone. But when I headed down the hall toward her room, I found her standing in plain view kissin' a giant of a man with black hair. I checked at the desk and found out his name is Buck Holester. I thought you'd want to know."

William slammed the law book down so hard the large volume bounced. "One of the damn miners came with her! That jaded woman has to be driven out of town. I'll need to take care of this Mister Holester as well."

"You wantin' Kelly and me to handle it?"

"Not now. Stay around the boardinghouse so I can get in touch with you. I'm going to the house. I'll be back later."

"Milly?" William called as he knocked on her bedroom door. "Are you in there?"

"Looking for me?" Milly asked from the bottom of the stairs.

Why is the woman never where she's supposed to be, William wondered angrily. "Yes, dear," he replied. "I have marvelous news." He went back down. "Summer is in town."

Tears of joy filled Milly's brown eyes. "Oh, William! How wonderful! Where is she?"

"According to the note I received, she's staying at the Tremont. She'll be here at three this afternoon."

Milly smiled. "I would never have thought she'd come down so early."

"What do you mean?"

"Nothing, Willy. I must talk to the cook. I want to serve something very special when she comes."

Milly took off toward the kitchen, barely able to contain her excitement. She couldn't wait to see

Summer and hear all about her marvelous adventures in the wilds.

William waited until Milly left the kitchen before cornering her again. "Dearest, will you invite Summer to dine with us tonight? I regret I have a client coming to the office and I won't be back until supper. I'd very much like to visit with Summer."

"After the things you've said?"

"How many times do I have to apologize? Rest assured, I will be on my best behavior. I know it's important to you. I have come to accept that you and I will never marry, and I'm trying the best way I know to make amends. What more can you ask of me?"

Milly could feel nothing but exasperation. Still, she said, "I'm sorry, William, and you're absolutely right. You have acted the perfect gentleman as of late. Thank you for welcoming her."

"Well, I must be on my way. I only came home to tell you the good news."

"Thank you. You know, as soon as Summer is rested we will be leaving to return home."

"Yes," he said sadly, "I understand that. I shall miss you, but I realize now that it's for the best."

When Summer arrived, the two women hugged, kissed, and cried. Milly laughed while wiping tears from her cheeks. "I have never seen you looking better, my dear. Obviously your little jaunt agreed with you."

Looking at Milly's mint-colored silk suit, Summer was glad she had bought the new dress. Milly led her into the opulent parlor, a room Summer found stuffy and overcrowded.

"Oh, Summer, you simply do not know how much I've missed you. I can hardly wait to hear what you've been doing. Tell me all about it while we have tea."

After they were seated with their tea served in delicate china cups and a variety of pastries placed on the table to choose from, Milly turned to her friend. "Now, I want to hear everything. I've waited so long." She leaned back in her chair and made herself comfortable. "Start from the beginning, and don't leave out a single detail. How were you kidnapped, and why?"

"Milly, it's a story even I would find hard to believe."

Summer started at the beginning and soon had Milly laughing. At other times her face showed concern and worry, especially when Summer got to the part about the cave-in.

Summer glanced at the window and was surprised to see it getting dark outside. "Milly, I hate to leave, but I really must."

"You can't desert me now. Did Buck survive?"

"Yes, and I'll finish telling you the rest tomorrow. Oh, Milly, you have no idea how often I needed your advice."

"Believe me, darling, I've had similar feelings. I even thought about going up the mountain and joining you. Summer, you must have supper with us. William is looking forward to seeing you."

"I'd hoped he'd be here this afternoon. I wanted to tell him that I'm turning down his proposal of marriage."

"Then tell him this evening. He's quite expecting it, you know. I told him. But I think you should explain it to him yourself."

"You're right, of course. Unfortunately, I have nothing to wear."

"Then hurry upstairs with me. I still have all your clothes."

Summer quickly glanced through her clothes. Having forgotten what she'd brought, she oohed and ahhed over the lovely silk, brocade, and velvet gowns, most of which had never been worn. Prior to coming to the Colorado Territory, she'd spent months with dressmakers, preparing a wardrobe that would make William proud.

Then Buck Holester had stolen into her room and swept her away, leaving these lovely clothes behind. She could hardly wait for Buck to see her dressed in her finest. She laughed to herself, just remembering how she'd trekked all around camp those first few days with nothing on but that nightdress.

"Very well, Milly, I'll be back for supper, but I have to hurry because it's getting late. Angus and Buck will be worried." She pulled out a violet watered silk gown.

"Oh, I didn't think about that. Of course they would be there. How else would you have made it back? Did Charley remain at the mine?"

Summer didn't want to talk about Charley at the moment. "Tomorrow you must come to see me at the Tremont House, and we'll have the entire day to talk." She looked at her friend. "Milly, I would rather William knew nothing of what I've told you."

"I don't trust William, Summer, and I think it would be wise if he didn't know Angus and Buck are with you. I know you're in a hurry, so we'll discuss it tomorrow."

Summer wasn't the least surprised when Buck opened his hotel room door the minute she opened hers. He looked magnificent in his new gray trousers and satin vest over a white shirt, and she could see he'd been to the barber. Summer felt guilty for having agreed to dine with Milly and William. How could she have been so thoughtless?

Buck followed Summer into her room. "That day

dress is most charming." He paused to look it over properly. "You were absolutely right about the clothes you have not being good enough." He made himself comfortable on the nearest chair. "I was beginning to wonder when you'd return."

"I'm sorry, darling, but Milly and I started talking and the time passed too quickly." Feeling more than a little nervous about informing Buck of her plans for the night, she walked to the bed and laid down the watered silk gown.

"So you did buy something for tonight," Buck said with a grin. "Should I go to my room and let you astound me when I see you in it?"

Summer felt wretched. "This . . . I didn't . . . this is one of the dresses I brought from Philadelphia." She turned and faced him. He was in such a jovial mood. "Buck, please don't be upset, but I told Milly I'd have dinner with her and William tonight. To-morrow night we can—"

"You did tell Nielson you won't be marrying him?"

"He wasn't at the house. I plan on telling him tonight."

"I see."

Summer could tell he was peeved. "Buck, I'm trying to do what I think is right. I won't be gone long."

"It's getting dark out, so I guess you'd better get ready."

"Yes, I guess I should." Summer expected Buck to leave, but he didn't budge an inch.

When Summer put on the violet dress, hard un-giving jealousy twisted in Buck's gut. The decol-letage was deep, showing a good degree of bosom and leaving her creamy neck and shoulders ex-posed. The tight bodice was molded to her body, and the full skirt practically floated. He watched her place his diamond necklace around her neck.

Her toilette complete, Summer turned stiff circles. "Do I meet with your approval?" she asked, trying to keep her voice light.

She was without a doubt the most beautiful creature Buck had ever seen and it infuriated him to know she had dressed for William, not him. "Send the banker a note and be done with it."

"Buck, don't order me," Summer warned. "Why are you doing this? After tonight we'll be together for the rest of our lives." Summer gasped. "You don't trust me, do you?"

"May I ask why they didn't come here to dine with us, or why I wasn't asked to supper since we are supposed to be getting married?"

Besides the jolting realization that Buck placed no faith in her, Summer knew she couldn't tell him about Milly's warning. At least not until she found out more details. It would be just like Angus or Buck to confront William. "I haven't told them about us."

"I think that deserves an explanation."

"I'll tell them, but—"

"When?"

Summer looked into his hard eyes. His whole attitude was making her angry. "I don't think it would be proper until I've at least informed William of my decision regarding him. Milly will be here in the morning, and I'll tell her then." She didn't bother to hide her annoyance. "You'll like her," she added.

Even though he knew in his gut he wasn't being fair, Buck still said, "I liked her the first time I saw her."

"That's right," Summer snapped at him. "You were going to take her instead of me, if I remember correctly."

They both knew their tempers were leading them into treacherous waters, but neither seemed able to stop.

"I love you, Summer, but I don't like you being in the house of the man you came here to marry. If by tonight you haven't told your friends that we're to be wed, then I am going to be sorely tempted to find solace elsewhere."

"And I don't like being given ultimatums!"

Buck rose and left. He was standing in the middle of his room, fists clenched, when he heard Summer's door open and close. Even though he knew his jealousy was uncalled for, it took every ounce of control he could muster to keep from going after her and taking off for the mountains.

By the time Summer's buggy stopped in front of William's house, her anger had dissipated and she was chiding herself for agreeing to come. Buck had every right to be angry. He had expected her to inform William she would not be marrying him. She was tempted to turn around, but didn't. She should have thought of these things before agreeing to come to supper.

When the maid led Summer into the parlor, Milly was seated on the sofa and William stood by the window. Even dressed in fine attire, William didn't impress her. One glance made Summer wonder what she could ever have seen in him. He was slender and his hair well groomed, but his facial features reminded her of a hawk. There was an effeminate quality about him when he moved toward her. She didn't even remember him being so short.

"My dear Summer. It is so good to see you." William raised Summer's hand, and kissed her knuckles. "I had forgotten just how lovely you are," he said honestly. She looked more mature and was now one of the most beautiful women he'd ever seen. "Please have a seat by Milly," he said, leading her to the sofa. "Supper will be ready shortly. Would you care for some port?"

"Yes, please."

William pulled the tassel and a butler immediately stepped into the room.

"We're ready for our drinks, Henry." He instructed the gray-headed man as to what he and the ladies wanted before taking a seat on the brocade chair.

"So," William said after the drinks were served, "it is my understanding you have been teaching some miners how to become gentlemen. A seemingly impossible task. Were you the least bit successful?"

"Yes, they are very bright men."

William's eyes found Summer's decolletage, and he decided then and there that if he could, he would enjoy the pleasures she had freely shared with the backwoods miners before he shipped Miss Caldwell out of town.

Summer knew that to delay informing William of her reason for being here would be a mistake, especially after Buck's threat. "William, it was so nice of you to let me dine here tonight, but I came only to decline your offer of marriage."

William took a sip of his drink. "Yes. Well, I'm not surprised. Milly had already informed me. But I have a confession to make. While you were gone, I came to realize I wasn't in love with you. You see, I've fallen in love with Milly."

Summer's eyes were round circles as she looked at her friend.

"However," William continued, "she has also turned down my proposal. So it would appear that if I am to marry, I must look elsewhere."

Poor William, Summer thought before taking a quick drink of her port. She felt guilty.

"Summer," Milly said, "I must tell you what I've been doing while you were gone. William has been such a gracious host."

William expelled a grunt. He wanted to hear about Summer's escapades, not Milly's.

Even after they had gone into the dining room, Milly monopolized the conversation. She talked about everything from the social affairs she'd attended, to the plays she'd seen at the Langrishe Theater, to William's political career and even William's aunt's funeral. Summer came to realize she hadn't missed anything. Her life in the mountains had been much more exciting.

William was being driven to distraction. Every time he tried asking Summer a question, Milly would say they could talk about that later. Later never came. After dinner, Summer said she had to return to Tremont House.

"Milly, you will come to see me tomorrow?" Summer asked as William placed her cloak over her shoulders.

Milly smiled. "Bright and early. I'll also see that your clothes are delivered."

When Summer left, she ordered the driver to hurry. She was anxious to tell Buck that she'd told William everything. Now all she wanted was to be held in his strong arms for the rest of her life. Tonight had made her see just how important that was. Buck was right. He was the one she should have dressed for, not William. Pride could be a terrible thing.

It had been almost two hours since Summer left, and whether she liked it or not, Buck had made up his mind to go to William's house and fetch her.

He'd procured the address over an hour ago from the desk clerk. Buck threw on his coat. He'd had a long talk with himself about trusting Summer and letting his jealousy get the better of him. True, he didn't want Summer remaining under William's roof any longer than necessary, but she'd already had plenty of time to tell the man she wasn't going to marry him. Besides all that, Buck now had another concern. He was worried about her coming home alone so late at night.

The knock on his door startled Buck. He knew it couldn't be Angus because he'd taken off hours ago for a night on the town. Thinking it had to be Summer, he flung open the door and was surprised to see a marshal and a dark-skinned man standing before him.

"Is this the one?" the marshal asked the stranger.

"Yep. That's him. Don't let them fancy clothes fool you, Marshal. He's the man who stole my horses a couple of days back."

The marshal drew his gun on Buck. "Mister, you're going to jail. We don't take to horse thieves in this part of the country. Now I don't want no trouble, but if you don't come peacefully, I'll pull the trigger."

"The man's lying! I never stole his damn horses."

"We'll let the judge decide that."

Summer let out a sigh of relief when she arrived at the Tremont House. She hurried up the stairs. Coming to a halt in front of Buck's room, she tapped on the door and waited. A moment later she rapped on it harder. Still no answer. Summer tried the door and, finding it unlocked, entered. Buck was not in his room. Summer was furious. Had he left so soon for his so-called solace? Could she have hurt him that deeply, or was he just looking for an excuse?

Going back into the hall, Summer tried Angus' door, but there was no reply there either. Not knowing what else to do, she went to her own room and lit the lantern. She'd change her clothes and wait.

By the time an hour had gone by, Summer's fury had turned into deep hurt. She loved Buck with an intensity of passion that was almost frightening. How could he go to the arms of another woman? There was no doubt in her mind that that's where he was because, as he'd proven many times, he always did what he said he would. She even remembered the encouragement the women had given him when they rode into town this morning. Going to the chest of drawers, she pulled out the lapel watch she'd bought. It was already two in the morning. Tears began flowing down her cheeks. Why couldn't he have waited?

When Summer awoke, it was already daylight. She had been determined to wait up for Buck's return so she could confront him. Rising from the chair she'd fallen asleep in and ignoring her cramped body, she marched out of her room and into Buck's. No one was there. The bed wasn't even mussed.

Chapter 17

⌐◦◦◦⌐

"Milly," Summer said as she marched into her friend's bedroom, "I want to leave immediately for Philadelphia."

"Immediately? Aren't we being a bit hasty?" Milly motioned the maid to remove her breakfast tray. "Bring a tray for Miss Caldwell, Jenny."

"I couldn't eat a thing," Summer insisted.

"Nonsense. And Jenny, bring coffee also." Milly slid out of bed, then put on the satin and lace robe that matched her nightdress. "Come over here and sit down, Summer." She motioned to a small table and two chairs. "I can see by the look on your face that something has happened. You've been crying."

Tears started tickling down Summer's cheeks again, and Milly handed her a handkerchief.

"Now, tell me what has you so upset."

"Oh, Milly, Buck spent the night with another woman," Summer sobbed.

"Ah. So you fell in love with the black-headed devil, and now he's broken your heart. Does he love you?"

"I thought he did, but how could he do something like this? Milly, we were supposed to get married!"

"Married?" Milly clapped her hands and

laughed with delight. "This is wonderful."

"I'm glad you think so."

Still smiling, Milly studied her friend. She would never have believed Summer would actually wear a plain calico that was completely out of fashion. Yet oddly enough, it was quite becoming. "I have a feeling that when you were telling me your story yesterday, you left something out. Now I want to hear the rest, and this time include everything."

Summer blushed.

"You won't shock me. Start from the cave-in."

Summer continued her story, and without realizing it, ate most of the breakfast the maid had returned with. The tears flowed again when she came to the part about the fire and Charley's death. Even Milly had to brush away a few.

"Oh, Summer," Milly said when the tale was finished, "I had no idea." She leaned over and patted her friend's hand. "But I must admit, I envy you. Even with the sad parts. Oh, Summer, what an adventure you've had, and what a love you've shared with Buck. I haven't been fortunate enough to find such a love."

"Love? How can you call it love?" Summer blew her red nose, and Milly handed her another handkerchief.

"Because, my dear, that's exactly what it is. From all that you've told me, Charley, Angus, and Buck are, or were, three charming and wonderful men. But Buck was the most hesitant to face marriage and certainly to give his love. Though you might find it hard to believe, there are men who love only one woman in their entire life. I believe Buck is one of those men. I also believe you are of a similar nature."

"If that's true, why did he turn to another woman?"

"I don't know that he did, nor do you. But running away isn't the answer. If you love him as much as you claim to then you should be willing to fight for him. I have a feeling Buck isn't sure of your love either, not from what you've told me. Only by forgiving him, no matter what he's done, will you finally prove how much he means to you."

"And what about the next time he feels an itch?"

Milly laughed softly. "Somehow I doubt that there will be a next time. It sounds to me as if you're well matched in bed. Now, I want you to stay here. If you still want to go home after that, we will."

"I really don't want to lose him, Milly." Summer sniffled.

"Good." Milly went to the side of the bed and pulled the tassel.

"Yes, ma'am?" Jenny said when she entered.

"Miss Caldwell will be staying with us for awhile. See that the blue room is prepared and her things are brought over from the hotel."

"Yes, ma'am."

"As soon as your room is ready, Summer, I want you to take a rest. I'll send a message to the Tremont saying you're staying here. If Buck Holester is half the man I think he is, you won't be here for very long."

When Summer was settled in her room, Milly dressed and went downstairs to face William. She found him in his study.

"It is my understanding Summer has moved in," William said in a harsh tone of voice. He continued to lean over his desk, pretending to be examining some papers laying there.

Milly crossed her arms over her voluptuous bosom. "I hope it's all right with you, William. She won't be here very long."

"And then?"

Milly decided it would be better to tell William what was in store, let him have his temper tantrum, and be done with it. Besides, he'd eventually find out anyway.

"Well?" William asked impatiently.

"And then Summer will be marrying one of the miners."

William couldn't hide his shock. "That rubbish could never give her the life she's accustomed to. Are you in favor of this, Milly?"

"I will not stand in her way. She has a right to happiness."

"And just where will they live? I certainly hope not in Denver. I have no desire to have them meet me on the street and act like they're old friends!"

"I would be careful of what you say, William. The day may come when you would very much like to have them as friends, especially considering your political hopes."

"What do you mean by that?" he asked, finally giving her his full attention.

"Nothing. I expect you to treat Summer as a welcome guest."

The minute Milly left, William smiled. This was turning out much better than he had expected. Who better than he to console Summer when her lover turned up dead? And Milly wouldn't be the least suspicious. He tapped his finger on the desk. First he had to get rid of Holester. But he'd have to move fast. He went in search of Milly.

William finally located the worrisome female in the linen closet. "Very well, my dear, I will make every effort to be hospitable to our guest. I'll even see to the hiring of a personal maid for her."

"How very kind of you, William," Milly said. "But it's really not necessary. We aren't likely to be here long."

"But I insist," he responded. "Now, I am going to my office. Lamb would be preferable for supper. Seven sharp?"

Milly expelled a sigh of relief when William left. She was counting the days until she would be rid of the insufferable man.

William's first stop was at a small house on the outskirts of town where an actress lived. Now in her early forties, Tula Baker was still an attractive woman, even though her waistline had become ample. On more than one occasion, William had taken advantage of her need for money.

She gave him a broad smile when he entered her parlor. "It's been a while," she commented.

"I'm here on business, Tula."

"You usually are. The last time was when you wanted me to find out about Henry Hogen. A political problem, wasn't it? I heard he was found dead between Denver and Golden."

"Are you insinuating something?"

"Not at all." She smoothed back her brown hair.

"For your information, I was planning on using what you told me as a means of holding something over his head if he became too much of a problem. Nothing more. Besides, you were paid well by both of us."

"What man do you want me to take to my bed this time?"

"I don't. I want you to work in my house for a few days as a maid. Do you think you can adequately handle such a position?"

"In the theater I had to do everything, including dressing hair."

"Then report to my house as soon as possible. Tell Miss Stern I hired you to be Miss Caldwell's personal maid. I want you to keep your ears open and report what you've heard nightly. You will be well compensated, as usual."

After arriving at his office, William sent a note to Ernie. An hour later the dark-skinned man arrived.

"Holester is in jail?" William asked.

"Yep, and the marshal isn't believing a thing he says."

William pulled a handkerchief from the sleeve of his dark frock coat and mopped his forehead. It was an insufferably hot day already. "Did anyone at the Tremont see you?"

"No, it was late and the desk clerk was in the back."

"Good. Tomorrow night, I want you and Kelly to break Holester out. The Federal Circuit Judge will be arriving the following morning."

"Why break him out? It's my word against his, and he has no way of proving who those horses belong to."

"I don't pay you to ask questions. I want the man dead. Take him out of town and hang him."

Ernie's black eyes lit up with pleasure. "Why not tonight?"

"There are circumstances that would make it too soon." William had made arrangements to spend the latter part of the evening with his new mistress, and when the hanging took place he wanted to be home, right under Milly's nose.

Discovering Buck and Summer were not in, Angus went to his own room to catch some sleep. He'd had a most invigorating night. A slow smile creased his lips as he undressed. But though he had thoroughly enjoyed the lady he'd been with, he'd not felt any love. Strange how life had a way of playing tricks on a man, he thought as he climbed into bed.

It was early afternoon by the time Angus awoke. He wasn't surprised to discover Summer and Buck still hadn't returned. He decided that after he had something to eat he'd go see Howard Jackson and take a look at some of the property Howard had talked to him about buying.

When Summer awoke from her nap, she didn't feel much better. She pulled the tassel beside her bed and waited. Since Milly hadn't awakened her she felt sure Buck hadn't made an appearance. Her shoulders slumped. She had honestly thought Buck would come after her.

When the maid entered the room, she announced her name was Tula, and that she had been hired by Mr. Nielson as Summer's personal maid. A few minutes later two other servants arrived carrying water.

"Miss Stern thought you would like to freshen up," Tula said.

Tula struck Summer as being slightly intimidating, though it did feel good to be pampered.

"Tula," Summer said authoritatively as she climbed out of the tub and allowed the maid to place a large towel around her, "from now on I will be attending to my own bath. I require only a little help in dressing and undressing. If I think of anything else, I'll let you know."

"Yes, ma'am. I'm very good at doing hair."

"Well, when I'm ready, we'll see how good you are." The woman seemed honestly hurt at the way she'd been spoken to, and most willing to do what was required.

"Do you know if I had a caller while I slept?" Summer asked in a softer tone.

"I haven't heard of any. Are you expecting some-one in particular?"

"No." Summer went to the chifforobe and began yanking out her mountain dresses and tossing them on the floor. She hesitated a moment at the dress she'd made for the dance, then jerked it out and added it to the others. The cotton undergar-ments followed along with the two coats and a pair of red slippers.

"Shall I have these laundered?" Tula asked.

"No, they're to be thrown away, unless you want them."

Tula bit her lip to keep from showing just how pleased she was at her good fortune. She could sell the items for a nice sum.

"I want these things removed from my room before you dress my hair," Summer ordered.

"Yes, ma'am."

By the time Tula returned, Summer was already seated in front of the diamond glass mirror. Tula set to work. After brushing the lustrous hair until it crackled, she parted it in the middle and smoothed it back. It took a while to form the tight curls all around the base of the lady's long neck. It was quite the fashion, and Tula was pleased with her handiwork.

"That's lovely," Summer complimented. "You are indeed accomplished."

Summer stood and studied her reflection in the mirror. The dress she had selected was white. The full skirt had an abundance of pink embroidered flowers and bright green leaves scattered about. She hardly looked like a woman who had lived in the mountains. Summer felt strangely saddened. She knew that if Buck didn't want her any longer, she would eventually return to being willful and bored. Without him, she had nothing. She went down to join Milly for tea.

The two women sat outside in the lovely garden behind the house, enjoying what little breeze there was. Milly wasn't sure what to think at this point. She had sent a message to the Tremont House and had expected Buck to arrive by now. She knew he hadn't checked out because the clerk had said he would give Mister Holester the note as soon as he returned. Perhaps he'll arrive this evening, she thought.

"I told William this morning about your possible marriage to Buck."

To Summer's shock, Milly pulled an already rolled cigarette from her bodice. "Milly! What if someone sees you? Whenever did you start smoking cigarettes?"

Milly inhaled deeply before letting the smoke trail back out. "Summer, you have always been a bit stuffy, though from what you told me about the mountains, I honestly thought you'd changed."

Summer suddenly broke out laughing. Maybe she wouldn't return to her old self with Milly around.

"Now that's what I like to see. Laughter always makes things look a little brighter." Milly smiled. "I have been smoking off and on for some time, but since coming to stay with William I find I do it a lot."

Summer picked up one of the small cakes covered with almonds. "I thought you said William wasn't to know about Buck?"

Milly couldn't tell Summer everything about what William had said; it would only make her more upset. "I changed my mind. I decided he would feel more secure if he knew you were to marry. William was most distraught at discovering you were living with three miners, and immediately became concerned that his social status as well as his political aspirations would be jeopardized should anyone find out."

"But I would never do such a thing. It would damage my own reputation."

"I know, but you don't think like Willy. Then to make matters worse, he didn't tell me you were safe. I just happened to overhear his conversation with the man he hired to locate you."

"Why did he do that?"

"I've asked myself the same question many times." She took another long draw on her cigarette. "He claimed it was to keep me here because he'd fallen in love with me. However, that doesn't really make sense. Had I believed you were dead, why would I stay?"

"You don't care for William much, do you?"

"If you recall, I never have. Even less now. I'll be glad to get away."

"Milly, I'm so sorry you've had to go through all of this."

"I don't mind in the least, especially if Buck comes through, as I expect him to. I would suggest you say nothing to William about Buck being rich." Milly put out her cigarette. "Just how wealthy is he?" she asked out of curiosity.

"I have no idea. I guess I never thought about it."

"Well, considering how long they went without money, a little might seem like a lot to him. So if you do marry Buck, you might be wise not to plan on living in luxury. Considering all the things he bought you, there might not be much left. Personally, I know absolutely nothing about mining, or the price of gold, but I bet William does. So I say again, tell him very little.''

As the day drew to a close, Angus couldn't understand why Buck and Summer had been gone so long. He even went to the desk and asked if a message had been left for him. Upon hearing there wasn't one, he went to Buck's room and tried the door, surprised it wasn't locked. Nothing looked disturbed. He then went to Summer's room, only to find it empty of everything. Angus was becoming more worried by the minute. Something wasn't right. He would have gone to William's house to confront him, but try as he might, Angus couldn't remember the man's last name. He'd just have to wait. If nothing turned up by tomorrow morning, he was going to tear the damn town apart.

By the time Summer went to bed, she'd given up hope of Buck coming after her. She was hurt and angry. She was also tempted to go to Buck tomorrow and have it out with him, but her pride wouldn't let her. She had done nothing to deserve any of this except come for supper, while he'd spent an entire night and day out!

As Jenny brushed Milly's hair before bed, Milly was feeling quite mystified. At supper William had played the part of the perfect gentleman. He'd asked Summer questions, but nothing the least bit embarrassing. He'd seemed in the best of spirits, almost as if he were placating them. When he departed shortly after the meal, he excused himself by saying he knew they had a lot to talk about. Milly was more inclined to believe he was off to see a mistress. Also, Milly just couldn't understand why Buck had not replied to her note. She decided to try another tack. If she couldn't get anything out of Buck, she would pay Angus Comstock a visit early tomorrow morning. Perhaps he would shed some light on what was going on.

"Jenny," she said to her maid when the brushing was complete, "have my breakfast ready early in the morning. And I'll need your help to get dressed. I heard of a new seamstress who is supposed to be able to do wonders with material, and I want to see her before it gets too hot."

"Yes, Miss Stern."

"How is the new maid William hired getting along?" Jenny was Milly's eyes and ears among the servants.

"If you don't mind my saying, that's a strange one. She hardly talks to anyone, unless it's to ask questions."

"What kind of questions?"

"She asked me what my duties were, and what you expected of me. I have an awfully strong feeling she's never worked as a servant before."

"How interesting." Milly stood and Jenny helped her into the nightdress.

"She also asked Gloria if she'd overheard any of your conversation with Miss Caldwell in the garden this afternoon. The woman is nosy."

"Thank you, Jenny, for the information. Warn cook and the other servants to be careful what they say to her."

"Yes, Miss." She fluffed the pillows and turned back the sheet. "Will there be anything else?"

"No, and thank you again."

So, Milly thought, William has planted a spy in our midst.

It was nearing eight the next morning when Milly directed the driver of her coach to let her off at a small dress shop on Fourth Street. After getting out, she told him not to wait, but to be back in an hour. Milly entered the shop and spoke briefly with the owner. When she was convinced the carriage was out of sight, she left. It was only a short distance to Front Street and the Tremont House.

"Is Mister Holester in?" Milly asked the desk clerk. The man grinned and Milly was convinced he had nothing in his mouth but teeth.

"Not that I know of, ma'am. Mister Comstock was here a few minutes ago asking if Mister Holester had left him a message."

"And where is Mister Comstock now?"

"I believe he returned to his room. He wasn't in a very good mood. I wouldn't want to tangle with that man."

"What room is Mr. Comstock staying in?" Milly watched the young man's grin quickly fade.

"I'm not allowed to give out that information. Besides, it's not . . ."

"It's not what?"

"Ladies don't usually—"

"I'm quite aware of what ladies do and don't do, young man. But just to set your mind at ease I want you to send someone immediately to Mr. Comstock's room and tell him there is a lady here to see him and that it's urgent."

"I'll attend to it right away."

From Summer's description, Milly recognized Angus the minute he stepped into the lobby. Summer had said he was a handsome man, but Milly had brushed it off, thinking Summer said that because she was so fond of him. Now she regretted not having met Angus Comstock sooner. He was well over six feet tall, broad-shouldered, and had a wonderful head of red hair. She turned in his direction.

"Mr. Comstock? I'm Milly Stern, Summer's

friend." She watched his gaze cover her from head to foot, liking the twinkle in his eyes.

"My pleasure," Angus said after kissing her offered hand. Studying the lovely lady standing in front of him, Angus silently thanked Summer for her lessons. "If you've come to inquire about Summer, I'm sorry to say I have no idea where she is."

"I do. She's staying with me at William Nielson's house."

"I see. Then she's all right?"

"She's all right, but quite upset. That is why I came to see you."

"Has Buck been there?"

Milly was surprised at the question. "Why, no. I thought you could tell me where he is and why he hasn't been by to see Summer."

"If you're not adverse to going in a man's room, Miss Stern, it would be a good place to talk privately."

"I agree completely. And please, call me Milly." She felt a rush of excitement when he took her elbow and led her away from the lobby. He was so tall and big! Suddenly she felt ashamed of herself. She'd come to solve Summer's problems, not her own.

When they were comfortably seated in the two-room apartment, Milly told Angus everything. The entire time, Angus had his elbow on the arm of the chair, slowly rubbing his chin. He was not only listening intently, he was also studying her. Milly knew he was deciding whether she was trustworthy or just plain nosy. He was cautious. A most admirable quality in a man, she thought.

"To be perfectly truthful, Milly, I haven't seen Buck since the day before yesterday, the same day they had their fight. I will say that Buck often takes off for periods of time, then finally shows back up.

But I can't picture him doing it without at least leaving some kind of a message. I was just about to search the town for him. Now I'm even more convinced that something isn't right. If he decided to leave, it would have been with Summer strapped across his saddle. I have a hunch Mr. Nielson is behind this."

"I can't imagine how. William didn't know Buck was in Denver." Nevertheless, Milly told Angus about William's comments regarding Summer. Though he didn't move a muscle, she knew Angus' anger was growing by the way his eyes were changing from hazel to brown.

"That son of a bitch," Angus said when she finished. "That man has to be the culprit. I bet the only reason I'm safe is simply because he has no idea I'm here. If he's hurt Buck, your lawyer friend is a dead man." He watched Milly's reaction. She looked a bit shocked, but certainly not displeased over the prospect. "The question is, how are we going to find out?" He thought a minute. "Is William at his office now?"

"I doubt it. He usually doesn't go there until later."

"Does he have a clerk working for him?"

"Yes."

"Then I know where to start."

"I must return to the shop before my coach arrives. You will keep us informed, won't you?"

They both stood. Milly was sorry to have to leave.

"Most assuredly. And thank you for coming by. Tell Summer Buck wouldn't have left without her, and that one way or another, I'll find him."

"William's office is on G Street, just off of Larimer."

Angus guided her out of the room. After seeing

the lady off, Angus ordered his horse to be brought to the front. Mounting, he headed directly to William's place of business.

As Angus entered the office, a tall skinny man looked up from the books surrounding him. Jack Stapelton, William's clerk, was perched on a stool and made no effort to get down.

"Mr. Nielson in not in his office right now," the man stated sharply. "I suggest you come back later. And you will need an appointment. Mr. Nielson is a very busy man."

Angus moved forward until the only thing that separated them was a narrow table. "I didn't come to see Mr. Nielson, I came to see you."

The man looked surprised. "Why would you want to see me?"

Angus placed his hands on the table and leaned forward. "Because you are going to supply me with some information, my friend."

The man gulped. "I'm not allowed to give out information of any kind."

"Then you must not be adverse to getting the hell beat out of you."

"Well . . . ah . . . what kind of information?"

Ten minutes later, Angus was on his way to O'Leary's boardinghouse. He wasn't worried about the clerk saying anything to Nielson. Angus had told the man that if he did it would probably cost him his job—not to mention the fact that one night he'd wake up with a gun in his face.

Chapter 18

"**S**ummer," Milly said as she entered the parlor. "I thought you might sleep late this morning."

"Milly, I have made a decision. I'm . . ." Summer stopped when she saw Milly raise a finger to her lips, silently telling Summer to be quiet.

"That's nice, dear, but whatever it is, I'm sure it'll wait until tomorrow. The heat is going to be unbearable today."

Summer cocked her head questioningly.

"I have a marvelous idea. William has excellent horses. How would you like to go for a ride?"

"Milly, I want—"

"Good! Now you run right upstairs and change. I'll make sure you get a well-spirited horse, the kind you've always enjoyed. We won't be gone long."

Summer wanted to refuse, but didn't because of the look on Milly's face. She knew her friend wasn't particularly fond of riding, so there had to be a good reason for suggesting a jaunt. "I'll hurry."

Thirty minutes later they'd left Denver behind. This is ridiculous, Summer thought. Milly hasn't said a word and now we're in the middle of nowhere. Summer glanced ahead. They were approaching a creek bed that had a wide sandy

bottom and was fringed with feathery cotton-
woods. What little water there was trickled down
the middle. She glanced over at Milly, who sat atop
a small black mare that wasn't nearly as frisky as
the stallion Summer rode.

"Where are we going?" Summer asked.

Milly laughed. "Why, to water the horses, of
course. This is called Cherry Creek. It's said to be
dry."

"I can certainly understand why. All right,
Milly," Summer said as the horses lowered their
heads to drink, "what is all this about?"

Milly brushed a strand of hair from her eyes. "I
went to the Tremont House this morning, Summer,
and had a talk with Angus."

"I suppose he excused Buck's actions?"

"Summer, I hate to be the bearer of bad news,
but Buck is missing. Angus hasn't seem him since
the morning of your argument."

"He probably took off to his mountains," Summer said bitterly.

"Angus doesn't think so."

"Milly, who would want to harm Buck? Besides,
it would probably take an army of men to pin him
down." She pulled the horse's head up and they
crossed the creek.

"You are letting your bitterness blind you, Summer Caldwell," Milly said angrily. "I'm sure Angus
is aware of everything you said, so why is he so
worried? As for pinning Buck down, a gun, or even
a bullet could accomplish that very quickly."

Summer clutched the pommel. "Milly, are you
trying to scare me?"

"If that's what it takes." Milly didn't like seeing
Summer's face turn pale, but she needed to understand the seriousness of the situation.

"Then I will repeat my previous question. Who

would want to harm Buck? I don't believe he even knows anyone in town."

"William Nielson."

Summer's mouth became as round as her eyes. "That's preposterous. William is nothing more than a harmless prissy." A blackbird suddenly swooped down, and the stallion shied away.

"That's what I thought," Milly replied when Summer had the steed settled. "But then I started wondering why he hired Tula to find out about our conversations and keep an eye on you. Jenny said she seriously doubted Tula had ever worked as a maid before. At first I didn't believe William would go to such extremes, but talking to Angus brought other things to mind. William is a very ambitious man and has changed in the short time I've lived here. When he found out I had overheard that you were alive, he stopped doing any business at home. Even that short little man with the strange square glasses doesn't come by anymore. The thing that—"

Summer jerked her horse to a halt. "What was the man's name?"

"I have no idea. William never introduced him and he always rushed the man into his study."

"Was he bald?" Summer almost whispered the words.

"Yes, he was, and—"

"Oh, my God! Did you tell Angus?"

"Well, no. I didn't think about it until just now."

"Milly, that fits Toddle's description. But it couldn't have been. How would they have known each other?"

"Are you talking about the man that caused all the trouble at the mine?"

"Yes. Milly, we have to hurry and let Angus know about this."

"And then we're packing up our things and leaving William's house," Milly added with finality. They jerked their horses around and took off at a full gallop.

When Milly and Summer arrived at the Tremont House, Angus wasn't there. They left a message and headed toward William's home. They had every intention of searching his desk for anything that might provide some clue as to what was going on. To their aggravation, William hadn't left the house.

Summer and Milly put on work dresses and hiked their skirts up at the sides to assist in the packing. It was another hour before Jenny came with the news that William had gone. Summer ordered Tula to help Jenny pack Milly's clothes. That way Jenny could keep an eye on her.

Milly waited in the parlor to delay William should he suddenly return, and Summer entered the study. She searched through the desk, making sure to put everything back in its proper place. Finding nothing incriminating, she looked around for anything else that could contain information. The room wasn't large and had only a desk and two chairs. Law books and various other reading material lined one wall. The effort was fruitless. Summer joined Milly in the parlor.

"Well?" Milly asked expectantly.

Summer shook her head. "I'm going to check his room."

Again, Summer's examination provided nothing. She was heartsick. All they could do now was wait and pray Angus would be more successful in finding something that could lead them to Buck.

Angus had been following Ernie around most of the morning and was starting to think it served no purpose. However, when Ernie met his partner Kelly at the Goose Neck Saloon in the rough section of town, Angus decided to follow them inside. It was a small place and reeked of dirt and stale beer. The customers looked seedy. Angus was glad he hadn't worn his city clothes. He stepped up to the bar and ordered a whiskey. Ernie and Kelly took a table in the back. By looking in the mirror behind the bar, Angus had no trouble keeping an eye on the pair. They put their heads together and spoke in quiet tones, every now and then looking around to be sure no one could overhear them.

When they left the saloon, the men went to a mercantile store. Looking through the window, Angus saw them purchase a length of good rope. Kelly was laughing when they came back out. He fashioned one end of it into a loop, placed it around his neck, and laughed all the harder.

"You're crazier than a damn snake," Ernie lashed out. He spit tobacco juice onto the road. "You want everyone to get suspicious?"

Following behind them, Angus' concern grew.

"Will you be going out later?" Milly asked William. They were all seated in the parlor waiting for supper to be announced.

"No, no. I plan on spending the evening with you two charming ladies. I thought that after we've eaten, we might play dominoes. I must warn you, Summer, Milly is very good at the game."

Summer smiled, hoping it didn't look weak.

"I think that is an excellent idea." Milly continued fanning herself.

The evening passed with excruciating slowness. By the time Summer went to bed, her head was throbbing. Her worry over Buck's safety was all-consuming. He had to be safe. He just had to. She'd never forgive him if he was sitting on some mountain nursing his pride. But if he was in danger, it would be her fault. None of it would have happened if she had given way to his desire to be married in the mountains. But no, she had to talk to William and Milly. Never would she have suspected William to be devious. She took some small consolation in the fact that they'd be leaving his house tomorrow. But she still wanted Buck. He was the one who made her feel alive.

It was a dark night, and Angus could barely see the two men sitting on their horses on Market Street, across from the jail. They had another horse as well, saddled but riderless. Angus looped his leg around the saddle horn, waiting to see what they were going to do next.

Nearly an hour later, the marshal opened the door, the light from the lantern inside silhouetting his body. "I'll be back in a little while," he said to the man inside. "Just going to take a look around."

When the marshal was out of sight, the two men dismounted and pulled bandannas over their noses. Revolvers ready, they walked across the street and entered the jail. Angus swung his leg down, stuck the toe of his boot in the stirrup, then pulled his rifle out of the scabbard.

A few minutes later the men ran back out with another man in front of them. Angus didn't get a look at his face, but he sure as hell recognized his body. From what he could see, it looked like Buck's hands were tied behind him. Angus didn't dare ride forward for fear his partner would be shot.

The three men mounted, and with one holding the reins to Buck's horse, they rode off. Angus followed, making sure to stay out of sight.

Ernie and Kelly pushed their horses hard. They

didn't slow down until they were well out of town. Feeling safe, they turned their attention to their prisoner.

"Ain't you lucky," Ernie said. "Now you don't have to go before no judge. We're going to hang you instead."

Kelly laughed. "Maybe a couple of times. But you ain't gonna know when we decide to make it the last time."

"Ain't you got nothing to say?" Ernie persisted.

After smoldering for the last couple of days, Buck's temper was at the bursting point. He'd already devised a plan for escape. But he'd damn well return and make sure these two got their just reward.

"Why you doing this?" Buck asked.

"Ain't nothin' personal," Ernie replied. "I got my orders and it pays well."

They pulled up to a tall, lone tree.

"Since I'm going to die, don't you think I got a right to know who wants me dead?"

"Sorry, can't do that," Ernie replied.

Kelly rode under a sturdy limb. A hangman's knot had already been tied on the end of the rope. The first time he tried swinging it over the limb, he failed. And the second time.

"What the hell are you doing?" Ernie demanded.

"It's too damn dark to see."

"Hell! Give it to me."

As Ernie handed the reins of Buck's horse over to Kelly, Buck gave his mount a hard kick in the ribs. The horse bolted forward, yanking the reins from Ernie's hands.

The sudden movement caused Ernie's horse to shy and Kelly's kicked. Before they could get their horses around to chase after Buck, a shot rang out, killing Ernie immediately. The next shot took care of Kelly.

Angus jammed his rifle back into the scabbard. Leaning over his horse's neck, he took off after Buck. Angus knew that with the reins hanging down, the animal could stumble and break his neck as well as Buck's.

It was a hard chase, what with both men encouraging their horses to go faster. Angus had to yell, "Buck! It's me, Angus!" several times before Buck heard him.

By the time Angus managed to grab the loose reins and bring the horses to a halt, the animals were lathered and their sides heaved.

Buck laughed. "What the hell took you so long?"

"What the hell were you doing in jail?" Angus leaned over and untied Buck's hands.

"Ernie back there told the marshal I'd stolen his horses. Was that you shooting or them?"

"Me. I just sent Ernie and his pal to the devil."

They dismounted and started walking back, allowing their horses to rest. "Hell," Angus said. "After that walk to get a doctor for Charley, I swore I'd never do it again."

"Beats sitting in a cell. Ernie said someone hired him to kill me."

"Did he say who?"

"Nope."

"You know the marshal's going to be after you now," Angus said.

"Yep. Have you seen Summer?"

"No, but I saw her friend Milly. Summer is staying at William's house." Angus relayed everything Milly had told him, and how he had tracked Buck down. "You've got to ride to safety, Buck, at least until we can find a way to get you out of this damn mess."

"Do you think Summer is safe?"

"Not for much longer. However, they're moving out tomorrow. No telling what the bastard is going to think of next. You're a wanted man, Buck, so you're going to have to stay out of sight."

Buck nodded. "Ernie's buddy strangled the deputy. Now I'll be wanted for that murder, too. Though it's tempting as hell to kill William, it isn't going to prove my innocence. Somehow, you've got to get proof he's behind all this. We'll also need a place to meet so I can find out what's going on."

"I bought some land by the Platte River. There's an old shack on it. I'll meet you there at night in a week." Angus handed him a bag of gold. "You might need this."

"Don't tell Summer. She's better off thinking the worst of me. I may be a wanted man for the rest of my life. Maybe I should head for California. Always wanted to see what the place looks like."

"I'll see you in a week, partner." Angus told him how to get to the shack.

Summer was finishing her toilette, when she heard a light tap on the door. Tula went to answer it. One of the young maids stepped inside the room.

"You and Miss Stern have a gentleman caller waiting in the sitting room, ma'am."

Was it Buck, Summer wondered excitedly. She started to laugh with joy, but saw Tula out of the corner of her eye. "Has Miss Stern been informed?"

"No, Miss Caldwell. I was going to her room next."

Summer was too excited to wait on Milly. "Then tell Miss Stern I'll meet her downstairs. Tula, that will be all."

Tula hurried off to find William.

Summer left her bedroom; it was all she could do to keep from running down the hall and stairs. But when she finally reached the sitting room, it wasn't Buck standing there.

"How do you do, Miss Caldwell," Angus said in a most gentlemanly fashion. "I hope I'm not imposing by calling this morning?"

"No. Not at all, Mister—"

"I'm crushed that you don't remember my name. But I'm sure a lady of your rare beauty has many gentlemen callers. Fox, Brandon Fox."

He smiled, and Summer saw the old twinkle in his eyes. She knew Buck was safe. Summer returned his smile.

"I understand we have a caller," Milly said as she entered.

"Yes, Milly. You remember Brandon Fox. We met him yesterday on our ride."

"Of course. Won't you have a seat, Mister Fox?"

"As I was telling Miss Caldwell, I don't want to inconvenience you. I merely stopped by to ask for the privilege of escorting you lovely ladies to supper tonight."

"That's impossible," William said as he rushed into the room.

Milly quickly made introductions. "I for one see nothing impossible about it, William," Milly said with a light air. "Actually, Mister Fox, Miss Caldwell and I are moving today, and would quite enjoy dining with you. Isn't that so, Summer?"

"Yes, that would be quite nice."

"Milly, why don't you go alone? Since Summer is bespoken, I don't think it proper for her to leave."

"I disagree, William. That rogue certainly hasn't made an effort to contact Summer, and I think she needs other interests." Milly smiled apologetically at Angus. "Please excuse our manners, Mister Fox. Miss Caldwell and I would be most delighted to accompany you. We will be staying at the Tremont House."

"Then I shall arrive at seven with my carriage, unless that is too late."

"Seven would be fine," Summer answered.

Angus made a slight bow and left.

"I don't like this at all!" William went to the sideboard and poured himself half a glass of port. "From what I heard, neither of you even know the man." He gulped down his drink.

"Willy, how did you know we had a caller?" Milly asked innocently.

"I just happened to pass by and heard a man's voice. And I don't have to explain my actions in my own house."

"I was just curious. But that's beside the point. Summer and I shall probably be receiving more callers once it's known we are about town."

"Ladies do not stay in hotels unchaperoned. What's made you decide to go?"

"But we are chaperoned. We have each other. It didn't seem to bother you when we arrived. Oh, and I will be taking Jenny with me. I need a servant."

"What about Tula?"

Milly headed for the doorway, Summer following.

"Jenny is quite capable of taking care of the two of us," Milly said over her shoulder.

When they were walking down the long hallway, Summer started laughing. "It's such a beautiful day, don't you think, Milly?"

Milly laughed. "Apparently so."

Knowing he'd accomplish nothing by sitting at

home fuming, William went to his office and sent for Ernie. It was time to see how they'd managed with Holester. When an hour passed and Ernie hadn't appeared, William scribbled out another note telling him to report to the back of the house as soon as possible. He handed it to his clerk for delivery. William picked up the newspaper and left for the day. The clerk headed straight for the Tremont House, anticipating the money he would receive.

When William returned home, trunks were already being loaded in the carriage. He ordered a maid to tell Miss Caldwell she was wanted in his study. There was always more than one way to get something accomplished.

"You wanted to see me, William?" Summer stood just inside the door, her head high and back ramrod straight.

"Yes, my dear." He motioned to the chair by his desk. "Please, come sit down." He admired the way the silk day suit molded her high, firm breasts and trim waistline. "I'm afraid I have some bad news."

"I prefer to stand. What news?"

"Very well." He stepped behind her and closed the door. "There is something in the *Rocky Mountain News* that I think you will want to read."

Summer moved to the desk and looked down. Staring up at her was an article about the death of the marshal's aide. A description of Buck followed, along with the announcement of a two thousand dollar reward for the return of the culprit, dead or alive. She sank down on the chair.

"There, there, my dear." William placed a hand on her shoulder. "I thought that fit the description of your miner. Now I know for sure. Believe me, that sort of man isn't worthy of you. You would be wise to keep your relationship with the rogue a secret."

Summer stood so fast, she knocked William away. "You, of all people, dare to make accusations against the man I love? Compared to you, the man is a saint. You are vermin. Damn vermin! I don't know what all this is about, but I know you're behind it. If anything happens to Buck, one way or another I'll kill you. I've already killed one man since I came to Colorado and I won't hesitate to do it again."

William gasped. He'd never heard Summer talk like this. She looked him straight in the eye, and her beautiful face hardened. "My dear, you're distraught and don't realize what you're saying."

"I know exactly what I'm saying, and you would be wise not to forget a word of it."

In the privacy of Milly's room, Summer told her friend about the article and what William had said.

"Good heavens!" Milly exclaimed. "I'm surprised you didn't break out in tears."

"I'm not sad, I'm furious. Milly, I know Buck is alive. Angus as much as told me so this morning. That means Angus has to know where he is. I have to go to Buck and beg him to take me with him."

"You can't do that! Buck will be a hunted man for the rest of his life."

"Only here. We can leave and go somewhere else."

"Summer, please. Don't do anything until we've talked to Angus. There is an awful lot we don't know yet."

Summer said no more. One way or another, she would find Buck.

By five o'clock, Milly and Summer had completely moved out of William's house. Summer and Milly weren't sure what to think when William did everything he could to assist them. The carriage had to make several trips before all their belongings were properly transferred. During the whole procedure, William was his usual smug, superior self.

When the women were finally gone, William sat in his parlor, enjoying his solitude. He had come to accept the inevitable. He knew when it was time to back off quietly. Since there was to be no marriage between Buck and Summer, it was doubtful anything would ever be mentioned about Summer's past. So his political career was still intact. In the late edition of the paper he'd read that Ernie and Kelly's bodies had been found, and that Holester was now being blamed for that also.

William's only regret was that he hadn't been able to sample Summer's charms. Feeling a need for a woman, he reached behind him and pulled the tassel.

"May I be of service?" the butler asked when he entered.

"Send Tula down."

Angus arrived promptly at seven. As the carriage headed for the restaurant, he told Summer and Milly about Buck.

"And Buck's all right?" Summer asked excitedly.

"He's fine, Summer."

"I have to see him."

"He doesn't want to see you. He's on the run."

"Did he say he doesn't love me?"

"Well . . ."

"Either yes or no."

"You would only slow him down and make him an easy target."

Summer leaned back against the cushion. Buck loved her. "There is something else I found out, Angus."

"What?"

"William knew Toddle."

A dead silence fell.

"That son of a bitch," Angus muttered. "I'd like to personally hang the bastard, but he's the only one who can save Buck's neck. I only wish the note he sent Ernie had said something about Buck."

"We could threaten to ruin his political career," Milly offered.

"He wouldn't exchange a noose for his political career. I'm afraid that at the moment, our friend William has the upper hand, and damn it, he knows it."

Chapter 19

While Angus spent his time trying to find some wrongdoing that he could hold over William's head, Summer was making her own plans. Though Angus had not come right out and said it, several comments he'd made convinced her that Angus had arranged to meet with Buck.

As soon she and Milly were settled in the hotel Summer went out and purchased a powerful stallion. She had deliberately selected a black mount, and boarded it at the livery stable. She excused herself by saying she needed to spend time alone and couldn't think of anything more pleasurable than to go for morning rides. She didn't tell Angus or Milly that she had also purchased a Western saddle and had a seamstress make her a pair of black riding pants that actually looked like a skirt, allowing her to sit astride.

Each morning, before Milly arose, Summer rode for at least an hour over every type of terrain until she felt capable and competent. If Buck had to stay on the run, she wouldn't be the one to slow him down. Sometimes she found it hard to stick to the regimen. She'd been feeling vaguely sluggish and out of sorts lately—particularly in the mornings. But she had only to think about Buck to give her all the motivation she needed.

Milly, Summer, and Angus now dined together each night, and Angus would tell them what he had found out about William, which unfortunately amounted to almost nothing. Apparently, William was very careful to keep his coattails clean. Angus had, however, found out a great deal more about Ernie. The man's record for nefarious activities stretched back for years. But he'd been very clever at letting others take the blame for his wrongdoings.

By Tuesday night, Angus looked tired and worried. "It has been a week," he said as he pushed his partially eaten meal aside, "and I'm no further along at trying to find a solution. The strange part is that I have a very strong hunch something is right under my nose, but I can't see it."

"You've done everything possible," Milly said soothingly.

"But everything possible isn't good enough. I paid a visit to the marshal today."

"Why?" Summer asked. "If anything happens to you, Augus..."

"There's is nothing to worry about. Because of my gambling days, I've never put much trust in the law. But since I haven't been able to accomplish much on my own, I decided to have a talk with him."

"And?" Summer encouraged.

"He seemed like a good man, so I ended up telling him almost everything."

"Not the shooting!" Milly face had turned white.

"No, but I explained how Buck was set up. He listened, but found it hard to believe a man like Nielson could be involved in such underhandedness."

"Will the reward be removed?" Summer asked.

"No."

Summer's shoulders slumped.

"At least it's one step in the right direction. I'm sorry to say, it may take months or even years before we find a means of putting William's neck in the noose. But one of these days he's going to slip up, and I'll be waiting."

"What you say about Buck is only true to a point," Milly said. "From what I understand, Buck has money from the mine and he can go elsewhere to start a new life."

"I'm sure he would rather it be his choice," Angus answered.

The waiter arrived with the desserts Milly and Summer had ordered.

"By the way ladies, I won't be dining with you tomorrow night." He gave them a full smile. "A man does have an occasional need."

Summer was surprised at the hurt look that flashed across Milly's round face. Was it possible that Milly had feelings for Angus? But why not? Angus was a fine-looking man. Summer realized she had been so wrapped up in her own problems she hadn't taken notice of what was staring her in the face. The interesting part was that Angus was one of the very few men who had paid little or no attention to her beautiful friend. That was strange because Angus had always been a flirt.

As she ate her peach cobbler, something else occurred to Summer. Angus was lying. If he wanted to bed a woman, that wouldn't have to interfere with their meal. And why would he make a point of telling them? To make Milly jealous? She doubted that. Angus would charm, not flaunt. Her gaze drifted toward the man sitting across from her. His face was strained, and showed worry, not pleasure. Buck! Tomorrow night Angus was meeting Buck! Summer's smile was cold. Angus wouldn't be alone.

When Angus' horse was delivered to the front of the Tremont House the following night, Summer was down the street waiting. She was dressed completely in black so it would be difficult to be seen. Her hair was covered with a black, wide-brimmed hat. Even her gloves were black. When Angus rode off, she followed. Soon, she would see her beloved Buck.

Going at a full gallop, it wasn't long before they were far out of town. Only the silhouettes of occasional trees could be seen against the dark sky. It was a long ride. Summer prayed her horse's hoof didn't get caught in some prairie dog hole. As she continued to follow Angus, she wanted to yell out her joy, and anticipation filled her soul. It seemed like a lifetime since she and Buck had been together.

A cloud drifted across the moon, and by the time it had passed over, Summer had lost sight of Angus. Panicked, she urged her mount to go faster. She was passing a big oak when she was suddenly knocked from the saddle. Summer hit the ground so hard, she was sure every bone in her body was broken. She shook her head, trying to get her mind to work. What had caught her? A low branch?

"Climb to your feet, Mister," a deep voice commanded, "and make it fast."

"Buck?" Summer whispered. "Buck?" she said excitedly as she jumped to her feet.

Buck was as astounded as Summer. God, how he had dreamed of holding her in his arms and making love to her. But for her own sake, he had to make her leave. There was already a bounty hunter on his trail.

"How did you know I'd be here?" he barked out.

"I guessed that Angus was coming to meet you. Oh, darling, I've missed you so. I've been such a fool. I want to find the nearest preacher and get married. Buck, I love you so much." She reached up to kiss his lips.

It was all Buck could do to steel himself and shove her away. "I don't want you here, Summer, and I certainly don't want to be shackled with a damn wife."

"I don't believe you. Please, Buck, at least let me talk to you. Are you all right? Is there anything you need?"

Angus rode up, leading her horse.

"What I need is for you to get the hell out of my life."

Summer grabbed the reins that Angus held out to her. "I won't go, not until you at least talk to me. I'll follow. Buck, I know you love me."

"It's no use, Buck," Angus said. "Let her come to the shack."

Buck yanked his horse around and rode off. As soon as Summer was mounted, she and Angus followed.

After tying their horses in front of the line shack, Angus and Summer entered. It contained just one small room with a hard-packed dirt floor and no furniture except a low, wobbly table. Buck had already lit the candle.

Summer stared at the man she loved. His blue-gray eyes were hard, a short beard already covered his chin and jaw, and lines were etched across his forehead. He wore soiled, dusty buckskins. She ached for him.

"I'm sorry, Buck, but I've come up with a blank. Summer did find out that William knew Toddle, but whether they where in cahoots with each other

in trying to take over our mine, I have no idea."
Angus went on to tell Buck about his conversation
with the marshal and what he'd found out about
Ernie.

"So we've reached a dead end," Buck said in a
matter-of-fact tone.

"It looks that way, partner."

"Then I see no reason not to go blow William's
head off."

"I thought the same thing, but like you said, he's
the only one who can clear your name. I need
something to force him to make a confession."

"Just what kind of a man is our dear William?"
He gave Summer a sadistic grin.

Summer lifted her chin. "Clever," she replied.
"And if you want to know if I slept with him, the
answer is no. You are the only man I have, or will
ever share my bed with."

"Then you've got a long dry spell ahead of you."

"Will you meet me here next week?" Angus
asked.

"I don't know. Like I said, I'm thinking about
heading out for California. It's getting too damn
hot for me around here."

"If you head out, let me know where you settle,
and I'll send your money to you. I'll know your
answer if you're not here when I return."

Buck nodded.

"If you have nothing more to say to Buck, Angus, I'd like to talk to him alone."

"I'll wait outside."

"No, I can find my way back."

Angus hugged Buck and left.

"Now, just what is it you have to say, lady? Make
it quick. I have to be going."

"To begin with, I want to say how sorry I am
that I caused all this trouble. You would never have

been in this position if I hadn't insisted on seeing William. I have hurt for you, and desired you more than I could have ever thought possible. Milly said she thought we were both the type of people who only love once in our lives, and I've come to believe that. I will never be a complete person again without you. I love you more than life itself. If you want me to leave, I will. I would never do anything that would jeopardize your life."

"Fine. Get the hell out of here."

"Are you saying you no longer love me?"

"That's right, teacher. I had my fun with you, now it's finished."

"Then I'll say the same thing to you that you once said to me. Kiss me first, then look into my eyes and say you don't love me."

"Go to hell."

"Afraid?"

Buck reached out and yanked her to him. His kiss was hard and punishing, but she didn't pull away. Then, as much as he wanted to, he couldn't let her go. His kiss softened, and his passion grew as her arms circled his waist and her hand cupped his hips, drawing him to her. He groaned, his need for the woman he loved banishing all sense.

She drew back, her lips barely touching his. "Please, Buck," she muttered, "make love to me. It seems like a lifetime since we've been together. I love you so much, darling, can't we at least spend tonight together?"

He loosened the chin strap and removed her hat. "What a magnificent woman you've turned out to be. Had I any inkling, I would have taken you that day we saw the elk and not wasted so damn much time."

Summer laughed with delight as he began unbuttoning her blouse. "We'll just have to spend the rest of our lives making up for it. You still haven't looked me in the eye and said you don't love me."

Buck grinned as he slipped the blouse off her creamy white shoulders. "I've loved you so damn much it frightened me. But not anymore, Summer Caldwell. You will always be a part of me." He gently kissed her shoulder and then brought his lips down to the swelling of her full breasts. "God, how I've wanted you," he said before reclaiming her lips.

They undressed, admiring each other's nakedness in the candlelight. Buck gently laid Summer on the ground, then trailed his mouth over her body. He felt her squirm with delight as his tongue caressed her navel, and he nipped her flat stomach and suckled her breasts. Raising her legs, he slowly entered her, then remained still until neither one of them could stand the sweet agony a moment longer. Their movements became demanding as they strived to give each other total fulfillment as an expression of their love.

All night they made love and shared tender words, but soon it would be dawn. The candle had long since gone out as Summer lay wrapped in Buck's arms.

"Buck," Summer said softly, "we love each other too much to be apart. Please, let me go with you. I have practiced using a man's saddle, and I know I can ride as hard as you can. I won't complain or slow you down, and if I do, I promise to let you go on alone."

Buck thought about the bounty hunter. As much as he wanted Summer by his side, he couldn't take the chance of something happening to her, nor could he subject her to the grueling pace of trying to make a run for it. "All right, darling, we'll head for California. Now get some sleep because we have a long ride ahead of us today."

Summer snuggled up to him.

"Summer, I love you above anything else."

"I know, darling," she said, her eyelids heavy. She was so happy. She and Buck would now have an entire lifetime to spend together. Nothing would ever part them again.

When Summer awoke, Buck was not in the shack. Realizing how late she'd slept, she dressed in a hurry so they could be on their way. She rushed outside expecting to see him, but he was nowhere in sight. Neither was his buckskin horse. She tried convincing herself he hadn't gone on without her, but after waiting an hour, she knew the truth. She also knew his decision was based on a concern for her safety, but it didn't help to relieve her misery.

As Summer slowly rode back toward Denver, a hard ball of hate steadily grew inside her. She became very calm and her eyes were green stones. William had destroyed her life and the man she loved.

She went over everything she could remember that Angus had said about the man called Ernie. One thing kept coming back to her mind. Angus said Ernie always managed to escape trouble by letting someone else take the blame. Would Ernie have worked for William without knowing that, should he get caught, he could blame the man who'd hired him?

By the time Summer entered Denver, she'd coldly calculated her every move. She stopped at the first gunsmith shop she saw. It didn't take long to purchase a revolver and have the man show her how to use it. The fellow was also helpful about telling her how to reach O'Leary's boardinghouse, where Angus had said Ernie had been living.

Seeing Summer's dusty, black clothes, Mr. O'Leary looked at her suspiciously. "We don't rent rooms to single ladies," he informed her.

"I'm not here to rent a room, Mr. O'Leary. I'm looking for a man by the name of Ernie, and I've traveled a long way. I was told he lives here. He killed my husband and took his money. I don't care about the money, but I want to see the man hang for what he did."

Mr. O'Leary's face softened. "I'm sorry, ma'am, for what I just said. As for Ernie, I'm afraid you're too late. He up and got himself killed not too long ago."

Summer leaned against the wall as if to support herself.

"Are you all right, ma'am?"

"I'll be fine," she said weakly. "Do you still have any of the man's things? There was another man with him, and perhaps there would be a clue as to who he was. I think his name is . . . ah . . . Bill."

"Sure it wasn't Kelly?"

"No, that wasn't the name."

"Ernie didn't have much, but I stuffed what little he had up in the attic. You're welcome to take a look."

"Thank you."

Mr. O'Leary took her upstairs and, after pointing to a small pile in the corner, he left her alone. The first thing Summer noticed was that there was no money. She wondered if Mr. O'Leary had also gone through everything. Summer searched pockets and pulled out everything from the two small satchels, but came up empty-handed. She saw a worn holster that had fallen off to the side, but there was no belt. She had dismissed it earlier, but out of curiosity she leaned down and picked it up.

Why would he have saved something as useless at
that? She reached inside and felt something
smooth. Pulling it out she discovered a neatly
folded piece of paper. Summer opened it and read.

Henry Hogen will be leaving at three tomorrow afternoon, headed for Golden. Make
sure he doesn't get there alive.

W. Nielson

A cruel smile spread across Summer's lips. William had slipped up. She refolded the paper and
went back downstairs.

"Did you find anything?" Mr. O'Leary inquired.

"Not really."

"Sorry, ma'am."

Summer went outside, mounted, and turned her
horse in the direction of William's office.

"Is Mr. Nielson in?" She asked the clerk when
she entered. Her jacket was hung over her arm,
hiding the revolver gripped firmly in her hand.

Jack Stapelton looked her up and down, showing
disgust at her appearance. "Yes, ma'am," he replied in a snippy tone, "but he's with a client. Let
me see when I can make you an appointment." He
opened a large ledger.

"That won't be necessary. I'll wait."

"But you can't do that. Mr. Nielson has a very
busy schedule."

"Tell him Summer Caldwell is here. He'll see
me."

The man scurried away and disappeared behind
a closed door. He came back out a few minutes
later, the look of disapproval still on his face.

"Mr. Nielson said he'd see you in a few minutes.
Try to make it quick; he has a luncheon appointment with the governor."

Summer smirked. "I shouldn't be very long." She sat on the bench along the wall.

When a man and woman left William's office, the clerk motioned for Summer to enter. William was standing behind his imposing desk when Summer stepped into the room. She closed the door behind her.

William gave her a smug smile. "My dear, what has happened to you? I've never seen you dressed in such a fashion, and your hair is an absolute mess. Have you found another miner to romp with?"

"Why not? You certainly showed me no interest." She watched William's eyes light up and his tongue circle his thin lips.

"I didn't realize you were interested."

"Come here, and I'll show you."

William stepped from behind his desk, and Summer let her jacket fall to the floor, exposing the revolver. She smiled when William's face turned white.

"My dear," he said nervously, "put that away. You might hurt someone."

Summer lowered the muzzle until it pointed to his groin. "According to Milly, that's what you think with."

"I don't know what you're talking about."

"Don't take another step," Summer warned as he tried to edge back to the desk. "You have destroyed just about everything I hold dear in this world. Your man Toddle killed Charley and tried to kill Buck. I hope Toddle's hanging was slow."

Williams hands grew clammy.

"But that wasn't good enough for you. You still wanted the man I love killed. But it didn't work. Buck is alive. I just left him this morning." She held up her left hand with the piece of folded paper in it. "This is a note you wrote to your friend, Ernie, telling him to also kill a man by the name of Hogen. You should never have signed it. It's my guess that Ernie had every intention of handing it over to the marshal if you tried to get rid of him."

"What . . ." he cleared his throat, ". . . what do you plan on doing with it?"

"Nothing, because I can't think of a reason why I shouldn't kill you. But it will be one bullet at a time, and you know where the first one will land. And if I don't, I'm sure some night Buck will pay you a visit, or maybe even his partner, Angus, will. You see, he's in town also. I forgot. You met him. He was the man who came calling."

William's mind flashed to the huge, redheaded man. He glanced down at Summer's hand holding the revolver to see if it was shaking. Maybe he could duck behind the desk. Her hand was perfectly steady. She could pull the trigger before he even had time to move. "Now don't be so hasty, Summer. Perhaps we can make some kind of a deal." His own hands were starting to shake. "I'm sure there is a way we can get all the charges dropped against your friend, Buck. After all, I am a lawyer."

"How?"

"Well . . . let me think." He was having a hard time making his mind work. The revolver was still pointed at his groin. "I will say I overheard Ernie and Kelly planning how they would get horses by saying Buck stole them."

"What about the dead deputy marshal?"

"Ah . . ."

"Think quick, my hand's getting tired."

"At the time Ernie also told Kelly they probably couldn't make the charge stick, and they would have to get Buck out of there before the Circuit

Judge arrived, or they might be the ones standing trial."

"Let's go see the marshal. If you're not convincing, you're a dead man."

"What do I get out of this?"

"Your life. I still have the piece of paper and if that doesn't do it, I'll shoot you."

"How do I know you won't hand that paper over to the marshal, or that you'll keep your word, or that one of your miners won't kill me?"

"Though I hate the thought of you getting away with everything, Buck's life is even more important. I'll give you the piece of paper when all charges are dropped, and my word that none of us will do you any physical harm. You'll have to settle for that." Summer motioned the revolver toward the door. "Now let's get going."

Summer remained behind William, gun pointed at his back as they marched down the street. William was humiliated as people started pointing, then laughing. By the time they reached the jail, a crowd had formed.

"What is all this about?" the marshal asked with a big grin.

"Mr. Nielson has something to tell you, marshal," Summer replied.

"Can't we close the door?" William demanded. "There is no need for all these people to hear."

The marshal closed the door. He was beginning to have doubts about William. After meeting with Angus Comstock, he'd ridden over this morning and talked to a real estate man by the name of Howard Jackson. Jackson verified how wealthy Buck Holester and his partner were, and that they were both good men. It didn't figure that Holester would steal horses. It made a hell of a lot more sense that Ernie and his pal had set Buck Holester up. What Nielson had to do with all this was another question. "Would you be willing to sign a piece of paper stating what you tell me is the truth, Mr. Nielson?"

"Absolutely."

"Well, you're a lawyer, I'll let you write it all out." He went over to his desk. "Here's paper, pen, ink, and a piece of blotting paper."

When William was finished, Summer asked to read what had been written. Satisfied, she handed it back to the marshal. "Does this clear Buck Holester?"

"As far as I'm concerned. He could have killed Ernie and Kelly in self-defense. We'll see what the judge has to say. He'll be here in the morning."

Summer handed the revolver to the marshal. "Here," she said, "I really have never fired one of these things."

"Summer?" William called before she left. "Have you forgotten something?"

"I'll see you tomorrow afternoon, after I've heard what the judge says."

Well into the night, Summer, Milly, and Angus worked diligently at trying to copy William's handwriting. It was Milly that produced what looked like a perfect replica of the note. If William tried anything else, they'd see he paid for it.

The next day, the *Rocky Mountain News* reported how Summer had marched the prominent lawyer, William Nielson, down the street, and heralded her as a true woman of the West. At court Angus explained exactly how Kelly and Ernie had lost their lives. When the judge heard they'd been about to hang Buck, he dropped all charges, and Buck was a free man. But Summer could find no happiness. Buck didn't know he was free, and she might never see him again. Furthermore, William was getting away with not having to pay for his crimes.

When Summer left the Tremont House that afternoon, she bumped into a man, dropping the fake note she intended to return to William. The man dressed in buckskins picked it up, but instead of handing it to her, he tipped his hat.

"Miss Caldwell?"

"Yes. My note—"

"The name's Sam Hogen, ma'am."

Summer gasped. "Are you related to Henry Hogen?" Summer realized her mistake as soon as the words left her mouth. Her gaze fell on the note the man was still holding.

Sam Hogen had been looking for Summer because he'd read in the newspaper about what she'd done to William Nielson. Now seeing the horrified look on her face and her preoccupation with the note, he slowly unfolded it and read. *He didn't bother to ask. He was a desperate man.* "Thank you, Miss Caldwell." He handed the paper back. Worried at what repercussions this could have, Summer watched the stranger walk down the street. But as she made her way to William's house, she started thinking, that perhaps her meeting with Hogen had been downright providential.

The butler smiled broadly when Summer arrived at the house and led her directly to the parlor. A few minutes later, William joined her.

"Won't you have a seat?" William said in a most congenial tone.

"There's no need. I came to give you the paper, not to visit." She handed it to him.

He quickly read the words, then tore the paper into shreds and stuffed them into his vest pocket. "You look quite lovely today. Green has always been a most becoming color for you. I must say, my dear, I never gave you credit for being so clever. Tell me, would you have really pulled that trigger?"

Summer smiled sadistically. "Without a moment's hesitation."

"I see. You've changed a great deal since coming to Colorado. You're not the sweet little innocent I once knew."

"Thank you, William. That's probably the nicest compliment you could give me. My only regret is that you won't have to pay for your crimes. But someday, William, you will get your just reward."

"Perhaps, but only time will tell." He pulled a lace handkerchief from his sleeve and dabbed his mouth. "When I become governor, it will be a simple matter to take care of anyone who stands in my way, and that includes you and your friends."

"Have you read the newspaper? There's quite an article about me marching you down the street at gunpoint. They referred to me as a true woman of the West. Don't you think that is going to put a damper on your so-called political career?"

"Not at all. I will simply make a joke of it. Now if you don't mind leaving, I have things to attend to."

"Good-bye, William. I hope I never have to see your face again."

"The feeling is quite mutual, my dear."

As Summer rode to the old line shack on the appointed night, she begged God to make Buck be there, waiting. It was the only chance she'd have of telling him he was a free man. Angus rode silently beside her, both of them not wanting to express their feelings.

When they arrived, there was no horse in sight.

"We might as well head back," Angus said. "He's not coming."

"Maybe he's just late. We have to wait."

They dismounted and went inside. An hour later, Buck still hadn't made an appearance.

"Summer, it's no use," Angus said gently. He rose from the hard ground and stretched.

"You can go back, but I'm staying until morning. I can't give up hope, Angus."

"If you can wait, so can I."

Not until the sun streaked through the cracks between the boards did Summer finally accept the obvious. She leaned her back against the old wall and stared out the open door. She wanted to cry, but there were no tears left.

"I'm going to go looking for him," she said quietly.

Angus moved over until he was sitting beside her. He placed his arms around her shoulders and drew her against him. "Darlin', you'd never find him. I'd have a better chance than you, and I know it's hopeless. If he's hiding in the high country even a cavalry couldn't locate him, and if he's taken off for California we'd have no idea where to look. There is one thing you can be sure of: Buck knows how to take care of himself. He'll be all right."

"But we can't just let him wander around, thinking he's a wanted man. Oh, Angus, I miss him so. Isn't there anything we can do?"

"Only wait and hope he writes. Right now, Angel, I'm more worried about you. You've been looking peaked lately. What are you going to do? You're a wealthy woman, now that you own a third of the mine. You can have anything you like."

Summer laughed sadly. "Except the one thing I want most. There's something I've never told any of you."

"What's that?"

"I don't need money. I'm already a wealthy woman in my own right. And while I'm telling truths, I think I'm pregnant."

Angus was silent for a moment. "We'll go see a preacher in the morning and get married."

"No, Angus."

"Your babe needs a legal name!"

"No, Angus."

"Then you should return to Philadelphia so you can be with your family."

"I'm not going to do that either. I'm staying here in the territory I've come to love. I'll wait for Buck."

He leaned forward and tilted her chin up. "What if he never returns?"

She smiled gently. "I'll have something to remember him by."

"Do you want to return to the mine?"

Summer stood and walked to the door. She gazed at the mountain peaks in the distance. "No, I think I'll stay around Denver."

"Is your mind made up?"

"Yes."

He went over and joined her. "You know, Buck used to talk a great deal about Colorado someday becoming a state."

"Really? I didn't know that."

Angus laughed. "When did you ever have time to talk about it?"

Summer laughed with him. "Not very often. We were too busy doing other things.

"You remember when Buck came to Denver during the winter and returned with that mare for you?"

She nodded.

"Well, Buck bought up a lot of land during that trip, and he purchased even more the day we arrived. He said between the two of us we could just about own Denver. He told me once that he had over five hundred acres near the foothills with a house that only needed few repairs. He never got around to telling you, but that's where he planned on the two of you living. Far enough away to be in the open, but still close to Denver. He even said with a little adding on, the house would hold twelve kids."

Summer spun around, her face lit up with excitement. "Do you know where it is?"

"No, but I can sure as hell find out. What do you say we ride back to town?"

Chapter 20

Two days later, Angus, Summer, and Milly made the trip out to Buck's spread in the foot-hills. When they found the house, they separated, each looking in different rooms. To Summer's delight, the last owners had left behind a good deal of furniture, and she even found an old cradle and rocking chair in one of the rooms, both in good condition.

"Come here, Milly," she called. When Milly joined her, she smiled. "This will be the baby's room."

"When Buck said there was a house, I had no idea it was so big," Angus commented when he joined the women.

Summer took off to inspect the attic.

"She'll be happy here," Milly commented.

"What are you going to do now?"

Milly pulled a pre-rolled cigarette from her purse. "Do you have a match?" She expected to see Angus frown his disapproval. Instead, he smiled broadly.

"I'm beginning to suspect you have hidden qualities," he said as he struck a match and held it out to her.

"You've been too worried about Buck and Summer to see just what my qualities are." She inhaled deeply. "I think I'll stay here with Summer. Like her, I really have nothing to return to in Philadelphia, and she's going to need help when the baby arrives. Angus, do you think she's going to be all right?"

"With you and me to watch over her, she'll be fine. Of course she'll never give up hope of Buck's return."

"I want to move in immediately," Summer announced excitedly as she rushed back into the room. "And I'll hire men to fix this place up as good as new. Angus, can you take care of that for me?"

He laughed. "As soon as we get back to town."

"I'm curious. Who could have left such a fine house and furniture?" Summer went to the cradle and pushed it gently, watching it rock back and forth.

"A man who was wiped out of business by the big fire last year. he decided to pack up his family and return to the East."

Summer looked up and smiled. "We have so much to do, I guess we had better go to town and get things started." She went to the door then stopped. "Angus, do you plan on returning to the mine soon?"

"Not right away, but eventually I'll have to check on how things are progressing."

Summer nodded.

With Angus, Milly, and Jenny's help, everything moved at a fast pace. Because Summer was in a family way even though it didn't yet show, Angus insisted she have servants. The repairs were made, the house was cleaned from top to bottom, and additional furniture was moved in. Within two weeks, Summer and Milly were residing comfortably in the beautiful home. Summer tried to get

Angus to move in also, reminding him there was plenty of room. He refused, claiming it wouldn't look right.

Two nights later, on May 19th at eleven P.M., William sat behind his desk planning his future. He felt reasonably confident that no one would believe anything Summer Caldwell might say if she decided to cause him more trouble. After all, he had a reputation in Denver. And with the damaging piece of paper destroyed, and Ernie and Kelly out of the picture, she could prove nothing.

He was smiling when he heard the study door creak open. Looking up, William saw a short, husky man dressed in buckskins step into the room. He was holding a shotgun.

"Just who let you in?" William demanded as he stood. "If you're seeking legal advice you can make an appointment at my office. Now get out of my house."

The man gave him a lopsided grin. "You remember Henry Hogen? I believe you and him had some differences."

"Yes, I remember him. I understand he was gunned down."

"I'm his brother." He turned the shotgun towards William, and moved forward.

William couldn't stop the side of his mouth from twitching. "What does that have to do with me?"

"You're the one who had him killed."

"That's ridiculous. Why would I want to do that?"

The stranger stopped and raised the barrel of the shotgun just enough so that it was pointing at William's face.

Perspiration was starting to run down William's temples. "You have no proof."

"Just looking at you is proof enough."

"You can't do this! It's murder!" Raw panic took over as he saw the man's finger curl around the trigger. "You don't understand. I didn't mean to! It was an accident!"

The stranger pulled his finger back.

William's body slumped to the floor just as a thunderous noise, began to build. Thinking it might be a tornado, the stranger ran out of the house.

No one was prepared for the torrent of water that rushed down Cherry Creek and spilled into the Platte River. It swelled and thickened, sweeping away huge trees, houses, and businesses. The muddy waves of water grew higher, drowning all other sounds, taking people, livestock, buildings, furniture and equipment. The *Rocky Mountain News* building disappeared, including the lot it stood on. Meanwhile, ominous dark clouds split open overhead and the water reaped its destruction.

When the deluge ceased, one million dollars worth of damage had been done. The few buildings and houses that still stood were full of mud and water five feet deep. Three ranchers up the Cherry Creek lost over four thousand sheep.

Fortunately, that night Angus had stayed at Summer's house.

Two weeks later, a tall, bushy-faced man stepped up to the crowded bar on the western slope of the Rockies. He was a big man and the customers quickly made room for him. He ordered a bottle of whiskey. The bartender set one in front of him, along with a dirty glass, then collected his money.

Buck was on his third shot of liquor when he began listening to the man beside him talking about a flood in Denver. He had a copy of the *Common-*

wealth and was pointing out different things that had been reported. "All them people killed! Hell, no one had a chance. That water just came out of nowhere!"

Buck jerked around and snatched the paper away. The man said nothing. He didn't want any trouble with the stranger.

As Buck read the long article about all the people dead or left stranded, his throat constricted. He slammed the paper down on the bar and rushed out. Let the law catch him, he didn't give a damn. He had to find out if Summer was safe.

Buck rode hard, night and day, only stopping long enough to rest his horse. When he entered Denver he was appalled at the sights that confronted him. Hardly anything was standing, but the town was already in the process of cleaning up and starting to rebuild.

Buck sat atop his horse, staring at where Nielson's house used to stand. There was nothing covering the ground but dried mud.

Buck spent three solid days searching for Summer and Angus, but even the *Colorado First* couldn't come up with any information. They ran a list of the dead, but the only name Buck recognized was the real estate man, Howard Jackson. It was widely believed that many people had simply been washed down the Platte River meaning their bodies would never be recovered.

The following week Buck remained drunk, not sure if he even wanted to live. All he could think about was the woman he loved lying dead somewhere. He cursed himself for not taking Summer with him, even though at the time he'd thought he was doing the right thing. But in the back of his mind remained the faint hope that Summer was still alive.

When Buck finally sobered up, he knew he had to ride to the mine. Just *maybe* Angus had taken Summer back up the mountain. Afraid he wouldn't find her there either, he was more than a little tempted to delay his departure. However, after a visit to the bathhouse and a change of clothes, he mounted his horse and rode out of Denver.

It was a bright, warm day when Buck headed toward Golden, but there was only sadness in his heart. At the last minute he changed direction and headed south. He'd take one last look at the house where he'd planned to live for the rest of his life with his beloved Summer.

Summer stood in the middle of the baby's room, eyeing the clean, white walls, the wooden floor polished to a bright shine, and the furniture, sanded and beeswaxed. Now it was just a matter of hanging the fluffy white curtains she'd made, and another room would be completed.

As she headed toward the open window, Summer noticed dust rising in the distance. She smiled. It was probably Angus coming to see how things were going, but—more importantly—wanting more of the new cook's marvelous meals.

Summer climbed onto a wooden stool, ready to feed the curtains onto the rod. She paused and looked out the window again just in time to see a lone rider top the distant hill. She was sure the afternoon heat was playing tricks on her, because against the blue sky it looked like he was wearing a Stetson.

Trying to get a better view, she squinted her eyes to help block the glaring sun. Slowly she stepped down from the stool, her gaze remaining on the man. Her breathing became shallow, and the curtains slipped from her hands onto the floor.

As he continued forward through the long grass, she could clearly see he was riding a big buckskin. Summer's heart began beating wildly against her breast.

"He's come home," she whispered, almost afraid to say the words aloud. When he brought his horse to a halt in the shadow of the tall oak tree standing at the edge of the meadow, Summer darted out of the room. "Milly," she hollered, "Buck's come home!"

Buck sat staring at the big house, remembering how he'd planned to spend a lifetime here with the woman he loved. He still had a hard time accepting the loss of what might have been.

Suddenly a flame-haired woman ran out of the front door, the skirts of her blue cotton dress whipping behind her. He sat very still, not wanting his hallucination to vanish. As she continued to close the distance between them, her hair worked its way loose from the bun atop her head and flew wildly.

"Buck!" she called. Her voice snapped him back to reality. It wasn't a dream!

With a burst of laughter, he kicked his horse in the ribs and rode hell-bent for leather toward her. Yanking back on the reins, he was out of the saddle before the stallion had come to a full halt. The horse continued on toward the house, but Buck paid scant attention. His mind was on the woman who ran into his waiting arms.

"You've come back to me!" Summer cried before Buck's lips joined hers.

Though loath to do so, he finally had to push her gently away, needing to prove to himself that she was all right. His gaze fell from her shiny hair to her lovely green eyes, glowing with love. Her cheeks were flushed with happiness.

"I thought I'd lost you," he groaned, unable to go another moment without feeling her back in his arms. "God, woman, how I love you!" He captured her full lips, the same lips that had haunted his dreams, night after night.

Even though there was a reward for his capture, he wasn't sure he'd ever be able to ride out of her life again. He savored her kisses and caressed her back, his need growing with every passing moment. He was surprised when Summer pulled away.

"Buck," she said, her breathing heavy, "I have to tell you something."

"Can't it wait?"

She sat down in the tall grass, and he joined her.

"Surely it can wait," he muttered, before pulling her close to lie beside him.

"No, it can't." Summer reached over and brushed grass from his thick, black hair. "Darling, I understand why you rode off without me at the old line shack, and it was a very noble deed. But before we make love, and before you try pulling any tricks like that again, I want you to know you're no longer a wanted man."

Buck raised up on his elbow and cocked a dark eyebrow.

Now that Summer was able to take a good look at him, it broke her heart to see the hard lines etched on his handsome face. She didn't have to be told he'd been living in hell since their parting.

He pulled her back into his arms. "It won't work, darlin'," he said, already hating the words.

"I'm telling the truth," she whispered. "That's something I would never lie to you about."

With all his heart, Buck wanted to believe her, but it seemed impossible. "How did it happen?" he asked suspiciously.

Summer quickly related the story. "I wanted to go looking for you," she finished, "but Angus said it would be impossible to find you."

Buck finally believed her. "Well, I'll be damned," was all he could say. After the hell William had put them through, he wished he'd killed the man the first time the idea had come to mind.

"You don't seem very happy," she said.

Seeing the worried look on her face, he smiled. "I guess it just takes a little getting used to. Besides, I have more important things on my mind."

"Milly is in the house, but I doubt she'll come looking to find us."

Buck broke out laughing. "Summer, my dear, you've turned into a hussy."

She grinned back at him. "Are you complaining?"

"Not for a moment."

She began unbuttoning his shirt. "Oh, how I've missed you, Buck Holester."

After their wild passion had been satisfied, the two lovers rested beneath the oak tree, watching the sun dip behind the majestic mountain range.

"Just take a look at that sky," Buck commented. "Have you ever seen anything prettier? All pink, red, and purple. And smell the grass. As sweet as a man could ask for. This is damn good cattle country."

"Mmm," Summer agreed as she snuggled closer to the man she loved. "It is beautiful. Before we go to the house, you might be interested in knowing that—as of late—Angus has been showing Milly a considerable amount of attention."

"Oh? You think something might come of it?"

"I wouldn't be surprised." She ran a long fingernail down his naked chest. "Are you still planning on making me an honest woman?" she crooned.

Buck pulled her closer and kissed her nose. "I have every intention of us paying a visit to the preacher first thing in the morning."

"Good. It wouldn't be proper to have our child out of wedlock."

There was a moment's pause before Buck asked in awe, "Are you telling me I'm going to be a papa?"

"That's what I'm saying." She rested her head on his chest. "In about five months."

Gently he ran his hand along her stomach. "You don't even show!"

"You just didn't notice. My dresses are already becoming too tight around the waist."

Buck became very quiet. "Summer," he finally said, "do you ever think you'll want to move back to Philadelphia?"

"Never, my love. My home is right here by your side—in Colorado."

Buck raised up and pulled her across his lap. "How did I ever manage to find me such a woman?" he asked, grinning from ear to ear.

Summer laughed. "If you'll remember, it wasn't easy."

He lifted her in his arms and stood. "But well worth it, my love. Let's go home, Summer."

She nodded, then wrapped her arms around his strong neck. "Home is such a wonderful word," she said softly.

He started walking toward the big house—and their future together.